I0693058

# The Amazing Wolf Boy

## Roxanne Smolen

Published by: moonRox, Inc.
Cover Design: Y. Nikolova at Ammonia Book Covers

Copyright © 2011, 2014 Roxanne Smolen. All rights reserved. No part of this publication may be reproduced, stored in a retrieval system or transmitted in any form or by any means, electronic, mechanical, photocopying, recording or otherwise without the prior written permission of the copyright holder, except for brief quotations used in a review.

This is a work of fiction and is produced from the author's imagination. People, places, and things mentioned in this novel are used in a fictional manner.

ISBN: 978-0-9915673-1-7

Thank you for supporting author rights.

For more information about Roxanne Smolen please visit www.roxannesmolen.com

# Contents

*For Aurora, who loves werewolves and vampires as much as I do.*

# ONE

I'll never forget the night my life ended.

It was Christmas Eve, 2007, and I was in France with my parents at *Maison Kammerzell*, one of those fancy historic restaurants. The room glowed with plastic icicles. Ropes of apples and mistletoe hung from the ceiling. My tie felt like a noose and my suit coat a straitjacket.

We were dining on *le Reveillon*, a holiday feast of roast capon, which is a castrated chicken, and *boudin blanc*, which always tastes like vanilla pudding to me. My mother waved her hands as she described in detail the Christmas decorations at the Charity Ball she chaired. I love my mother, I really do, but give her a glass or two of wine and she can outtalk an auctioneer. My father listened with a rapt expression, letting her build up steam. I thought about my DS back in the hotel room. Out the window, beyond the reflection of red and gold holiday lights, I saw a full moon.

As if someone threw a switch inside my head, my senses came alive. The room rang with the sharp clink of china and crystal. The string quartet, whose

1

classic Christmas Carols had gone all but unheard in the hectic atmosphere, now played sharp and clear.

Scents rose from my table and mixed with those from surrounding tables. I put down my fork, staring at my plate. My nose told me that the poor, mutilated rooster I'd been eating was stuffed with rosemary. The bird reeked. I couldn't believe I'd put that in my mouth. It made my skin crawl. For real. I could see the hair on the back of my hands stand up.

Hair on my hands? When did that happen?

Before I thought of a satisfactory explanation, agony gripped me. I clutched the sides of my head. It felt as if my skull cracked open. As if someone pulled off my face. My teeth ached so bad I couldn't close my lips. Drool dribbled down my chin. I covered my mouth with my hands and froze.

It didn't feel like me. The nose was flat. The jaw protruded. I ran my tongue over my teeth. They were long and sharp. Like fangs. I leaped to my feet, almost knocking over my chair. While my mother prattled on about the ball, I rushed from the table.

My only thought was to hide. It might have made sense to yell for help, both my parents are doctors, but I didn't want the other diners to see me. So I zigzagged through the tables with my napkin to my face, dodging curious stares. Panic churned the over-spiced food in my stomach.

I reached the lobby. A couple came in arm-in-arm through the door, and another couple greeted them. They laughed and shook hands, blocking the exit. Couldn't get out there. A man stepped out of the men's room, while two others went inside. Couldn't hide there. Too busy. The smell of leather and fur radiated from the coatroom. When the coat-check girl turned her back, I ducked inside.

Excruciating pain wracked my body. Every muscle clenched and twisted. I felt as if my bones shrank and elongated at the same time. Sweat poured from my skin. I tore off my suit coat and unbuttoned my shirt, gasping as the cool air hit my chest. Trapped in a sort of mental haze, I climbed behind the mink and sable wraps.

My father's voice snapped me to wakefulness. "I'm looking for my son, Cody."

It sounded like he was at the front desk. I could walk that far. Still sweating, I got to my feet.

All four feet.

I yelped, and the sound that burst from my throat was not human. I stared at sleek silver paws. As I stumbled forward, my pants slid from my hindquarters.

"Cody? Are you in here?" my father called.

Before I saw him, I smelled him—from his shampoo to his shoe polish to the residue of dinner that clung to his pores. He stood in the doorway of the coatroom, his face unreadable. Then he said, "For crying out loud."

Not knowing what else to do, I barreled past him into the restaurant lobby. My paws clattered on the smooth floor, and my hind legs skittered sideways. I saw wood paneling and spiral staircases. People stood everywhere. Someone screamed. The maître d' shouted something I couldn't understand.

Then I caught a puff of chilled, fresh air. I scraped and skidded toward the door, trying to spread my weight over four legs, and accidentally slammed my shoulder into a man's hip. He fell, and the impact bounced me into a twenty-foot Christmas tree. One of my hind feet snagged a strand of holiday lights; the tree swayed and tinkled.

I bounded out the open door, leaping for freedom, and hitting the pavement on all fours. Lights flashed and dazzled my eyes. The sound of traffic roared. The stench of motor oil and hot rubber rose in swells. Pedestrians came from all directions. They trampled me and cussed, or jumped back like I was something scary. I scrambled to get out of the way.

I scented water and remembered passing a fountain on the way to the restaurant. I headed toward the smell at a trot, thinking it would be quieter there, and caught my reflection in a storefront window.

I was a dog. A large, silver dog with a short yellow tail. How could it be true? It had to be a dream. *Keep to the sidewalk. Try to look inconspicuous. Just a big fluffy pet wearing a necktie.* My tongue lolled to the side. I closed my mouth but it dropped open again as if my teeth were too large to contain.

The fountain was not as deserted as I hoped. It was a meeting place for lovers. Some of the girls squealed and pointed. Several couples hurried away. Maybe they thought I had rabies. I stood there, not knowing where to go or what to do. I felt scared and confused.

But also intrigued. I smelled fear on the people who stared at me, tasted their mingled scents on the breeze. I wanted to chase them just to see how fast and how far they'd run.

What was wrong with me?

The wail of sirens rose over the street noise. Weird sirens, not normal ones like in Massachusetts. I never missed home more than at that moment. If I could just wake up, I knew I would find myself in my own bed. That thought held me, and I must have spaced. A moment later, two cars screeched to the curb. Several uniformed men hopped out. One held a lasso on a stick. They walked in my direction.

"I need help," I shouted. "Something's wrong."

Only, that's not what came out. I frowned, replaying the rough sounds that burst from my throat. The men surrounded me, holding their arms from their sides like they were fences. I decided to try talking again. Maybe if I said something in Dog it would come out as English.

"Woof," I barked. "Woof, woof, woof."

The nearest guy tried to loop his lasso over my head. I dodged. He swung again, and I backed into one of the men. He wasn't a very good fencepost— he went down beneath my weight.

I spun about, intending to speed away, but my hind legs ran faster than my front. I skittered around the fountain like I was running on ice. The bystanders scattered. The men spread out, cornering me. A growl rose in my chest; my teeth bared themselves. Without thinking, I jumped. No, I soared. Right over their heads. Came down running and didn't stop.

I heard shouts and the thud of heavy footsteps, but after a while, the sounds faded. I didn't slow down. My nose led me to a brick-paved alley, and I tore through it, trying to catch up with myself. It was like if I could run fast enough, far enough, I might leave the nightmare behind.

After a time, pain overcame my horror, and I limped to a halt. My overexerted muscles screamed, and my paws felt raw and stone bruised. I was still in the labyrinth of byways, enmeshed in the rich odors of garbage. I saw recessed doors and bicycles leaning against walls.

Townhomes. Everyone asleep. Visions of sugarplums dancing in their heads.

My holiday dinner curdled in my stomach. I was thirsty. Someone left out a dog bowl, and the water was almost irresistible. I refused it. I would not drink like an animal. With an almost drunken stagger, I continued walking.

The alley was bright. I looked up at the brilliant, full moon.

Tears burned my eyes. I wanted to cry. But I was sixteen years old. I hadn't cried since I was a kid. Besides, if I started, it might sound like I was howling, and I couldn't handle that.

In a doorway, I curled into a ball and put my paws over my muzzle.

🐺 🐺 🐺

I awoke to a frigid dawn. I was human. I was also naked. All I wore was my necktie from the previous night.

My body convulsed with shivers as I stumbled down the alleyway. I had to get to my parents before I died of exposure. There was no traffic so early in the morning. The street lamps were still lit. I stood in the shadows, searching for a signpost, a landmark, anything familiar. I didn't know Strasbourg well, although I'd visited before.

While I considered how to get from point A to point B, a squad car pulled up the alley behind me. An early riser must have seen me streak past their window.

As the police officer stepped toward me, I raised my arms over my head and shouted, "I'm an American."

His eyes were amused. At least, he didn't draw his gun. "You look cold," he said in a thick French accent. His gaze settled on my shriveled shrinky dink.

I dropped my hands, covering myself. "I was...I am..." I wanted to tell him I was mugged and my clothes were stolen, but I was shivering so hard, I couldn't get the words out.

He opened his trunk and removed a long, heavy coat. Perhaps he didn't feel it was cold enough to wear such a garment. He tossed it to me, and I put it on. The coat was as icy as the air. If anything, I felt colder. He ushered me to the car. I balked. I didn't want to go to jail.

"My parents are at the *Sofitel*," I managed to say.

"*Oui.* Your family contacted us regarding your disappearance and your mental aberration." He pushed me inside with a practiced hand atop my head and slammed the door.

The car was so small I had to slouch to fit. The backseat smelled like vomit. There was no heat. The officer got in front and spoke French into his radio. I hugged my arms and puzzled over what he'd said.

Mental aberration? Is that what had happened? Had I only thought I was a dog? That would explain my father's annoyed reaction when he saw me in the coatroom. The idea comforted me, as if being crazy was better.

By the time we reached the police station, I felt warm within the coat. The officer helped me out of the vehicle and up the stairs. Noise burst to greet us as he opened the door. The station was crowded despite it being dawn on Christmas morning. I walked at his side past the front desk, garnering more than a few stares. He led me down a corridor decorated with a line of threadbare tinsel taped to the wall. The floor was gritty and cold. We stopped at an office with

8

Captain Jean Luc Boudreaux stenciled on the window. Inside, I saw my parents get to their feet. My mother's eyes were puffy as if she'd been crying.

"Mom." I wanted to go to her and hug her, but the look she shot me was not inviting.

My father handed me a fleecy jogging suit. I slipped on the pants, and then passed the coat to the officer.

He accepted with a nod.

A bald man I assumed was Captain Boudreaux stood from the desk. "So we find zee little boy and all is well, no?"

Wincing at the words *little boy*, I sat to tie my shoes. I felt invisible. No one spoke to me. My father signed a pack of paperwork. I imagined it like a receipt, like he was pulling a wayward puppy out of the pound.

And just like that, we were free to go. Before I knew it, we were back at the hotel.

I wanted to talk about the night before, wanted to figure out what had happened, but I was still getting the silent treatment. My mother paced the room, avoiding my eyes. I stood at the door, wondering how to broach the subject.

At last, I said, "Am I crazy?"

"Don't ever think that," said my father.

"I must be." I took a step into the room and held out my hands. My palms were raw from a night of running on all fours. "I thought I turned into a dog."

"A wolf," Mom snapped. "You turned into a wolf."

Her tone was both disgusted and accusing, as if it were my fault, as if I'd been playing around. I was so taken aback it took a moment for her words to sink in.

"Wolf?" I remembered the full moon. "As in werewolf?" *But aren't werewolves vicious monsters?*

She stopped to face me, straightening her shoulders. "Your father and I have talked it over, and we feel it would be better for everybody if you went to live with your uncle in Florida."

"What?" I stood there, dumbfounded. "I can't live with him. I only met him once."

"It's for your own good."

"But what about my life? What about school?"

"They have schools in Loxahatchee," she shouted.

*Loxahatchee.* As if there *were* such a place.

Tears filled my eyes for the second time in as many days. "I can't believe it. I can't believe you'd send me away." I expected them to take me to a doctor, or even a psychiatrist. But this?

"We already have your ticket," my father said. "We'll arrange for a car to pick you up at the airport and take you to Bob's house."

Uncle Bob. The black sheep. The only thing I knew about him was that he sometimes hit my mother up for money.

"You aren't coming?" I said, sounding like the little boy the captain had branded me.

My parents turned away.

So there you have it. My life was over. Not literally, of course. But as I stared out the window of the jumbo jet at the spreading void of Everglades below, I knew nothing was going like I planned.

# TWO

I stood on my uncle's porch, suitcase in hand, and pounded the door. No response. I felt like an idiot. Guess I wasn't expected. Or maybe this wasn't the right place.

My car and driver were gone. There were no other houses in sight. What looked like solid jungle bordered the yard. I walked along a wooden rail and peered through a curtainless window. The shadows inside were still.

With a groan, I sank onto a porch swing that hung by rusted chains. I was tired, and I hadn't eaten since the capon the previous night. The jogging suit made me sweat in the Florida heat.

Miserable, I looked at an orange and purple sunset. It would be night soon. Would I change into a wolf again?

I winced and pushed the thought from my brain. Where was my uncle, anyway? Probably at a party. It was hard to remember it was Christmas Day.

Maybe he hoped he could avoid me. Maybe I wasn't wanted.

Daunted by that thought, I walked around the

side of the house. A window was open. Pale curtains fluttered like ghosts. I leaped for the frame and caught the sill, but couldn't pull myself up. Grit stung my hands. I wiped my palms on my chest. I returned to the porch, stomped to the door, and knocked until it rattled. In desperation, I tried the knob. It was unlocked.

"Hello?" I stepped inside.

The house smelled like a dog. I wondered if Uncle Bob had a pet. One look around the dim interior and I realized why he hadn't locked the door. There was nothing to steal.

A battered recliner sat in the middle of the living room. Beside it was a metal TV table with a twelve-inch television on top. Probably black and white. I longed for the forty-two-inch plasma sitting in my room at home.

On top of the TV, a large jawbone gripped a stack of newspapers. Like a freaking paperweight. I wondered to what animal it had belonged. Maybe an alligator. My shoulders sagged. I dropped my suitcase, closed the door, fumbled for a light switch and found one that turned on a chandelier in an empty dining room. Only two of the bulbs lit.

A folded note was stuck to the television screen with black electrical tape. Leaning closer, I realized that it was addressed to me.

*Cody, I couldn't wait any longer for you to arrive.*

*I have somewhere to be tonight. I know you under-
stand. Your room is to the right. Make yourself at
home. We'll talk in the morning. I'm glad to have you
here, boy. — Uncle Bob*

Relieved, I picked up my suitcase and went to my
room. I hesitated at the door. There was a wrought
iron bed. No sheets. No pillows. No blinds on the
windows. I sat on the mattress. My mom said she
would ship my things when she got back from vacation. I hoped she wouldn't, hoped she would recon-
sider my banishment.

Besides, where would I keep anything?

With a sigh, I peeled off my soggy sweatshirt and
put on a tee with *Recycle America* printed on the
front. The closet had no hangers, so I hung the
sweatshirt on the bedpost to dry and set off for the
kitchen. It was easy to find—I just followed the draft.
The window above the sink was open. Beyond it, the
sky darkened. My stomach did a somersault, and I
wasn't sure I could eat.

I needn't have worried. The cupboard held a couple of mugs and a large jar of instant coffee. There
was a white Formica table in the corner. It had four
chairs, two of them tucked against the wall. There
were coffee-ring stains on top along with a chromed,
old-style toaster. Maybe there was bread. I searched
the cupboard again, and then turned to the refrigerator. It held three beers and a bottle of ketchup.

"Cripes!" I slammed the refrigerator and stormed

into my room. I decided to call my mom, had the cell phone in my hand. I didn't know whether I would beg her to take me back or tell her off for sending me to Podunk land.

A sudden sharpening of my senses stopped me. I froze. I heard crickets and birds, smelled dust and the rich damp earth. Muscles squirmed beneath my skin. It was happening again. Oh, God, I couldn't stand it. I yanked open the bedroom window, climbed outside, and sprinted for the line of palm trees. My legs felt like they shattered with each step. I dove for cover, and then writhed in agony. I thought it would never end.

Then it did. I looked at my silver paws and placed them over my eyes. I needed help. But there was no one. There was nothing I could do.

A breeze ruffled my fur. I smelled flowers, stagnant water, and rabbit spoor. I heard insects in the brush and opossums in the trees. A bird let out a screech that made me feel I was in Africa.

The wind invited me to run with it. I refused. I didn't want to wake up naked and lost again. Drenched in sweat, I stood and stepped out of my shoes. My bulky jogging pants slipped off my narrow hindquarters. Then I realized I still wore my T-shirt. I tried to grab it with my teeth, but only succeeded in spinning. I tried again and spun the other way.

A snarl twisted my muzzle. This was ridiculous. I threw myself onto my back, then wriggled and kicked, my hind legs digging my chest. The shirt

15

would not come off.

I sat defeated in my *Recycle America* tee. The amazing wolf boy. No wonder no one wanted me.

The tears started. I couldn't stop them. I cried like I hadn't a friend in the world. It sounded like I bayed at the moon.

🐕 🐕 🐕

I awoke in the bushes, covered in dew. The sky was a soft gray. Birds sang in the trees.

My eyes burned, and I rubbed them as I looked toward the silent house. A blue pickup with an extended cab sat in the gravel driveway. I wondered if it belonged to my uncle. I heard that my mother sent Bob money to buy a truck. At the time, I assumed it was a tricked-out show vehicle. This one looked like it was accustomed to hard work.

I dressed in a hurry, crossed the yard, and climbed through my bedroom window. A clatter came from the kitchen. My stomach fell. I was as apprehensive about seeing my uncle as I was about turning into a wolf.

I went to the kitchen. Uncle Bob stood at the sink making a cup of instant coffee with hot tap water. He had steel gray, over-the-collar hair and a thin build.

I cleared my throat. "Good morning."

"Cody. Good to see you, boy."

He held out his hand, and I shook it. His palms were calloused. I wondered what he did for a living.

"Hey, you got tall," he said with my mom's smile.

I tried to smile back, but it felt like a grimace. Yeah, I got tall, seeing's how the last time he saw me I was four years old.

"You have grass in your hair," he said.

My hands jerked up, and I stammered, "Oh, I was, ah—"

"Want some coffee?"

"No, sir," I said, and then blurted, "There's nothing around here to eat."

He slurped. "What, you didn't eat last night?"

I frowned. Had he expected me to exist on airline food?

"I ate." He patted his stomach. "Had me a nice rabbit dinner. Nothing better than fresh caught."

"You like to hunt?"

"Sure. Don't you?"

I'd never been hunting in my life. But I hoped to fit in, so I said, "I fish." Although I hadn't since I was ten.

"Fish?" He scrunched his face. "To each his own, I guess. Why don't we go into town and get some breakfast."

"Can I go like this?" I indicated my damp sweat pants and stretched out tee.

He shrugged. "This is South Florida. You can go in your skivvies if you want."

We walked together into the gray morning. My nose twitched with flower-scented humidity.

"This will give me a chance to show you around."

Uncle Bob circled the cab of his truck.

I sat shotgun and buckled in. The first thing I noticed was the truck didn't have a radio. The second was a baseball bat on the floor. I didn't think it was there for sport. A knotted leather cord dangled from the rearview mirror. Feathers and animal fangs decorated its length.

"What's that?" I motioned.

He winked. "Trophies."

I nodded like it was normal to keep mementoes of road kill. I saw why my parents considered him a black sheep.

We lurched along the rutted roads that led out of the neighborhood, and finally pulled onto asphalt where we picked up speed. Outside my window, the landscape turned alien. It wasn't like I'd never been in Florida. I visited Miami Beach plenty of times—blue water, white sandy beaches, high-rises. This was nothing like that. One minute we'd be in a jungle so thick you couldn't see past the trees. The next, we'd be in a flat expanse of scrub and sawgrass that stretched for miles.

As if he sensed my bewilderment, my uncle said, "This here's the northernmost tip of the Everglades. We got our share of 'gators. They're surprisingly fast on land so don't antagonize them. We're also getting a nasty population of Burmese pythons."

"Snakes?" Was this a joke? "I thought they lived in the rainforest."

"Well, people think they can dump any old thing."

His voice trailed.

"Like that myth," I said. "Alligators in the sewers."

"Except this ain't no myth." He grew quiet for a long moment, and then said, "It's happening all over South Florida. People take things as pets and then tire of them. I heard they're finding Japanese lionfish off shore. They're that fish you usually see in home aquariums. If they don't get them out of our waters, the buggers will ruin the reefs. They're vicious predators."

I added to the list of things I knew about my uncle. He liked to hunt, he was an environmentalist, and he didn't listen to music.

We passed a few crossroads. None had street signs.

Uncle Bob motioned toward one. "That way takes you to Belle Glade and the sugarcane fields. When they're harvesting, it smells like burning syrup. If you go down that road, you'll run into the back end of the safari park. It's a four-mile preserve, sort of a drive-through zoo. All kinds of animals."

"Do they ever get out?"

"I never heard of a lion getting loose, but you'll see a runaway monkey from time to time. And their peacocks are everywhere. You probably heard them last night."

I winced. I'd heard plenty of strange sounds last night, but I hadn't been myself.

Bob pointed down another road. "That way leads to the Sunspot nudist camp."

I sputtered. "As in no clothes?"

"They're nice people. Don't go bothering them."

I shook my head. "Never met a nudist before."

"They're like anybody else." He grinned. "Only nekked."

We stopped at a traffic light. There weren't many other cars on the road.

"This is Southern Boulevard," Uncle Bob told me. "You'll find most of what you need along here."

I nodded and hoped I wouldn't be around long enough to need anything. He was right, though. There were stores and chain restaurants I recognized. It was like a regular city, only in miniature.

We pulled into a parking lot for the Coffee Café. The pavement was cracked; foot-high grass sprouted through the fissures. There were only two other cars. One of them was a convertible with leather seats baking in the heat. The other had Sheriff stenciled on the side.

I hopped from the truck and circled around. If this was anything like home, cops usually knew the best places to eat. Uncle Bob seemed pensive as we approached the door.

Almost as if he'd been waiting for us, the sheriff came out the diner. He had white hair and a mustache. "Morning, Robert. Who do we have here?"

"Hello, Brad," my uncle said with no trace of a smile. "This is my nephew. He'll be staying with me."

"How do you do, sir?" I said.

He looked me up and down, ignoring my out-stretched hand. "Well, young man. Let me know if you have any trouble settling in."

"Thank you, sir." I moved to step around him.

He blocked the door. "We like to think of this here town of Loxahatchee as the town that doesn't ask too many questions. But that's not to say anything goes. I like to keep things quiet, you know what I mean?"

"Yes, sir. I do," I said.

"Excuse us, Brad," my uncle told him. "The boy is mighty hungry."

We stepped into the café. It smelled of coffee and pancake syrup. The room was dim compared to the bright morning.

I stood in the entryway and replayed the conversation with the sheriff. I had the impression Sheriff Brad didn't much like my uncle—and by extension, me.

From across the room, a waitress called, "Bobby, nice to see you, hon. I have a table for you over here."

We squeezed into the booth she indicated. It was by a window that overlooked the street. Stripes fell through the slats of the blinds, the light tinted pink by a transparent Santa Claus painted on the glass.

"How was your birthday? Good?" She poured a cup of coffee for my uncle.

"Wonderful. My sister surprised me with the best gift ever." He gave her a wide smile. "Anne, this is Cody. He's staying with me now. I want you to set

21

him up with a tab, and I'll tally up at the end of the month."

They both looked at me as if I should gush with enthusiasm over my uncle's generosity.

"Umm. I don't really like coffee," I managed to say.

Uncle Bob laughed. "Then get him chocolate milk. What kid doesn't like chocolate milk?"

"One chocolate milk coming up," Anne said over her shoulder as she hurried away.

They looked so pleased I didn't have the heart to tell them I didn't care for milk either. I rarely ate breakfast at home, just grabbed a Dew on the way to school.

When Anne brought my food, however, I was ravenous. I had eggs, sausage, pancakes, and a bowl of white soupy stuff my uncle called grits. It all tasted great. I couldn't get it in my mouth fast enough.

My uncle chuckled as he snagged a piece of my toast. "I guess I forgot what it's like to be a growing boy."

I nodded and polished off my milk.

"After winter break, we'll take you over to Seminole Bluffs and get you signed up for high school," he said. "It won't be like those prep schools you're used to, but it has a good reputation."

I set down my fork, suddenly losing my appetite. My prep school was going to get me into Harvard. I planned to become a doctor like my parents. How would that happen now? How could I go to a normal high school, act like a normal kid?

How could I have a normal life?

I sensed his eyes upon me and scrambled to hide my emotions. "Do they have extracurricular activities? I was president of the Science Club at home."

"Sports." He shrugged. "Home of the Hawks."

My shoulders deflated. I liked sports, but I'd never be mistaken for an athlete. Too thin. And in spite of my dad's assurances that I would grow to be taller than him, I was average height. Still waiting for that growth spurt. Uncle Bob stared at me, so I cast about for something else to say. "Will a bus pick me up?"

"Don't think it comes out my way, now that you mention it." He rubbed his chin, frowning thoughtfully. "Do you have a driver's license?"

"I have a learner's permit," I told him.

"Good." He stretched and draped his arm over the back of the booth. "I saw something the other day you might like. Hope it's still for sale."

I looked at him, my stomach doing a little flip. Was he buying me a car?

"Finished?" He motioned at my empty plate. "Let's go have a look."

# THREE

We left the café and drove along a side street lined with pink and aqua houses. Icicle lights hung from garages. Deflated plastic snowmen lay puddled on the driveways. A flock of wild parakeets flitted from tree to tree like a green cloud.

Uncle Bob pulled the truck up to a house with a yard sale. Rows of folding tables filled the lawn. Grass grew around their legs and gave the impression that the tables were permanent fixtures. They were piled with everything from clothing to dishes.

A man came out of the garage with yet another box of stuff to add to the disorder. He wore cut-off jeans and a Dolphins football jersey. His dark hair hung in a long ponytail down his back. I thought he looked Native American.

Uncle Bob got out of the truck and slammed the door. The man glanced over, and his broad face broke into a smile. He hugged my uncle like a brother. They slapped each other's backs.

"Open for business the day after Christmas?" Uncle Bob said. "Aren't you cutting the holidays a bit short?"

He shrugged. "Ah, well, it's not my religion." Then he looked at me. His eyes narrowed.

"Cody, my nephew," Uncle Bob told him. "He's down from Massachusetts."

"He has your aura." The man nodded as he circled me. "Yes, indeed."

Uncle Bob draped his arm across my shoulders and dropped his voice. "Cody, Howard here is a friend. Best friend you can have. If you ever get in trouble, anything at all, he's the man to see."

"Day or night." Howard raised his hand in a solemn promise.

I nodded and wondered how friendly either of them would be if they knew my secret. "Thank you very much, sir."

"Welcome." He glanced about as if he just noticed his yard. "I'd like to stand around and chat, but I have more junk to display."

"Need a hand?" asked my uncle.

"No, I've got it. Why don't you two look around?" Howard returned to his garage.

As if that were his cue, Uncle Bob set off through the cramped rows. It wasn't easy to keep up. I couldn't imagine why we were there. Howard labeled his wares junk, and he couldn't have been more right. He must have an army of kids to accumulate so many cast-offs.

My uncle cocked his head as he peered beneath the tables. "Here it is. This is what I was telling you about." He pulled out a rickety bicycle.

I took a step back. "It's a bike."

"Yeah. You'll need something to get around on."

"But it's a bike. I don't need a driver's license to ride a bike."

"You need identification. I don't want you to pedal around without ID." He rolled the bicycle back and forth. Both tires were flat. "Howard! How much?"

"Twenty-five dollars," Howard called back.

"No, no, no. How much for me?"

"Thirty."

Uncle Bob sat on the bike. It gave an ominous creak. "I'll give you ten."

Howard raised a hand in acceptance and disappeared once more into the depths of his garage.

With a wink and a grin, Uncle Bob handed me the bike and slapped me on the shoulder. "What else does he have around here? Do you need anything?"

I could have laughed. What could I possibly need? Here I was in South Florida with a suitcase full of winter clothes. "Hangers. For the closet."

Bob slung a thick, red blanket over his shoulder. It looked hand woven. He peered into a box. "Hey, bed sheets. How about these?" He pulled out a set of mustard-yellow sheets printed with Scooby Doo.

I made a face. No way would I sleep on something like that.

"Ah, come on." He laughed. "What kid doesn't like cartoons?"

We ended up with quite a haul. Besides the bike and bedding, we picked up some bowls and plates for the kitchen and some extra towels for the bath. I found a decent pair of jeans and a few T-shirts.

Howard claimed we owed him eighty-eight dollars, but Uncle Bob talked him down to twenty-seven. We packed everything into the back of the pickup and said good-bye.

As I climbed into the truck, I felt dazed. Everything happened so fast. It was like if I bought those few things, I was agreeing to stay. Only I couldn't stay. I wanted to go home.

"Just one more stop." My uncle smiled as he drove back toward Southern.

I bit my tongue. My frustration erupted in an overwhelming anger at Uncle Bob. Deep down, I knew it wasn't fair. He was trying to be nice. My exile probably messed up his life as much as mine. The people I should be mad at were my parents—but every time I tried to be, I saw my mother's puffy, red eyes. I couldn't blame them. I couldn't blame anyone.

Uncle Bob pulled into the lot of a Walgreens Pharmacy. Red and green bells hung from the streetlights, and silver tinsel decorated the window. He backed into a spot, parked across the line, and took up two spaces. It didn't matter. No one else was around.

"Coming in?" he asked as he hopped down from his seat.

I shook my head. "I'll keep an eye on the bike."

He thumped the car door as if soothing a rhinoceros. "Won't be but a minute."

27

He hurried into the store. I unlatched my seatbelt and slouched. Sweat trickled down my back. It was hot and humid. The morning haze burned off and left the sky a brilliant blue. I glanced at my watch. It was still set for France. Six o'clock. My parents would be getting ready for dinner. I took out my cell phone. The screen said it was twelve noon.

Without really planning to, I dialed my mom's number. It rang four times. When it went to voicemail, I said, "Mom, this is Cody." Then my voice failed. I hung up without another word.

Tears burned my eyes, but I blinked and nurtured my anger. I leaned out the window toward the lazy flow of passing traffic and listened to other people's music. I wished I'd put some tunes on my phone, wished I had my mp3 player. When I packed for France, my parents told me I could bring either my iPod or my DS. I chose the DS. Now I rued the day. Total ruage.

Down the street, a Volkswagen Beetle pulled into a shopping center. I noticed it because Beetles weren't common anymore and because it was painted lime green. The car parked and a girl got out. She wore black and white striped tights, a purple miniskirt, and a black tee cut to reveal her midriff. Her hair was short and angular. She was the most interesting thing I'd seen in this backwoods town. She went into Video Stop, a store where you bought and traded used videos.

My uncle wrenched open the driver's side door.

It startled me. He flipped his seat forward and piled some bags into the backseat. I glimpsed a box of Cap'n Crunch cereal and a jug of chocolate milk.

He climbed in and started the truck. "Anywhere you want to go while we're out?"

"No, sir," I said, my thoughts still on the girl.

"Then we'll head home." He beamed at me like it was a special treat.

We took a different route back. This time, we passed through orange groves. Fruit filled the trees. Their branches drooped. It smelled phenomenal, like perpetual breakfast. Then we reached a patch with the trees picked clean. They appeared diminished somehow.

Uncle Bob slowed to get around a pair of horses. "We've got some nice stables here. That's how the Council hopes to lure more residents. Like it isn't already crowded enough."

I looked in the side-view mirror at the girls riding the horses. They wore shorts and tank tops in spite of it being winter.

There were worse places to be exiled. But none of the girls were for me. I was the amazing wolf boy. Astound your family and mystify your friends. I wasn't the kind of kid anyone would date. I thought about Video Stop girl.

Minutes later, we pulled onto the gravel drive of my uncle's house. Trees rustled in the breeze. Birdsong filled the air.

"Do you own this place?" I asked.

"No. I rent. You know how it is. I don't want to be bogged down if I have to move on." He pulled the bags from the back. "Get the door for me, will you?"

I skipped up the steps and opened the front door. Unlocked again. Bob carried the bags into the kitchen and set them on the table. He'd gotten other things to eat—Spaghetti-Os, bread, peanut butter. He also bought a dozen coat hangers and a couple of twenty-six-inch bicycle inner tubes.

"You're probably used to a live-in housekeeper to cook and clean for you," he said as he put the food into the cupboard.

"No," I said. "Mom handled everything." I didn't add that we had a cleaning service come in three times a week.

"We don't have anyone on staff here, either." He looked at me. "We don't even have a dishwasher. So here's the thing. You clean up after yourself or you don't. But the rule is, you don't complain about it. The place gets to be a mess, you don't complain. You want something, you either get it or you don't complain. You need help, you ask or—"

"Don't complain," I said. "Got it."

"Good." He clapped me on the back. "Let's go get the rest of your stuff."

We went to the truck where he loaded me up with clothes, towels, and bedding. The blanket made my nose itch, and I wondered if its last owner had been a horse. I carried everything inside. But as I reached my room, I stopped.

Evidence. That's what I held in my arms. Physical proof that I lived there. If anyone saw this, I would be lost. I sat on the edge of the bed, afraid to set the stuff down, and thought about running away. My dad always gave me my allowance via a debit card. I had enough in the account for a bus ticket home. I could live in the bathhouse. My parents would never know I was there.

Until my friends came calling.

I groaned and thought about my friends, all of them enjoying holiday break with families who didn't want to send them away, all of them looking forward to nighttime without worrying about what kind of monster they might become. This was a nightmare. How could anyone turn into a wolf? It was impossible.

I sat up straight. Yes, it was impossible. This couldn't be real. And if I was stuck in some sort of dream, all I could do was keep moving forward until I woke up.

In the spirit of my new resolution, I made my bed with the Scooby sheets and placed the thick, red horse blanket on top. I stared at it and hoped no one would ever come into my room. Then I went outside to look for my uncle.

I found him in the backyard by a tool shed. The bike was upside down. Uncle Bob knelt beside it. He grunted as he tightened the chain. I noticed he'd repaired the tires. I also noticed his shed was better stocked than shop class when I was a kid. There were three cabinets on wheels, each drawer labeled, and racks of wrenches on the walls.

I crouched at his side. "How's it going?"

"Almost done," he said.

I tried to picture myself wheeling up and down Southern Boulevard. "Maybe we should have bought a bicycle lock."

He smiled. "No one's going to steal this beauty."

I thought he was probably right.

He set the bike erect and bounced it a couple times. "Want to take it for a spin?"

"Maybe later," I said. "It's not really my thing." I couldn't remember the last time I'd been on a bike.

He turned away with a sigh. I recognized the sound—I'd stretched his patience. I wasn't being the appreciative guest.

Keep moving forward, I told myself.

He wiped his hands on a shop cloth and put away his tools. Then he locked the toolshed with a heavy padlock. It figured he would lock his tools but not the house.

"I keep the key here." He showed me a notch in the roof. "In case you need anything."

"I don't know much about tools," I said. "But I'd like to learn."

"I'd like to teach you." His face eased into a smile. "Are you hungry? I make a mean grilled peanut butter sandwich."

I nodded. "Sounds good."

We ate our sandwiches in front of the television

as we watched women's volleyball. I didn't even know they televised that sport. Despite the spectacle of bounding booties, however, I couldn't keep my mind on the game.

I worried about the coming dark. Would I change again? I thought werewolves only changed during the full moon, but last night was the day after. Would I change every night for the rest of my life?

I needed more information. If I had my computer, I could surf the Web. But, no, I was out here in the Everglades with nothing and no one. I would re-search the old-fashioned way. Tomorrow, I would look for a library.

First things first. I couldn't risk shape changing with my uncle around. I had to either find an excuse to leave the house or get him out of the way.

So it was a relief when, later that afternoon, Uncle Bob said, "I'm going out tonight. Would you like to come along?"

"Ah, no. Thanks," I said.

"Come on. It will be great. I'll show you a good place to fish."

"No, really," I said. "I think I'll just hang out here and relax."

"Another time, then."

And just like that, he was in the truck and down the driveway—and I was alone, sitting before his flickering black-and-white TV as I awaited the night.

# FOUR

I rocked on the creaking porch swing until the sky turned purple and the crickets came out. It was like waiting for a bomb to drop. I was scared, and the more scared I felt, the angrier I got. I was not going to change into a wolf. I didn't deserve this.

I stomped into the house, made a cold Spaghetti-O sandwich, and ate it over the sink. The kitchen window was open. It let in a variety of smells I wouldn't have noticed before, from night blooming jasmine to the garbage can behind the shed. I faced the growing darkness as if to stare down an enemy.

My muscles itched to move. I wanted to burst out the door and run as fast as I could, feel my legs stretch beneath me, feel the wind in my face. But I figured that was the wolf in me, eager to get out. So I compromised—I walked. I walked from the kitchen to my bedroom and back again. I turned on every light I could find. Occasionally, I checked to see that hair hadn't sprouted from my knuckles.

I'd left the television on and soon heard the beginning of a football game. Purdue and Central Michigan. I tried to watch but couldn't hold still, so I turned up the volume and paced. It was a maddening game. Central Michigan scored four times in the third quarter and still lost. I yelled at the referees, yelled at the sportscasters, tore at my hair, and shredded my uncle's newspaper. I don't think I ever felt so angry in my life—and I'm not even a CMU fan. With my rage barely in check, I kept walking.

Sometime after midnight, exhaustion set in. I collapsed face down on my bed, aching and sweaty. The horse blanket itched where it touched bare skin. I didn't mind. At least, I still had bare skin. That filled me with intense pride. I was human. I had beaten this thing.

With a tired grin, I sat up, pulled out my cell, and called my mom in France.

My father answered. "Hello, Cody."

"Hi, Dad. Where's Mom? Is she okay?"

"Yes, she's…" he hesitated, "taking a shower."

I heard the lie. She didn't want to talk to me. I let it slide. "I'm calling with good news. It's the middle of the night, and I haven't turned into a wolf."

"That *is* good news."

"I can come home now."

He hesitated again. "That's a little premature, don't you think, son?"

"I can control it. I promise it won't happen again."

There was a moment of silence as my life flitted across my eyes.

Then my dad said, "It would be better if you stayed in Florida for a while. Spend some time on your own. How are you getting along with Uncle Bob?"

A crushing disappointment hit. They didn't want me. It had nothing to do with my turning into a wolf. They'd waited for an excuse to get rid of me.

"Cody? Are you there?"

"Yeah. I'm here."

"Is there anything you need?"

Why did everyone keep asking that? I rubbed my eyes. "My computer. I need my computer."

"I'll see to it." His voice was cheerful. "Hey, thanks for calling. It's good to hear from you."

"Yeah. Enjoy your vacation."

"We're cutting it short, actually. Going home to-day."

Home. I winced. A lump grew in my throat.

"Goodbye, son."

"Yeah."

My shoulders sagged. I sat on the edge of my bed, staring at the phone. *Call ended.* It might as well have said *life ended.*

What had I done to make my parents hate me? I got decent grades. Never been arrested. Of course, there was the time Mickey Martin and I said we were spending the night in his tree house, and we really went to a party. They were angry about that. But hate?

Maybe I was just no good.

I lowered my face to my hands. I ached all over.

Sweat poured from my body and chilled me. Fever-ish. Over the past year, I'd gotten unexplained fevers. Missed a lot of school because of them. I peeled off my shirt, crawled under the scratchy blanket, and fell into a fitful sleep.

🐕 🐕 🐕

I awoke to the sound of slurping. Sunlight poured through the window. The blanket and sheets lay in tangled heaps on the floor.

My uncle stood in the doorway, drinking coffee. "Morning. Tough night?"

"Guess so." I sat up and rubbed my face. My hair felt stiff and stuck up all over. But the fever was gone.

"I need to go to work," Uncle Bob said. "I have my own business, the Fix-It Guy. Home repairs, light carpentry, that sort of thing. Maybe you'd like to come along. We can make a day of it."

"That's really nice, but I kind of planned on biking to town today. I need to learn my way around."

"Oh. Okay, then. I'll be back around five." With a nod, he left.

I listened to him rinse out his cup. Then the front door slammed, and his truck backed down the gravel drive.

I climbed out of bed and stretched, feeling pretty good. Feeling very good, actually. Strong enough to pull the ears off a *gundark*. I went over my plans for the day. My dad was right—I wasn't clear of this thing just because I beat the wolf for one night. I needed information. I needed the Web. The library should have Internet access. I showered, ate, and hopped on my bike.

By the time I pedaled out of the neighborhood and reached the paved road, I felt like I was back in the shower. My hair dripped into my eyes, and my shirt clung to my back. I wasn't used to the bike, wasn't used to the humidity. My newfound energy had all but left me. But the land was flat. The road was smooth. I made good time the rest of the way into town.

Southern Boulevard was way busier than the previous morning, but still not up to big city standards. As I merged with the slow-moving traffic, I set landmarks in my mind. I passed the Coffee Café and the street that led to Howard's place. To my right was the Walgreens we stopped at. Across the way, I saw the Crestwood Shopping Center. A green Beetle sat in the parking lot.

Video Stop girl.

I copped a left so fast, a driver honked at me. My bike coasted as I glided up the driveway and onto the sidewalk. The car was parked near a light pole. I leaned my bike against a wall, wiped my palms against my jeans, and stepped toward the store.

A bell dinged as I opened the door. Cool air swept over me. I stood in the entrance and looked around. Movie posters covered the walls, and racks of used DVDs stood in rows.

From behind an Entertainment magazine, a girl said, "Welcome to Video Stop."

The girl I saw before. She had black, spiky hair and wore a T-shirt with *Spear Britney* printed across the front. I wanted to stand there and stare.

But that would be too weird.

So I walked slowly up and down the aisles, one eye on her. I decided I could get information here as easily as I could at the library. I picked up a copy of Teen Wolf with Michael J. Fox and took it to the counter.

"Hmm." She tapped the cover. "You know, if you're interested in werewolf movies, you might like the Ginger Snap series."

She came around the counter and brushed by me. She smelled like fresh mangoes. Maybe her hair gel. I followed her, feeling self-conscious. She plucked a DVD from the wire rack and held it out.

"I just like to watch movies about werewolves," I said. "I don't really care about them or anything." I took the movie from her without looking at it and backed smack into the shelves behind me, which caused an avalanche of DVDs.

"Hmm," she said. She knelt to pick them up, and her miniskirt rose up her thighs.

I tore my eyes away and knelt beside her to help with the mess. "Sorry. I didn't mean to do that."

"That's a relief." She pursed her lips as if holding back a laugh.

"Uh, I'm Cody. What's your name?"

39

"Brittany." She stressed the *tany* as if I might get her mixed up with the other one.

"You're really knowledgeable about movies. You must like working here."

She shrugged. "I only work on school breaks. My mother thinks it will keep me out of trouble. Of course, she didn't know *you* were coming in today."

She cocked a brow at me, but her eyes sparkled, and I knew she wasn't angry. Together we restocked the upper shelves. Many of the movies didn't have their original cases, which made it difficult for me to spot their titles. Brittany was a lot quicker at alphabetizing than I was.

She stood back to look at our handiwork. "So, do you want to buy Ginger Snap or not?"

"Yeah. Sure."

She breezed past me again, and I breathed in her scent. "Cash or credit?" she asked.

I felt a sinking sensation. Were my parents angry enough to cancel my debit card? Brittany stood behind the counter, brows raised, looking at me.

I handed her my card. She swiped it, watched the screen, and then handed it back. The transaction went through without a problem.

"Come again." She smiled a perfect smile.

I took the bag and backed toward the door. "Sorry about..." I gestured with my thumb, "all that." I bumped into a rack labeled *New Arrivals*. This time, I only dislodged one movie. As I bent to pick it up, I knocked over a life-sized cutout of Darth Vader.

"It's all right. I'll get it." She hurried toward me. "Just go."

"Sorry," I murmured and slipped out the door.

I walked to my bike and leaned against the wall. As far as first impressions went, I'd done worse. Like the time I was shooting baskets and wanted to show off in front of Meredith Taney by hanging from the hoop. Only I missed, seeing how I'm not that tall, and my watch tangled in the net. I just swung there until the backboard came down on my head.

At least, Brittany didn't seem to think I was a total dork. Closing my eyes, I thought about her smile. She wore purple lipstick. I wondered what it tasted like. Then I looked at the bag with the movies and realized I had no way to play them.

*Dork.* I shook my head, pulled the bike around, and rode into the street. The Café looked good for lunch. It was busy, but Anne remembered me and gave me a hug. I sat at the counter with a turkey sandwich—fresh sliced, not that pressed stuff—and declared it my new favorite. She seemed pleased.

Anne gave me a cup of chocolate milk to go, and I headed back to my uncle's house. The afternoon was sweltering—probably in the mid-seventies. I was used to snow. But I kept Brittany's smile with me as I pedaled, and it passed the time.

When I reached the neighborhood, I decided to tour around. It was tough going. The dirt road was full of small rocks and seashells. The homes were set back from the street, some of them big, some small, some with immaculate lawns, others not so much.

As I approached one house, a dog yapped. An old lady tended a flower garden. The heavy floral scent hung in the humid air. Beside her, the tiny dog barked like he wanted to take my leg off. I frowned. Usually dogs loved me.

I leaned on my pedals to pick up speed when the little dust fluff darted out. I stopped before I ran over him.

"Oh, dear." The lady hobbled toward us, one hand on her hat. "Roscoe, come here. You naughty boy." She caught the dog in her arms. His growl sounded like a wind-up toy. Black eyes glared from a mound of tan fur.

"Ferocious," I said.

"I'm so sorry, young man. I've never seen him act like this."

"No harm done."

"You must be Cody. I've heard so much about you. I'm Edna Binkley. That's my husband, George, on the porch. He's confined to a wheelchair. Stroke, you know."

I blinked. "How do you know my name?"

"The whole town was abuzz about you. But now they're all talking about that mauling instead."

"Really? I haven't heard about a mauling."

"Gruesome," she said with obvious enjoyment. "A woman's body was found down North Road ripped to shreds. Some sort of animal attack. The authorities figure she'd been dead at least two days. Poor thing."

She continued talking, but a sound buzzed in my head and covered her words. I was a wolf two days ago. Had I murdered a woman? I didn't think I hurt anyone. Yet both times I became a wolf, I fell asleep. What if I hadn't slept? What if I blacked out instead?

"So you see why the safari is under investigation," Mrs. Binkley said.

"Yes, ma'am," I murmured. I felt like I might puke right there in the street. "Well, I better go."

"All right, dear." She smiled, and her little dog glared knowingly in her arms. "Bye, now."

I made it back to my uncle's house and left the bike in the yard. I stumbled up the porch steps. How could this be happening? How could I go in just a few days from a normal kid to a monster that killed people?

Once in my room, I fell onto the bed. My head spun. I went over the night I turned into a wolf. I'd made it to the tree line, and I remembered I howled at the moon. Then nothing.

Except during that nothing, I apparently mauled a woman to death.

I considered going to the authorities. But what would I tell them? They thought a wild animal was involved, not a kid. They'd probably laugh. Give Mrs. Binkley something more to gossip about.

My parents must have known this would happen. That's why they got rid of me. I couldn't go home. I had to live a life of secrecy. I had to keep away from people.

The thought brought an image of Brittany with her spiky hair and perfect smile. I felt like she'd just broken up with me. Like I'd lost her—which is crazy because I never had her in the first place.

A thought came to me—wolves mate for life.

"She's not my mate," I told the ceiling.

Somehow, I didn't believe it.

My cell rang. I fished it out of my pocket. It wasn't my parents. It was Mickey. I stared at the phone, wanting so much to answer, wanting so much to hear my best friend's voice. But I couldn't. I had to make a clean break. I winced and turned off the phone.

After a while, my uncle came home. I walked out to greet him. He carried a sack of hamburgers.

I stood in the kitchen doorway ready to go into my usual spiel of how red meat was bad for you and I never ate it. A throwback from having doctors as parents. But it smelled good, and I was hungry. I figured just this once wouldn't hurt. Hunkered down at the table, I dug in.

My uncle chuckled and took a couple burgers for himself. "How was your day?"

"Fine," I said between mouthfuls. "Anne says hi."

He nodded. "I made a few calls and found out we can't register you for school until January fourth."

"About that, I was thinking I would drop out of school. I'm old enough. I could work for you, learn how to be a Fix-It Guy."

"Your parents wouldn't thank me." He smiled. "We'll enroll you as planned. And I expect good grades. You probably already know more than most of those kids."

"That isn't the problem," I blurted, and wished I hadn't. I could never tell him what the problem was. I floundered around for a change in subject. "I met Mrs. Binkley today."

"Nice lady."

"Her dog hates me."

"Roscoe? Just give him a good growl. Establish dominance."

"She told me there'd been a mauling down on North Road. A woman."

"I heard."

"What do you think happened?"

"I really don't know."

"Do you think a lion escaped from the safari?" I asked, still hoping, still grasping for alternate explanations. "Or maybe one of those Florida panthers came out of the Everglades and got her?"

"No. That wasn't it."

"But what if—"

"Damn it, Cody. Forget about it. It has nothing to do with you." His eyes flashed. There was something feral in them.

I sat back. That was the first time Uncle Bob raised his voice to me. He was hiding something, I was certain. He knew something about that murder. I wondered what.

# FIVE

I spent the next week at Uncle Bob's side learning to fix things. He seemed glad for the company. I was nervous and jumpy, expecting Sheriff Brad to connect me to the mauling. I wasn't afraid of punishment. If I killed someone, I deserved to be jailed. But I didn't want Brittany to find out, didn't want her to think I was a monster.

So I filled my days with physical labor. We put up a split-log fence, patched the roof of a barn, and blacktopped a driveway. The sun was bright, and I learned to wear a hat. I met my neighbors, and made an effort to remember all their names. Something my dad taught me. They were friendly in return.

In the evenings, my uncle and I would dine at the café, and then we would go home and play gin rummy by porch light. It kept me busy and exhausted. But at every free moment, I thought of Brittany and how she smiled at me.

Friday morning, the dreaded day of school registration arrived. Uncle Bob drove me to Seminole Bluffs. The school had an expansive concrete courtyard with small holes cut in it for trees to grow through. The only grassy area I saw was a football field. Home of the Hawks.

We walked to the office. My uncle carried a FedEx envelope with my birth certificate, medical records, and some papers my parents' lawyer drew up. I felt sweat gather on the back of my neck and wondered if I should have gotten a haircut. Maybe they didn't care about things like that in public schools.

A woman greeted us at the counter. She wore a sweater draped over her shoulders as if she were cold and a pair of glasses on the end of her nose.

"I'm Bob Nowak," Uncle Bob said. "I called earlier about enrolling my nephew, Cody Forester."

She accepted the envelope and then looked at me, her eyes crinkling above her reading glasses. "Hello, Cody. We expected you. We've got your transcripts right here."

"That was quick." I felt like my old school had been eager to get rid of me.

"We need this to complete the registration." She slid a four-part form to my uncle.

While he filled in the blanks, a man stepped up.

He loomed over me. "Cody Forester? I am the Vice Principal, Mister Overhill. May I see you in my office for a moment?"

With a frown, I stepped into a room filled with photos and diplomas. Mr. Overhill closed the door. "Have a seat."

As I looked for a chair, I wondered what was up.

If he wanted to give me a standard welcome speech, he would have done it in the lobby.

He sat behind a desk and folded his hands. "Why are you here?"

I looked at him. I wanted to ask the same thing.

"You come from a rather prestigious school," he said. "You got good grades. Until last year. Can you tell me why your grades dropped?"

I gulped. I knew very well why my grades had fallen. I'd missed school because of the fevers.

As if a light went on, I realized that my unexplained fevers had something to do with my becoming a werewolf. Maybe wolf-ism was like a virus warping my genetic code. My body tried and failed to fight it off. I wasn't about to explain that to Mr. Overhill. I fudged for a suitable excuse.

He took my silence as an answer. "We don't abide drug use here at the Bluffs. I can refer you to several county programs if you admit to a problem."

"I don't have a problem."

"I see. Well, you obviously have some sort of problem. Moving from a private to a public school. Moving to Florida by yourself. So I ask again. Why are you here?"

I glared. I rarely talk back to an adult. It doesn't get you anywhere. But it was all I could do to keep my words level. "I'm at this school because this is where my uncle lives. The reason I live with my uncle is private."

His eyes narrowed. "We don't like troublemakers

at the Bluffs."

I wondered if he'd been talking to Sheriff Brad. I stood. "I'll keep that in mind."

He walked around his desk and opened the door. I stepped into the cool lobby.

"Get a haircut," he murmured as I passed.

At that moment, I knew they'd have to tie me to a chair before I'd cut my hair.

Uncle Bob looked up at the shuffle of my feet. "A couple of questions. Your birth date is October thirtieth, 1991. Right?"

The question didn't surprise me. He never sent a card. "Right."

"And you were born in Massachusetts?"

"D.C."

"Ah." He scribbled on the form. "That should do it."

"You're all set, Mister Nowak," said the woman with the crinkling eyes. "Cody, we'll see you bright and early Monday morning. Stop by here, and I'll give you your schedule."

"Thank you," I said, already walking away. I had to get out of the building.

My uncle hustled to catch me. "Nice school. It's practically brand new."

"I don't like it," I said. "I don't want to be here."

"You haven't tried." He blew out his breath and squinted as we stepped into the sunlight. "Let's give it until summer. If you still can't stand it, we'll try something else. Get you a tutor, maybe. But I can't let you quit. Your mother would kill me."

Then my mother shouldn't have kicked me out of the house, I thought, blaming her for the first time.

We drove home in silence. I memorized the route. I figured it would take close to an hour to cover the distance by bike. We pulled up the driveway. A large box sat on the porch.

Uncle Bob frowned. He cut the engine and came around the truck. Then he looked at me and grinned. "Dude. You got a Dell."

"A computer?" My jaw dropped. "They left a brand-new computer on the porch?"

He shrugged. "No one bothered it. Here, let me help you get it inside."

He held the door as I carried the box into the house. I felt excited, but a little disappointed, too. I'd hoped my parents would send me my old computer. It was a gaming machine, a real screamer. My friends dubbed it *The Heart-Stopper.*

I dumped the package on my bed and sat beside it, missing my friends. I wondered what kind of rumors they would spread when I didn't return to school. Kids were brutal. Mickey would be on my side. But after a while, even he would forget me.

I tore open the cardboard to find a laptop. Sleek and thin. Top of the line. I pulled out the spec sheet and ran my finger down the list. It had Wi-Fi, of course, but also a cellular card, which meant that I could get online from almost anywhere.

The manual said I could surf a hundred hours a

week and pick up a thousand emails without going over my cap. So the first thing I did after configuring the software was check my email.

I had seventy-five messages waiting, all from my friends. They wanted to know if I'd made out with any French girls, when I was coming home, and why I hadn't answered my mail. I didn't know what to tell them, didn't want to say where I was and why.

As if my fingers were made of lead, I deleted the emails one by one. Each click felt like the fall of an ax.

"How's it going?" Uncle Bob said from the doorway.

"Fine."

"What do you say we go out for dinner and celebrate your enrollment in school?"

I glanced at my watch. I hadn't realized it was so late. "All right." I left the laptop to charge.

We drove into town. My uncle jabbered on about how he never had a computer and maybe I could give him a few pointers, and about how he saw a nice book bag at Howard's but he held out for one that had Scooby Doo printed on it. I stared out the window and let his words wash over me.

I got a new computer. That should constitute a good day. But I didn't think I could get more depressed.

That is, until Monday, the day I had to go to school.

🐕 🐕 🐕

The alarm on my watch woke me before dawn on Monday. I rushed to the kitchen for a quick breakfast and was surprised to find my uncle at the table with a cup of coffee and a newspaper.

"You're up early," I said.

He sipped and smacked his lips. "Good morning to you, too. What time do you need to be at school?"

I pulled a jug of chocolate milk out of the refrigerator. "My first class is at seven thirty, but I have to get there early to pick up my schedule."

"I'm headed in that direction. I'd be happy to give you a ride. That is, if you can stand to be seen with a parental figure."

"That would be great." Relief washed through me. I didn't relish arriving at school sweaty and exhausted from riding my bike fourteen miles. "Can you pick me up again at three?"

"Not a problem."

"Thanks." I opened the cupboard. A bright green face and black eyes peered out. I jumped back. "There's a lizard in my bowl."

"Wave your hand at him. He'll move."

I snatched a dishtowel and flicked it at the creature. It settled deeper beneath the rim. I danced back and forth as I snapped the towel, careful not to get too close. I didn't want it to jump on me.

My uncle set down his cup. "What are you doing?"

"I'm trying to get it out of there. The thing must be a foot long. It's not like those little black ones."

Uncle Bob folded his newspaper and got to his feet. "Aw, it's a baby." He placed the newspaper on top of the bowl and carried the lizard to the open window. "They're great to have around. A natural pesticide."

I wondered which I would rather have in the house—lizards or bugs. I grabbed a clean bowl and sat down with a box of cereal.

"We have all kinds of lizards around here. You'll get used to them." Uncle Bob returned to the table with his newspaper. "The ones I don't like to tangle with are those spiny tail iguanas. They're tan, about five feet long. Look like a dinosaur."

"I feel like I'm on the set of Animal Planet."

He laughed. "Any rural area has wildlife. That's why I moved here."

"Do you ever close that window?"

"Never. I want a way to get inside in case I can't open the door."

I couldn't imagine when that would be. He never locked the house.

I finished breakfast, and he drove me to school. We got there before the buses, so I had time to scout the campus before it got crowded. I found a place to leave my bike if I rode in by myself. I saw the student parking lot, and stared at it a moment in longing and disappointment. My father hinted he might buy me a car this year. The only way I'd get one now was if I

53

got a job and bought it myself.

As I passed the lot, I smelled cigarettes. Three guys with physiques like gorillas stood together, smoking. I knew better than to make eye contact. Their kind meant trouble for regular guys like me. I'd been pushed around plenty of times. Being the president of the Science Club made me somewhat of a geek. So I knew not to antagonize gorillas. But before I could look away, I noticed the car next to them. It was a green Beetle. Brittany's car.

I froze in place, my heart racing. Brittany went to school here. Maybe I would bump into her in the hall. Would she remember me?

"Hey, jerk. Who do you think you're staring at?"

I registered the words as background noise. I imagined myself walking into class to find Brittany there, her hair black and shiny, an empty desk beside her.

Someone grabbed the front of my shirt. "I said who are you staring at?" one of the gorillas growled in my face. "Are you dense or what?"

"He's lost," another said. "Aren't you, new kid?"

"Is that right?" said the one creasing my shirt. "You lost? Do you want me to call your mommy for you?"

That just hit me wrong. All my anger about my parents and my unjust banishment welled up in me. I didn't want trouble. Heck, I didn't want to be there at all. And I didn't appreciate having it thrown in my face.

Usually I keep my head down and try to talk my way out of trouble. This time I looked up. Just looked. After a moment, the gorilla's gaze wavered. His grip on my shirt slackened.

"Keep your eyes to yourself," he muttered, and banged into my shoulder as he and his cronies walked away.

After they left, I felt both glad the exchange hadn't escalated and sorry he hadn't taken a poke at me. I'd never been in a fistfight, but with my increasing bad mood, I wondered what it would be like.

The school office was mass confusion. Voices vied for attention as students jostled for their place in line. I regretted not coming sooner. But the smiling woman I'd met before caught my eye and motioned me to the side. She still wore reading glasses on the end of her nose.

"Good morning, Cody," she said.

"Morning. What's going on?"

"Everyone complains about their schedule." She flipped her hand as if dismissing the chaos. "This is for you. Your first class is trigonometry."

I looked at the slip of paper she handed me. I had already finished trig one and was due to start trig two, but I didn't tell her that.

"I put you in Lunch B, which is at twelve thirty. I hope that isn't too late. As requested, your electives are Shop and Physical Education."

"PE?" I recoiled. I hadn't suffered through PE since I was in grade school. "I didn't ask for that."

"Why, yes." Her smile lines creased. "It was on the form your uncle filled out."

Of course. I pinched the bridge of my nose, practically hearing him say *what kid doesn't like Phys Ed*. "All right. Thank you."

"You're welcome. Come see me if you have any questions."

I pushed through the office and into the streaming hallway in search of my first class. The school was big, but I knew better than to ask for directions. I remembered too many times when I sent a new kid to the wrong side of the building at my old school.

I found my trig class. A couple of girls were already in the room. I sat in the back row. Only people who liked attention sat in front.

Kids trickled in. Like radar, their eyes snapped to mine. They didn't smile. I knew the look. *New kid*. I slouched a bit more in my seat.

The teacher showed up. He was short and narrow, like a miniature man in a suit. He didn't take attendance, just wrote some problems on the board. It was like I figured—I already knew the stuff. I'd ace the class, no problem.

As the rest of the students opened their texts, the teacher came down the aisle toward me.

"I have an extra." He gave me a discerning look and a workbook. "I understand that you're transferring from a private school."

"That's right."

"What are your thoughts so far?"

I looked at all the kids pretending not to listen, and then quoted the lady in the office. "Like anywhere else. Everyone complains about their schedule."

"Well, we're a young school. Got to learn to stand before we can march. But we have a good student body. We don't allow troublemakers."

I thought of the three gorillas in the parking lot.

"I don't know the reasons why you were asked to leave your last school." He held up a hand to quell my protest. "And I don't want to know. I believe people deserve a second chance. It's the third chance I have a problem with." With a tight smile that looked vaguely threatening, he walked away.

I sat, stunned. He thought my school kicked me out. Probably all the teachers thought that, talking about me behind my back. I opened my workbook with more force than necessary. Nearby students stared.

This was going to be a long day.

I had trouble finding my second class, World History, and got there just as the door closed. I stepped inside the crowded room. My stomach flipped.

Brittany was there, all eyeliner and lipstick, just as I imagined her. She was talking to the girl beside her, laughing, making me feel small and insignificant as I stood there.

"Thank you for joining us, Mister Forester," said the teacher. "There's a seat for you over by the window."

"Yes ma'am."

As I made my way to the back of the room, Brittany glanced up. She smiled at me. It was enough to blot out whatever the teacher said for the rest of the period.

The class ended and I hurried forward, but Brittany didn't hang around. I stepped into the hall and watched the back of her skirt sway as she dodged the growing crowd.

Third hour was gym. The three gorillas were there. I should have expected them. PE was probably their best class. They sneered at me, but I ignored them.

The teacher, Mr. Murgott, wore shorts and trailed an odor of BO. Everyone called him Coach. After taking attendance, he ushered us outside for some exercise. We staggered in single file. Some kids had dressed out, but others wore street clothes so I didn't feel too conspicuous. I followed the class onto a track surrounding the football field, careful to avoid my three friends.

"Take a lap," Coach Murgott ordered. "No screwing around."

I started at a trot, but soon found myself running. It felt good to stretch my legs after being cooped up inside. I thought about Brittany and the way she smiled when she saw me.

She recognized me. I knew I made an impression that day in Video Stop. Wish I hadn't knocked over Darth Vader, though. I winced, remembering, and then pushed the thought away.

That didn't matter. She was here. I couldn't believe it when I saw her in class. I wondered if there was a way to switch seats with the girl sitting beside her. Maybe I should play dumb and ask for her help with my homework. Maybe I should ask her out.

I ran faster, thinking of where I might take her. The Coffee Café? Nah, she'd want to go somewhere dressier than that. The Olive Garden.

Suddenly Coach stepped before me. "Hold on, boy. Pull it in here."

I slowed and circled around to stand beside him. I was panting, but not hard.

"Have you ever considered trying out for the football team?" he asked, eyes wide. "You'd make one heck of a wide receiver."

I looked across the field, unable to believe I'd left the rest of the class halfway down the track.

# SIX

The next morning when my uncle dropped me in front of the school, two guys approached. They had buzz cuts and button-down shirts.

The taller of the two wore glasses. "Hey," he said. "I'm Maxwell."

"Lonnie," said the other.

They seemed nervous. Their eyes shifted like they were goading each other to talk to me.

I looked at them. "I'm Cody."

"Yeah," Maxwell said as if agreeing with me. "New, eh?"

The kid had a knack for the obvious. Before I could ask where this was leading, the other kid spoke.

"Is it true you outran Efrem Higgins on the track yesterday?"

I screwed up my face. "Who?"

"Two things," Maxwell said. "Eff is kind of a good ole boy, born and raised in Florida. Him and his family still think the South will rise again. They hate New Yorkers."

"I'm from Massachusetts."

"Same difference, man," said Lonnie.

"Point number two," Maxwell counted on his fingers. "Eff don't like to be shown up. I mean, he's the freaking star of the football team. Twenty-seven receptions. He rules the school. Everybody loves him."

I got it. Efrem Higgins. One of the gorillas I met yesterday. "And I drew attention to myself."

"You're on his list." Maxwell nodded. "At first he blew it off, saying he had a stomach cramp or something."

"Yeah, but now he says he's going to break both your legs." Lonnie bounced on the balls of his feet like the circus was coming to town.

A sour taste filled my mouth. I gazed across the courtyard, expecting to see my doom. "Maybe I better stay out of his way."

"Maybe," said Maxwell. "Or maybe you don't care, with your reputation and all. Maybe old Eff finally met his match."

Me? I managed a smile. "Thanks for the heads up."

"No problem," Maxwell said. "Seeya."

"Seeya," Lonnie echoed.

As they walked away, I wondered what their stake was in all this. I guessed they were the kind of people that liked to look at car wrecks.

I spent the rest of the week playing keep away from Efrem Higgins. It wasn't easy, especially in PE. Fortunately, he didn't seem to want to start anything in front of the coach, and the coach was always nearby, trying to talk me into playing football. I didn't tell him that if I made the team it would be an instant death sentence. I was polite and non-committal and made sure I didn't run faster than anyone else.

Looking back, I honestly don't know how I ran so fast that first day. I was thinking about Brittany, and my feet just took off. I guess I could always run like that, but never had reason to. Why would I? I was expecting to become a doctor like my parents, and my classes were geared toward those ends.

All week long, Brittany ignored me in World History. It was fast becoming my most hated class. But Friday, just before lunch, she said hi as we passed in the hall. I was so amazed that I nearly walked right into Eff.

Fortunately, something warned me in time. In spite of the between-period commotion, I could hear him as if he stood next to me. I pulled up against the wall.

"What, are you chicken now?" he asked an unknown accomplice. "All I need you to do is distract him."

"I don't know, Eff. You're forgetting the lunch patrol. Can't we do this off school grounds?"

"I'll hit him quick. No one's going to catch us."

"We could get benched."

"I'll bench you if you don't help me teach this guy a lesson. He can't diss me."

It sounded like they were standing in front of the lunchroom. I considered running the other way, but that would just postpone things. Drawing my shoulders back, I rounded the corner to see a group of five burly football players in the hall.

Eff's face lit with a Christmas-come-early smile. He moved in, lowering his voice. "Hello, new kid."

"Eff." I nodded. "Interesting name, Eff. It fits you."

He blinked as if trying to work that one out. I stepped around him, hoping to reach the haven of the lunch patrol. But a hand grasped my shoulder.

I turned and stood nose-to-nose with Eff. We were the same height, but he was so muscular he outweighed me by about a hundred pounds. I met his eyes, but this time I was more scared than angry, so it didn't have the same effect. I sensed passersby streaming around us, trying to get out of the way, sensed the other four gorillas move up behind.

A booming voice chortled, "There you all are. I'm happy to see you getting along."

Eff stepped back. I looked over as Coach Murgott bounded down the hall toward us.

"Mister Higgins, I hope you are talking our friend here into trying out for the team," Coach said. "We certainly could use an extra pair of legs."

"Yes, sir." Eff narrowed his eyes at me.

The bell rang. "Where should everyone be?" Coach asked.

"Lunch," cried one of the thugs, smiling like he got the answer right.

The five football players walked together into the lunchroom.

I stood in the hall, heart racing.

"The way to show him what you're made of is to meet him on the field," Coach said. "The only language he speaks is football."

Anger flared, and my mouth filled with retorts. I didn't care if Eff knew what I was made of. I had no intention of meeting him anywhere. And the last thing I wanted to do was to play football. I clamped hard on my response, but I think he saw it in my eyes. "Excuse me, Coach."

I stormed off, skipping lunch. I thought of going outside to the courtyard and sitting in the sun. Instead, I went to the office. It was noisy, almost as crowded as before. I looked around for the woman with the reading glasses but couldn't spot her. Defeated, I sank on a bench. I'd promised Uncle Bob I would stick it out until summer, but I was barely making it through the week. What was I going to do?

"Cody? Is anything wrong?" The woman with the glasses sat beside me. She carried a cup of coffee and a brown paper sack.

"I was wondering if I could change my electives."

"Did you speak to your counselor?"

"We haven't been introduced."

"Oh." She set her coffee on the floor. "Let's see. You have PE."

I groaned. "Yes."

"They say you're doing well in that class. Coach Murgott likes you."

I looked away.

"A little physical activity must be nice. Work out your frustrations. It must be difficult settling in at a new school."

"Yeah."

"So PE isn't the problem. What's your other elective? Shop?"

"They're making birdhouses, for crying out loud." I said it like it was beneath me, but truthfully, I was way behind the other kids.

"I'm sorry, Cody, but we have so many students, once the schedules are set, it's hard to switch them around. You need a really good reason." She reached into her sack. "Would you like a tangerine? Home grown."

"Sure," I said. "Thanks."

She gave me the fruit, picked up her coffee, and with a fleeting smile walked away. I just sat there and watched the other kids, feeling left out and miserable. As I finished eating, the bell rang, and I went to class without running into any more problems.

It turned out that Maxwell and Lonnie were in my Shop class. I hadn't noticed them before, kept my head down too much. Besides, they were so nondescript they faded into the walls. They also looked harmless. At that moment, I was all about harmless, so I walked over and sat with them. They seemed pleased.

"We took this class because it's an easy pass," Lonnie said.

"Really?"

"Yeah, nobody ever fails Shop. You just have to show up." Smiling, he gave an exaggerated wink.

I smiled in return, relaxing for the first time that day. We turned to face our birdhouses.

"The roof goes on just like that," Maxwell said.

Lonnie frowned. "What about that big gap?"

"I'll just fill it in with putty. It's what my mom always does when she's baking a cake."

"She uses wood putty?"

"Frosting, toe fuzz. And you made that hole too small for a door. The birds will get stuck."

"Well, it can be a window, then."

"What?" Maxwell laughed. "What's a bird need a window for? You going to make little curtains, too?"

Lonnie punched Maxwell in the shoulder, and Maxwell shoved him back. They burst out laughing.

"No rough housing back there," called the teacher.

"Yes, Mister Conklin," they said in unison.

"I've got an idea," I whispered to Lonnie. "Why don't you cut a triangle from the bottom? It'll look like a keyhole. A door like no other."

"Nice." He nodded. "Maybe I'll get extra points for creativity."

We fell silent for a moment while Lonnie chiseled out the keyhole, Maxwell frosted his roof with putty, and I tried to tongue-and-groove my walls together.

"Guess your uncle must keep you busy," Maxwell said. "His business is booming."

"Think so?" I glanced up in surprise. I never

thought business was that great.

"Sure. Nobody does anything for themselves anymore."

"That's why I suck at this." Lonnie grimaced at the lopsided hole he'd made in his birdhouse.

"Anyway, if you get some free time tomorrow, you should come to the mall in Wellington. They have a great arcade. Every Saturday, there's a Tie Fighter tournament. Lonnie's won three times in a row."

"I'm a natural," Lonnie said.

"Sounds like fun," I said. "I'll try to make it."

Just then, Mr. Conklin gave the ten-minute warning, and we began putting away our supplies. I watched Maxwell and Lonnie from the corner of my eye. Part of me wanted to take them up on their invite, but a larger part warned me to stay away. I wasn't a normal kid. I didn't deserve to have friends. That thought led me to Brittany, and I winced as I imagined her screaming at the sight of my wolf.

I stayed away from the mall on Saturday. Uncle Bob had to work, so I spent the weekend with my laptop. I had fifty emails from friends back home, but I didn't read them. I didn't have to. They would want to know where I was, why I wasn't in school. I filtered them all as spam so I wouldn't have to look at them anymore.

I downloaded a calendar with the phases of the moon and set it as my wallpaper. I also set up a widget for the local news so I would know if there were any more animal attacks. Then I opened the Internet and researched werewolves.

I found out that present-day lycanthropes called themselves *therians*. They were all over the Web. There were even social networks devoted to *therians* and *otherkins*. But I didn't want to join a community. I wanted to find a way to stop becoming a wolf.

My research went nowhere. I felt anxious and alone. Time was running out. The moon would be full again soon.

# SEVEN

A week later in the middle of the night, the change gripped me. I was dreaming something stupid about all the classrooms looking like birdhouses, when for no reason I took a running leap off the roof. I came down in a barrel roll, and when I stood up, I went wolf, tearing through the woods.

The dream startled me awake. I lay in bed, sweating and shaking, half expecting something with teeth to be in the room with me. My bedroom was dark, but I could see through the shadows as if they weren't there. Sounds drifted through the open window. There was so much life in Florida. Crickets and field mice, opossum and armadillos. Bats flitted through the trees, making a kind of whistling sound. Higher in the open air, a nighthawk circled.

They called to me, tempting me to join them. I wasn't stupid. I knew it was the night before the full moon. If I climbed out that window, my humanity would be lost to the wolf. So I clutched my Scooby sheet to my chin and waited out the night.

A little after dawn, tires crunched over the gravel driveway. A door slammed, and footsteps came up the side lawn. A figure moved past my window. It was Uncle Bob. He had blood on him. Not drenched in it or anything, but I could smell it. I crawled out of bed, moved to the window, and peered out. He walked to the garbage can behind the shed, stripped off his bloody shirt, and dropped it inside. Then he closed the trashcan liner and dragged it to the curb for pick up.

After that, I heard him on the porch, stomping his boots like he stepped in something nasty. I stumbled into the living room, still pulling up my jeans, and met him as he came through the door. I squelched the urge to ask where he'd been.

"I don't feel well," I told him. "I think I'll call out of school today."

He chuckled and shook his head. "Oh, no. You aren't getting out of it that easily."

He walked past me on his way to the kitchen. He had a birthmark in the shape of a backwards C between his shoulder blades. I also noticed three deep scratches on the side of his neck. I smelled his blood. It wasn't the same scent as the blood on his shirt. I pictured him in a bar fight, but I never knew him to go to a bar.

From the kitchen doorway, I watched him make his customary cup of instant coffee. I wished I could talk to him and tell him why I couldn't go to school. I wished he could understand. Like that would happen. He'd probably lock me up somewhere. Maybe I'd be better off.

"No, really," I said. "I'm sick."

"Nah. You don't get sick." He sipped his coffee, looking at me over the rim of his cup. His eyes smiled.

My shoulders sagged. "I *can't* go."

"You can't cut every time you get the shakes. What do you think girls do? Do you think they take off just because they have a little visitor?"

That stumped me. What was he talking about?

He sat at the table with his coffee and newspaper, bare-chested. His movements made the cuts on his neck ooze. The coppery scent of blood filled the kitchen.

My stomach roiled. "I can't."

"You're going," he said from behind his paper. "Even if you're late."

I scowled, unable to think of a retort. "What happened to your neck?"

"Cat fight. You know how it goes." He grinned and gave me a wink.

A chill ran through me. I backed away and got ready for school.

We drove through town without speaking. I kept my eyes closed most of the way. Colors were too bright, and the jouncing of the truck made everything blur.

As we pulled to the front of the school, Uncle Bob said, "I'll pick you up at the regular time."

I got out and slammed the door. My life sucked. Shoulders hunched, hands in my pockets, I walked through the courtyard. The school buses were already there, and people hung out in groups. I noticed a crowd near the parking lot.

Then, with my hyper-hearing, I heard Brittany say, "Knock it off, Efrem. Leave me alone."

My stomach plummeted. I rushed toward the growing crowd.

"Where you going, goth girl?" Eff said. "How about a little kiss?"

"Stop it!"

I pushed through the bystanders and burst through to the front. Brittany hugged an armful of books, struggling to get away from Eff's half-embrace. He stood behind her making smooching sounds in her ear. She twisted, and he suddenly let go. I couldn't tell if he shoved her or if she overbalanced, but she fell, books scattering across the pavement.

I was so mad I heard sirens go off in my head. I stepped between them, glaring at Eff. "That's enough."

A gasp encircled the crowd as the onlookers took a collective step back.

Eff's face lit. "Oooh. New kid. I'm so scared."

The football brigade stood behind him, their ears perked, sensing an easy mark. But I wasn't easy. Not this time. I would never be the easy one again. "Walk away, Eff."

"What are you going to do, huh?" He sneered. "I've been waiting for this."

Eff glanced to the side, and his buddies stepped back as if to give him room. His eyes narrowed. He swung a fist at me. It was like in slow motion. I raised my hand and caught it—not deflected it. Stopped it cold. His eyes widened in a moment of surprise. With the heel of my other hand, I struck him flat in the face.

He flew backward ten or twelve feet. Might've gone farther, but he slammed into his friends. I stomped forward, and they dropped him like he was hot. He sprawled on the pavement, looking dazed. Blood gushed from his nose. I stood over him and growled.

Actually growled.

That snapped me out of it. Silence stood around me. I glanced about at surrounding faces, all of them looking shocked and amazed. I turned toward Brittany. She still sat on the ground, her books strewn about her.

If this were a romance novel, I would offer my hand to the beautiful damsel in distress. But this was a horror flick. I didn't want to turn into a wolf in front of her. I stalked away without a backward glance. I figured that if the jocks were going to jump me, they would have done it by now. The crowd retreated, murmuring and staring.

I clenched my jaw. The wolf inside me seethed, but it was tempered by the knowledge of where I was and what I'd done. I pushed through the front doors of the school and went to my first class.

The morning was miserable. Everywhere I went,

people stared at me, whispering, "There he is." "Did you hear what he did?"

The between-class crush no longer existed. A magical aisle formed before me wherever I walked.

When I went to World History, I kept my head down and avoided Brittany's eyes. It was ironic. All this time, I was hoping she would notice me. Now that she had, it was for the wrong reasons.

At the end of class, I went to the boys' locker room to dress out for PE. Eff wasn't around. I wasn't surprised. I busted his nose pretty good. I wove through rows of benches, making my way to my locker, trying to ignore the stares that followed, when Coach Murgott latched onto my arm.

In a quiet voice, he said, "Vice Principal Overhill wants to see you in his office right away."

I closed my eyes. It figured there would be reper-cussions. Probably I'd be expelled. I wondered where my parents would send me after Uncle Bob kicked me out.

Coach patted my shoulder. "I've already put in a good word for you."

I stared at him. "But he's your star player."

"You could be, too. Besides, I've seen how Eff taunts you. We all know he can be a bit of a jerk." He smiled and gave me a gentle shove.

I walked out wondering if Coach was tricking me. Like he'd fill me with false hope, and then I'd get to the office to find a firing squad.

The woman with the glasses greeted me with a

worried expression. She nodded toward the vice principal's door. "Go on in."

I licked my lips, but my mouth was so dry, it didn't do any good. I walked into Overhill's office.

Eff sat in a chair. He looked paler than usual. Bright white tape covered his nose. A man stood behind him. Probably his father. He glared at me as I entered. Behind the two of them, looking as stern as ever, stood Sheriff Brad.

Great. Not only was I being expelled, I was being arrested, too.

"Have a seat, Cody," Overhill said.

There were three chairs before his desk. I chose the one farthest from Eff.

"What do you have to say for yourself?" Overhill said.

My stomach quivered, but beneath my apprehension came a twinge of anger. I met his eyes. "A lot of people saw what happened."

"Yes. We've gotten a variety of stories. I want to hear yours."

I shrugged. "Eff was harassing a girl. He shoved her. She fell. I stepped between them."

"You hit a girl?" Eff's father bellowed.

"No." Eff mumbled around the wad of gauze up his nose. "Dad, he's eyeing. I was dust hawking do her."

Overhill cocked his head at me. "That's when you punched Efrem."

"I told him to walk away. He took a swing at me.

I pushed him."

"You didn't punch him?"

"No, sir."

"Hold out your hands." Sheriff Brad stomped over to me. He examined my knuckles. "They're clean. No marks."

"Thee? Ike I toad you," Eff said. "I fell. He couldn't ache my nodes. Ook at him. Inny 'ittle 'it head."

"That's enough of that kind of language," Overhill said.

From the doorway, a girl said, "You wanted to see me?"

I smelled Brittany—from her fruity hair gel to the mud on her shoes. My face went hot, and I wanted to melt through the floor, but I turned to look at her. I couldn't stop myself.

"Yes," Overhill told her. "Sit down."

Her eyes flashed. In a measured tone, she said, "I will not sit next to that moron."

Overhill blinked. "Which one?"

Sheriff Brad said, "Miss Meyer, we are trying to get to the bottom of an altercation that occurred on school grounds this morning."

"Simple," she said. "Mister Football, here, was shoving me around, and Cody stopped him."

Relief eased my frown. *She knows my name.*

"I see," said the sheriff. "Did you at any time feel you were in danger?"

She waved her arm at Eff. "What do you think?"

"Brittany," Overhill said in a cajoling voice, the

kind of voice my mother used when she was pointing out the ridiculous. "It has been suggested that Efrem pushed you down."

"He did."

"Did hot," Eff said.

"You lie." She glared at him, and then pointed at me. "If Cody hadn't shown up, you might have hurt me even more."

Overhill perked. "You're hurt?"

"Yeah." She focused her glare on the vice principal. Then she lifted the side of her skirt. Way up. Her thigh looked scraped and bruised, and a dark red abrasion showed near her hip.

I gasped, first at the beauty. Her leg was hot. Then at the harm. Eff had hurt her.

He *hurt* her.

I shot to my feet, a growl in my throat, my hands poised to strangle.

Eff's father got to him first. "That does it." He dragged his son by the collar. "Mister Overhill, thank you for your time. We're going."

I clenched my fists, breathing hard, glaring as they left the office. Overhill walked to the open door. "Carol, please have someone escort Brittany to the infirmary."

Brittany sputtered. "I don't need—"

He held up his hand, curtailing her. "You're injured. You should at least put some ice on it."

With a huff, she spun on her heel and went into the lobby. I watched her go. I wanted to be with her, needed to protect her. Her bruises raged in my mind. I relaxed my shoulders and tried to look nonchalant. "Are we done?"

"Well…" Sheriff Brad consulted a notebook. "Under the circumstances, I don't believe Mister Higgins will be pressing charges. However." He fixed me with a steely eye. "That's quite a temper you have, boy. We'll be watching you." He flipped the notebook shut and left the room, jingling as he walked. Maybe he had keys or loose change in his pockets.

Overhill sat on the edge of the desk. "I told you we don't like troublemakers here."

"I didn't cause this."

"No. But this vigilante stuff. The proper thing would be to get a teacher."

"And leave a girl to the mercy of a thug?"

"At least he'd be held accountable, not you." He looked at me. "Is this the sort of thing that got you in trouble at your last school? Are there sealed legal records I should be aware of?"

I pursed my lips, biting back a tirade. I'd never been in trouble. Not once. But Overhill wouldn't believe that. He already had me pegged as a problem.

"The sheriff is right," Overhill said. "You have anger management issues. If you don't learn to control yourself, things like this will follow you all your life."

"Things like helping people?"

"You're a superhero now? Is that how you see yourself?"

The bell rang. There was an immediate uproar

from the hallways beyond the office.

Overhill looked at me. "You may go."

I rushed out, welcoming the noise, the crush of bodies, the obscurity. That is, until an aisle opened as those around me backed away and stared. I didn't know whether to laugh or scream.

At lunchtime, I went through the line and carried my crappy meal to the back of the room as usual. I slouched in my seat, wondering how I could get away with cutting the rest of my classes, when someone dropped their tray on the table before me.

"Do you mind?" Brittany asked. "Nobody wants to sit with me, either."

I blinked, my mouth dropping open. "Ah."

She sat across from me at the empty table, the florescent lights turning her hair almost blue. Her lips were glossy purple. She smiled. "That was really cool, what you did."

Wow. She thought I was cool. Pleasure and embarrassment warmed my cheeks. "I don't usually get in fights like that. It's not me."

"I know." She nodded. "But that is your rep."

"I have a reputation?"

"They say lots of things about you." She looked at her tray. It held an orange, two apples, and a yogurt. She took a bite of apple. "Some say you hit your teacher with a car. Others say you picked up the car and threw it at your teacher. But most say you locked your teacher in the trunk of the car and pushed it over a cliff."

"I what?"

"You have cliffs where you came from, right? In Maine?"

"Massachusetts," I said, "and yes, we have cliffs."

"Florida must be quite a change for you. We don't have much of anything around here."

"I can get used to the weather."

"Wait until summer." She took another bite of apple, leaving bright purple kisses on the skin.

I cleared my throat, looking away. "So, what's with you and Eff? You two got some sort of a thing?"

She scoffed. "He asked me to go to Jana's birthday party."

A rock landed in the pit of my stomach. I tried to cover my dismay. "Someone's having a party?"

"Jana. It's a big deal. Most everyone in the tenth grade will be there."

"Eff asked you in front of all those people?"

"No." She drawled the word. "He asked me a couple days ago. In private. The party's in February. I guess he figured if he asked me early he'd catch me off guard. I said I wouldn't go with him, of course. He's still mad about it."

"So, you two aren't dating?"

"He's been trying to get me to go out with him since we were in eighth grade. You'd think he'd get the freaking message."

Smiling, I picked up my sandwich.

She nearly choked. "Don't eat that."

"It's just cheese." I opened it up. "Cheddar, see?"

"That part's all right, but don't eat that stale white bread. It's *processed.*"

She scrunched her nose as she said it. I stared, wishing she would do it again.

"Hold on." She opened her packet of silverware. With a plastic knife, she sawed two thick slices from her remaining apple, and then sandwiched the cheese between them. "Eat it like this. The perfect lunch."

"You're joking." I nibbled a corner. It wasn't bad. I shrugged and took a larger bite.

She seemed pleased. "You live with the *Fix-It Guy?*"

"Yeah. He's my uncle."

"How come you don't live with your parents?"

I looked at her, wanting to tell her the truth, wanting to tell her a lie. I pictured myself giving a witty reply—*well, after I set my teacher on fire...* But I wasn't witty. I was a monster.

With a shrug, I said, "I guess they just don't want me around anymore."

Brittany nodded, looking a little sad, and opened her yogurt.

For the rest of the day, I went through the motions of listening in class, but my mind was on Brittany. I replayed our lunch together in minute detail.

Kids continued to stare and hop out of my way. It didn't bother me. I even smiled once or twice. But when I got into Shop, Maxwell and Lonnie treated me like some kind of conquering hero. I had to put a stop to it.

"Look, it wasn't a big deal," I told them. "He threw a punch, I threw a punch, and it was over."

"Over is right." Maxwell chortled. "I heard his dad came to get him. I'd like to hear Eff explain what happened."

"Seriously," Lonnie said.

"Good thing you don't have to explain to your parents," Maxwell said.

"Yeah." I closed my eyes. I would have to tell my uncle. The thought soured my mood.

By the end of the day, the wolf in me raged. I rushed to escape the confines of the building.

A group of girls gave me a wide berth.

I yelled at them. "Yeah, that's right. Get out of my way."

They scampered like rabbits, giggling and flicking glances at me over their shoulders.

I looked for my uncle, but Howard was there instead. He leaned against the side of a truck the color of rust. He wore overalls without a shirt, and his hair blew about his bare shoulders.

I walked over to him. "Is Uncle Bob okay?"

"He bumped into an old friend. Taking her to dinner. He said to tell you that he'd see you in the morning."

"Oh." I winced and glanced over the emptying courtyard. "Great."

"Not a problem, is it?"

"No. I mean, it's his life and all. It's just that..." I lowered my voice. "I got in a fight today. Busted a guy's nose. I just figured it'd be better if he heard it from me first."

"I see."

"I know I shouldn't have, but I got so angry. I wanted to..." I made a wringing motion like I was throttling Eff's neck.

"We are all one child spinning through Mother Sky." Howard opened the passenger door, and slapped me on the shoulder. "Hop in, young *Mai-Coh*. I have what you need."

I climbed in, wondering what *Mai-Coh* meant. Probably Native American for *padawan*.

The interior of the truck was as rusty as the outside. The floor was bare of carpeting, and the plastic coating had worn off the dashboard. There was a gun rack behind my head. It held a polished staff with feathers tied to one end.

"This truck is ancient," I blurted as Howard climbed behind the wheel.

"But she purrs like a kitten."

He started her up. The engine roared, deep and throaty. Its power rumbled in my chest. I gained new respect for Howard's junk.

He didn't speak much as he drove. I didn't feel like talking anyway. When we got to his street with all the pink houses, I realized his place stood out like an eyesore with its tables and overgrown grass. I wondered if he caught any flak for that.

Howard parked in the driveway. "Come on in."

I followed him to the front door. I had never been in Howard's house, although I spent a lot of time in his front yard, it being my uncle's favorite place to shop. The first thing I noticed was that Howard locked his doors. Inside, I caught an odd odor, like herbs and rich soil.

Furniture filled the living room. Animal figurines covered every flat surface. *Brednie*, my mother called it. We passed through to the kitchen. A wooden drop-leaf table stood in the center with a pestle and mortar on top. On the wall, a clock shaped like a chicken clucked with each second.

"We'll go out back," Howard said. "It's stuffy in here. Just let me get a few things."

He opened a cupboard lined with crocks and mason jars. With his arms filled, he hip-checked the back door.

Howard's backyard was nothing like the front. It was a green oasis. There was a covered patio complete with lounge chairs and a propane grill, flowerbeds filled with plants I didn't recognize, and a square of grass the brightest green I'd ever seen. It should have been pleasant.

But the propane reeked. The unusual plants made me want to sneeze. Birds sang too loud, and the palm trees rasped like crinkling paper. The television blared from the house next door. Down the street, two little boys squabbled over a toy airplane. In the next cul-de-sac, a sweating man trimmed bushes with a gas-powered hedge-cutter.

"Have a seat," Howard said. "I'll just get this tea brewing."

I pursed my lips. I didn't care for tea. But I didn't feel like being alone either, so I sat on one of the lounge chairs and put my feet up.

Howard started the grill and set a pot of water on the flames. He moved through the flowerbeds, plucking a leaf here, a blossom there. He hummed as he worked. A singsong melody. After a few moments, he laid everything on a table beside the grill. His voice rose as he crushed the flowers between his fingers and dropped them into the simmering water. He did the same to the leaves. Then he opened the mason jars and added a pinch of this and a pinch of that. His song ended with an abrupt motion of his hands. He extinguished the propane flame.

A sweet aroma drifted to me. I breathed deeply. "Are you Seminole?"

"Navajo, actually." He smiled. "I'm a long way from the reservation."

"How did you end up here?"

He stirred the pot. "I took a vacation, decided I liked the weather."

I laughed. "That's not it."

"Part of it." He sighed. "I fell in love with a beautiful Miccosukee woman. They suffered me to live with her for a time, but I wasn't one of them, and the friction wore on our relationship."

"Why didn't you go home?"

"Sometimes you can't. You know?" He shrugged, ladling tea into a mug. "Besides, I like knowing she's nearby. We always return to our first loves."

He carried the mug to where I sat. I took it, sniffing. It smelled like a mountainside meadow.

"It looks like blood," I said.

"There's blood in it." He nodded. "Powdered."

My stomach quailed. I reminded myself that I had eaten blood soup once on a trip to Poland to visit my mother's ancestral home. In my lifetime, I'd eaten many things out of the ordinary. This was no different.

Blowing away the steam, I sipped from the mug. The taste of flowers hit first, but after I swallowed, the back of my tongue reported an earthy flavor, maybe mushroom. It didn't taste like blood.

"Good?" Howard asked.

"Yes." I took another sip. "What is it?"

"A restorative." He walked to the table and picked up the containers. "It has a calming effect. You might fall asleep."

Sleep would be nice, I thought, remembering I'd stayed up half the night before. I drank more tea. My shoulders relaxed. The cacophony around me faded into something less grating. Howard took his containers of powdered blood and mushrooms into the kitchen. I heard him clattering around. Then he came back out and sat next to me in one of the lounge chairs.

"Still angry?" he asked.

I smiled and drained my mug. "What is this stuff?"

"Just herbal tea. We've given it to our children for generations."

"Uh-huh. What kind of blood do you put in your herbal tea?"

"Snake."

I motioned around the yard. "Does everything here have medicinal properties?"

"Not medicines as you expect. All plants are our brothers and sisters. They talk to us and if we listen, we can hear them. They want us to be well." He stood. "Come on, I'll take you home."

I was comfortable and didn't want to get up. But before I knew it, we had pulled into the drive at my uncle's house. I thanked Howard for the ride and waved from the porch. As he pulled away, a crushing loneliness overtook me. I did *not* want to go into an empty house.

I sat on the porch swing. It creaked as it rocked. I thought about my lunch with Brittany and wondered if she would join me again tomorrow. I'd have to remember not to buy a sandwich. Thinking about the purple prints her lips left on her apple, I drifted to sleep.

🐕 🐕 🐕

I awoke abruptly. The porch was shadowed, and the sky was orange. My stomach cramped as if wolf paws clawed to get out. Tonight was a full moon.

I paced, wringing my hands. What would I do? I didn't want to hurt anyone. I had to run, had to go deep into the woods and hope nobody saw me.

With a desperate whine, I hopped the railing, crossed the side yard, and entered the tree line. Dry brush crunched beneath my feet. I smelled water nearby, heard the hum of traffic on the overpass at least a mile away.

I strode through palms and pine, hoping to be far from civilization before the change took me. Dusk masked fallen branches and gullies, but even in the deepening gloom, I could see. I felt like my senses were merging, like sight and smell and hearing were all one.

After a time, I looked behind. My uncle's house was dark, distant through the tree trunks. I should've left on the porch light, let it be a beacon back to my humanity. As an afterthought, I stripped off my shirt and hung it on a branch as a marker. I figured I would smell it even from a distance. It would lead me home.

Then I pulled off my jeans and shoes. I piled them at the base of the tree. The symbolism didn't escape me—I was leaving behind much more than my clothes. Tears streamed down my face. I felt like I was at a funeral. The death of me.

With my back straight and my jaw set, I walked into the woods.

# EIGHT

I continued walking in my undershorts and socks, passing from deep woods to fields of scrub. I sloshed through marshland and fought serrated plants with leaves that cut like razor wire.

Miles later, I came across a dirt road. I stared in disbelief. I'd tried so hard to get away, and here were signs of people again. My shoulders slumped, and I covered my face with my hands.

"Oh, God," I cried. "If you'll let me be a normal kid again, I promise to do anything you say. I'll even go to church. Just don't make me turn into a wolf anymore."

My muscles cramped in answer. A thousand pinpricks swept my skin, and I imagined coarse hair popping out. I tried to stop it. I tried to stay human, but I had no control. Without looking, without needing my eyes at all, I sensed the moonrise.

I moaned. "At least, don't let me hurt anyone."

I left the road and burst through a line of trees into a starlit field. It was like a hidden courtyard with tall pines on all sides. About halfway across, the pain in my legs dropped me. I curled into a ball and managed to remove my shorts. My face ached as my muzzle elongated. I panted through my teeth, struggling to take off my socks.

My toes felt like they were whacked with hammers. My feet contracted and shifted into paws. After that, the socks pulled off easily. They tasted good.

That brought a pang of guilt. I wasn't supposed to be a wolf. I had failed.

Dropping the wet sock, I looked around. My vision was clear even in the shadows. It was as if moonlight made everything glow. A variety of scents thickened the air. I smelled dirt and grass, flowers and trees. Beneath those scents, I recognized that of animals. Rabbits were everywhere. Deer ran to the east. In the surrounding stagnant water, I smelled fish and frogs.

Farther away, I smelled wolves. That surprised me. I didn't know Florida had wolves. But there they were—a male and the stronger scent of a female. I pictured them frolicking in the moonlight. The female smelled enticing. I wanted to go to her, but I fought to keep my head. They were wolves. I was the amazing wolf boy. They'd probably rip me to shreds.

I walked in the other direction. At first, my hind legs couldn't keep up with my front, but after a while, I caught the rhythm of my stride. I left the privacy of the courtyard and followed the dirt road, wondering where it led.

A breeze tickled my ears, making them twitch. I

listened for the approach of a car, but none came. The road was deserted. At one point, it widened and curved away from a cliff. Man-made, of course. There were no natural cliffs in the Everglades.

Bored, I turned off and headed deeper into the woods. Since I mastered the technique of walking, I decided to practice trotting. I felt clumsy and stupid. This must be why puppies always laugh at themselves. I wasn't in much of a mood for laughing.

I crossed a field and entered a thicket. The trees were old and gnarled. Twigs and rotten logs covered the ground. I'd gone a distance inside when I caught a whiff of something I couldn't identify. I mean, I recognized rabbits because I kept one as a pet when I was little. I knew deer because we had plenty of them in the hills back home. This scent was new.

I stopped, lifting my nose. A rustle came from the branches above. I looked up.

I was standing directly beneath a Florida panther. My fur stood on end. The cat leaned forward as if to pounce, gold eyes shining.

A growl rumbled in my throat. I didn't mean to do it. I'd rather keep quiet and tiptoe away. I growled again, louder this time, and even to me it sounded menacing. The panther settled back on its branch. Evidently, it wanted no part of a wolf.

I gave a snort of acknowledgement, kind of a sneeze, and kept walking. My shoulders tensed, and I expected to be struck down by the weight of the beast, claws sinking into my back, fangs at my throat. I kept my gait unhurried, listening. The panther did not pursue.

By the time I got out of the thicket, the whole thing seemed hilarious. Who did that cat think he was? Did he actually expect to beat a super-sized wolf? I was twice as big. I grinned, allowing my tongue to loll to the side.

As I walked, I passed a pungent, muck-filled gully. Mud sucked my paws. I danced and laughed with the sensation of moisture squishing through my pads.

A new scent grabbed my interest. Rabbit. I leaped, and it hurdled forward, daring me to chase it. I zigzagged over a field, filled with the thrill of the run, the exhilaration of the hunt. The rabbit sped before me, fur silvered by moonlight, fear thrumming in its veins.

I pounced and caught it. The small creature hung limp from my jaws, heartbeat like a drum roll, and I wanted so much to eat it. There was nothing like a fresh-caught rabbit dinner, as my uncle would say.

Humans don't eat this way, a voice whispered in the back of my head. Humans eat *Big Macs* and pizza with extra cheese. I recognized the words, but try as I may, I couldn't remember what they meant.

It didn't matter. I wasn't hungry, and the fun was in the chase, anyway.

I dropped the rabbit. It hit the ground running and took off through the grass. I watched it go, and then trotted into the trees.

The moon was low when I found the shirt. It hung from a tree like a flag, wafting a familiar scent. With a bounding leap, I snagged it with my teeth and pulled it down. It was stiff with dried sweat, rich with complex odors. I rolled on it, squirming on my back.

That was when the change hit. I yelped as every muscle in my body knotted and cramped. My skin felt on fire. I struggled to my feet, shaking, and felt a liquid sensation as my ears slid down the sides of my head.

What was happening? Where was the moon? Panic swept me and I howled, howled with all my remaining strength. Dry heaves cut short my cry. Foam erupted from my mouth. My muzzle retracted. I fell to my knees, choking, gagging, certain I was about to die. Then my spine straightened and took the pressure off my throat.

I gasped and groaned, then rolled onto my back. I remembered who I was. Even more, I remembered everything that happened throughout the night. I hadn't killed, hadn't hurt anything, human nor beast. I may be a monster, but I could control myself.

I found my clothes, dressed, and stumbled to the house. I ached all over like I was getting the flu. The light of pre-dawn showed an empty driveway, so I went in through the front door. I tossed my clothes into my closet and hopped into the shower. Cuts covered my arms and legs, and they burned with the touch of water.

As I toweled off, I heard my uncle come in. I

tugged on a fresh pair of jeans and hurried to the kitchen to greet him. "Morning."

"Yep," he said.

"Have a nice night?"

"The best." He grinned. "How about you?"

"Nothing special." I leaned against the doorframe with my arms crossed. I noticed the scratches on his neck were gone. He must be a quick healer. That reminded me. "I got into some trouble at school yesterday. Broke a guy's nose."

"I heard. You're kind of the talk of the town."

"Again?" I grimaced, remembering old Mrs. Binkley saying everyone knew I had moved to Loxahatchee.

"Did you used to get into scuffles at your old school?"

"I was usually on the receiving end. I mean, I'm not a wuss or anything. But I was into science and I got good grades, so that made me a target."

He nodded. "There's always been a thing between jocks and nerds."

I sighed. Yeah, I was a nerd once upon a time. What was I now?

"So you like science?" Uncle Bob asked.

"I like puzzles. Like to piece things together. Science is the ultimate mystery. If you can figure it out, you can know everything."

"That's some goal, knowing everything." He motioned. "Looks like you got a five o'clock shadow."

I blinked. "What?"

"A beard."

I ran my hand over my face and felt stubble. Honest to God stubble. I had a beard. I bit back a whoop.

How could I explain this?

But my uncle didn't seem to think my sudden hairiness strange. He turned to the sink, making his coffee. "There are some disposable razors in the medicine cabinet if you're interested."

"All right."

I returned to the bathroom grinning, staring at myself in the mirror. I had a beard. This was one side effect of being a werewolf I could get used to.

I knew how to shave. I'd been shaving once a month since I was fourteen, although I never really had to before. I finished the job with only one nick on my chin.

Uncle Bob knocked on the bathroom door. "Get a move on. It's time to leave."

I went to school in high spirits, in spite of not having slept nor eaten. In the hallways, kids still moved out of my way, but I found it funny. The talk of the town, that's me.

Brittany glanced my way during World History, but made no move to switch seats. I understood. I was still the new kid. I felt lucky she acknowledged me at all.

By lunchtime, I was ravenous. I got into the food line. The room echoed with voices. The lunch patrol broke up cliques of kids. In the back of the room, someone sat at my table.

It was Brittany.

My heart skipped, and my mind halted. *What should I eat?* I had to find something she would approve of. With my eyes on her, I pulled items off the ledge at random, loading my tray. I bumped into the person in front of me, trying to get them to hurry.

When the cashier told me I owed ten dollars, I paid without looking. Part of me warned that I had just spent my food allowance for the next week.

Brittany smiled as I approached and patted the table in front of her, inviting me to sit. The room seemed suddenly quiet. I felt lightheaded, my stomach leaping like we were having a secret rendezvous instead of lunch in a crowded cafeteria.

"Hi," I breathed as I slid in across from her.

She looked at my tray. "Hungry?"

I looked down. I'd bought pizza, French fries, a ham and cheese on rye, and an apple. And Jell-O. Three servings of Jell-O. I felt my face color. "You can have some, if you want."

She snagged a fry. "Yuck. Tastes like cardboard." She took another.

Smiling, I took a bite of pizza. "I didn't get breakfast this morning."

"I never have breakfast. I'm too busy getting Butt Crack off to school."

"Who?"

"My little brother."

"Oh," I said around mouthfuls. "What's his name?"

"Butt Crack."

"What's his real name?"

She looked at me. "Butt. Crack."

"Oh."

"He's such a pest. You know how brothers are."

"I'm an only child."

"Lucky you," she said. "I have an older brother. He works as a graphic artist in Jacksonville. That's what I want to be. My sister is married and has a two-year-old daughter. She named her Miley. Do you believe it?"

"I thought that name was copyrighted."

She opened her yogurt. "I think everyone should have their own name. Like the Indians used to do."

"Oh, like Fat Goose in Tree."

She laughed. "I'm so glad you understand."

Her laugh was like the tinkling of a fairy. I could listen to it all day. She watched me for a moment, making me wonder what kind of dumb expression I had on my face.

"You're pretty smart in World History," she said.

"It's just a matter of memorizing dates."

"Yeah, but Napoleon? Give me a break."

I shrugged.

"I had a really cool teacher in American History last year," Brittany said. "She taught us about the Salem Witch Hunt and voodoo and things."

"Do you practice voodoo?"

"No." She smiled, drawing out the word. "What's really interesting is what they do with bits of hair and fingernails. That's DNA. Only they hadn't discovered DNA in those days, so how did they know to use it?"

"Well, I—"

"One word." She leaned forward. "Aliens. We were obviously seeded here by creatures from another world. Or at the very least, we were visited by them."

"Right," I said trying to follow the conversation.

"You don't believe me."

"On the contrary," I said. "I've watched enough sci-fi to know anything is plausible if you say it with enough conviction."

Her eyes sparkled. "We should be study partners."

"Ah, sure. Whenever you like."

"How about today? Do you have a car?"

I blinked. "No, I—"

"That makes it easy, then. I'll take you to my house, and I'll drop you home whenever you like. Deal?"

I grinned. "Deal."

I don't remember anything else that happened the rest of the day. I walked through my classes like a zombie. By the time I got into Shop, however, the shock had worn off. While Mr. Conklin droned on about the proper use of a saw, I told Maxwell and Lonnie what happened.

"Brittany." Lonnie nodded. "She's hot."

"Seriously," said Maxwell. "She's double hot."

"So what's your issue?" Lonnie asked.

I frowned. The issue was I was a werewolf and couldn't afford to let Brittany get too close. Then another problem occurred to me. "My uncle picks me up after school. Only I can't reach him to tell him what's going on. I've got no bars on my cell."

Maxwell shrugged. "Take a leak."

I frowned. "What?"

"No one gets bars in school," Lonnie said. "They've got like a cell phone blocker or something."

"Only the block doesn't work so well in the boys' bathroom nearest the office." Maxwell gave an exaggerated wink. "Go up and get a bathroom pass."

"It has to be an emergency, though," Lonnie said, "so walk kind of hunched over."

I looked at Mr. Conklin. "Here goes nothing."

Maxwell gave me a little shove.

I swallowed my smile, hunched my shoulders, and walked to the front of the room with short, hurried steps. "Excuse me, sir, but I need–"

Without looking at me, Mr. Conklin tore a pass from a tablet and handed it over. Just like that, I was down the hall and into the bathroom next to the office.

I called my uncle.

His muffled answer sounded like I woke him. "Nyello."

"Uncle Bob, this is Cody."

I could almost see him sit up in bed. "Another fight?"

"No. I'm okay. I just wanted to let you know I'm

going to a friend's house after school, so don't pick me up."

"That's fine."

"And don't hold dinner for me."

There was a long pause. A frown crept into his voice. "Are you planning to be back before dark?"

Cripes. How could I have forgotten? Tonight was the night after the full moon. "Yes, sir, I will."

"All right, then." He hung up.

I leaned against a stall, my smile spreading. I was going to be with Brittany.

# NINE

When classes ended, I rushed out of school and into the student parking lot. Part of me braced for a letdown, and when I saw Brittany leaning casually against her lime green Beetle, at first I couldn't believe she'd showed. She smiled at me, and the day lit up like sunlight couldn't wait to touch her.

I stood mesmerized by her face, pale and perfect beneath her spiky black hair. Her lips shone bright pink today. She wore a sweater that clung to every curve, a short black skirt, and tights with pink peace signs on them. There was a hole at her knee. The memory of bruises and scrapes on her leg dampened my mood.

She broke the spell by walking around to the driver's side. I climbed into the passenger seat. The car's interior was faded beige, but only the roof and the seats remained that way. Bumper stickers covered the doors and the entire dashboard. *Friends help you move, real friends help you move bodies. All generalizations are false, including this one. If you are telepathic, think HONK. Suburbia: Where they tear out the trees and then name streets after them.* They layered one another, cut out around gauges and door handles. The effect was like a steamer trunk my mother bought once. *Decoupage*, she called it.

Brittany started the car; music rattled the speakers. I recognized *The Pink Spiders*, although I didn't usually listen to them.

"Seatbelts," she said as she buckled her own.

I hurried to comply. "Nice car."

"Thanks. It's old, but I love it." She looked behind as she pulled out of the parking spot. "My dad got it for my sixteenth birthday. Sort of a peace offering, I guess. I don't see him much."

"He doesn't live with you?"

"He lives in Georgia, thank the maker. That's where I'm from. Only been in Florida a few years. My mother, my little brother, and I live with my dad's father. Grandpa Earle. You'll meet him. He's cool."

I nodded, trying not to stare. I couldn't believe I was in the car sitting next to her. Her scent rolled over me. I smelled her skin, her breath, her hair gel, and the fabric softener on her sweater. She smelled great.

*The Pink Spiders* turned into *Death Cab for Cutie.* I relaxed, bobbing with the music. I resisted the urge to hang my head out the open window and catch the breeze. I'd never been happier.

We stopped at a light.

"There's that new tattoo parlor everyone's talking about." She motioned. "As if we needed another."

"You don't like tattoos?"

"They're fine. On other people. As an art form, they can be amazing. I saw a tat of a girl's boyfriend once, and you could recognize him. But they're just so permanent. I might get one, and two months later, I might not be that person anymore. I can't be restricted like that."

"You don't have to get someone's face." I couldn't bring myself to repeat the word boyfriend.

"Same difference. Say I got a butterfly with *green* wings."

She emphasized the word green, and with a start, I realized she had green eyes.

"Two months down the road, I decide my favorite color is purple. Green and purple don't go." The light changed, and she made a left turn. "Butterflies are lame, anyway."

I chuckled, although I wasn't sure she was joking. I could hear my uncle say *what girl doesn't like butterflies*. After a moment, I surprised myself by asking, "What about piercings?"

She flashed a smile. "Body piercings are all about other people's pleasure. Think about it. That's all they're for. And I'm just not into making everyone else happy. I'm still trying to figure out me."

"Me, too," I murmured.

She smiled again. I sighed, memorizing her lips and the curve of her nose.

"You like *Drop Dead, Gorgeous*?" she asked.

"They're all right." I tried to get my mind back into

103

the conversation. "I prefer *Lamb of God. Green Day.*"

"*Tool?*" she asked.

I nodded, and she pressed seek on her XM until she found the station. All *Tool* all the time.

Moments later, we were out of the city. I saw stables and barns. And a sign that read *Sunspot Naturist Resort.*

I kind of yelped. "You live at a nudist colony?" Embarrassment coursed through me. I couldn't take my clothes off in front of her. Not unless she did it first.

"We live next to it." She leaned forward as she pulled onto a narrow dirt road. "Grandpa Earle sold them some land a while back. He wasn't too happy about it. But what can you do, you know?"

Through the trees, I saw a white, two-story house with an overhanging roof and a screened-in porch. In the shaded yard, a man sat on a lawn chair.

Brittany pulled around the side to a carport and parked next to an old camper. Its tires were flat, and it was coated with dust.

"You like camping?" I asked.

"Never been. Grandpa Earle took my brother a couple times when we first moved down. But being the butt crack he is, he wore that out right quick." She hopped out and stepped to the front of the Beetle to retrieve her books from the trunk. "I keep saying I'm going to get a backpack for all this."

"My uncle got me one with Scooby Doo on the front," I blurted, and then wished I hadn't. She laughed, and I shrugged. "Well, who doesn't like Scooby Doo?"

She laughed again. "Where are your books, now?"

"I finished everything in school."

"You're quick," she said. "Come on. I'll introduce you."

We came around to the front of the house. Brittany dropped her books at the steps. A dog squeezed out from under the porch. A beagle mix.

Brittany slapped her leg. "Come on, Haff. Heel, boy."

The dog whined, but didn't come closer.

"Haff?" I asked.

"Short for half-breed." She frowned. "I don't get it. He's usually so friendly."

The dog scrambled back into his hidey-hole. I felt self-conscious, knowing exactly why the dog didn't want to meet me.

We walked toward the man beneath the trees. The yard was big, and the grass was skimpy under all the shade. I smelled oranges, and I looked up to see some of the trees still had fruit in them, too high to pick.

We approached the man, who held a rifle in his lap. Brittany seemed to take that in stride. "Grandpa Earle," she said, "this is Cody. Cody, this is Grandpa Earle."

"How do you do, sir?" I shook with him, aware of the wrinkles on his hand.

"You live around here, boy?" he asked.

"Yes, sir, I do."

"He lives with the Fix-It Guy," Brittany said.

I noticed she raised her voice when speaking to him.

Grandpa Earle nodded. "Good man. Good worker."

"Yes, sir," I said.

"'Course, he ain't been around as long as me. I been here since 1963. Okeechobee Boulevard was one lane. I remember when MacArthur Dairy would come down that road there and deliver the milk. Butter, too, if you had a hankering. Now you got to go into town and get your own milk. Can you imagine that? And then you got to pump your own gas in order to get back."

Brittany's cheeks sucked in. She looked like she was stifling a smile. "Times change, Grandpa." She put her hand on his shoulder.

He patted her fingers, smiling at her. "Praise the Lord for my two little pleasures."

The scene made me uncomfortable. I didn't have grandparents, and I wasn't used to talking to senior citizens. But watching Brittany with him, I realized she didn't care about his rumpled clothing or his trips down memory lane. She was fine with him the way he was.

My senses prickled. I smelled people approaching. A man and a woman stepped out of the surrounding trees. They were naked, shining white in a patch of sunlight.

"Gerk." I stared, unable to think of anything more intelligent to say.

In an instant, Grandpa Earl whipped up his rifle and shot at the couple.

I jumped at the sound. They jumped, too. A puff of dust exploded from a tree trunk near their heads. Turning tail, they ran, their behinds quivering.

Grandpa Earle let out a whoop.

Brittany shouted, "We talked about this."

He waved a hand. "Ain't no law against shooting albino deer."

I covered my mouth, wanting so bad to laugh but figuring it would fuel Brittany's outrage. I'd never seen naked people in person before. These two were kind of sagging and dimpled, not like in magazines at all.

Brittany held out a hand to her grandfather. "Give it to me."

"No," he said. "I need it. You know how many snakes we got around here."

"But you aren't shooting the snakes."

He hugged the rifle, looking stubborn.

She jammed her fingers into her hair, making it stand straight up, and then closed her eyes as if composing herself. "Did Butt Crack get home all right?"

"He's here," said Grandpa Earle. "I told him to do his homework before he saw his friends."

"He'd better."

"You're too hard on the boy. He's a good kid."

"I know. And I want him to stay that way."

A car rattled up the driveway. It was Sheriff Brad. Apprehension seized my stomach. I glanced at Brittany. If anything, she looked bored. The sheriff climbed out of his patrol car and slammed the door. He walked toward us, lips pursed beneath his mustache, pockets jingling with each step.

"Hello, Sheriff." I tried to sound nonchalant.

He ignored me. "Now Earle, you can't be shooting at people with that pellet gun of yours. We're getting complaints."

Grandpa Earle scowled. "I ain't hit none of them."

The sheriff nodded. "Well, I appreciate that."

"Come on," Brittany whispered. She took hold of my arm.

I tingled where she touched me. As we walked to the house, I struggled for something to say. "Does that happen a lot?"

"The sheriff showing up?" She shrugged. "They're friends."

"No, I mean the naked people."

"Oh." She chuckled. "The Sunspot has nature trails running along our property. Sometimes folks get off the trail and wind up in our yard."

"So your grandfather shoots them."

"Been at it all day, by the look of him." She glanced over her shoulder. "He never did want to sell that tract of land."

We got to the porch steps. I picked up her books

and noticed she was reading *To Kill a Mockingbird*. I'd read that last year at my old school. This year it would have been *The Catcher in the Rye*.

She held the door so I could enter. The porch was larger than my uncle's living room. It had white wicker furniture and a variety of potted plants. Ceiling fans chugged, wobbling as they spun.

Brittany ushered me into her house. The blinds in the living room were drawn, making the room feel cool in spite of the warmth outside. I smelled dinner cooking. Something spicy. Music played above us.

"Just drop the books on a chair." Brittany tossed her purse down as well.

I stacked the books and followed her to the kitchen. I blinked at the brightness. Everything was yellow. The walls. The curtains. Even the air seemed yellow after the dimness of the living room.

Brittany took the lid off a large slow cooker and stirred the contents. "Ham hocks and white beans. I hope you're hungry. She made too much, as usual."

"Who? Your mother?"

She nodded. "She puts dinner on before she goes to work in the morning. She has two jobs, so she doesn't get home until after midnight. I only see her on Sundays, and then she's so worn out, she hardly talks to me." She tapped the spoon and carried it to the sink to rinse. Then she shouted, "Butt Crack, get down here. Now!"

Thunder rolled down the stairs, and a kid appeared in the kitchen doorway. He was small, even

Roxanne Smolen

shorter than Brittany, and his hair hung like a mop over his eyes.

"What?" he asked.

She faced him. "You have been home for half an hour and there are breakfast dishes in the sink."

"I'll do them when I get back."

"Back from where? You aren't going anywhere."

"Yeah, the guys are waiting."

"This is a school night."

"I got to go. Volleyball." He grabbed an apple on his way out the door. "I'll be home early. Promise."

"I don't appreciate your slackitude," she called after him. Then she shook her head. "That kid."

"He plays volleyball?" I asked.

"He *watches* volleyball. Spying from the bushes."

I must have looked baffled because she laughed.

"Every winter, the Sunspot hosts a festival. People come from all over the country. It's a big thing. They have arts and crafts, and weenie roasts. Skin cancer seminars. And volleyball competitions."

"Nude volleyball?"

"Conjures an interesting picture, doesn't it?"

I burst out laughing. "Wow. No wonder he's in a hurry."

"I hope he doesn't get caught. They've already called the sheriff on us once today." She motioned across the room. "Have a seat. I'll get the book." To my stunned expression, she said, "World History anyone?"

My face warmed. I crossed to a breakfast nook

110

and sat at a table with a ruffled yellow tablecloth.

Brittany set her book before me. "So what's your secret for memorizing events?"

"I make a song out of them."

"You mean, just make everything rhyme?"

"Yes, but tune is important, too. I don't know about you, but when I try to remember a song, it's the melody that triggers the lyrics."

Outside, Sheriff Brad's car pulled away. Grandpa Earle came into the house. He sat in the living room and turned on *Judge Judy* full blast.

Brittany rolled her eyes. In spite of the noise, we spent the better part of an hour making up ridiculous and somewhat raunchy songs about Napoleon. I loved watching her laugh. I wanted to touch her face and stare. I wanted to kiss her.

Then I caught a newsbreak from the other room. "Coming up at five. The body of a young woman was found this afternoon along North Road, the victim of an apparent animal attack. But in an alarming twist, authorities now suspect a person or persons unknown armed with a jawbone and a straight razor."

*Another murder?* My stomach clenched, and my thoughts whirled. It wasn't me. I remembered everything I did the night before, and it wasn't me.

Was it?

# TEN

I glanced around Brittany's yellow kitchen as if looking for an escape. The words of the newscaster rang in my ears—*body of a young woman...person or persons unknown*.

"Are you all right?" Brittany asked.

I thought I was going to be sick. Sweat trickled down my neck. My hands shook. I was losing control. If I didn't get out of there, I would turn into a wolf in front of her.

"I didn't realize it was so late," I murmured, unable to keep the alarm out of my voice. "I have to go."

"Can't you stay for dinner? I'm making beer biscuits to go with the beans."

"No, really. I promised I'd be back before dark."

She stood as if offended. "All right."

Without looking at me, she left the kitchen. I hurried after. In the living room, Grandpa Earle sat sound asleep in front of the blaring television.

Brittany skipped down the porch steps and across the yard. The sun was low, and gold light glinted through the trees. My vision swam, and I could have kicked myself. What was I thinking, going

112

to her house the day after a full moon?

I walked to her car, one foot ahead of the other. Her dog, Haff, appeared from nowhere to growl and bark at me. My lip rose, and I gave it a sidelong glance. It took off yelping like I'd kicked it.

I climbed into the passenger seat. Brittany buckled in, and then changed the radio back to the indie station. She backed out of the carport. I knew she was disappointed. She probably planned to have me stay for dinner, wanting to cook for me. I was ruining everything. With a groan, I leaned against the door and let the breeze from the open window dry my sweat.

"You look feverish," she said.

"Not feeling good."

"I'll get you home." She nodded and smiled.

My heart nearly burst. I wanted to tell her everything—why I was ill, why my parents kicked me out, and how none of it mattered now that I met her. I wanted to tell her how much I liked her. Of course, I couldn't.

We pulled onto the dirt road and turned opposite the direction we came in. The temperature dropped with the sun, turning the wind cool and refreshing. The road met another, forming a T, and we turned left. After a while, I saw flashing lights and two green and white cars parked on the grass. Orange cones blocked the street.

Brittany slowed to get around them. "This must be where they found the body," she said.

We were on North Road. Had she gone that way out of curiosity? Several men stood at the edge of the trees. Not all were in uniform. They milled about like they were at one of my mom's cocktail parties. All they needed were champagne glasses.

I smelled fur a moment before four police dogs and their owners stepped out of the woods. My heart nearly stopped. I stared ahead, picturing the dogs lunging through my window, foaming at the mouth to get at me. How would I explain that? But we were past the cones and picking up speed before anyone saw we were there.

"I wonder who it was," Brittany said. "They only said she was a young woman."

It occurred to me that there was a good chance she knew the deceased. The killing was so near to her house.

"It was probably a jogger," she said. "We have a lot of joggers around here."

"Do they run at night?"

"Doubt it. That's a good way to turn an ankle."

"Do you jog?"

She laughed. "It's not my thing."

"Stay inside tonight. Really."

She glanced at me. "All right."

We got to my uncle's house. His truck was in the drive. I stared at the front door, reluctant to go inside, afraid to let him see me like this.

"Here we are," Brittany said. "Feel better."

"Thanks." I looked at her, wanting to tell her to be

careful, to watch out for her little brother, but the words tangled in my mouth, and all I said was, "Seeya." I opened the door of the Beetle and got out.

Her tires crackled on the gravel as she pulled away. I looked at the house, and my stomach twisted.

I would turn into a wolf tonight. There was nothing I could do to stop it. I was weak. Hopeless. Angry at myself, I stomped across the porch and through the front door.

Uncle Bob sat before his old black-and-white, watching the news. "Cute girl."

I glared as if he'd ridiculed me. Yeah, cute girl. Too bad she'll never like me. I wanted to yell at him to mind his own business, wanted to pack up my things and run. But that would be stupid. I stormed into the kitchen.

I was sweating harder than ever. At the fridge, I grabbed the chocolate milk and drank from the jug. I remembered Grandpa Earle on his lawn chair, talking about the good old days. I understood. I hadn't wanted my life to change, either.

"I thought we could spend some time together tonight," my uncle said from the kitchen doorway.

I set the empty container on the sink. I couldn't meet his eyes. "Not tonight," I said, my voice sounding husky. "I have to go."

Without looking at him, I pressed past and left the house. He could have stopped me, but he didn't try. I grabbed my bike and took off, pedaling as fast as I could. I wasn't sure where I was going or what I would do when I got there.

I followed the winding street out of the neighborhood and stopped at the two-lane highway that led into town. The long stretch of asphalt spread before me. I turned away from civilization, riding on the shoulder of the road. Only one car passed. For a wild moment, I half-hoped it would be Brittany, but the car kept going.

I came to a dirt road jutting off through the brush. It felt familiar, so after a moment's hesitation, I followed it. It was rough. Broken seashells and bits of coral packed the dirt, and it gave me a workout in spite of my wolf super-strength.

Before I knew it, I found the tree-enclosed courtyard where I had shifted the night before. I guess something inside me knew it would be there. I hopped off the bike and walked it through the tall pines.

The scent of the trees and grass felt comforting. This was my safe place. No one would find me here. I laid my bike on the grass and took off my shoes. As I undressed, I draped my clothes over the bike to keep them out of the morning dew.

Moonrise was coming. I used the time left to me to scout around the enclosure, searching for the underwear and socks I'd stripped off the night before. When I found them, they looked like rags. I could have left them there, but it wasn't cool to litter in your own home. I laid them next to my bike.

The change hit. I didn't fight it. I was so wound up over the murders and my fears that Brittany would never love me that I welcomed becoming something else.

But if I thought turning into a wolf would make me oblivious to my problems, I was wrong. As I shook the last traces of humanity from my fur, I felt an overwhelming need to know who was poaching in my territory. I turned my back to the bike and kicked a little grass up as if to bury it, and then headed to the murder site.

There was no one there, of course. The only barrier was yellow tape; that was easy enough to avoid. The place reeked of boots and pants legs. And death. There was a lot of blood. The brush was trampled, but whether from the victim putting up a fight or from homicide detectives afterward, I couldn't tell.

I followed the victim to the road where there was more blood. Apparently, someone attacked her on the street and dragged her into the woods. It would take a really large animal to drag a woman that far. The only animals I smelled were police dogs. Could the murderer be a man?

The area was so sullied with odors it was difficult to identify just one. As I moved away, however, I picked up the woman's scent. I followed it. The dogs hadn't been down the road, so I was in fresh territory.

The woman was indeed a jogger, just as Brittany surmised. She'd run right past the narrow dirt road that led to Brittany's house. My hackles rose. The murder had taken place practically in her backyard. That meant the murderer had been nearby, too.

*Brittany needs my protection.*

I cut through the trees and angled toward her house. The grounds were wild with growth. A man would need a machete to get through. That would be a good deterrent.

I came across a septic tank site and an old well with a few rotten boards across the top. Farther along, I found a shed so overgrown with vines and saplings it was nearly invisible. It stank of humans. I circled around. Soda cans littered the ground. A few sat on a log like targets. Pellet gun practice.

The human odor intensified as I entered the yard. Squares of light outlined the house. I recognized the kitchen's yellow curtains. On the floor above, a figure passed a window. It was Brittany.

Relief washed through me. She was safe. Now, my mission was to keep her that way. I prowled the yard, liberally leaving my scent, marking the area as mine. Let the cowardly dog, Haff, deal with that.

I remained on the property, keeping a watchful eye, as the moon rose high over the treetops. A short time later, the back door opened, carving a yellow slice from the darkness. Brittany stepped into the light. Quickly, I leaped into the dry brush, trying to conceal myself. She must have heard me because she looked my way. She looked for a long while. Maybe she only sensed I was there, or perhaps my eyes caught her light. At last, with an air of giving up, she stuffed a bag into the garbage can and closed the lid.

Ham bones. My mouth watered.

After she went inside, I approached the cans. Wooden stakes corralled them so they wouldn't tip over. No problem. I identified the can I wanted. Standing on my hind legs, I took the handle in my teeth and twisted it to unlatch the lid. I nosed it off and pulled out the bag of bones.

Careful not to tear the plastic, I carried the bag to the trees. I chuckled to myself. Brittany made my dinner after all. The ham hocks were warm and delicious. I was still munching when a minivan pulled up to the carport. My ears twitched, and I lifted my nose.

A woman got out of the van. She wore rubber shoes and a thin sweater that smelled so strongly of antiseptic and medicine I wanted to sneeze. She strode across the porch and unlocked the front door. I heard Grandpa Earle's voice. The door closed on his greeting.

I relaxed after that. Even dozed. Just before the moon set, I returned to my safe place. The courtyard made me feel like I'd come home. I rolled in the damp grass, allowing myself a moment to relish the scents. Then I shifted back to my other self.

Tired and aching, I pulled on my clothes and walked my bike to the road. It was still dark as I rode the long stretch of asphalt to my uncle's house. When I got there, I skidded to a halt in the driveway, frowning.

Uncle Bob had pulled his pickup onto the side yard. He was wrestling a bundle from the truck bed. It looked like a body.

My stomach plummeted. Had he killed someone? I didn't know whether to call the sheriff or to back away and pretend I hadn't seen. He pulled the bundle from the truck bed with a wet plop. I smelled blood.

Oh God. What should I do?

Quietly, I leaned my bike against the porch and walked toward him. Uncle Bob must have been so intent on dragging the tarp behind the house, he didn't notice me because he jumped when I spoke.

"What happened?" I said in a low voice.

He looked frazzled. "It was an accident. I didn't mean to do it."

A runlet of blood drizzled from the tarp. I closed my eyes. "I can't believe this."

"I'll call Howard," he said. "He'll help me. He's good at butchering."

"You're going to butcher it?" I shouted.

He avoided my eyes. "Well, we can't just leave it here."

My head whirled in confusion. My uncle was a good man. He took me in after my parents threw me out. What was he doing with a body?

"Open it," I said.

Uncle Bob frowned. "But—"

"I want to see."

He woofed a sigh. I braced myself as he grabbed

the corner of the tarp. With a flap of noise and a burst of foul odor, he flipped the side open.

I stiffened. I saw a mound of black feathers and thin, pink legs.

"An ostrich?" I squeaked. "You killed an ostrich?"

A giggle burbled up my throat. It was a stupid bird. Had I actually thought my uncle killed a person?

Right then, I heard the jingle of Sheriff Brad's pockets as he came around the house. I considered flipping the tarp closed and pretending it wasn't there, but that probably wouldn't fool him for long.

My uncle faced him with a cold smile and narrowed eyes. "Out and about early, aren't you Brad?"

"Well, I wouldn't have stopped if I hadn't seen you were already up." He nodded at the bird. "Got a bit of a problem?"

"It came out of nowhere," Uncle Bob said. "Shocked the heck out of me."

"Don't see any damage to your truck."

My uncle's smile widened. "It's a lightweight."

"Maybe it's from that safari," I said. "We get a lot of their peacocks."

"I thought so, too, at first." Uncle Bob leaned over the carcass. "But they tag all their animals. I don't see a tag on this one."

"There are some ostrich farms north of here," said the sheriff. "People thought there'd be good money in the meat. Maybe it escaped."

Bob straightened and shrugged. "Guess I should contact them."

Roxanne Smolen

"If it were me, I'd have a barbecue and leave it at that." Sheriff Brad looked my way. "I saw you over at the Meyer place."

"Yes, sir," I said.

"You spend the night there?"

"What? No!"

"I just saw you ride up on your bike."

My mind blanked. "Uh."

"Some people like to jog," my uncle said. "Cody, here, likes to ride his bike a bit before school."

"That right?" Sheriff Brad folded his arms. "You must be just getting in yourself, Robert. Looks like a fresh kill."

Uncle Bob met his stare in silence. I fished for a plausible story. Uncle Bob gave me an alibi. What could I say for him in return?

Before I could think of anything, the sheriff turned away. "I'll be seeing you, boys," he said.

As he left, realization struck. Sheriff Brad was following me.

# ELEVEN

I didn't go to school that day. It was a tough decision. On one hand, I wanted to see Brittany so bad it made my back teeth ache. And other parts, too. Just thinking about her did things to my body I could never tell my mother.

On the other hand, I had a belly full of ham bones. They felt like rocks.

Howard stopped by mid-morning. He chanted over the dead ostrich, something lilting and incomprehensible. He then announced that he wanted to save the feathers and tasked me with pulling them off. It wasn't difficult, but I had to wear work gloves because, as it turns out, feathers are sharp. The carcass reeked, and I didn't enjoy sitting next to it for a couple hours in the growing heat.

As I worked, I noticed its neck was broken, the skin torn almost like bitten, but the rest of it appeared to be in good shape. Not what you would expect after being hit by a truck. When I finished plucking, I watched Howard butcher the bird. It was cool. I'd seen internal organs before, of course, but never in something so big.

123

Roxanne Smolen

Later that day, a Big Brown truck delivered a package from my parents. I didn't want to open it, but my uncle hung over my shoulder like it was Christmas. It was filled with lightweight clothing and even a few swimming trunks. Like I knew anyone with a pool. At the bottom of the box, I found three pairs of shoes and some rolled up posters from my room. And my mp3 player. I was glad to see that.

There was also a note.

*Contrary to what you must believe, I do love you, and I only wish the best for you. – Mom*

Tears filled my eyes, but I couldn't cry in front of Uncle Bob and Howard, so I acted mad instead. I piled everything back in the box and shoved it on the floor of my closet. Except the iPod. I kept that.

We ate ostrich all weekend. It tasted good. Not like chicken at all. My uncle never gave details of how the bird died. It seemed to upset him.

🐕 🐕 🐕

When I arrived at school on Monday, Maxwell and Lonnie were waiting for me.

"Eff's back," Maxwell said.

I nodded. "Old raccoon eyes, eh?"

"Nah. You should see him." Lonnie laughed. "The black has slid under his chin, and his cheeks are green and yellow."

"He looks like a ghoul." Maxwell chortled.

I frowned. The worse Eff looked, the more humiliated he'd feel—and the madder he'd be at me.

"Just wanted to give you a heads up," Maxwell said, "you know, in case he tries to get even or anything."

I nodded. "Thanks."

Eff and crew glared at me all through PE. I had to admit, he did look like a ghoul. I'd have to remember to punch him out again right before Halloween. The thought brought a chuckle. I guess they knew I was laughing at him because their glares intensified, and they put their heads together as if planning something.

All thought of Eff and his anticipated payback whooshed out of my brain when I saw Brittany sitting at our table at lunch. After three days without seeing her, I felt like an addict getting the shakes. I'd brown-bagged an ostrich sandwich, so I bypassed the line, hit the machine for a couple of Dews, and hurried over to her.

She put out her hand. "Give me your phone."

I handed her my cell and sat down, watching her program her number into my contacts.

"There," she said. "Now you have no excuse not to call."

I took back the phone, staring at it in amazement. "Does this mean we're, like, um…"

She made a tsking sound and flipped her head. She'd dyed her bangs cherry-red over the weekend, and they fell over one eye. "No," she drawled. "It means we have to study twice as much. We have a history test coming up, and I need to practice our Napoleon songs."

I leaned back, my heart pounding so hard it hurt. Okay, she wasn't interested in anything boyfriend-girlfriend. At least, she wanted me around.

So we went to her place after school. I felt more at ease this time. I even walked into the kitchen without being shown the way.

The slow cooker held something spicy again. "Vegetarian chili," Brittany said, stirring the pot. "All fresh. My mother and I went to the Farmer's Market yesterday."

"In January?"

"Sure. Florida has lots of winter crops. They'd burn to a crisp in summer."

That sounded ominous. I wondered what I was in for, turning into a wolf in the summer heat. "Well, I'm glad you got to spend Sunday with your mother." I knew how much I missed mine, even if I was still sore about being kicked to the curb.

"Yeah, it's confusing, right? I don't know whether I want to spend more time or less time together. She drives me crazy. But we had a nice day yesterday. She didn't even complain about my hair."

"I like it, by the way."

"You do?" She looked at me through her red swag and smiled.

I sighed. I couldn't help it. She was that cute.

"Too floppy, even when I gel it." She brushed her bangs out of her eyes. "I swear, someday I'm going to shave my head."

"Then you could tattoo your scalp. Little snakes coiled all over. It'll look like hair until you get close."

"Tattoos aren't my thing."

"Henna, then. I can do the artwork."

"That actually sounds cool."

I grinned, pleased to have impressed her. We sat at the kitchen table. I had math homework because I'd missed school on Friday, and she had her history book. We'd just settled when Grandpa Earle came in.

"Ah, the fix-it boy," he said without looking at me. "You here again?"

"His name is Cody, Grandpa," Brittany said.

He poured a glass of water from a pitcher in the fridge. "The faucet in the bathroom is drippy."

"We're studying," Brittany said with exasperation.

"It probably needs a washer," I said. "I'll bring one the next time I come by."

He looked at me. "You should keep your tools on your belt."

"Yes, sir." I smiled.

A lesser guest might feel putout about being asked to work around someone's home. I felt accepted, like I was already one of the clan. Watching Grandpa Earle shamble out of the kitchen, I decided I kind of liked the old guy.

We studied for a couple of hours. Brittany was smart. I doubted she needed coaching in history. To change things up, I asked for a hand with my math. So there we were, two people acting like we needed help when neither of us did. It was slower but more enjoyable working together.

The sky darkened. It was a relief to feel I didn't have to shift tonight, that the moon had no hold on me. I watched Brittany's face as she bent over my Trig worksheet, wanting to spend as much time with her as I could.

"Do you have to get back?" she asked as if just noticing I was staring at her.

"No, I can stay."

"Good. Let's get dinner before Butt Crack comes down and eats everything." Her eyes sparkled as she said it, so I didn't think she was really speaking ill of her brother.

She opened the pot, and steam puffed up. She nuked a couple of sticks of butter until they were soft. Then she pulled out a breadboard and sliced off the tops of four round loaves of bread. She used a spoon to hollow them. It was like watching someone carve a jack-o-lantern. The loose chunks of bread went into the chili, instantly thickening the broth.

"The secret to a good bread bowl is buttering the inside," she said as she painted a loaf with the soft butter and a brush. "Otherwise, it gets soggy."

Her brother appeared as if he'd teleported. He gave me a nod of acknowledgement, and then leaned over his sister's shoulder as if to make her hurry.

"Stop, Butt Crack," she said. "Geez. Have one."

He snatched the bread, smiling in triumph, and ladled vegetables inside. "Any cheese?"

"No." She handed me a bowl. "Here, Cody. Just push him out of the way."

I was struck by how casual dinner was. Not the white linen affairs of my home. In spite of that, I was not about to push anyone out of my way.

"Is Grandpa awake?" Brittany asked.

"Asleep." Butt Crack ladled until cooked tomatoes dripped down the sides of his bowl. "I saw a black bear today."

"An actual bear?" I blurted. I didn't know Florida had bears. Alligators, panthers, pythons. What kind of place was this?

Brittany dropped her paintbrush in the sink. "Don't tell me you were hanging out in the Glades again."

"Nope. It was closer to town."

"Well, it better stay away. Somebody will shoot it. Poor thing."

"Yeah." Butt Crack looked thoughtful. He carried his bowl back upstairs.

I took his place at the pot, and then moved aside for Brittany. She handed me a plate to hold my vegetable-laden bread and led me to the front porch. We sat together on the wicker furniture, eating and counting fireflies. The chili was good, spicy and full of peppers and squash. A few months ago, I would have said it was ideal, but lately I craved a little more meat with my meals.

After we ate, we played gin rummy. I told her about the ostrich and how I thought it was a body, which she thought was hilarious. She kept trying to steer the conversation to my home in Massachusetts, but I didn't want to talk about it. My life there seemed opulent compared to what I had now, and I didn't think I could describe it without sounding like I missed it. I mean, I did. But if somebody came up to me and offered to turn back time, I wouldn't let them. This day was perfect, and I wouldn't leave Brittany for anything.

Around eight o'clock, after she'd beat me two hands out of three, she drove me home. I wanted so bad to kiss her goodnight, but I was afraid to spoil things. I knew she liked me as a study partner; that was as far as it went. So I thanked her and got out of the car.

The house was dark. Uncle Bob wasn't home. I booted my laptop and searched *how to fix a leaky faucet*. It looked straightforward. With a flashlight in hand, I went to the tool shed. I unlocked it with the hidden key.

My mouth dropped open. There must have been a million tools in that shed. There were five kinds of wrenches, one of them two feet long, and twelve different screwdrivers. There were even a couple of machetes. All the drawers were labeled—three-eighths this and five-eighths that. How was I going to choose what I needed?

"Can I help you find something?" Uncle Bob said.

I jumped at his voice, then wailed, "Grandpa Earle has a drippy faucet."

"Earle Meyer? How do you know him?" His face eased. "Ah, the cute girl."

My shoulders drooped along with the flashlight beam. I didn't want him to know that I had a thing for Brittany. After all, she didn't have a thing for me.

"Newer faucets don't use washers," he said, "but I happen to know the Meyers have an old one like us. I'm not sure what size you'll need. I'll give you a couple of the most common. It's just a matter of taking off the handles. Come on, I'll show you."

Wishing I could have figured it out myself, I followed him into the kitchen.

"First thing," he said, "turn off the water. Then close the drain and lay paper towel in the sink. Next, you take the screws out of the handles. This screwdriver is a six-in-one. You change the bits like this. When you take out the screws, lay them on the paper towel so you can see them."

I leaned close, watching him work. He removed the handles, and then used an adjustable wrench to take out the insides.

"You know, people relationships are tough," he said. "I don't want to see either of you hurt."

I wanted to say no problem, but it wasn't that easy. I knew in my gut that I would love Brittany until

I died. But if she ever found out about my little problem, I was likely to be the one who got hurt.

"I realize things are tough for you right now," Uncle Bob said. "Your body's changing, and you have urges you never felt before."

I groaned. Was he saying what I thought he was saying? I had *that* conversation with my dad two years ago.

He looked at me and smiled. "I'm here, that's all. If you ever want to talk."

"Thanks." I took the tools and went to my room.

Tuesday after school, I fixed Brittany's bathroom faucet. She beamed at me as if I'd performed brain surgery. Grandpa Earle was already down for his nap, so we couldn't tell him. That was all right. I didn't do it for him, anyway.

🐕 🐕 🐕

For the next couple of days, I had to watch my step at school. Literally. It seemed the entire football team was gunning for me, tossing objects in my path as I hurried between classes, trying to trip me. Once as I was walking through the halls, a book came skittering across the floor at me. Another time it was an apple. Then the halls would boom with laughter to make sure I knew who'd thrown it. Often it was Eff himself.

It was stupid and petty and totally not beneath him. It was also not without precedent. I remember at my old school, James Dawson flung a handful of pencils at the feet of his lacrosse rival. The kid wrenched his back and had to sit out the entire season, and James didn't make the team anyway.

Jocks. They're a different breed. But what Eff and his beefy friends didn't know was that I had enhanced hearing and reflexes. They weren't going to trip me up no matter how many times they tried.

Thursday at lunch, Brittany threw me a curve. "We have to put our study sessions on hold."

I was watching how delicately her throat moved when she swallowed her yogurt, and at first I didn't register what she said. "Stop studying? Why?"

"Tomorrow is my niece's birthday. Miley. I told you about her. She's turning three. So Butt Crack and I are driving up to give her a present. If we go right after school, we're sure to get invited for dinner. My sister's a great cook."

"Where do they live?"

"Kissimmee."

I frowned. "Kiss who?"

She laughed and shook her head. "You really are a newbie. Anyway, it takes a couple hours to get there, so I won't be back until late."

"Well, tell little Miley happy birthday from me. What did you get her?"

"That's the problem. I don't know whether to buy clothes or a toy."

"Kids want toys," I said. "There's nothing worse than opening a gift and finding clothes."

"You think so?"

"Sure. You buy clothes to please the parents, not the kid."

Brittany smiled. "I'm going to the mall this afternoon. Can you come with?"

My heart somersaulted. She actually wanted to be seen with me in public. This was *way* better than studying. "No problem. I'll even help you pick out a birthday card."

We drove out to Wellington. It's a small town, and I expected the mall to be rundown, but it was state-of-the-art. It had two floors and palm trees growing under skylights. I saw a lot of kids, and remembered Maxwell and Lonnie inviting me to the arcade for a Tie Fighter tournament. Apparently, this was a designated hang out.

I was so proud to be with Brittany. I wanted to hold her hand, but didn't have the nerve. We walked along the storefronts. She made fun of the dresses on the mannequins. Then she made fun of the people going in to buy them.

"Look at them. They're probably getting ready for Jana's party," Brittany told me.

"You mentioned her party before. Who's Jana?"

"She's this really rich girl. She has all these stables and a gazebo and stuff. Every year she throws a formal birthday party. February twenty second. It's huge. Like *event of the year* huge. The stores will actually run out of decent dresses." She laughed and nudged my arm. "I heard last year she had life-sized ice sculptures. Can you imagine ice sculptures in Florida? I would've gone just to watch them melt."

"You weren't invited?"

"Sure, I was. Everyone is. Our entire grade. It just isn't my thing, that's all."

I felt a sinking sensation in my stomach. February twenty first was the next full moon, which meant Jana's party fell on a waning moon. There was no way I could attend that party. I hoped I wouldn't be expected to go.

We went into Planet Toys. Contrary to my advice, I had no idea what to buy a three-year-old girl—although I knew better than to suggest anything stereotypic, like a doll. Fortunately, all the toys had age groups printed on the boxes. We ended up with a barnyard set. It was bright and bulky, and sure to be a hit.

As we left the store, I saw Eff coming out of a clothing shop a few doors down. He stopped to stare, looking at first surprised and then angry. He might have started something right then, but he was with a woman, likely his grandmother. I pretended I didn't see him and walked at Brittany's side, carrying her bag.

We went into Annie's Hallmark for wrapping paper and a card. Brittany froze in the doorway, and then stepped to a display of snow globes as if drawn to them. She seemed entranced. Then she shocked me further by pulling down a globe with fairies in it.

My uncle would say *what girl doesn't like fairies.*

That just goes to show how little I know about girls because I did not expect it.

"Look," she said breathlessly, holding the thing so I could see.

I will never forget the look of pure delight on her face as she shook the globe and tiny flower petals swirled among the fairies. It played a tune. I didn't recognize it, but Brittany hummed along. I promised myself that if I had to go without lunch for a month, I would buy her that snow globe.

The next morning, I told my uncle I didn't need a ride into school and would take my bike. It wasn't as tiring as I expected. In fact, the quiet of early morning was enjoyable.

That would not be the case, I knew, on the long haul to the mall. But I was excited to buy Brittany a gift. Something she really wanted.

After school, I hopped on my bike. The sky was blue and cloudless, and the air was warm in the sun but cool in the shade. I paced myself, hoping to keep my newfound super-strength in reserve for the ride back.

I was tired when I finally made it to the mall. It was late afternoon, and the parking lots were filling up. I had to ride halfway around the back before I found a bike rack. It felt good to stand up and walk.

I bought the snow globe first thing—checked it over, made sure the music played fine. At my insistence, the clerk stuffed the box with tissue paper. I didn't want anything to happen to it on the way home.

I sat in the food court with a tall drink and people-watched for a time. The mall was crowded, like there was nothing better to do on a Friday afternoon. I caught sight of Eff walking with two of his football thugs. He was texting on his cell and didn't notice me.

After a while, I picked up my bag and headed outside. The setting sun turned the sky bright orange. I hummed the tune the snow globe played as I skirted the parking lots and made my way to the back of the mall where I'd left my bike. I wondered if I should wrap the present, but no, I wanted to keep it casual.

There was no one around. I was beginning to think I'd walked the wrong way when I saw the rack and my lone, beat-up bike. I quickened my pace.

With a squeal of tires, three cars leapt the curb, blocking me in. Doors opened even before the vehicles came to a stop. Jocks swarmed out as if from clown cars with a dozen occupants. They all wore white T-shirts and football-player hair. Then I saw Eff, his face lit with awful glee and a two-by-four in his hand.

# TWELVE

A groan escaped me as I glanced around at the closing half-moon of football thugs. My heart rate shot from zero to a hundred in about a second. I placed the snow globe on the ground and stood over it, hoping I could protect it.

Eff rushed me, swinging the two-by-four like a baseball bat. I took the blow on my arm and struck out with my fist, aiming for his nose. I clipped another kid instead.

The guy next in line socked me in the jaw, and I staggered. I took a punch to the ribs. Then a round-house that snapped my head back. An arc of blood shot out.

Someone gave an appreciative, "Yeah."

I stiff-armed him in the throat. Someone else clobbered my ear. Knuckles caught me square in the mouth, and I swear every tooth loosened. It felt un-real, like I was watching a movie. But unlike the mov-ies, these guys didn't take turns. They crowded me, each getting their licks in.

I held my own for a while. But a hard punch to my brow caused my vision to flash. I nearly fell. Another punch and another burst of light. I looked up, gasping for fresh air, aware of blood streaming from my nose. Above the heads and flying fists, I saw Eff's two-by-four swing as if he intended to brain me. I raised my arm to deflect the blow and heard something crack. I didn't think it was the wood.

I dropped to my knees. Apparently, this put my face out of the comfortable range for punching, so they started kicking. Thuds came from all directions. I rolled on my side, arms over my head and knees to my chest. After a while, it didn't hurt anymore.

Their kicks tapered to a distant pummeling.

Someone said, "Knock it off, Eff. You're going to kill him."

And just like that, the beating stopped. I didn't move. I felt a terrible wrongness in my body.

"I got an idea," a voice said.

Someone fumbled with my zipper. This alarmed me more than getting beat up, but there wasn't a thing I could do to stop them. They yanked off my pants and shirt, and then dragged me to the wall.

"Here. Pose him with this. Fairies."

"Perfect," Eff said.

Something cool and smooth was shoved into my arms. Brittany's snow globe.

Oh, God.

I tried so hard to open my eyes. I wanted to glare at them, wanted to tell them to back off. But my face felt thick and wet. My mouth wouldn't work.

Someone snickered, and then the globe went

away. The plastic bag rustled.

"Here, let me package this back up for you," Eff said. "Oops."

I heard the bag fall, heard the globe pop as it struck the ground.

Laughter surrounded me. High-fives all around. Then tires screeched nearby. I smelled exhaust.

Hands lifted me, tossed me through the air. I landed on something cold and rough. A truck bed. They were taking me away. For the first time, I was afraid they intended to murder me.

For the first time, I wished to become a wolf. I imagined their faces when they came around the pickup to find a full-grown wolf in the back. I tried to shift, delved deep down inside, even though it wasn't the full moon, wasn't even full dark. The bouncing of the truck threw off my concentration. All I could do was to wait for the end.

I must have blacked out, because the next thing I knew, water poured over my body. Wind gusted, and I swayed gently.

Swayed?

The sensation jerked me awake. I was cold and in more pain than I ever imagined. My arms stretched over my head. I tried to move and swayed again. I opened one eye to a slit and looked around. Darkness. Nighttime. It was raining.

I was just thinking how unusual it was to rain at night in South Florida when lightning struck nearby.

Thunder reverberated in my chest.

I wanted to run, needed to get out of there, needed to find shelter. My legs moved, but my arms wouldn't. With my swollen eye, I peered upward and saw knots binding my wrists. I was strung between two trees.

Dear God. I was in the trees during a storm.

Lightning flashed again. I thrashed in spite of the pain. The ropes held.

"Help," I cried, but my lips were so smashed they wouldn't let the word out.

Thunder boomed. The clouds pulsed with electricity. In the light, I made out a house and a yard. With a sick dawning, I realized I was at Brittany's. They'd hoisted me until I was even with her bedroom window. She only needed to glance outside to see my broken and bloodied body.

I didn't want her to find me like this. I struggled with new vigor, trying to pull my rain-slicked hands free. A grinding sensation in my left forearm stopped me. I remembered breaking my arm under the blows from Eff's two-by-four.

I stilled. I wasn't getting out of this. The driving rain buffeted my body. Lightning flared all around. I smelled it in the air. I started to bawl like a baby, but the tears stung my eyes and my ribs grated every time I took a breath. Instead, I made myself small so the storm wouldn't find me.

I awoke to the sound of barking. Brittany's dog, Haff, I assumed. My eye opened a bit. The air was gray. Early morning. I thought it was still sprinkling, but it might've been runoff from the trees.

Cold, so cold. Shivers wracked my body, and with each shake, I ached worse. The dog kept barking. He was right beneath me.

Then Brittany came out the back door. I groaned, wishing I were anywhere but there.

"Oh, my God," she said. "Oh, my God. Butt Crack, get out here."

A door slammed. Then her brother said, "Holy crap."

I guess I lost a little time. The next thing I knew, the ropes were jerking and I was swaying. The pain was so bad, I couldn't help crying out.

They lowered me to the ground. I flinched when my bare back touched the grass. Man, all I had on was my underwear. Why did everything happen to me? Excruciating heat gushed into my arms as I flexed my fingers. I heard whimpering. It sounded like my voice.

"Call 9-1-1," Brittany said.

"No," I croaked, surprised I could speak. "No hospital, no police."

"At least, let me get my mother. She's a nurse. She can help."

"Please don't."

I heard tears in her voice. "Why?"

Because I'm different, I thought. Your mother

won't *get* me. She might have to call a veterinarian.

"Secret," I whispered. I was shaking so hard, I wasn't sure she understood.

"Get a blanket," she cried in a squeaky voice.

Butt Crack tore away. The next thing I knew, I was sitting up, and they were wrapping something warm and dry around my shoulders. The dog growled, foraging in the bushes.

"My mother is in the shower getting ready for work," Brittany said, and I understood her to mean she couldn't take me into the house.

"The shack by the old well," I said.

"What shack?" she said, sounding both frightened and exasperated.

"I know the one," said Butt Crack.

They got me to my feet. Movement made me nauseous, and if I'd had anything in my stomach, I might have barfed right there. Holding my breath, I shambled barefoot over the stick-strewn lawn. It took forever, but at last, I made it to the shack I'd seen the night I was patrolling the yard.

Butt Crack stacked magazines and comics so I could sit on them. By the time I got inside, I tasted blood. I didn't have enough strength to swallow, so I let it trickle down my lips.

Brittany knelt to tug the blanket around me. "Who did this to you?"

"Eff," I said, "and friends."

"Oh, God. You're bleeding." Her voice quavered. She stood beside me. "I'm calling a doctor."

"No." I latched onto her hand. My thoughts whirled. *If you're ever in trouble. Day or night.* "Call Howard."

Her voice cracked. "Garage Sale Howard?"

I thought I nodded, but I wasn't sure.

I must have lost a little more time, because I woke to someone lifting my eyelids. Howard's face came into focus.

I tried to smile. "Got any tea?"

He looked grave. "You have to come to my house. It's going to hurt."

I winced at a sharp pain in my ribs. "I know."

He helped me to stand, and I shuffled out of the shack. Rain drizzled onto my upturned face. Something important occurred to me.

"My bike," I panted. "I left my bike at the mall."

"We'll get it. Don't worry." He ducked under my arm, supporting my weight.

To my surprise, Brittany ducked under the other. I looked at her, and then at her little brother who stared back with wide eyes. A powerful mix of gratitude and shame grasped me, and I almost buckled.

"Thanks," I croaked, although I knew it would never be enough. Tears burned my eyes, and I fought to keep them out of my voice. "Don't tell my uncle, okay?" I didn't need more witnesses.

"Got to," Howard rumbled near my ear. "He's my friend. And he's been searching for you all night."

They didn't take me through the yard like I expected but through the trees to a clearing where

Howard left his truck. There was a trail just wide enough to drive through. Maybe that was how Eff got me there unnoticed.

I leaned against the side of the truck, thinking that if I could just stretch out in back, everything would be fine. But Howard pulled open the door with a creak and a rattle. He half-lifted half-pushed me into the cab and across the wide bench seat.

Brittany got in beside me. The truck shuddered as she slammed the rusted door. Then she slipped her arm around me and cradled my head on her shoulder.

It felt wonderful. It was almost worth the pain and misery just for that moment. I wished I could have paid it the attention it deserved, but I must have fallen asleep because after a time I heard her voice calling me as if from a dream.

"Cody, wake up. It's time for more tea."

She helped me lift my head and pressed a mug of warm liquid to my mouth. It burned my lips but soothed my throat. My stomach reached for it hungrily.

"Thank you." I laid back.

"Do you need another blanket?" she asked.

I realized I was in Howard's house, recognized the smell of herbs and plants. I was on a couch with a pillow at my head and one of Howard's hand-woven horse blankets draped over me.

Beneath the blanket, I wore a jogging suit. It was dry and warm. I flashed to the first time I turned into a wolf and my father brought a fleecy jogging suit to the police station. This one wasn't as thick, but it was just as comfortable.

"No, I'm fine," I murmured.

"All right." She sounded anxious. "You rest. I'll be right here."

I wanted to thank her again, but it was starting to sound lame. Enough was enough. I fell asleep, my face turned toward her scent.

I awoke to a soft patting on my cheeks. Moisture ran behind my ears. Brittany was cleaning my face. She dabbed my eyes and nose with something that smelled like cucumbers. I imagined her putting a salad into a blender and turning it into a tonic. It felt good, and I didn't want her to stop, so I pretended I was still asleep. Slowly, she worked her way over my lips and down my chin.

Somewhere far away, a door slammed.

"Did you find it?" Howard asked.

"It was still in the bike rack," my uncle said. "The rain washed away the blood and most of the scent."

"What were you planning to do?" asked Howard. "Track them down and kill them?"

Uncle Bob made a growling noise so full of anguish and rage I nearly opened my eyes with alarm. "They hung him in a tree," he said.

I tensed, trying to hear their conversation, almost resenting Brittany as she noisily rinsed her rag in a bowl and continued patting my ears and neck.

After a moment, Howard said, "The cool rain

cleansed his wounds and kept the swelling down. The ropes held his arm in traction. I couldn't have set the bone any better."

"Are you saying they did him a favor?"

"I'm saying the boy will heal. And your life with him is too rich to risk."

Brittany splashed her rag into her bowl, wringing it out, and then placed it like a compress on my forehead. She stood. It sounded like she walked into the kitchen.

"How's his fever?" Howard asked.

"He's so hot," she said. "Are you sure he doesn't need a doctor?"

"A fever means the body's fighting back. It's a good sign."

There was a pause, and then she asked, "Did you get Cody's things?"

"I did," my uncle said. "His shoes were gone, probably wrapped around a power line somewhere. But his clothes were in a pile. I found this underneath them."

A bag rustled. My stomach plummeted. They found the snow globe. I hadn't wanted her to know I bought it, hadn't wanted her to find out what happened to her gift.

Brittany made a sort of choking sound. Then she said in a thick voice, "Throw this away for me."

My mouth dropped, and tears blurred the slit of my eye. It sounded like she was trying not to laugh.

She wasn't pleased that I bought her a gift or disappointed that it was broken. She was amused.

Glass clinked at the bottom of a trash bin. Humiliation heated my face and knotted my throat. What an idiot I'd been. Brittany would never want me to be anything more than a friend. I was a freak.

The amazing wolf boy.

# THIRTEEN

Night fell. No idea how I knew. Probably something to do with the pull of the moon. I woke a couple of times to see Uncle Bob dozing in a foldout chair. Brittany must have gone home. I couldn't sense her.

Once I woke drenched in sweat and shaking so bad I thought I'd gone into convulsions. Someone draped another blanket over me.

By morning, both blankets were on the floor, and I was sprawled over Howard's couch. I opened my eyes—both eyes, I was pleased to note. Sunlight drew hazy shadows across the ceiling. I took a careful breath. My ribs felt good.

Green smells and birdsong drifted through the screen door in the kitchen. Someone clattered about out there, and after a moment, I recognized my uncle's tuneless whistle. He came out carrying a couple of mugs.

"Hey." He smiled. "I brought you some tea. Think you can sit up?"

"I'll try." With a grunt, I propped myself up on an elbow and swung my bare feet to the floor.

149

"How're you feeling?"

"A bit shaky." I reached for the mug, and sharp pain shot through my left arm. I grimaced and sucked in a shout.

"Yeah, we had to tape that," Uncle Bob said.

Sure enough, when I pulled back my sleeve, white tape covered my forearm. I took the tea in my right hand. It was sweet and flowery and as clear as water—not the snake blood tea I had before.

"So." He sat on the metal chair across from me. "Who was it?"

Embarrassment rose to my cheeks. "Football jocks. Felt like most of the team." I had a vision of them crowding around me, faces eager, shoulders straining their shirts.

Uncle Bob frowned. "How'd they get the jump on you? Didn't you know they were there?"

"They came up in cars. Kind of blocked me in."

"Ah." He nodded like he'd found a missing piece of puzzle.

"Are you telling my parents?" I asked.

He took a sip of coffee. "Not unless you want me to."

"I don't."

"Then don't worry about it."

Someone knocked at the kitchen door. "Anyone home?" Brittany said in a hoarse whisper.

"Come on in, Brit," my uncle called.

I ran my fingers through my hair. I picked up the blankets and bundled them on the couch. She came around the corner almost on tiptoe like she was expecting to find me on my death bed.

Uncle Bob stood. "Morning. Have a seat. You want some coffee?"

"Yes, please," she mumbled. Her eyes never left me. "Wow, Cody. You look a lot better."

Then it struck me. I *was* better. Healing at an extraordinary rate. How to explain it?

"Howard's tea." I shrugged. "It's a Navajo thing."

She sank onto the chair. "He should market it."

I grinned. The thing about grinning is you use muscles all over your face, and I was aware of every one of them. It hurt worst around my ears.

Brittany didn't smile back. "I thought you were going to die. I hardly slept all night. So I rush over here and you're...you're..."

"What?" Uncle Bob held out a cup of coffee. "You going to be mad at him because he's feeling better?"

"Of course not. It's just that—"

"We all heal fast. Runs in the family." He jiggled the cup. "Two sugars, right?"

"Oh." She looked dazed. "Thank you."

I barely had time to reflect on how much Brittany and my uncle had bonded when Howard came down the hall. He smelled like he'd just gotten out of the shower, which made me aware of my own rank stench.

"Good morning," he boomed. "How is our young *Mai-Coh* today?"

"I think he's going to be all right," Uncle Bob said

as he slurped his coffee.

"Let's take a look." Howard knelt and rested his large hand on my forehead. "Fever's gone. Eyes are clear. Can you sit up straight?"

He lifted my sweatshirt, and Brittany hissed through her teeth. A purple and black swath darkened my mid-section. Howard pressed gentle fingers over my side. "Take a breath. Deeper." He smiled. "No creaks."

"That's good, right?" I tugged my shirt in place.

"Very good." He got up and clapped my uncle on the back. "When a fox walks lame, the old rabbit jumps." They strode to the kitchen.

I looked at Brittany. "What does that mean?"

She laughed her tinkling laugh. It made me feel lighter. Like she was magic.

"Sorry I scared you," I said. "I'm sorry about everything."

"You were quite a sight."

"How's your brother?"

"He was pretty shaken up. He stayed home the whole day."

I drank the cooling tea. "Do you think he'll tell anybody?"

"Well, he didn't tell Grandpa. And he won't tell our mom. No one tells her anything."

"Why not?"

"She can't take it. She works six days a week at Doctor Gutman's, the pediatrician, from nine to three, and then at Palm West Hospital from three-thirty to midnight. It's hard. On all of us."

I nodded. "Both my parents are doctors. I rarely saw them either."

"They must be rich."

"I guess. We used to go on these fantastic vacations. I've been all over the world."

"What's your favorite place?"

"Africa," I said. "I'd love to go back."

She returned my smile, but her eyes were sad. I wished I could revise my answer.

"I'm glad I'm here," I told her. "And I'm glad you're with me."

She glanced down, and then looked at me through her red swag of hair. Her face was pink.

"Do you need a refill?" Uncle Bob peered around the corner, holding out a coffee pot.

Brittany lifted her cup and he topped it off. "Mmmm," she said. "I smell sausage."

"I thought you only ate health food." He smirked.

"It's my one vice."

"Only one? That's good to know. Breakfast will be ready in a few minutes."

I cleared my throat, breaking into their conversation. "Do you think I could wash first?"

"That's a great idea," he said. "Let me help you."

Howard called from the kitchen, "He can use the guest toothbrush. It's in a mug on the sink."

Brittany looked incredulous. "*Guest* toothbrush?"

"Well," Howard said. "They don't know it's used."

The three of them laughed. I felt out of the loop.

"It's Sunday, right?" I said as Uncle Bob set me on my feet. "I haven't been out of it for like a week or anything?"

"No, nothing like that." He put his arm about my waist and guided me down the hall. "It happened on Friday?"

"I went to the mall. After school."

"From now on, don't go that far away by yourself. I thought you were caught by… It doesn't matter. You're safe, now."

He waited until I latched onto the sink before he closed the door. I peered in the mirror. My face didn't look as bad as I expected. My eyelids drooped a bit, and my lips had scabs. But my teeth were fine. In fact, they looked whiter than ever.

I turned on the shower, then started the strenuous task of taking off my clothes. My body was stiff and sore, but the only real pain was in my arm. The hot water spray felt amazing. I wanted to stand there for an hour. But I knew they were holding breakfast for me, so I washed and shampooed, groaning every time I reached for something, and got out as quickly as I could.

A clean tee and some drawstring shorts lay folded on the corner of the sink. Someone had snuck them in. Refusing to use Howard's community toothbrush, I swabbed my mouth with toothpaste on my finger. When I left the bathroom, I felt like a different person.

I walked by myself down the hall and through the

living room. Once in the kitchen, I was greeted by broad smiles.

"There he is," said Uncle Bob. "Sit down, boy."

"Hey, you really clean up nice," said Brittany.

"Hope you're hungry." Howard placed a plate of scrambled eggs, grits, and sausage before me.

"Starved." I felt like a kid on Christmas morning.

Then Brittany reached over and patted my hand. In front of everybody. I knew she meant it in friendship, but I was so proud and so happy, I thought I would burst.

"A hungry stomach makes a short prayer." Howard served the other plates. "Dig in."

We ate in silence. The food was delicious.

"More coffee, anyone?" Howard stood and walked to the counter.

"Me," said Uncle Bob.

"Of course, you. I meant anyone other than you. Brittany? You want some more?"

"No, thanks." She stood. "I'll clear the table."

"No, no, I'll get it," said Howard. "I believe Bob has something to say." He raised his brows at my uncle.

"Ah, yes." He squirmed a bit in his chair. "I want to talk to you two about the three Rs. Revenge, retaliation, and retribution. I think you should let this one slide."

"What?" Brittany shrieked.

"Even a small mouse has anger," Howard said over the sound of running water.

155

"I'm not your mouse," she snapped, and then waved her arm at me. "They could have killed him. In fact, I don't know how he's still alive. And you want to let them get away with it?"

"You know how it is," Uncle Bob said. "First they do something, then you do something back, then they do something more until finally someone gets killed. I know neither of you want that on your conscience."

He sounded like he was speaking from experience. Had he hurt someone in anger? I thought about the growl in his voice as he spoke last night. He'd sounded angry enough to want vengeance. Maybe he planned to take action himself.

"I should have called 9-1-1 when I found him in that tree," Brittany muttered. "I should have let the sheriff see what I saw that morning."

"But you didn't," Uncle Bob said, "and I'm glad for it. There would have been police reports and court dates, and obviously he wasn't hurt as bad as we thought."

She turned to me, eyes pleading.

Her outrage touched me. Perhaps it *would* have been better if she'd called 9-1-1. I was beat up pretty bad. But I couldn't go to the authorities now. They'd never take me seriously. There would be questions about why I was healing so fast.

That left physical retaliation. I saw Uncle Bob's point. It would go back and forth until somebody died. Even the wolf inside me didn't want to kill. I was sure that no matter how angry Brittany felt she wouldn't want that either.

"I promise," I said slowly, "to try to keep my cool."

"That's all we can ask." Uncle Bob grinned and tapped a short drum roll on the tabletop.

"You're a better person than I am," Brittany said, although she didn't sound like she admired me for it.

"If you'd like to take tomorrow off from school, I'll understand," my uncle said.

"Actually, I'd rather go, if I'm able. Show them they can't keep me down."

Uncle Bob beamed. "That's my boy."

Howard finished rinsing the dishes, and the four of us played Yahtzee. Brittany cheered up after a while. No one brought up my bike or the snow globe, which suited me fine.

I thought about the promise I'd made to Uncle Bob. It was ambiguous, but I meant every word. I wondered if I would feel the same when I saw Eff.

# FOURTEEN

My uncle dropped me off for school the next morning. I felt tired and achy, unsure if I could make it through the day. Uncle Bob assured me that he would be nearby, and to call if I needed an early pick up. I hoped I wouldn't have to.

I got a few stares as I went to my first class. That wasn't too unusual. I'd been gawked at for one reason or another since I started school. However, the snatches of conversation I caught stumped me.

"He's such a faker."

"I told you. It's been *Shopped*."

I was too worn-out to give it much thought.

Those stares were nothing compared to what I received when I walked into PE. Eff and his thugs gaped like they'd seen a ghost. I figured all I had to do was say *boo* and they would scatter.

I scowled as I passed, savoring the confusion on their faces. I'd toyed with the idea of pretending they'd beat up the wrong guy, but decided to go the *you can't hurt me* route.

Fortunately, it was Volleyball Monday. No one wanted me on their team, as usual, so I joined the other rejects on the grass. Eff watched me the whole time, even to the point of missing a few volleys. He looked skeptical, angry, and scared at the same time. Maybe he thought he'd be charged with attempted murder. Premeditated since there'd been so many of them.

I didn't run into him again until midday. Eff and three others stood like an iceberg blocking traffic outside the lunchroom. I faced them with my back straight and my eyes narrow, wondering if I should have stayed home after all. I could handle their glares, but I wasn't up to a shoving match.

Then someone slipped their hand into mine. It was Brittany. A wave of warmth washed through me. "Hi." She smiled. "Been waiting long?"

"No," I said. "I just got here."

"Good. Let's go. I'm starving half to death." Holding my arm, she led me past Eff's murderous gaze.

Suddenly, everything seemed funny. The floor felt like it was made of some bouncy material, and my head felt like a helium balloon bobbing along. I was grinning for all I was worth, so I kept my eyes on her so Eff wouldn't think I was taunting him.

Of course, she let go of me as soon as we were through the lunchroom door.

"That jerk," Brittany said. "I can't believe I ever thought he was cute."

My head returned to my shoulders with a snap. "You what?"

"How are you feeling? How's your arm?"

I grimaced. "It's like the bone is itching."

"Howard said it was broken." She shook her head as if she still couldn't believe I didn't see a doctor. "You'd better eat something."

We went through the food line with Brittany taking charge of the tray. She carried; I paid. We got to our table with a selection of fruits and yogurt, as well as a turkey on pumpernickel that she cut in quarters so I wouldn't have to open my mouth too wide.

I smiled at that, watching her, pretending we were a *couple*. I knew I was fooling myself. She probably picked up her nursing skills from her mother.

As we ate, a girl I didn't recognize came to our table. She ducked low to look at my face. She wore flowered leggings, and her hair flopped from a tail on top of her head.

Brittany gave a little frown. "Hello, Jana."

"Well," said Jana, "I don't know if you know about this or anything but there's a My Space called Cody the Fairy and it has photos and stuff so I saved them." She lifted a wine-colored BlackBerry.

My heart dropped into my stomach.

"Let me see that." Brittany took the phone. Her pale face turned paler. "When did these go up?"

"Saturday. I got them from Maryann and she got them from Josh. They're so obviously phony because—" She motioned at me.

I held out my hand. "I want to see."

"Cody. No." Brittany held the phone as if protecting it. Her eyes sparkled with tears.

I waggled my fingers. "Let's have it."

She handed over the BlackBerry. My mouth fell open. There in disgusting detail was photographic evidence of how badly I'd been beaten. There were close-ups of my face—I couldn't believe it was my face—and shots of my blackening ribs. Then the pictures pulled back to show me sitting in my shorts with the fairy snow globe in my lap.

Heat rushed through my body. I couldn't look at Brittany.

"It's been *Shopped*," I said, realizing what all the talk was about. All I could do now was go along with the suggestion that the photos were altered.

I handed the BlackBerry back to Jana. As she took it, her fingers slid over mine. She gave me a smile that would have melted my socks a few weeks ago. Now I was with Brittany.

"Thanks for letting us know," I said.

"Sure." She cocked her head, and her ponytail swung to the side. "You're coming to my party, aren't you? My birthday party?"

"Oh, you're *that* Jana." When would I stop hearing about *the* party?

"See you then." With a pop of gum, she flipped her tail and strutted off.

I stared at the table. Brittany's gaze pressed for answers, but I couldn't look up. I wanted to crawl in a hole somewhere. Now I would hear the questions. I looked so bad in the photos—how could I heal so fast? She'd figure out I was a freak.

"I want you to know," she said softly, "that was the sweetest present I never got."

I was so surprised I met her eyes. A tear rolled down her cheek, making me even more self-conscious. "Too bad it was smashed," I said.

She nodded. "I saved part of it."

I blinked, taken aback. But she'd laughed at the gift. Hadn't she? "Um, saved?"

"The glass is gone, of course. But I managed to glue one of the fairies back on, and it still plays Wind Beneath My Wings."

I couldn't believe it. I'd bought it for her, but I felt like she'd given *me* a gift. "I can get you a new one."

She shook her head and wiped her cheeks. "It's perfect the way it is, even though it reminds me of finding you in that tree."

"Yeah. In my underwear."

"At least now I know the answer to that age-old question, boxers or briefs. I also know what to get you next Christmas. Undershorts with Scooby Doo on them."

"No, no, no."

"Okay, then how about this? I'll get a pair with oranges all over them and *Welcome to Florida* printed on the butt."

"Or a bull's-eye."

With a sad smile, she walked around the table and gave my shoulders a hug. "I have to go to class. Try to stay out of trouble."

I watched her walk away, a dazed grin on my

face. Then I realized I had to get to class, too.

My uncle picked me up after school. He'd bought a couple of T-bones for dinner. He planned to break out the grill. But I fell asleep before he had the chance. I slept until dawn. We had the steaks the next night.

The night after that, we ordered pizza with double pepperoni and sausage. Evidently, my uncle felt that eating meat would help me get my strength back.

I bundled the empty pizza box with the rest of the trash and carried it outside. The breeze was cool, and the sky held an early sprinkling of stars. My stomach was full, and I felt more like myself than I had in days. As I approached the garbage cans behind the shed, I hummed to myself, trying to remember the little tune Brittany's snow globe played.

"I know what we did to you," someone said from the darkness.

I froze, recognizing Eff's voice.

"It wasn't Photoshopped," he said. "We beat you to a pulp. And yet, here you are taking out the trash like nothing happened."

Memories of the assault thrummed through me—visions of faces and fists, echoes of pain. I felt fear, a haunting terror that I would be attacked again. Why hadn't I smelled him waiting there? I had all kinds of extra perceptions. Why hadn't I put them to use?

I tipped the pizza box into the can, wondering if I should run. Did he have a gun? Would a gun kill me?

Maybe he needed silver bullets.

The sheer stupidity of that thought struck me, and I almost laughed. Silver bullets? Really? He was alone. He wouldn't shoot me without an audience.

"Where are all your football buddies?" I asked. "Aren't you afraid to come after me without back up?"

"I'm off the team."

"Oh?" Good, I thought. Double good. May your life be as screwed as mine. I looked at him. He was a shadow behind the shed, but I could see him clearly. "What'd you do, tell Coach what happened? They say confession is good for the soul."

"I didn't confess!" His shoulders slumped. "Coach had us turn in our cell phones. Anyone with your picture on them got the boot."

"Must've been half the team." I thought about Jana and her BlackBerry. Most of the school had seen those photos.

"Me and four others." His eyes met mine. They seemed wide and solemn in the darkness. Hurting. Then his voice hardened. "You ruined my life."

"Yeah? Well, you tried to end mine."

"That wasn't the plan. I got carried away."

"You could have stopped."

He hesitated. "I know."

"Is that an apology?"

"No." He sneered.

"Fine. I'm going back inside." I turned to leave.

He spoke to my back. "No one can heal that fast. There's something weird about you, and I'm going to find out what it is."

I scoffed and walked away.

🐕 🐕 🐕

The next morning, my uncle caught me staring out the kitchen window at the shed. "Anything wrong?" he asked.

I hesitated, not certain I wanted to tell him. "Last night when I took out the trash, Eff showed up."

"He what?" Uncle Bob nearly dropped his coffee cup. "Why didn't you yell? I would have heard you."

"He didn't try to hurt me, or anything. I think he just wanted to talk."

"That kid's dangerous," Uncle Bob said. "Stay away from him."

I knew he was right. Eff was a piece of work, and I hated him. But deep inside, part of me felt bad for the guy. His entire future must have been tied into becoming a professional football player, just like I was going to be a doctor. Both our futures had been taken away from us.

Then I remembered Eff saying he would find out what made me different. The idea felt ominous. But it wasn't very likely, was it? I mean, who was going to follow me around on just the right night and see me shift into a wolf? I read comic books. I knew how to handle a secret identity.

I also recognized *famous last words* when I heard them. I'd better be careful.

I went to school in a thoughtful mood. As usual, when there was a juicy bit of gossip to spill, Maxwell and Lonnie met me at the drop off out front.

"Hey, when did you become a snitch?" Maxwell wailed as I hopped down from my uncle's truck. "What were you thinking?"

"Not cool, man," Lonnie said.

"Hold on," I said. "What's not cool?"

Maxwell sighed like I was in second grade. "Are you saying you didn't get Eff kicked off the football team?"

"What?" I didn't consider anyone would blame me. "I didn't have anything to do with it."

"That's not what the school thinks," Maxwell said.

"Seriously," said Lonnie.

I stared at them, amazed at their anger. For weeks, we'd been laughing together at Eff's expense. Now they defended him? "He must have broken the rules. Coach wouldn't have banned him otherwise."

"But who told Coach?" Lonnie asked.

"You're giving me more power than I have."

"Aw, come off it," Maxwell said. "Everyone knows you hate each other."

I wanted to slug him. "You hate him, too."

"Look, I'm not an Eff fan, right?" Maxwell said. "But even I know he's the backbone of the team. We won't win a game without him."

"It's not okay, man," Lonnie said.

I shoved my fingers into my hair. "But it's okay for

him to beat me up?"

"Did he?" Maxwell yelled in my face.

"Does it look like he did?" I yelled back.

"No." He scowled. "But it sure looks like we'll be in last place next season."

He and Lonnie stormed off.

I gazed at the street. My uncle was gone. If he'd still been around, I would have gotten back in the truck and left. There was no sense in staying in school. I was never going to fit in, never going to have friends. If it weren't for the prospect of not seeing Brittany again, I would have gone into the Everglades and become a hermit.

As I walked into school, I found the curious stares had turned to glares of animosity. I wanted to make a big sign that said *I Didn't Do It.* Jana said hi twice as we passed in the halls, but I was so angry I didn't answer. Even lunch with Brittany didn't cheer me up. She seemed tongue-tied and distracted.

"They say one of the kids' parents is appealing the coach's decision. Says it's circumstantial." She spoke in a low voice, like we were at a funeral. "So, maybe it will blow over."

I couldn't look at her. She was the one who voted to get even. I guess the prospect of losing a few football games changed her mind.

By the end of the day, I was in as bad a mood as I could get. I jumped into my uncle's truck and slammed the door. Uncle Bob kept glancing my way as he drove.

Finally, he asked, "Do you want to talk about it?"

I hadn't planned to tell him, but it tumbled out of my mouth anyway. "Eff and a few others were kicked off the football team for having pictures of me on their cell phones."

"Well, that's good. Isn't it?"

"No. Because now every game they lose will be tacked up to me."

"Ah," he said. "Football season is a long way away. They'll calm down by then."

"No. They won't."

We didn't speak for a while.

As we pulled into the drive, he cleared his throat. "I hate to do this to you, but I have to go back to work. I won't be home until late. The project I'm working on is running into overtime."

"Don't worry about it."

He shrugged. "Got to make a living."

"Yeah."

"I'd feel better if you stayed indoors. In case Eff is still nosing around."

"Right." I wanted to yell *I can take care of myself.* Though, obviously, I couldn't. That's what everyone thought.

I climbed out of the truck and up the porch steps. I didn't relish going into an empty house. I was afraid of being alone. For a moment, I imagined having a dog to greet me at the door.

Who was I kidding? Dogs hated me. Everyone hated me.

As usual, I had finished my homework in class while the other kids asked questions. That left me with nothing to do. I decided to wash a load of clothes. Uncle Bob had a laundry room, but I'd never seen him use it. He seemed to prefer buying replacement clothing from Howard. I'd never done laundry before, but I knew enough to separate the lights from the darks. I started the machine, and then played Internet solitaire while it washed.

As dusk fell, someone tapped at the door. It startled me, and my thoughts went immediately to Eff. The smart thing would be to ignore it, but that made me feel like a coward. So I stomped to the living room and wrenched open the door.

Brittany smiled at me from the porch. She shook a bag. "I brought peace offerings. I realize it seemed like I wasn't on your side before, but I was only trying to make you feel better. Lame, I know. Anyway, I was at work today and I saw this movie, and I thought I *had* to get it for you because I know you like werewolves, and can I come in?"

"Um, sure," I said, a bit stunned by her rapid-fire greeting.

She stepped inside, glancing around. I saw the room as she must have seen it—a battered recliner, a kitchen chair, and a twelve-inch black-and-white television on a metal TV tray.

She raised her brows. "You *do* watch movies, right?"

"In my room. On my laptop."

Roxanne Smolen

"Good. I hope you have a microwave." She pulled a package of popcorn out of her bag.

"Yeah. We do." I closed the door and led her to the kitchen. "You had to work today?"

"No, I only work on holidays. Since the eighteenth is Presidents' Day, I stopped in to see if they needed me. And they do. I thought maybe you could come and keep me company. Unless, of course, you're still mad."

"I'm mad, all right. But not at you." I relaxed, realizing it was true.

"Well, let's not worry about it now. Presidents' Day is more than a week away." She placed the popcorn in the microwave. "Do you have a bowl?"

"Good question." I stood on my toes to search the cabinets. All I found was an old, square cake pan.

"Perfect." She dumped the popped corn inside. "What do you have to drink?"

"Chocolate milk?"

"Yum. You get that, and I'll carry this."

I grabbed two coffee cups and the jug of milk and followed her down the hallway. She paused at the doorway to my room. I closed my eyes, picturing the red horse blanket, the Scooby sheets. At least, my dirty clothes were in the laundry room.

"You weren't kidding about liking Scooby Doo, huh? I can tell." She sat on my bed and fluffed the pillow.

I set the milk on the floor. "What movie did you bring?"

"*Underworld.* It has vampires and werewolves. Can't go wrong." She set the laptop at the foot of the bed and booted the DVD. It played Coming Attractions.

I sat on the other side of the bed. Since it was a twin, our shoulders touched even with the popcorn between us. I tried not to move for fear that she'd lean away.

"Do you like werewolves?" I asked.

She scrunched up her nose. "They aren't believable. I mean, bones and muscle rearranging by themselves? No way can a human body change shape like that. Just like vampires. How can their fangs pop out? Snick." She made vampire fangs out of her fingers. "On the other hand, zombies are probably real."

"What?" I burst out laughing.

"Some people in my neighborhood make me very suspicious. I'm sure my third grade teacher, Miss Ellison, was of the undead persuasion."

I wasn't sure if she was serious or not. "Speaking of teachers, all of mine are having fits over something called an FCAT."

"Oh, yeah. Part one is coming up next week."

"I've heard of an MCAT. That's to get into medical school. But never an FCAT."

"It's an annual test. The state wants to find out how well the teachers are doing so they test *us*. If we fail, they know the teachers aren't doing a good job."

"That's dumb. We could sabotage them by failing

171

on purpose."

"But then we would lose privileges, like football teams and bands."

I nodded and stuffed my mouth with popcorn.

"If the FCATs are here, Jana's party won't be far behind. All the girls will be giggling and having their dresses altered." Brittany glanced at me. "Don't ask me to go. It's not my thing."

"Okay."

She sat up, nearly knocking over the cake pan. "That was easy. Didn't you plan to ask me?"

I shrugged. "It's not your thing."

The main menu came up, and I leaned forward to hit Play. Brittany stared at me. "Did you ask someone else?"

"Hmmm?" I settled back and ate more popcorn.

"It's all right. You can tell me."

I made a shushing sound and pointed at the screen, feigning interest to cover my thoughts. Of course, I hadn't asked anyone else. I couldn't go to the party even if I wanted to. It fell on the night after a full moon. The wolf would still affect me.

The werewolves in the movie were snarling and vicious. Every time they came onscreen, Brittany booed. I felt uncomfortable with the reminder of how the world saw me. It didn't matter. No one was going to find out.

Halfway through the movie, my uncle came home. I didn't hear him come in. He just appeared from the darkness of my doorway, making me jump.

"What are you two up to?" he asked as if he couldn't tell.

"Watching werewolves," Brittany said. "Want to join us?"

"Werewolves." He snickered and shook his head.

I realized he was covered in dust—his clothing, his hair, even the creases around his eyes. He hadn't told me what his big project was. How did he get so dirty?

"I'm not much for horror flicks," he said. "Think I'll take a shower."

"Good idea," Brittany said. "You look like you've been digging graves."

My uncle laughed, moving away. The sound chilled me. Was that what he'd been doing?

# FIFTEEN

The following week school was chaotic. Classes were pre-empted for the FCAT. The tests weren't hard, but the stress left me drained. I blame that as much as anything for losing track of the day.

"Tomorrow is Valentine's Day," I blurted as I rushed into the living room.

Uncle Bob looked up from the television. "Kind of snuck up on you, eh?"

"Well, yeah. I mean, except for exchanging cards in kindergarten, I never—"

"Did you buy her a present?"

I shook my head. Buying a gift for Brittany hadn't worked out so well last time. "I thought I'd make her a nice dinner."

"Good thinking. The way to a lady's heart, and all that. But I didn't know you could cook."

"I've seen people cook. How hard can it be?" I sat in the chair next to his big old recliner. "Do you think you could arrange to be... gone?"

He laughed. "I'll tell you what. Not only will I be gone, I'll even drive you to the grocery store to pick up the things you need."

"That was going to be my next question."

He switched off the TV. "Let's go."

He took me to Publix, a grocery chain that seemed to be popping up on every corner. As we went through the door, a large Valentine's Day display greeted us.

"You see?" I pointed. "Now that's a helpful reminder."

"You should get flowers for the table."

"I don't know."

"Sure. What girl—"

"Doesn't like flowers." I laughed. "All right, but not roses. I want to keep it casual. In case she hates it."

"She won't." He rummaged through the stand. "Here's a nice assortment. Daisies, carnations, and one rose. You put the flowers in water, but take the rose out and lay it on her plate."

I grinned as I pictured it. "Perfect."

I put a box of spaghetti, a jar of marinara, and some shredded mozzarella in the cart. I found sesame breadsticks. I added a two-liter bottle of Dew.

"How about some ice cream for dessert?" my uncle asked.

"I think she would rather have cake."

"Great. They have a terrific bakery here."

"I want to do it myself," I said. "I want to make everything from scratch." So I bought a chocolate cake mix and a can of fudge frosting. I even got a bag of chocolate chips to sprinkle on top.

As we got into line to check out, I noticed a bin of

videos selling for a dollar. I decided to buy one. It couldn't be too romantic, though. After all, we were just friends. I picked out *Homeward Bound*, a movie about two dogs and a cat crossing the country to get back to their owners. The cover got a ten on the cute-and-cuddly scale.

After we got home, I called Brittany. "Hi." I felt suddenly unsure.

"Hi."

"Do you want to come over to my house tomorrow night?"

Her voice smiled. "Anything special?"

"No. Just dinner and a movie."

"Sounds great. What time?"

"How about six?"

"I'll be there."

We hung up, and I stared at the phone, wondering what I was getting myself into. I'd never cooked anything other than heating things up in the microwave. That night, I was so nervous I hardly slept.

The next day, my uncle picked me up after school, and then dropped me at home. He took off again without a word of advice. I would have liked some, although come to think of it, he didn't cook much either.

I got out my trusty cake pan and the mix. Reading the box, I found that the recipe called for eggs and vegetable oil. I was surprised and a little dismayed. I didn't have any oil. Looking in the refrigerator, I found a stick of butter. That would do as a substitute. Butter would probably taste better, anyway.

I mixed the batter with a fork until it was smooth, poured it into the cake pan, and put it into the oven. Then I took a shower.

When the cake was done, I placed it on the windowsill to cool. I'd seen that in a movie. The cake was dark, almost black, and more lopsided than I expected.

Around five o'clock, I found a saucepan for the marinara and put it on the stove to simmer. I couldn't find a large pot for the spaghetti, so I fit the noodles in a skillet, covered them with water, and put them on to boil as well.

I pried the cake out of the pan. It fell out like a brick, clattering onto the plate. I don't know what I expected, but that wasn't it. I spread frosting all over, trying to even up the slanted part. Then I poured chocolate chips over the top.

Everything was going fine.

Time to set the table. I got out two wine glasses. There were no napkins, so I used a couple of my uncle's disposable blue shop cloths.

I'd stashed the flowers in the refrigerator to keep them from the lizards that roamed the kitchen, and I brought them out. I had a moment of panic when I realized there were no vases in the house. I ended up rinsing out the empty marinara jar and putting the flowers in there. I laid the single rose across Brittany's plate.

I was proud of how the table looked.

Brittany's car pulled up the drive. With my laptop and the new movie in hand, I met her at the door. "Come in." I grinned. "You look really nice."

She did, too. She'd changed her hair since school that day. The red bangs were gone. Now her hair was wispy and purple on top. Her lips were dark and glossy. She wore a black miniskirt and sandals that crisscrossed to her knees.

"Thanks." She smiled. "Something smells good."

"Dinner is almost ready. I brought my laptop out here. I got a new movie." I handed it to her.

She gasped. "This was my favorite when I was little. How did you know?"

The words *when I was little* rang in my head. Had I bought a kid's movie? "Well, I knew you liked dogs. We can watch something different, if you'd rather."

"No. It will be fun to see it again." She dropped her purse onto the recliner. No coat to deal with—another perk of South Florida living.

I moved the TV and placed the laptop on the metal stand.

"I think something's scorching," she said.

"Oh! Have a seat. I'll be right back."

I rushed into the kitchen. The spaghetti was sizzling, and I took the skillet off the heat. Most of the water had boiled away, and the spaghetti had merged into a single fat noodle. With lines.

"Rats," I said.

"Is everything all right in there?" she called.

"Fine," I lied.

I grabbed a lump of butter and plopped it into the pan. I figured the grease would separate the spaghetti, but all it did was turn the noodles gold.

"You know, I was thinking," she said, "since neither of us is going to Jana's party, maybe we can do something together that night."

"Hmmm?"

I slid the noodle onto my serving plate, brown butter and all. What was I going to do?

"Yeah, it will be great," she said.

"No, I'm busy that night."

"What?"

"Busy."

Using a sharp knife, I sliced the thick noodle into half-inch chunks. Then I smothered the whole thing with mozzarella and topped it with the marinara.

"Dinner's ready," I called. "Come and get it."

She appeared at the door. "That looks interesting."

"It's my own creation. I call it…spaghetti balls."

"Wonderful." She sat at the table and lifted the rose. "For me?"

"Happy Valentine's Day." I set the serving plate onto the table.

"I've never met anyone like you." She looked at me like she couldn't figure me out.

My cheeks warmed. "Well, you're the nicest

179

study partner I've ever met."

She lifted her wine glass. "Are we having wine?"

"Only the best." I opened the bottle of Mountain Dew and held it out with a flourish.

She laughed.

We served ourselves spaghetti. It was gooey with cheese. The noodles were a bit gummy, but the butter gave them an interesting flavor. Brittany had seconds.

I was relieved things were going well, and happy to have her with me. I thought it was the best night of my life.

Until I brought out the dessert.

"Yum, double chocolate," she said. "You made this yourself?"

"Old family recipe." I tried cutting the cake with a butter knife. No good. "It came out a little tough."

"Get a sharper knife."

I got the largest, sharpest knife in the drawer and tried again.

"That's strange," she said. "Maybe you need a cleaver."

More like a buzz saw, I thought. Even I knew cake shouldn't be like a rock. Pressing with both hands, I put my weight into it. The cake snapped in two. Crumbs shot over the table like gravel.

"It's ruined," I said.

"Don't be silly. You can't ruin chocolate." She took the knife from me and somehow chiseled the cake into small squares. "Crunchy cake. It's good."

It nearly broke my tooth. I felt terrible. I'd wanted everything to be perfect.

Then Brittany said, "This is the best Valentine's Day ever."

My chest swelled with love for her.

She insisted on helping me wash the dishes, and we had fun splashing each other with sudsy water. Then we sat together in the big old recliner and watched the dog movie. Brittany cried at the end.

In spite of that, I thought the evening went pretty well.

# SIXTEEN

Monday was President's Day. No school. My alarm clock sat in silence. My pillow felt soft. Parakeets squawked outside my bedroom window. Something fell in the kitchen. Probably a lizard scurrying about. It wasn't my uncle. His scent was gone.

My senses were in overdrive, as they always were approaching the full moon. They felt almost natural, like the wolf was part of me. In two days, I would shift. The thought sickened me, so I pushed it out of my mind. No sense in worrying. Nothing I could do to stop it.

I showered, ate, and hopped on my bike. The sky was clear, the breeze warm, and the ride into town barely tapped my new super strength. Parking outside the Video Stop, I hurried inside. Cool air smelling strongly of plastic chilled my damp skin. Brittany sat behind the counter. She smiled at me, and the room lit up.

"Hi," I said. "How are you?"

"Glad to see you. I could use some company."

"Quiet morning?"

"The worst." She stretched and yawned. "Everyone's probably sleeping in."

Was that a dig? It was nearly noon. "Sorry I'm late."

"I was beginning to think your uncle grabbed you for his big project." She brought a tall stool around the counter and went back for another. "He's running out of time."

"Why? What's he doing?"

"You don't know?" She looked at me. "He's at Jana's house making one of those fake waterfalls with all the rocks and the koi pond and everything. He needs to get it done before the big party."

"Whoa." That *was* a big project. I remembered my parents doing that back home. The landscaper had a mini-bulldozer. "That's a lot of work for one man. I wonder why he didn't ask me to help."

"He probably didn't want to distract you from the FCAT last week."

"They were testing the teachers, not me."

"But you were doing the work." She smiled. "You probably got a hundred percent."

"You, too."

"Not me. I don't like to score higher than eighty. High enough to keep my mother off my back, but not so high as to draw attention."

"You throw your grades?" A laugh threatened my better sense.

"I didn't one year. My father got mad. He said he wouldn't have a snooty show-off for a daughter."

I went cold. "What did he do?"

"What he always did." She shook her head. "It doesn't matter. He lives in Georgia."

I wanted so much to take her hand, to comfort her about what was obviously a bad memory. I wondered what kind of father would yell at a kid for being smart. Brittany and her family lived with her dad's father after the divorce. Grandpa Earle must take the mother's side.

The pause in conversation made me uncomfortable, so I got up to browse the sci-fi aisle.

After a moment, Brittany walked toward me. "See anything good?"

"Yeah. You have a nice selection."

"Pick out something. We can make Thursdays our standing movie night."

My heart sped. *A movie night?* We spent the last two Thursdays watching DVDs. Had she thought of them as dates? It sounded too good to be true. Nothing would make me happier than to have a standing date.

But this Thursday was the full moon. I couldn't.

"Sorry," I said. "I'm busy this Thursday."

"You said you were busy on Friday."

"That, too."

"All right." Brittany sighed. "How about Wednesday?"

"I can't," I said, then trying to diffuse her sharp look, added, "But we can do something tomorrow night if you want to."

She started walking way, then stopped and turned back. "You're going out with her, aren't you?"

I blinked. "Who?"

"Jana. I've seen how she looks at you. Rich girls always fall for the bad boys. It ticks off their fathers."

I moved close, smiling and dropping my voice. "You think I'm a bad boy?"

"Cody, just go. I've got work to do."

I glanced around. "I'm the only one here."

"I'm serious." She stomped back to the stools and dragged them out of sight.

I felt a hot surge of anger. I wanted to grab her waist, lean her back against the counter, and kiss her hard on the lips. I'd show her how a bad boy acted. I'd show them all. So, rich girl Jana had a thing for me, did she? I wondered how she'd feel when she found out my parents could buy hers.

With my fists clenched, I approached Brittany. She studied a shipping invoice and did not look up. I wanted to shake her and roar *look at me*.

But that was the wolf talking.

"I'm not going out with anyone," I said.

How could she accuse me? Didn't she know how much I loved her?

"Leave," she said, her voice crackly.

I honestly didn't know what I was supposed to do. I didn't know what I'd done wrong, how to talk my way out of it. If she had just looked up from that invoice, I would have begged her forgiveness. I would have promised her anything.

185

But she didn't look up. So I left.

Warm, muggy air enveloped me as I stepped out of the store. The traffic sounds of the shopping center grated against my ears. My inner wolf raged. I should go back. I should yell, force her to listen.

I guess I growled, because a man getting into a red Camaro, a really nice Camaro, gave me an odd look. I went to my bike, which still leaned against the wall. No Camaro for me. No sir. I scowled at the man. There was something about the way he watched me that made me want to bare my teeth. I took off across the parking lot, pedaling like the devil himself was behind me.

That night, I called Brittany, but only got her voicemail. I didn't leave a message. I was still mad and didn't want to say anything I might regret. Besides, we'd see each other at school the next day.

But she wasn't interested in talking to me. She wouldn't look at me all through World History, and at lunch, she sat with a bunch of girls. I was so angry I couldn't eat. I kept watching her, catching glimpses across the crowded room. It was unfair. She blamed me for something I didn't do. Why wouldn't she give me a chance to explain?

By the time I got home, I was afraid to call. She hated me. She'd never speak to me again. There was no hope of her ever being my girlfriend.

I barely slept, just tossed and turned like I was sweating out a fever. My stomach was queasy, and my muscles ached. At first, I thought I was heartsick over Brittany. But it was the full moon nearing. I half wished to turn into a wolf and stay that way.

When I saw my uncle the next morning, he looked as bad as I felt.

I poured some milk. "How's the project?"

He gave a weary smile. "I'm putting the finishing touches on it today."

"I could stay home if you want, lend you a hand."

"Nah. Thanks, though."

"All right." I rinsed my cup. "I think I'll bike it to school today."

"Are you sure? You don't have to."

"Yeah, it's good. Why don't you get an extra hour of sleep?"

"I'll do that." He nodded, frowning.

I knew that look. My mother got it when she suspected I was keeping something from her. Unlike her, he didn't lecture. So I rode my bike to school. It felt good to get rid of the excess energy. But at the sight of Brittany's green Volkswagen in the student parking lot, I became tense and anxious again.

I don't know how I got through the day. I wanted to snap everyone's head off. Lunch was again spent by myself. I couldn't wait for school to end.

I stopped at the Coffee Café on the way back to the house. Anne, my uncle's favorite waitress, acted glad to see me—and I was happy to spend an hour with her. I wanted to be with normal people, wanted to say *hey, look everybody, I'm human just like you.*

Of course, I wasn't. So I ate a bloody hamburger,

had three refills of chocolate milk, and soaked up all the attention Anne would give me. Eventually, the time came to leave. If I went home, either the house would be empty, which I hated, or my uncle would be there to question my leaving at nightfall. So I went straight to my hidden courtyard. I walked my bike through the thicket and stood there, taking in the familiar scents of pine, grass, and dirt. Birds made a racket in the trees. Field mice scurried through the underbrush.

I dumped my bike and sat beside it, unwrapping the tape from my arm. Would I have a broken leg as a wolf, or would the shift mend the bone? When I turned back to human, would my arm automatically heal? Maybe I would have a wolf leg instead of an arm.

That would be weird.

I shook off that train of thought and instead spent my time searching for the pull of the moon. It was like a stream of energy fortifying me. It made sense that I should be able to tap its strength whenever I wanted. After all, the moon was always there, even when it shone on the other side of the planet.

The sky fell to purple. Moonrise was minutes away. I stripped, tossing my clothes over the bike. With my senses focused, I faced the moon head on, holding out my hands as if to shield myself from the first beams.

The change overtook me. My muzzle elongated, feeling like it was pulling off my face. My ears tugged toward the top of my head. I fell to my knees, crying out as my injured arm twisted and stretched. I licked my foreleg until the pain dulled.

At last, I got to my paws. I ached like I'd been beaten with a two by four all over again. My fractured front leg balked at holding my weight. No chasing rabbits tonight. I limped through the trees and onto the road. Before long, I found myself at Brittany's house.

As I approached the yard, I smelled wolf. My hackles rose, and a low growl issued from my throat. Someone had been there. Three distinct scents. They circled the property and crisscrossed the woods. It was almost as if they'd left me a message. They wanted me to know about them.

Rage swelled my chest, and I growled again. No one had the right to be there except me. I spent the rest of the night tracking the wolves through the trees. But the trail ended, masked by the scent of humans.

🐕 🐕 🐕

When I went to school the next day, I was determined to talk to Brittany. I planned to ask her out to a real movie Saturday night.

But she avoided me. When I saw her in class, she was busy. When I tried to catch her in the hallways, she scurried away. I felt crushed. What good was my life without her? It made no difference that I wasn't at fault. All that mattered was her smile when she saw me, the touch of her hand on mine. I would never have those things again.

I went home dejected.

The moon was full that night. I sat in my clearing, awaiting the pain, itching to be out of my skin. I didn't want to be me any longer. I felt lost.

After I shifted into a wolf, I continued to sit there. A swirling wind tousled my fur. It brought with it all sorts of scents. Deer and panther. Swampland. Loxahatchee was on the northern tip of the Everglades. There was plenty to see and do, adventures I never imagined. But all I wanted was to be with Brittany. Even if she never spoke to me again, I needed to watch over her, needed to keep her safe.

So turning my back on the enticing smells, I went to her.

The moon climbed high. Shadows fell crisp. The wind drew music from the night. As I feared, I found the trace of a wolf in the grass. One of the three. He'd returned to the house for a reason. I growled at the thought. How could I protect her if I was only a wolf a few nights a month?

Just then, the back door opened. Brittany stepped out with her bag of garbage. I should have jumped into the bushes—but I couldn't. I had to see her, even if she didn't know it was me. So I stood in plain sight, gauging her reaction.

She froze like a doe. I held perfectly still so I wouldn't spook her. I was too large to be mistaken for a dog. Almost too large to be a wolf.

Moonlight turned her features silver, like a statue carved from crystal. I expected her to yell or to throw something to chase me away, but she did neither. She stared at me for a time. Then she edged forward, dropping her bag into the can. She backed away, leaving.

Panic gripped me. I stepped toward her, wanting to cry *stay with me*, but she was through the door and gone. The deadbolt sounded like a gunshot.

I couldn't stand it. All the heartache and confusion of the past few days balled up inside me, rising up my throat like bitter vomit. Lifting my head, I bayed at the moon. Long and forlorn. I howled again, releasing my pain.

Brittany stood at the kitchen window, watching.

🐺 🐺 🐺

Friday, I caught her in the hall outside World History. I grasped her arm so she wouldn't run away. "I'm not going out with another girl," I said.

She met my eyes. "Okay, then. Where *are* you going?"

"I can't tell you."

"Is it a secret?"

That sounded like a trap, and I hoped that by not answering I wouldn't step into it. Of course, it never turns out that way.

"That's the thing." Her voice rose. "Friends don't

keep secrets from one another."

"So what are you saying? I'm not your friend?"

"I have to go."

"You aren't being fair," I wailed. "There are things about me you don't understand."

She pursed her lips, and I faltered. Even angry, she was beautiful.

"Look," I said, "it's just this one thing. I'll tell you anything else you want to know."

Brittany paused. "If I was hiding something and you asked me flat out about it, I would tell you."

I stared at her, knowing it was true. But she didn't have a secret like mine. If I told her, she'd call me a monster and I would lose her. If I didn't tell her, I would lose her anyway. "Brittany, please. Can't you just trust me?"

She wrenched her arm from my grasp and walked away. I stood there dumbstruck in the middle of the hall with kids streaming to either side. I felt like cutting the rest of my classes, but that wouldn't do any good. I stuck it out.

At lunch, I grabbed a Dew and sat alone at my table. I didn't look to see if Brittany showed up. I wished I had someone to confide in. Someone like Uncle Bob, who always listened and never judged.

"Hi," said a voice.

I looked up, trying to place the face. "Jana, right?"

"Right."

"Happy birthday."

"Oh, thanks." She smiled, showing deep dimples. "Are you coming? To my party, I mean."

I shook my head. "Sorry. I'm busy."

"Come on." She swung her hips and tossed her ponytail. "We'll have fun."

From the corner of my eye, I saw Brittany. She walked toward me, then stopped, her face falling. My insides wrenched. She was coming to speak to me, and here I was with this stupid, insignificant—

"Cody?" Jana giggled.

The wolf snapped, and my voice roared. "I don't want to go to your stinking party."

She looked alarmed, then outraged. If looks could kill, I'd be a smear on the table. She stormed away, ponytail swishing.

My head bowed into my hands. Brittany had been coming to see me. I blew it again.

I managed to get through to the end of the day without yelling at anyone else. Just before Shop, Lonnie and Maxwell grabbed me in the hall. The last time we'd spoken, they blamed me for getting Eff kicked off the football team.

I was glad to see them, but feigned disinterest. "Are you two talking to me again?"

"Come with us," Maxwell said.

They led me to the bathroom near the office.

Lonnie pulled out his phone. "Have you seen this? There are new photos on your fairy page."

I took the phone, expecting to see more shots of

me posed with the snow globe. Instead, I saw pictures of me tied in the trees. Good photos. Taken with a good camera. With a zoom.

My stomach fell. Someone had come back. Someone took pictures of me in Brittany's yard. I remembered her dog barking.

I scrolled down. There was a shot of Brittany and me together, her face streaming with tears, my eyes swollen shut. There was Butt Crack hanging onto the rope, looking horrified. Me in close-up, grimacing in pain. Me on the ground with Brittany kneeling at my side.

Rage built deep in my gut. Someone was in her yard. They might have hurt her, and I would have been powerless to stop them. Powerless.

I wasn't powerless now.

With shaking fingers, I handed back the phone. My vision dimmed as if light were seeping out of the room. All I could see was the photo of Brittany looking anguished, tears on her face. Burned indelibly into my mind. I slammed out of the bathroom and turned toward the exit. The main door would be unlocked.

"Where are you going?" Lonnie called after me. "We have to get to class."

"Tell Mister Conklin I'm sick." I walked out right past the office. I didn't care who saw me. My mind was so full of hate and rage, I could barely think.

It was one thing to post photos of me on the Internet. They shouldn't have involved Brittany. Now the whole school would know what I put her through.

Now, *I know*, I thought, remembering her stricken face.

A growl escaped me. I clenched my fists, hating Eff for hurting her. I wanted to tear him apart. As soon as he came out that door, POW!

No. Too crowded. I'd go to his car. I couldn't wait to see his face when he saw me standing there. But once I reached the parking lot, I realized I didn't know which car was his.

Too public, anyway. I needed to take this off school grounds.

Then I thought of the waning moon. I would be a wolf tonight. A smile spread across my face, and the beast inside me howled. I would pay Eff a little visit in my wolf form. Scare the crap out of him. Bite him a little. Maybe a lot. Maybe leave him as bloodied as he left me.

I stomped away from school. It would take a couple of hours to walk all the way to my hidden courtyard, but I was up for it. The animal in me made me strong. It nurtured my rage.

I imagined Eff snapping photos as Brittany lowered me from the tree, imagined him smiling as he zoomed in. That was premeditated. He went back there to gloat.

Well, maybe there will be pictures of Eff in the news tomorrow. Just one more unexplained attack.

With a snicker, I stepped up my pace. I was halfway through town when my phone rang.

It was Uncle Bob. "Hey, boy. I'm waiting outside the school. Where are you?"

"I'm walking. I cut my last class."

"Are you okay?"

"Sure."

A pause. Then he said, "Where are you? I'll swing by and pick you up."

"I don't need you to pick me up," I snarled. I didn't want him to mother me, didn't want him to be reasonable.

Uncle Bob's voice grew stern. "I expect you to come home. Do you hear me? Whatever you're doing, stop and come home."

My shoulders sagged, and I looked to the moon for strength. After a moment, I said, "Fine."

It was nearly five o'clock when I got back.

My uncle held the door. "Where you been, boy? I was worried."

"Why can't everyone just leave me alone?" I pushed past him and went into the kitchen. Standing in front of the open refrigerator, I chugged milk from the carton.

Behind me, Uncle Bob said, "You're my responsibility. I care about you."

I rolled my eyes.

"What happened?" he asked.

Good question. What should I tell him first? Should I tell him about Brittany ditching me, or how Jana wants me dead? Maybe I should tell him that in two hours I would turn into a wolf. I took another swig of milk. "Eff posted more pictures."

He sighed. "Yeah. I saw them."

I slammed the milk carton onto the counter. "What, you have a MySpace page now?"

He chuckled. "Me? Of course not. Howard does."

I glared at him, wanting to slug him in the mouth. I felt like they'd been spying on me, felt like everyone knew my business before I did.

"Come with me tonight," Uncle Bob said. "Don't do anything in anger."

"Yeah. Right," I muttered.

"Your mother wouldn't want–"

That did it. I couldn't stay there a moment longer. I rushed out of the house, not even bothering to close the door, hopped on my bike and roared away. I half-expected him to pull up behind me and force me into his truck, but he didn't. So much for caring about me.

I turned down the long, asphalt road, pedaling as fast as I could. The sun had set. Between the growing darkness and my mounting agitation, I wouldn't have been surprised if I turned into a wolf right then. That would be funny. A wolf riding a bike.

I wondered how to find Eff. Just wander around and hope I caught a whiff of him? Then I remembered Jana's party. He was sure to be there. Most everyone in the tenth grade was expected to show.

Perfect. I would wait to catch him ducking out to have a smoke. Better yet, I could storm the party and chase him around in front of everybody. I'd make it an event they'd never forget.

197

I grinned as I imagined the screams.

By the time I reached the courtyard, it was pitch dark. I didn't bother to walk my bike through the trees, just tossed it to the side of the road. I stepped to the center of the clearing. The moon rose. It pulled at me. I stripped off my shirt. Then I kicked off my shoes and stepped out of my jeans and shorts.

The shift hit before I had time to take off my socks. I stood with my arms outstretched and welcomed it. My skin prickled and stung as the coarse fur broke out. My face elongated, and my fangs grew painfully, making me drool.

I heard a sound behind me. I spun about, teeth bared, a snarl in my throat.

Brittany stood at the line of trees, looking horrified.

# SEVENTEEN

Brittany's hands flew to her mouth. Our eyes met. The shock of seeing her momentarily stopped my transformation. I stood there with my muzzle half-elongated, drool dripping from my fangs, and knew how she must see me. A monster. A sideshow freak.

Then I realized I was naked.

*Oh, crap.*

I tried to shout, "Don't look at me," but it sounded like a dog with a bone caught in its throat.

Panic and shame rose like engulfing fire. I ran for the tree line. My legs shifted, and I fell on my face. I scrambled on all fours. Brittany didn't move. She looked afraid, which was worse than having her angry.

All thoughts of revenge and of finding Eff at the party left me. I wanted to cry. How could I face her again? How could I go to school?

Head bowed, I walked away. This was the worst day of my life, worse than when my parents kicked me out, worse even than when Brittany found me beaten in the trees. There was no way to fix my life. I had no life. I was the amazing wolf boy.

Grass grew tall around me. Its saw-toothed edges dragged at my fur. Muck sucked my paws. I realized with a start I'd left the woods and ventured into swampland.

I also realized another wolf tailed me. The thought brought more confusion than alarm. There weren't supposed to be wolves in Florida. I looked it up. Yet I'd come across the scents of several wolves in the few months I'd lived here.

Ahead, a pond stretched into darkness. Moonlight shimmered over its still surface. I lay on its bank, paws over my muzzle.

The other wolf sat a short distance away. He watched me. I almost wished he would start a fight. I wouldn't raise a paw to stop him. After a while, he moved forward, skirting the edge of the pond. My ears twitched, but I didn't lift my head.

Without warning, the wolf pounced into the water, coming up with a fish flapping in his jaws. He dropped it at my side, held my gaze for a moment, and trotted away.

I watched him leave. Was this was some strange ritual among wolves? Perhaps he was welcoming me into his territory.

The fish stirred and gasped. I nuzzled it until it flopped into the water. I watched the pond for hours, but it never resurfaced.

In the early hours of morning, I made my way back to my hidden courtyard. Brittany was gone, of course. But my clothes were folded neatly on top of my shoes to keep them out of the dew.

🐾 🐾 🐾

The temperature dropped a few degrees as a cool front passed through the area. Rain spattered the kitchen window. The view looked as dismal as I felt.

I heated a mug of chocolate milk in the micro-wave and sat at the kitchen table, staring at it. I pictured the scene with Brittany like a third party, seeing both her horrified face and mine with drool and fur. God, why did everything happen to me?

A quiet rap sounded at the door. For a moment, I considered not answering. But my uncle was still asleep. If he woke, he would want to know where I'd been all night. So I pushed heavily to my feet and went to the door.

Brittany stood there. My heart wrenched at the sight of her. She wore no makeup, and her eyes were red.

I'd hurt her again, I realized, wishing to somehow take back the night.

Afraid she might yell, I hurried outside and closed the door behind me. But she didn't yell. Instead, she walked to the porch swing and sat down. Tentatively, I sat beside her. We rocked in silence.

"So," she said after a moment. "That was a big secret."

"Yeah."

"I thought you were a dog when I saw you at my house."

I looked down at my hands.

She paused then said in a rush, "I know I shouldn't have followed you, and I don't blame you for being mad. I really thought I would catch you with another girl."

Was *she* apologizing to *me*? "I don't want another girl." A tear fell down my cheek. *Damn it.* I looked away so she wouldn't see.

"I still can't—" She shook her head. "You're a werewolf."

"I don't want to be," I blurted. "I'd stop if I could."

She put her hand over mine. "I would love to be a part-time wolf."

I stared at her. Had I heard her right?

"Run through the woods, no rules, no problems." She gave a faint smile. "What's it like?"

I searched for words, wanting to tell her, but I couldn't even explain it to myself. "Different."

"You should hear yourself when it happens. There's kind of a wet, gloppy, crackling sound." She crinkled her nose in the way that I loved. "Gross."

A strange mix of embarrassment and relief washed over me. I let out a breath. "I don't hear it. I guess I'm preoccupied with the pain."

"It hurts?"

"Yeah. Especially my arm." I showed her that I'd taped it again.

"I didn't think of that."

Her brow furrowed, and I saw she was working things out, probably understanding why I healed so fast.

We rocked for a few minutes.

"If you bit me, would I turn?" she asked.

"I don't think so. No one bit me."

Brittany frowned. "That doesn't jive with the movies at all."

Right. If this were the movies, I really would be a monster. I'd be ripping people apart instead of watching over her while she slept.

"Well, there's only one thing to do." She slapped her knee. "We have to go shopping."

I stopped the swing. "Huh?"

She stood, clutching her purse. "Would it be okay if I cleaned up in your bathroom?"

"I think so," I said, still confused about how shopping would help me. "Uncle Bob is asleep."

"I'll be quiet."

We went inside, and she disappeared into the bathroom. I wrote a note for Uncle Bob and left it under his coffee cup. He was probably mad at the way I spoke to him last night, and I didn't want to make matters worse by ducking out without a word.

Brittany's reaction to finding out I was a werewolf confused me. Acceptance was the last thing I expected. How long would it last? It didn't matter. All I wanted was to be with her, and I would take whatever time she gave me.

She came out with her eyes painted black and

203

her lips dark purple, smiling. "Ready?"

"Sure. What's the plan?"

"Think about it. You weren't bitten. This isn't a virus; it's more like a curse. If you're serious about not wanting to be a wolf anymore, we need more information."

"You're going to help me break the curse?"

"Of course. What's a girlfriend for?"

My head buzzed, mulling that one over. I must have looked dazed, because she took my arm and pulled me from the house to her lime green car.

The day was wet and cold, and I wished her little Volkswagen had heat. I folded my arms and stared straight ahead as Brittany backed the car down the gravel drive.

"You all right?" she asked.

"Yeah," I said, "it's just..."

"Just what?"

I looked at her. "You're amazing."

She laughed. "You're pretty amazing yourself. A werewolf. Wow. I just want to tell all my friends about it." She glanced over. "I know I can't, of course. Don't worry about that."

I nodded but still felt the weight of impending doom. Not for me, exactly. I had the sense that knowing my secret might be dangerous for her.

But Brittany's scent filled the car. She was happy with me again. I settled back and allowed myself a tentative smile.

"Where are we going?" I asked.

"*Awakening*, my all-time favorite place. There are other metaphysical shops, of course, but this one sells *quality* items. You know? The finest crystals. The purest candles."

"Great," I said. "I love that kind of stuff."

And so it was that I entered my first metaphysical shop. I smelled smoldering sandalwood as I opened the door. The smoke made my eyes water and the back of my throat itch. I stepped cautiously, glancing about, taking in all the *quality* items. I saw vials of essential oils, candles of every color, and unicorn figurines. A display of wind chimes sang in the breeze of a fan, and prisms dangled before a spotlight.

Brittany bounded down a narrow aisle. I followed, careful not to brush anything. I'm not exactly clumsy, but I have a history of knocking things over.

The clerk, an older woman in her thirties, held out her arms theatrically, giving Brittany a hug. Her skin was like leather, and her long hair was as coarse as a horsetail.

"Marta," said Brittany, "this is Cody."

"Bright blessings to you," Marta said.

What do you say to that? "Interesting shop," I murmured.

"I'm very proud of it." She nodded.

Brittany smiled. "We're just going to look around."

"Of course." Marta returned to the register.

Brittany studied both sides of the aisle as she drifted toward the far wall. I edged sideways behind

205

her, holding my breath as I passed the breakable objects.

She glanced up as I approached. "I want to find a stone that will repel negative energy."

"How about quartz?" I said as if I knew what she was talking about, surreptitiously reading the label on a bin of small rocks.

"Interesting choice. But even if you wore it against your skin, it wouldn't be strong enough. I was thinking of tourmaline or obsidian. You wear them in a medicine pouch."

That sounded Native American. "Maybe we should talk to Howard."

"That's an excellent idea. We'll do that later." She stepped away. "This is what I was looking for. Which stone do you prefer?"

"Unless they cancel each other out, I vote that we take one of each." It wasn't like I believed in all that mystical holistic stuff, but I was desperate. I would do anything for a normal life. More than that, I wanted to stay on Brittany's good side. "Where are the pouches?"

"Over here by the necklaces. Ooh. Look at this one. *Earth Calm Pendant.*" She read the label. "The talisman creates a Scalar Resonance circuit which grounds the wearer to Earth's energy field."

"Would that disrupt the moon's energy field?"

"It's worth a try." She kept the pendant, then pulled a small rawhide pouch from a mass of others hanging by cords from a hook. "Help me find the candleholders."

They weren't hard to spot. She chose four and handed them to me. Then she knelt before a wire basket filled with chunky, three-inch candles. She filled my arms.

"Keep these burning at all times. I mean it." She walked to the register.

The candles smelled strongly of peppermint. I stifled a sneeze and followed her.

"Can you get us a prism?" Brittany asked Marta as she approached the counter.

"Sure, honey. What size room?"

"Small." Brittany looked at me.

"Ten by twelve." I shrugged my armful of candles and candleholders onto the counter and took out my debit card. There was no telling how much we spent. Nothing was marked.

"Tourmaline, obsidian, white candles," Marta said. "You're exorcising one nasty demon."

I hardly breathed as she tallied up. To my relief, the prism took the bulk of the bill. We got out of there without wiping out my savings.

As we walked to her car, Brittany dialed her cell.

"Hello? Yes, this is Brittany Meyer. May I speak with the Grandmaster, please?" After a moment, she said, "Grandmaster, are you available today? No, for a friend. I can be there in fifteen. Thank you."

She returned the phone to her purse and hopped in the car. I climbed in shotgun. Before I had a chance to buckle my seatbelt, she leaned over to tie the medicine pouch around my neck.

"It's supposed to hang level with your heart," she said. "Wear it even when you're sleeping."

I tucked the pouch under my shirt. "I don't feel any different."

"Give the stones a chance to warm up."

She handed me the *Earth Calm Pendant*. It was on a long chain, and I slipped it over my head. "Good," she said. "We'll put the prism in your window and set the candles on the compass points."

"Okay. Let's go."

"We have one more stop. The Sunspot."

I nearly swallowed my tongue. "The nudist colony?"

"Oh, relax. We'll be along the outer edge. Clothing optional."

"I don't know, Brittany. Why do we have to go there?"

"Because you need a reading of your future, past, and present. We're fortunate to have an actual grandmaster in the area."

So just like that, I got my first look at a naturist resort. Part of it was like regular woods, and part was so beautifully landscaped with exotic plants it was like we were driving into Eden.

I saw only a few naked people along the way. My face went hot. They looked miserable and cold. I hated to tell them there was a reason people invented clothing.

Brittany pulled up to a white trailer with a red-wood deck. A sign read *Tarot Card Readers*.

"A fortune teller?" I asked.

"Certified." Brittany got out of the car.

I circled around to stand beside her.

She looked at me. "She has an office in Palm Beach. This is her home."

"What do you hope to learn here?"

"I don't know. Let's find out."

With a double hold on my arm, she tugged me to the wooden deck. The door of the trailer opened before we reached it, showing a woman with frizzy red hair. She wore clothes. "Brittany, dear, how nice to see you again," she said. "Is this your friend?"

"Yes, Grandmaster. This is Cody."

"Ah, Cody Forester from Massachusetts, living with Bob Nowak."

"You're a psychic?" I asked.

"Not at all. I'm a gossip." She stepped aside to allow us to enter. "I'm told you punched Efrem Higgins in the nose."

"Nice place." I knew as soon as I spoke that I was rudely changing the subject, but actually, I was just surprised. It looked like a normal home. Regular furniture. A little cramped. I don't know what I expected.

"Come in. Have a seat." She walked to the dining area and sat at a round wooden table. "I usually throw from a Thoth deck in a standard Celtic Cross formation, but I'm open. Do you have a preference?"

"No. That's fine." I sat across from her feeling out

of place. "I've never done this before."

"Ooh," they both crooned, exchanging smiles.

I knew then I'd walked into some kind of trap.

"Well, you're in for a treat, dear boy." The grandmaster reached for a bundle wrapped in a white silk scarf. The Tarot cards. "I want you to shuffle these. Don't frill the edges, just move them slowly in your hands. Caress them. As you do, think of the question foremost on your mind."

I shied from the stack. It occurred to me that if the grandmaster was as powerful as Brittany believed, she might be able to discern my secret. "I don't know if this is a good idea."

"Come on, Cody," Brittany cooed, leaning toward me. "Everybody's waiting. Shuffle the cards."

Since the whole operation was to please her, I picked up the deck. It's crazy, but they felt warm. Like they were alive. For a moment, I wondered if the grandmaster had popped them into the microwave, trying for an eerie effect.

I cut the deck several times and mixed the cards thoroughly. The two women stared at my hands as if expecting me to tuck a card up my sleeve. I tried not to think about being a werewolf. I told myself that the important question was whether Brittany liked me. But the wolf kept creeping into my thoughts until I realized it might be risky to keep handling the things.

"Done." I set the stack in the center of the table.

"Excellent," the woman said. "The Tarot knows your heart better than you yourself. But do not place too much emphasis on a single card. You must look at the reading as a whole, because each image is modified by its brethren. Now we begin. The first position is the Present." She flipped over a card. "*The Hermit*, which represents introspection and virginity."

"Great." Embarrassment made me squirm.

Brittany chuckled.

"Now, now. Virginity merely means the beginning or untried. It is modified by your Immediate Challenge." She placed another card crosswise over the first. "*The Tower*. Shocking revelation."

"That sounds ominous." Brittany sat literally on the edge of her seat.

I winced. The darn cards must have picked up on my inner wolf.

"The third illuminates your Distant Past, the foundation from which you spring. *The Moon*."

Of course.

She frowned. "Often *The Moon* brings illusions, visions, but in this position it means madness."

"I'm insane?"

"No, dear boy. I believe you are unduly affected by the phases of the moon. In fact, the double blue moon in January and March of the year 1999 was particularly eventful for you." She looked at me as if expecting me to expand upon that.

"I was eight years old." I pulled a face. "The most that happened to me was I came down with a fever and was out of school for a couple months."

As I said it, I realized the wolf was shaping my

life even then. I didn't want to think about that, didn't want to know, and I didn't want to hear more of what the grandmaster had to say.

She placed another card. Something about desire. Brittany slid her hand over mine. It felt comforting. I gazed at her and traced her perfect nose with my eyes. She had a few freckles. I hadn't noticed them before.

Another card.

Brittany gasped. "*Death*."

"Meaning transformation. Very ambiguous. I cannot see if you will transform into something more or revert to something less. Let us look further into your Immediate Future. *The Hierophant*. Worldly problems." She sat back, a thoughtful expression upon her face.

"What does it mean?" Brittany asked.

"It means your friend is not concerned about himself. None of this." She gestured at the pattern of cards. "None of it is about him. He senses evil and wants to stop it."

"Evil?" What was this about? I wasn't worried about evil. Except maybe the murders of those poor women.

"It's closer than you think." The grandmaster leaned over the images. "Madness. Shocking revelation. I fear you are in danger. No, not you. Someone you care for."

"What?" I stiffened.

She added to the pattern. "Inner Feelings. Represented by *Temperance*. Moderation. But External Influences draws *The Devil*, signifying pleasure and abandon. The evil is not within you. It is tracking you. It enjoys the game."

"Can we get back to someone I care about being in danger?" I asked.

"Your Hope and Fear." She turned the card theatrically.

"*The High Priestess*," Brittany said. "Knowledge."

"You want to know but are afraid of what you might learn."

"Know what?" I said.

"What the evil is," said Brittany.

"Or whom." The grandmaster looked at each of us in turn. She whispered, "The Final Outcome," and turned a card.

"Oh, no," cried Brittany.

"*The Hanged Man*. A time of Trial and Sacrifice. You must release something dear to you, for it can hurt you in ways you cannot expect. Dangerous. Let us draw three more for clarification. *Judgment* meaning rebirth or resurrection. *The Fool* giving us Infinite Possibilities. And the final card. *The Chariot*. War, Struggle, and Victory." She smiled. "So, you have a difficult time ahead, but in the end you will win."

"Okay, but what did you mean by dangerous?"

"Danger can mean anything from being kidnapped by a mass murderer to making poor life choices."

I pointed. "This one means sacrifice?"

"As previously mentioned, please do not dwell on a single card. Look at the reading as a whole. I believe that while you face a period of turmoil and revelation, you will prevail."

I glared. Not if it meant sacrificing Brittany.

We left the grandmaster abruptly. I think Brittany noticed my soured mood. We didn't speak on the way home, each entertaining our own thoughts. In my uncle's driveway, we sat in silence for a moment.

At last, I said, "Why did you take me there?"

"I was hoping for something that would make you stop being a werewolf. For a while, I thought we were on the right track. All that talk of transformation and moon madness." Brittany looked at me. "What did she mean about you wanting to stop evil?"

"I have no idea. I don't go hunting for trouble."

She nodded, then motioned to the house. "It doesn't look like your uncle is home."

"He's gone a lot." I didn't much like being alone. You'd think I'd be used to it, me being the only child of two doctors. But Uncle Bob was out more and more. I was beginning to think my presence cramped his style. "Do you want to come in?"

"I can't stay long."

Brittany handed me one of the bags with the candles, and we walked slowly to the porch. The wind was damp and chilling. I opened the door and held it for her.

"Doesn't he ever lock up?" she asked.

"Nope." I smiled. "Don't tell anyone."

We went to my room and dumped the bags onto my bed. One of the brass candleholders bounced to the floor. I checked it for damage.

She handed me her keys. "Find due north."

"You have a compass on your keychain?"

"Of course."

She apparently didn't find that unusual, so I shrugged and found due north.

Brittany placed a chunky white candle on the point. Then she went around the room setting down more candles—south, east, and west. "Do you have matches?"

"Ah, no."

"You'll have to get some. You need to keep these lit at all times, even when you're not here."

"Uncle Bob won't like that." I wondered about home insurance.

"It's necessary. That way, you'll have a haven to come back to. White purifies. You'll feel a difference in the room soon."

I felt a difference just having her there. "What about the prism?"

"It will reflect dark spirits from your window so they can't enter. We need a small nail or maybe a thumbtack."

I frowned. My uncle would have what we needed in the shed, but I hated to rummage through his things. "Let me check the junk drawer."

I hurried to the kitchen and opened the drawer. It

overflowed with rubber bands, bits of electrical wire, and mini-golf pencils. In the back, I found a small hammer and a prescription bottle filled with nails. I even found a book of matches.

"Got it," I called as I rushed to my room. I stopped in the doorway.

Brittany sat on my bed, putting the extra candles in a bag. She was so beautiful. I wanted to kiss her, wanted to lean her back against my pillow and touch her skin.

A flush heated my cheeks. I avoided her eyes. "Where do you want the nail?"

"Centered on top."

I thought belatedly that I might need a chair to stand on, but I must have grown a bit in the past few weeks. I had no trouble driving a nail above the window. She handed me the prism, and I hung it from its monofilament cord. Color danced over my walls.

Close beside me, Brittany reached up and sent it spinning. I looked into her face, inches from mine. My heart skipped, and my mouth went dry. I licked my lips.

She stepped away. "Got to go. I have a lot of things to do before my mother gets home."

"I'd be glad to help."

"Thanks, but it will be quicker if I do it myself. I kind of have a routine." She picked up her purse.

"Will I see you tomorrow?"

"Sadly, no. I already have plans. It's Mom's only day off." She smiled. "But maybe we can include you next Sunday."

"Shopping with your mother? I'll have to think about that."

"Will you turn into a wolf tonight?"

I was stricken by her matter-of-fact tone. "I don't think so. I feel pretty normal."

"Good. We don't need any more shocking revelations."

I stood on the porch as she drove away. When she was gone, the full impact of the day's events struck me. I was the luckiest guy in the world. She'd seen me, she knew what I was and still wanted to be my friend. I didn't expect that at all.

Humming, I went inside to make a grilled peanut butter and bacon sandwich. The day couldn't have turned out better. With Brittany's help, I knew I would break the curse. I would be normal again.

I ate over the sink, then wiped the skillet clean with a paper towel. Wind gusted through the window. The rain had moved on, and the temperature plummeted. I went to my room to light my candles. As I gazed at the prism, I thought it wasn't so bad living in Florida.

Had Brittany hinted that she wanted me to meet her mother?

I pulled my laptop from under my bed intending to check the weather. This was the coldest I felt since I moved here. It was kind of exciting. But the computer reminded me of the photos Eff posted on the Internet. That jerk. I still didn't know how to respond to his latest challenge.

Was Eff the evil the grandmaster was talking about?

My good mood deflated once more. Eff was a no-good jock, but I didn't think he was the evil that threatened Brittany. It was someone else, someone I didn't expect. A shocking revelation.

I booted the computer. The local newsfeed was on my desktop. My mood fell further as I read the headlines. *Two More Bodies Found.*

The story said one body was two days dead. The other was barely cold. The victims had their throats torn out and were partially disemboweled. Forensics now said that while both deaths looked like an animal attacks, the teeth marks were too large, and the slashes didn't match any known beast. The sheriff's department said they suspected a person or persons unknown armed with a jawbone. If the jaw were mounted on an axe handle or baseball bat, it would produce the type of wounds found on the victims. The attacks were officially classed as murders.

My mouth dropped. I stumbled from bed and rushed into the living room. The jawbone, the big old jawbone that my uncle used as a paperweight was gone.

"Oh my God," I said. "Uncle Bob is the killer."

# EIGHTEEN

The more I thought about it, the more likely it seemed that Uncle Bob was the killer—his strange hours, the fact that he had only one real friend. He used to invite me to go out with him, but he never did anymore. Not that I would, but still.

I remembered my uncle raising his voice to me when I mentioned the first murder. I'd heard about it from old Mrs. Binkley. My uncle's reaction surprised me. I thought he knew more than he was saying, but I was too preoccupied to follow up.

Then there was the morning he came home with blood on him. He threw his shirt away casually, like it happened all the time. There were scratches on his neck. Catfight, he said. I should have realized.

What should I do now?

I paced the room, wringing my hands. I could turn him in, but all my proof was circumstantial. People liked him. They'd believe him before they believed me. But I couldn't stay in the house with a serial killer.

The thought stopped me cold. My uncle was a serial killer. How could he do this to me? I thought he was a good guy. I *liked* him.

*This* was the evil from my Tarot card reading. The grandmaster had warned me—not what, but whom. But if she knew who it was all along, why didn't she tell me?

Maybe she meant someone else. Maybe I was wrong.

Frantically, I searched the living room—stacking newspapers, looking under the recliner. The jaw-bone wasn't there.

The killer would mount the jaw on an axe handle, the sheriff stated in the article. Either an axe handle or...

I sank to the floor. A baseball bat. My uncle kept a bat in the cab of his truck. He was a murderer.

How could I prove it? I needed to act normal and try to catch him doing something weird, something I could take to the sheriff. It was dangerous, but I would prevail. The grandmaster told me so.

That night I tossed and turned, listening for my uncle to come in. He never did. Eventually, I drifted to sleep.

🐕 🐕 🐕

When I woke the next morning, I checked my computer for news of another murder. No reports. I felt relieved, but not entirely convinced. Half-way to the kitchen, I smelled my uncle's coffee. I hesitated, then forced myself to enter the room.

"Morning." I avoided his eyes. "Have a nice night?"

"Great. An old friend was in town." Uncle Bob stared at me. "You mad because I didn't call in?"

I shrugged. "It's your house."

"No, no. It's what I would expect of you. I should do the same. It won't happen again."

Silence fell between us. I gazed outside. The sky was bright blue, and the breeze was cold and dry.

"Whatever happened to the jawbone that kept the newspapers from blowing around?" I asked.

He chuckled and slurped his coffee. "That old thing? I'm surprised you ask."

"I thought it was cool. I went to show Brittany, but it was gone."

He sobered. "I heard her come over yesterday. You okay?"

"Fine," I said, not sure what he meant. He couldn't know my little secret.

"I hope you don't have anything planned for to-day. I could sure use your help with a project."

"No problem. What are we doing?"

He drank again and smacked his lips. "Going to paint the front porch."

"But you rent."

"Part of how I keep the rent down is by doing re-pairs myself. I've been planning to paint for a while, waiting for cooler weather." He rinsed his cup and set it in the sink. "I'll start scraping. You finish break-fast and come on out."

I watched him leave. I was uncomfortable spending time with him, but it had to be done. Maybe he'd let something slip during conversation. Besides, I had to act normal. If he suspected I knew something, I might be his next victim.

I wolfed down a bowl of cereal and half a loaf of toast, changed out of my favorite T-shirt, and joined him on the porch. The paint he bought was pale blue. I slapped it on the railing.

There wasn't as much conversation as I hoped. Painting is hard work, and despite the coolness of the day, I was sweating. My thoughts drifted to Brittany. Her quick acceptance of my wolfish nature made her even more perfect. I pictured her with lips the color of the paint I slathered on the stairs. I wished she were with me.

Tires crackled and popped on the driveway, breaking into my thoughts. I so expected it to be her that at first I didn't recognize Sheriff Brad in his green and white car.

Uncle Bob climbed off his ladder. He'd been painting the overhang. "Hello, Brad. Can I help you with something?"

The sheriff slammed the car door. "I suppose you heard we found two more bodies."

"No, I hadn't. Were they in the same area?"

"One was a runaway from Jacksonville. Some kids found her in the woods. There were beer bottles around. It appears she knew the perp before he turned on her. Maybe met him somewhere local where teens gather. The older woman was from the Sunspot. Married. Here on vacation with her husband. She was jogging just before dawn."

"That makes four."

"Yep. It's a shame. Used to be a sleepy little town."

Uncle Bob's shoulders stiffened. "Maybe you should be out looking for the killer."

"I'm making the rounds, asking people if they'd seen anything out of the ordinary, asking where they were the past few nights."

"You plan to talk to every single person in town?"

"Eventually. I'm starting with those with a history of having a quick temper." He looked at me. "What about you, boy? You have anything to report?"

Was he giving me an opening? Did he suspect my uncle, too? I glanced at Uncle Bob. "Not me."

"You go to Jana's party?"

"No sir. I don't really know Jana that well."

"Well, you missed quite a wingding. I expect you'll hear all about it tomorrow at school."

"Yes, sir."

He gave a curt nod. As he walked back to his car, he said, "Don't be surprised if you see me again. I plan to be everywhere at once."

Uncle Bob stood next to me, watching the sheriff drive away. Anger radiated off him.

"I get the impression you two don't like each other much," I said.

"We have a history." Uncle Bob scowled. I

thought he would leave it with that cryptic remark, but he surprised me by continuing. "Shortly after I moved here, there was a rash of gas station robberies. Brad suspected me because I was the new guy on the block. He made my life miserable."

"Did they catch the robber?"

"It turned out to be some high school kid who'd lived here all his life. I don't think Brad ever forgave me for being an honest man." He slapped my shoulder. "How about I go out and get us a bucket of chicken? You hungry?"

"Yeah. Sounds good."

"Keep working. I'll be back in a jiff."

Thirty minutes later, we were sitting in lawn chairs and throwing chicken bones into the woods. If I didn't know better, I'd say my uncle was a great guy.

🐕 🐕 🐕

Sheriff Brad was right about everyone rehashing Jana's party in class the next day. The school split into two camps—those who went and those who wanted to know all about it. Even Maxwell and Lonnie were in the limelight. I heard them say there were two bands—the *Pink Spiders* and some local group. They also said there were white horses wearing bridles fitted with unicorn horns. I bet the girls loved that.

At lunch, Brittany sat with me as if nothing had happened between us. We talked about teachers and homework. I was in a great mood.

Then I saw Jana rushing to our table. She held out her BlackBerry. "Did you guys see the new fairy pictures?"

The lunchroom crashed in on me. I realized the pictures of me in the trees weren't going away. Worse, now Brittany knew about them. I remembered her tear-streaked face as she and her brother lowered me to the ground.

"Oh, please." Brittany slapped the table. She didn't even look at the phone. "Those photographs are fakes. Give me a break."

Jana sneered. "Sorry you missed my party, Brittany. You should have told me you had nothing to wear. I could have lent you something." She spun about and stormed off, ponytail swaying.

Brittany put her hand over mine. "I know that you're angry, and I know what he did sucks. Eff is a total jerk. I get it. But I want you to promise you won't start a fight."

I pulled back. "He already started it."

"All we can do is keep saying that he's lying. If you respond, it will look like there's something to it. People will ask questions. Like why you heal so fast. You can't retaliate."

"Unless I do it in my wolf form."

She leaned close. "If you so much as jump out of the bushes and scare him and they trace it back to you, they'll dump all those other murders on your head. The sheriff is desperate. You'll be all the evidence he needs. I'll never see you again."

I looked into her eyes. She was right. We couldn't risk it. I had to lay low. "And let Eff get away with being a jerk."

"Don't worry." She brightened. "He'll get his. Bullies always do. Are you busy after school? I thought we could stop by the bookstore and do some research."

"Anything we need is on the Internet."

"But you have to ask the right questions. I already Googled how to stop being a werewolf and didn't get any hits. We need old books where the information is compiled for us."

"Good thinking." I would have agreed to anything if it meant spending time with her.

🐕 🐕 🐕

*Y*e *Olde Bookstore* was in strip shopping sandwiched between a women's clothing store called Eve's and a weight loss clinic. The books propped up in its display window looked ancient and expensive. A bell dinged as we stepped inside.

Cold air hit me in the face. It was like walking into a refrigerator. The shop held a tang of old paper and dust. The girl at the front desk nodded at us. She wore a jacket.

Brittany walked down the aisles, me in tow. I'd never seen such an assortment of old books. The

226

leather bindings were faded, and the gold lettering was tarnished and worn. There were sections on the occult, sections on psychic abilities and ESP. No Shakespeare here.

We stopped at the area about shape shifting.

Brittany pulled several books off the shelves and carried them to a table. She patted the chair next to her. "Let's get started."

I thumbed through a book, reading at random. "How to become a werewolf," I said in a hushed voice. I felt like I was in a library. "One, rub a magic ointment over your flesh and then, two, place a girdle of wolf skin about your waist and, three, drink beer mixed with blood. Ugh. Sounds like something out of a college frat house."

"I've heard of the wolf skin belt before," she said. "It's supposed to be magical."

"I don't need to know how to become a wolf."

"We need to understand the process in order to reverse it." She put her book down and opened another. "Here's a different way to transform. In a deep forest, draw two concentric circles on the ground, one six feet in diameter and the other fourteen feet. Build a fire in the center of the smaller circle and bring a gallon of water to boil in an iron pot. Throw in a handful of aloe, hemlock, poppy seed, and nightshade."

"Sounds like my mom's recipe for Christmas punch." I grinned.

"You stir the ingredients counter clockwise, all

the while calling to the spirits of satyrs and were-wolves. Then you sit outside the edge of the larger circle and smear your body with fat from a fresh kill mixed with anise, camphor, and opium. Opium, hmm. That would do it." She chuckled, then read, "*But woe be to the wolf who treads upon the fourteen foot circle for he shall be trapped.*"

"How could a circle drawn on the ground trap a wolf?"

"You never heard of magic circles?" Brittany's eyes sparkled. "If they can hold a demon, they can hold a wolf."

I sighed. At least, she didn't think I was a demon. "How do you know," I murmured, "that I didn't kill those women?"

"You wouldn't hurt anyone as a human, and you never tried to hurt me as a wolf."

I waited, expecting her to ask flat out if I did it, but apparently, she trusted me. A smile crossed my face.

We browsed a few more books, the stack of rejects growing.

"Here's something," Brittany said. "It says here that those born on Christmas Eve are in danger of being werewolves because their birth is an act of blasphemy. To be rid of the curse, they must prove themselves pious beyond reproach."

"Pious? You mean like a monk?"

"When were you born?"

"October thirtieth." I frowned. "Wait a minute. I was a preemie. I was due around Christmastime."

"Maybe you were *supposed* to be born on December twenty-fourth."

"It was Christmas Eve the first time I turned. I was in France." I remembered the terror I felt, running down strange alleys, not knowing what was happening to me.

"Was there a full moon?"

"Yes." I felt a chill that had nothing to do with the refrigerated air of the shop. I snapped the book shut. "This is a waste of time. Let's get out of here."

We returned our stack to the shelves and left the bookstore. I was so immersed in memories of that cold night in France that I was shocked to step out into a sunny, Florida afternoon. We crossed the parking lot and sat in Brittany's little green car.

"You okay?" she asked.

"It's late. I should be getting home."

She nodded, but didn't start the engine.

"You know, there's something that always bothered me," I blurted. "Why can't I turn into a wolf on nights other than a full moon? It's still there. Even a new moon is near the Earth, especially in perigee. I should be able to tap into it."

She gave an uneasy laugh. "You want to be a wolf all the time?"

"No. I want to be able to change at will. If I can control it, maybe I won't have to shift at all."

🐺 🐺 🐺

The next day during World History, Vice Principal Overhill sent for me. I crossed the classroom with a sense of foreboding. I tried to catch Brittany's eye, hoping for a nod of support, but she had her nose so deep in a book it was like she didn't want to know what was happening.

I trekked down the hallway, dragging my feet all the way, and entered the vice principal's office. Overhill sat behind his desk with Sheriff Brad standing nearby. Eff sat before them, scowling.

What was going on?

"Come in," said Overhill. "Close the door, please."

I did, and sat in the chair next to Eff. My palms felt damp, and I resisted the urge to wipe them on my pants. "Is something wrong?"

Overhill steepled his fingers. "When you first came to the Bluffs, I believe I mentioned we don't tolerate troublemakers." He paused as if expecting an answer, then cleared his throat. "We have been made aware of an ongoing feud between you and Efrem Higgins."

A thousand comebacks clamored up my throat, and it was all I could do to keep my mouth shut. I didn't start the fight, and I wasn't responsible for it being *ongoing*. But here I was being called on the carpet for it.

Before I could choose a proper response, the sheriff stepped forward and opened a manila envelope. With a flourish, he laid out twenty photographs, covering Overhill's desk. I craned my neck to see. They were eight-by-ten glossies of me after Eff and his friends finished.

Seeing the images blown up with every detail enhanced, I was amazed I lived through it. My face looked like lunchmeat. There was more blood than I remembered. In one picture, my arm was clearly broken, and I ached just looking at it.

"These photographs were on the Internet," Overhill said. "Do you boys know about them?"

"Yes, sir," I said.

At the same time, Eff said, "No."

"No, Mister Higgins?" the sheriff roared at him. "I'm surprised to hear you say that, seeing how your email address was on the account."

I rocked back in my seat. What kind of idiot would use his own email to post that fairy page? Maybe he thought MySpace wouldn't give him up.

"L-lots of people know my email ad-dress," Eff stammered. "It doesn't mean anything."

The sheriff ignored him. He looked at me. "Son, is that you in those photographs?"

I stared at the desk. It would be easy to say yes, that Eff and his cronies jumped me. But then I'd have to explain how I healed so fast. Besides, I had promised Brittany I wouldn't retaliate.

A thought struck me. Had Brittany tipped off Overhill? She seemed cheerful when she said bullies always get theirs. Maybe she was trying to warn me off.

"It's me," I said with a sigh, "and it's not me. They've been Photoshopped."

Sheriff Brad snapped up a glossy. "This?"

"Come on. Someone posted those as a joke. If I'd been beat up that bad, I'd still be in the hospital."

The sheriff spluttered. "Are you telling me—"

"What's wrong with your arm?" Overhill asked.

I looked down at the tape, grasping for a lie. "I was helping my uncle move lumber. I didn't want to get splinters, so I covered my forearm."

"Why didn't you take it off when the job was done?"

"I thought it looked cool." It sounded pretty weak, even to me.

He crooked a finger. "Let me see."

Reluctantly, I stood and extended my arm. He examined it for a moment, then drew a pair of scissors from his top drawer. I flinched at the touch of cold metal against my flesh as the point of the scissors slid beneath the gauze and tape. He cut away my makeshift cast, exposing clean, unblemished skin.

Overhill looked at the sheriff. "Not even a bruise."

"Now, that's mighty peculiar. Perhaps this young fellow here can help clear things up for us." He tapped Butt Crack's picture.

I plopped into my seat. I didn't want them to question Brittany's brother. Not because I was afraid he would spill his guts. I was sure he would. I just didn't want him to go through all that.

"Of course, we can't talk to him without his mother being present. Nice lady, Missus Meyer. Have you met her? I'm sure she'd be interested in these happenings, seeing how you're friends with her daughter."

"That's right," Eff said. "You can't question me without my parents being here."

"But we aren't questioning you," said Overhill. "We're talking to Cody. You just happen to be in the room."

Sheriff Brad loomed over me. "You listen here, boy. Assault is a criminal offense. I expect you to press charges and bring the perpetrators to justice."

I hesitated. Wasn't that what I wanted, to get even with Eff? But the charges wouldn't stick. Not when I didn't even have a bruise.

"The photos are fakes." I looked up at the sheriff. "Like I said."

He held my gaze. I knew he wasn't buying my story.

"I see." He turned away.

"You disappoint me, Cody," said Overhill. "I expected a little more backbone from you."

Sheriff Brad looked at the pictures covering the desk. Instead of putting them away, he straightened the rows. "I can't for the life of me understand why you would protect a gang of thugs. Perhaps they're holding something over you. I don't know. I'm certain, however, that the two of you are hiding something. If I can't get your cooperation for assault, you leave me no choice but to prosecute Mister Higgins for possession of child pornography."

"What?" cried Eff.

I stifled a laugh.

Overhill looked stricken. "Pornography? You'll never make that fly."

"Oh, yes. These photos are of a minor in his underwear. Strictly speaking, they are illegal." He looked at Eff. "My deputy is currently on her way to your home with a search warrant. I expect she will find these images on your computer. Maybe even on your camera."

Eff blanched, cringing into his chair.

I almost felt sorry for the guy. How stupid could he be? I leaned away to stay out of the line of fire.

The sheriff moved close to Eff. "I thought so. The originals. Unedited."

It was my turn to cringe. My *Photoshop* explanation might not hold. I wasn't clear of the situation yet.

"Last chance, son," the sheriff told me. "Do you have anything to say?"

My mouth went dry. "No, sir," I croaked.

Overhill looked disgusted. "Get out of here. Both of you."

Eff and I hopped to our feet at the same time, and we nearly fought each other to get out the door. We walked side-by-side through the lobby.

"Truce," Eff whispered.

I nodded.

🐾 🐾 🐾

"Hey, study partner." Brittany grabbed my arm as I left school. "Where are you going so fast?"

I grinned with the roller coaster feeling I always got when she touched me. "Home, I guess."

"Want to come over to my house? We can work on our essays together."

I balked. Between the business with Eff and thoughts of Uncle Bob being a serial killer, my head was full. But the need to be with the girl I loved won out. "Sure. Let's go."

The car was sun-warmed in spite of the coolness of the air, and it felt good to get inside. I thought of my friends up north bundled in their heavy coats, and I chuckled.

"What's funny?" Brittany asked.

"I was thinking of how quick I got used to Florida weather."

"Have you ever been skiing?"

"A few times. Yeah."

"I always wanted to try that. Flying down a mountainside." She backed her car out of the parking space. "It's cold, I bet."

"Actually, I found it to be pretty sweaty work. Exertion keeps you warm."

"You don't sound like you enjoyed it."

I smiled at her. "I'd rather be here."

She merged into the logjam of kids leaving the

lot. I waved at Maxwell and Lonnie, wondering if they ever went anywhere separately.

As we drove into town, she said, "You were pretty quiet at lunch. Why haven't you told me what happened when Overhill pulled you into his office?"

"I didn't want anyone to hear us talking." I screwed up my face, trying to phrase my question in a non-accusatory way. "Did you tip him off about those pictures Eff posted on the Web?"

She stared forward as if concentrating on the road.

"If you did, it's okay," I added, "but I'm afraid it might blow up in our faces. Sheriff Brad is going to talk to your brother."

"Butt Crack? He won't spill."

"The sheriff might scare him."

"No." She glanced at me and grinned. "He's not afraid of Sheriff Brad."

"Eff is. Especially now that he's facing pornography charges."

"You're kidding." Brittany chortled.

"Don't know how that's going to work for him."

"Wow." Her eyes flashed with excitement. "That's going to spread like a muck fire."

Sure enough, Grandpa Earle met us on the porch. "What's this I hear about Efrem Higgins being picked up with child porn? Is he some kind of pervert?"

"I don't know, Grandpa," Brittany said airily. "You should ask your friend, Brad."

He scowled. "He's been busy all day."

"I'm sure it's not as bad as it sounds," I said, trying to hide my embarrassment. After all, I was the child in question.

Grandpa Earle ignored me. "It's a good thing you never got mixed up with that boy. He took quite a shine to you."

"He never had a chance." She crinkled her nose. "Why don't you take a nap, Grandpa? Cody and I are going to study."

"I never sleep during the day. You know that." He looked indignant, and I wondered if he was serious.

Brittany tossed her purse onto a living room chair and went into the kitchen. "Yum. Chicken leg soup. Just the thing on a chilly day."

She stirred the pot, fishing out the chicken bones. There must have been a couple dozen.

Feet thundered down the stairs, and Butt Crack burst into the kitchen. "Hey. What's for eats?"

"Hey, yourself." She poured a pint of cream into the soup. "That should thicken it up."

"Smells great," said Butt Crack.

She tapped the spoon and replaced the lid. From the living room, the television blasted.

Brittany asked her brother, "Anything interesting happen at school today?"

"I'll say." Hopping onto a stool, he pulled a bag of chips from the top of the refrigerator and opened them. "I was called into the principal's office. Made me look like a real bad boy, you know? But it was only Sheriff Brad. He was all bent about some photos he found on the Internet."

"Was your mom there?" I blurted. Those pictures would make the perfect first impression. A great ice-breaker.

"Nah, she couldn't get off work, so they had Grandpa sit with me. And get this. He fell asleep."

Butt Crack and Brittany convulsed with laughter.

I felt like the only one taking it seriously. "What did you tell him?"

"I said I didn't recognize the guy." He jabbed a finger in my direction. "And that's the truth. You looked like something out of a *Saw* movie."

His stance was angry, but his eyes were haunted, giving me a pang of regret. Poor kid. I probably gave him nightmares.

"I'm sorry, man," I said. "For all of it. You never should have been involved."

He shrugged, his sudden anger deflating. "No prob. It got me out of math."

"You were in a couple of those photos, you know," Brittany told him.

"Really?" He shoved a handful of chips into his mouth. "He never mentioned it."

He clomped back upstairs, taking the bag with him. I sat at the kitchen table, almost weak with relief. Disaster avoided.

Brittany sat with me. We started our history essays, reading each other's reports and sharing facts. I wasn't used to working in tandem, and I was really enjoying myself.

Until the news blared from Grandpa Earle's television. It reported another mauling. The murderer, in fact, was now dubbed *The Mauler.*

I felt the blood drain from my face. He struck again, and I was powerless to stop him.

"Cody? What's wrong?"

"Wait," I said. "I have to hear this."

The victim, a middle-aged woman, was found near Turtle Pond by a couple of fishermen. The authorities estimated she was dead almost a week.

My heart thumped against my chest so hard, I thought it was trying to break out and run away. I felt responsible, like I could have saved her somehow.

Why had Uncle Bob waited until I arrived to start killing? Did my moving in with him push him over the edge?

Brittany clucked her tongue. "I'm surprised the sheriff took time to personally handle Eff's case with everything else going on."

"I have to tell you something," I said. "It's a secret, okay?"

She nodded, her green eyes widening.

I told her my suspicions about Uncle Bob and all the reasons behind them. I even threw in the Tarot card reading and Grandmaster's cryptic warning. She never interrupted. When I finished, she sat in stunned silence for several long moments.

"I've known your uncle for a long time," she said in a voice barely above a whisper. "Longer than you, in fact. He's a nice guy. Soft-spoken. A bit of a loner."

Crud. She didn't believe me, probably thought I was out of my mind. Now she was going to yell at me for even thinking things like that about the man who took me in.

"A few weeks back, the *Discovery Channel* had a show about serial killers," she said. "Almost every one of them were nice guys. Quiet. Friendly, but without many friends."

"Then you agree with me?"

"I don't know. I don't want to believe." Brittany paced the kitchen. She looked so distraught, I felt sorry I told her. After a few minutes, she faced me. Her shoulders slumped in defeat. "Anything is possible."

"I don't know what to do," I said.

"The only way to be sure he's the one doing this is to catch him in the act."

"You want me to spend time with him?"

"He won't do it in front of us. We need to follow him." She lifted the lid on dinner. "We'll eat. Then I'll take you home."

Her brother appeared as soon as she opened the silverware drawer. He filled a bowl and sat at the table. I didn't think I had an appetite, but the soup proved me wrong. It was delicious. Chock full of chicken and chunks of vegetables. Butt Crack and I had seconds. Brittany, however, barely ate at all.

When we went out to her car, the cold air made me want to hug myself. It was dipping into the low forties, an event uncommon enough to make the news. Brittany put on a sweater, but all I had was the T-shirt I wore to school that day.

It would be cool if I could turn into a wolf and sit in the front seat masquerading as a pet wearing a thick fur coat. I shot the thought down almost as fast as it occurred to me.

Brittany didn't speak as she drove me home. Stewing, my mother would call it. I didn't mind. We both had a lot to think about. Like how would I sleep in a house with a killer? How could I follow anyone when I didn't have a car? What would happen to me if Uncle Bob were arrested? Would my parents take me away? Would I see Brittany again?

Even that thought fled as we drove up the driveway to find my uncle's truck gone.

"Think," said Brittany. "Where would he go?"

"Maybe he stayed late at a project."

"In this weather? I doubt it."

I sighed, staring at the dark house. "It's dinnertime. I bet he went to eat. The Coffee Café."

"All right."

We drove back into town, but my uncle's truck wasn't in the parking lot. We drove past Howard's house, but he wasn't there, either, although Howard appeared to be home.

We ended up cruising Southern Boulevard for a while. We never saw my uncle. But a funny thing. I spotted the same red Camaro three times. Almost like we were the ones being followed.

# NINETEEN

Over the next few days, I learned that Uncle Bob was the most boring person on Earth. He worked long hours, and spent most of his off time at the Café. He knew the names of nearly everyone in town, and always remembered personal bits, like where their kid went to college or whether or not their dog had pups. If he ran for mayor, he'd probably win.

So as we pulled up my driveway to find his truck gone again, I wasn't surprised when Brittany vetoed my suggestion that we track him down.

"Let's take a break." She climbed out of the *VW*. "It's too nice a day to spend cooped up."

I followed her to the porch steps.

"Did you repaint?" she asked.

"Yeah."

"Nice. I used to have powder blue lipstick." She sat on the porch swing, leaving room for me to sit beside her.

I found I couldn't stop grinning. We rocked back and forth, our shoulders touching.

"It's peaceful," she said. "All I hear are birds."

Of course, with my enhanced hearing, I heard

much more than random tweeting. I heard a field mouse building a nest in the underbrush, a beehive in a tree fifty yards away. "It's quiet at your house, too."

"Nah. I get traffic noise. Sometimes I hear music from the pool at the Sunspot."

I chuckled, imagining naked people doing belly flops and cannonballs into the water.

"Don't laugh," Brittany said. "You'd be surprised how noisy they are, especially this time of year."

"Oh?"

"I told you about the big festival they have every February. People come from all over the country. They have square dancing and campfire drum circles. DJ dances for the naked little kiddies."

I shook my head. "I can't imagine why anyone would want to be a nudist."

Her mouth quirked. "They prefer *naturist*. And it's a healthy lifestyle, when you think about it. The idea is to accept your body as is, just bare it all, and enjoy an afternoon or a week without modern devices. They have WI-FI but I can't always access it from my house. I have to use *JiWire* to find the nearest free access. They don't have cell phones. I mean, where would they put them? That in itself would drive me crazy."

I listened to her chatter, watching her lips move, her nose crinkle. Her skin was pale, almost too pale to be allowed in Florida, and liner made her green eyes stand out. Her lips were painted so deep a shade of violet they were almost black.

She was captivating. I know it sounds hokey, but there's no other way to say it. When I was with her, I couldn't stop staring. When I was alone, she occupied my thoughts. I wasn't complete without her.

I also wasn't listening very carefully, so I was surprised when she stopped speaking and looked at me, raising a brow into a perfect black arch.

"It's a yes or no question," she said.

I cleared my throat, my thoughts racing my heart. "Ah, yeah. Sure."

"Yes?" She leaped up. "How can you say yes?"

"I mean no. Of course not."

"So." Her eyes flashed. "You would be perfectly happy to have me join the Sunspot and show the world my booty."

"Not the whole world," I murmured. "Just me."

She blinked, and then grinned. "Yeah?"

"It seems only fair. You saw mine."

"I saw your *tail*. It was short and yellow."

I grimaced. Not a flattering picture. "If anyone should be a naturist, it should be me. It would make things a lot easier. I'm always afraid of misplacing my clothes."

"What's it like being a wolf?" she asked. "Is it just you, your personality, in a wolf body?"

"No. I don't think like myself at all. I mean, I might remember that I have a paper due in history or a math quiz coming up on Friday, but they're silly things. Mundane things. All that matters is the wind in my face as I run and the rabbit in front of me. And the smells. Everything is so distinct. I swear a wolf can smell color." I broke off, realizing I wasn't describing it at all. I couldn't describe it. "I don't know. When I'm a wolf, I just feel like I'm part of something big."

"Like nature?"

"Only there's nothing natural about a human becoming a wolf."

"There are worse things you could become." She looked away, her face sad and thoughtful.

I had the impression that someone had roughed her up in the past. Had it been her father?

"I won't let anyone hurt you," I said.

She smiled and nudged my shoulder. "Are you my bodyguard?"

"I'd like to be more."

"Maybe you better not make any promises until after you've seen my booty." She gave me a crooked smile.

Without thinking, I caught her face in my hand and kissed her. I don't know what came over me. I thought, oh crap, now I've done it. She'll never speak to me again. But she didn't pull away. She kind of melted into me. Her lips were soft and tasted like grape soda. Her breath brushed my cheek. Her fingers slid up my arm and buried themselves in my hair.

Then I heard the crackle of tires on the gravel driveway.

She leaned back. "Your uncle's home."

I scowled as he waved to us from his truck. What a time for him to show up. But even through my anger, my thoughts whirled. I kissed Brittany. And she kissed me back.

"Hey, kids." Uncle Bob climbed the wooden steps. "Got a lot of homework to do?"

"No," I said.

"Actually, yes." Brittany hopped off the swing. "I better get home. Talk to you both later."

"Wait," I said, trying for something witty that would make her stay.

Uncle Bob watched her drive away. "Hope I didn't scare her off."

"Not you. I can scare her off all by myself." I slouched into the house.

I spent the evening in my room replaying the kiss. What was I thinking? I knew she wanted to be friends. She'd told me often enough. I broke the rules.

It was just a kiss, a voice reasoned in the back of my mind. But it was more than that. The memory of it made my lips tingle. It made other parts of me tingle, too.

No! I had to apologize, try to salvage our friendship. The phone was in my hand. But I couldn't call. She'd driven away after I professed my love. Things couldn't be clearer than that.

But the next day, she sat across from me at the

lunch table, gossiping and laughing like nothing happened. Maybe to her nothing had. I felt a little annoyed that she could shrug off my kiss so easily, but mostly I was glad she was still speaking to me.

Friday, I got to lunch a little late. Brittany was already at our table as I strode up with my tray. "Happy Leap Day." Grinning, she slid a chocolate chip cookie in front of me.

"Aww," I said, "and all I got you was an apple."

"I like apples." She took a bite. "Do you have plans this weekend?"

"No. Why?"

"Well, we aren't getting anywhere with your *uncle* problem, so I thought we should put it on hold and focus on your other problem for a while." I blinked at her, confused. She leaned forward. "Hello? You're a werewolf. Remember?"

"Yeah. Right."

"Anyway, maybe we need to come at it from a different direction. Shape changing is common in North American folklore, you know."

"You mean Indians?"

"It's practically a tradition." She took a notebook from her purse. "I got this from the Web. The Mohawk word for skin walker is *Limikkan*. The Navajo had *Yenaldooshi* or *Yee Naaldlooshii*. Also *Mai-Coh*."

"*Mai-Coh*. That sounds familiar."

"The Hopi Indians had *Ya Ya*."

"Oh, yeah?"

"In the *Ya Ya* ceremony, the members could change into any animal they wanted by using a hide belt."

"Might be nice to be a bear."

"Yeah, it would. Let's see. The Yaqui had *Marea-Kame*. Both the Algonquians and the Cree had *Wendigo*. The list goes on. The point is that shape shifting is part of the Native American heritage. We should talk to them."

"The only Indian I know is Howard. He can tell us about staging a garage sale. But shape shifting?" I shook my head.

Brittany wasn't daunted. "There's a Seminole reservation down Alligator Alley. It's called Big Cypress. We could be there in a couple hours."

"I don't know, Brit. Isn't that where the tourists go?" I quoted a commercial from television. "Home of Billy's Swamp Safari."

"We wouldn't be there for that. We could ask around and—"

"Sure. Walk through the place yelling does anybody know about werewolves?" I stopped when I caught the look on her face. *Way to go, big mouth.* "It's a good idea. I just don't want to call attention to myself like that. If we go, we need a specific person to speak to."

She leaned back, tapping the table and avoiding my eyes. I shouldn't have shot down her idea. How could I make it up to her?

"Maybe Howard can help us after all," I said. "He

might know people from there."

"That's right." She brightened. "Let's stop by his place after school. If he can give us a couple names, we can go to Big Cypress first thing in the morning."

🐾 🐾 🐾

We found Howard sitting in a lawn chair in his front yard surrounded by the wares of his perpetual garage sale. Two elderly women rummaged through a stack of sweatshirts.

Brittany waved to them as we crossed the lawn. "Hello, Miss Morganstern."

"Oh, hello, dear," said one of the women. "How is your grandfather these days?"

"Pining for you," Brittany said. "You should stop by for a visit."

"Maybe I will." She chuckled. "Such a rascal."

We approached Howard. He looked as sour as the lemonade he sipped.

I said, "Hi, Howard. What's up?"

"Taxes." He glared at me.

"Uh, right. We need some information."

"Information will cost you one pair of jeans."

I blinked. "You want my jeans?"

He leaned forward. "I want you to buy some of mine."

"But I don't need anything." I thought about the box of rich-boy clothes in the back of my closet.

"Oh, here," said Brittany. "I'll buy this."

249

I stared at her. "A plastic ukulele?"

"Miley can play with it when she comes over."

"Twenty dollars," Howard said.

She cocked a brow. "I'll give you two."

He drank from his sweating glass, making a face. "Well, since it's for Miley."

"Fine." She handed him money from her purse. "We were hoping you could hook us up with the right people at the Big Cypress Reservation. Do you have friends there?"

"Apparently, I don't have any friends anywhere." He scowled. "Why do you ask?"

"We want to talk to someone about Indian Folklore," she said. "Shape changers in particular."

"For a school project," I said.

He looked me up and down. "Uh-huh."

"Who would we speak to about that?" Brittany asked.

Howard stood suddenly, knocking his lightweight chair onto its side. "You're a dollar short and a week late. You know darn well that the Big Cypress had its annual Seminole War re-enactment just last weekend. There would have been any number of people to talk to."

"Jana's party was last weekend," Brittany said.

"No excuse." Howard raised his voice. "The festival was during the day. The party was at night. Besides, did either of you even go to that party?"

"We planned to," I lied, wanting to lend Brittany my support. "Brittany spent all day getting ready. But

250

then... No, we didn't go."

"Uh-huh." Howard's scowl deepened.

Brittany said, "If you could give us a couple names—"

"I can't help you." Howard set up his chair, and then sat with such force I thought it would collapse beneath him.

His bad mood ticked me off. I remembered him saying he was in love with an Indian woman, and he stuck around to be near her. "What about the Miccosukee tribe? I'm sure you know people there."

He glared, and I stared back with the righteous air that said *yes, if you don't help me, I'll tell everyone the woman you love dumped you.*

"Every tribe has a Story Keeper," he said. "The Miccosukee Story Keeper is Chelsea Osceola."

"Where do we find her?" asked Brittany.

"It just so happens that I've been summoned to the Alligator Alley Indian Village tomorrow morning. On a Saturday, no less." He scowled as if tasting something bitter.

"Is that where Chelsea lives?" I asked.

"No one *lives* there," he said as if I were crazy. "It's a village they maintain in the Everglades to teach Miccosukee traditions to tourists. Open daily from nine to five."

"Okay," I said, although I didn't understand how that could help us.

"It's a public place. Must be why she..." He ran his hand over his face. "I'll be leaving at eight o'clock

251

sharp. I'll drive you down and introduce you if you want."

"That would be great," said Brittany.

I nodded. "See you tomorrow at eight."

🐾 🐾 🐾

The next morning dawned bright, blue, and breezy. I had a moment to appreciate Floridian winters as I stood on the porch waiting for Brittany to pick me up. I wondered if Howard would be in a better mood, wondered what had him so unnerved. He tended to be serious, but not grumpy. It wasn't like him to snap at anyone.

Brittany arrived, and we drove to Howard's house with the windows down, the breeze blowing, and *Lamb of God* turned way up.

I couldn't have been happier. Not because we were going to the Indian Village. I didn't expect the Story Keeper to give us any information we couldn't find on the Internet. I was just glad to be alive and to spend the day with my girl. If the opportunity arose, would I have the nerve to kiss her again? I leaned my head back and grinned.

Howard came out of his house as we drove up. We piled into his rust-colored pickup. He said nothing in greeting, just turned on News Radio. But his silence didn't make me uncomfortable. The wind was cool and filled with scents, and Brittany leaned her head on my shoulder as we rode.

An hour later, we pulled into the lot of the Miccosukee Indian Village. We parked beside five other cars next to a bright yellow gift shop. A sign stated the museum hours, although I didn't notice a museum. All I saw was tall, yellow grass and a ramp.

I helped Brittany down from the truck. She smiled, snagging my hand, and we walked together up the ramp to an elevated wood-planked walkway. Our footsteps scuffed the weathered wood. I liked the sound. Ahead, I saw platforms and huts.

The village had no walls. The buildings consisted of thick posts and thatched roofs. Inside, workers were setting up displays. Women sat on the floors weaving baskets or making necklaces out of beads.

A man approached. Most of his head was shaved, and he wore bits of fur and feathers in his topknot. "Howdy, Howard. What brings you to these parts?"

"Looking for Chelsea."

"She's here," he said. "Might try out by the cooking *chickee*."

Howard nodded. "*Shonabish*."

I took that to mean *thank you*. We continued clomping down the wooden bridges. Sawgrass rasped in the breeze. Black water shone in patches. The wetlands were deep enough to support airboats. A sign pointed toward the docks—*Airboat Tours $10*.

I caught a tantalizing whiff of sweet grease. "They have food here?"

"The Snack Shop. Must be getting ready for the

day," Howard said. "Fry breads. Frog legs. Smells good, doesn't it?"

"I'll say."

Brittany giggled. "You're always hungry."

"*Chehuntamo*, friends," said a man as he passed us on the boardwalk. He wore a snake draped over his shoulders. "Be sure to see the alligator pit. First show is in two hours."

I watched him walk away.

Then a deeper voice spoke behind us. "*Nokosi*. I did not recognize you without your bear claws."

Howard looked like he wanted to spit. "Have you seen Chelsea?"

The taller man smirked. "Yes."

Heat seemed to radiate off Howard. With apparent effort, he turned and walked away. I could tell the man was a rival of some kind, so I gave him a final sneer before following.

"Did you used to work here?" I asked Howard.

"No." He frowned like I'd startled him from his thoughts. "Why?"

"He said something about wearing bear claws."

"The last time I was here, there was an incident," Howard said. "I was provoked."

We entered a hut. It was large. I noticed rolls of tarps hanging from the ceiling, presumably as drop-down walls in case of a hurricane. Several women attended a star-shaped fireplace. They were having trouble getting the fire started in the breeze.

One of the women said, "*Chehuntamo*. Hello and

welcome. This cooking *chickee* was at the heart of every Miccosukee village. The star-shaped fireplace allowed several families to cook their meals at the same time."

Howard stared past her. "Hello, Chelsea."

A woman stood. Her dark hair was pulled into a bun, and she wore a long, red and yellow patchwork skirt. "You came," she said a little wistfully. Then she gave us a fake smile. "With friends."

"This is Cody and Brittany," Howard said. "They come to speak to the Story Keeper."

"I see," Chelsea said, her face stiff. "Let us go somewhere more private."

She left the cooking *chickee* and strode briskly away. She must've worn moccasins, because her feet didn't make scuffing sounds like our shoes.

The next hut had a table and chairs. As soon as we were inside, Chelsea rounded on Howard. "So, this is your trade-off?" she hissed. "You'll sign the papers if I speak to your friends?"

"Give me your papers." He sat at the table.

She pulled a packet from her pocket and handed it to him. Howard signed in several places marked with red stickies. When he finished, he looked anguished. "Chelsea, I never wanted this."

"I know," she murmured. "I need to be with my own." Silence fell between them. Then she added, "He's here."

Howard nodded. "I saw him." He climbed to his feet, and then looked at me. "I'll wait outside."

Chelsea folded the papers and pocketed them. She sniffled, avoiding our eyes. "Please sit. I am the Story Keeper. A Story Keeper is a tribal historian who memorizes oral stories of all that happened before. I carry the wisdom of our forbearers, which I recite during celebrations and ceremonies. If you'll just bear with me for a moment, I will pray."

She sat at the head of the table and closed her eyes. Brittany looked at me as if to ask if we were doing the right thing. I shrugged and chose a seat.

"Creator, it is I," Chelsea said in a soft voice. "Thank you for today's sunrise, for the breath within me, and for your countless creations. As the day begins, I ask Spirit Keeper of the East, Brother Eagle, be with me. Guide my step. Give me courage to walk the circle of my life. Spirit Keeper of the South, Wolf, be with me. Help me remember love and compassion for all mankind. Spirit Keeper of the West, Brown Bear, be with me. Bring healing to the people I love and to myself. Spirit Keeper of the North, White Buffalo, be with me. As each day passes help me to surrender the things of my youth."

I figured it was the Indian equivalent of *God help me to accept that which I cannot change*. I took Brittany's hand, and we waited until the Story Keeper focused on us.

"I will begin with the Joining of Two Nations," Chelsea said. "The Seminole and Miccosukee."

Brittany said, "If you don't mind, we have specific things we'd like to ask."

"And we're kind of in a hurry," I said. "Can you make them short stories?"

Chelsea gave a small smile. She was really pretty. I could tell why Howard was attracted to her. She spread her hands. "Ask away."

"We'd like to know your folklore about shape changing," Brittany said.

"We have many such stories. A medicine man could turn into any animal he chose by using a hide belt."

"What about shape changing that isn't so voluntary?" I said. "Like werewolves."

"Lycanthropy." She looked at me for several moments. "I can tell you that it is hereditary, passed on through the mother's side. The accursed child is born with a mark in the shape of a crescent moon. Usually on the back, although I've heard of it hidden on the scalp. He or she turns into a werewolf at age sixteen."

*Yeah, that fits.*

"You can tell a werewolf from a real wolf by its tail. Natural wolves have luxurious tails, while the tails of unnatural wolves are stubby and often yellow."

"Why is that?" asked Brittany.

"The devil cannot create a perfect animal as God can."

I blew out my breath. "Is there any way of breaking the curse?"

"These are specific questions," Chelsea said.

"We're doing a report at school," said Brittany.

"Yeah. Maybe we should be writing this down." I motioned at her purse, and she took out her notepad.

"There is a potion," Chelsea said. "Theriac of viper, aloe, wormwood, and vinegar."

"You drink it?" I asked.

"No, it is topical. Applied to the skin. The potion must simmer for two days and must be used on the night of the new moon."

"That's easy."

"Ah, but the person you are trying to cure will not voluntarily apply the potion. The wolf will want to remain a wolf. You need to trap them first."

I grimaced. "Like a bear trap?"

"Magical beings require magical means," she said. "A circle drawn in the dirt and bestowed with the power of Mother Earth will hold the creature."

Brittany nodded. "A magic circle."

I remembered reading about magic circles in the books at the bookstore.

Chelsea sat back. "I'm afraid I can't tell you more than that."

"Thank you for your time." Brittany put away her notes.

I stood. "It was nice to meet you."

"And I you." Chelsea smiled. "Take care of my friend, Howard, for me."

Brittany scowled. "He's our friend, too."

We left the hut. Howard sat on the edge of the boardwalk, his feet dangling over the swamp. I would have been afraid to tempt the alligators.

"Finished?" he asked. His eyes were bloodshot. He drove us back to Loxahatchee without another word. He even turned off the radio. It was a relief when we finally pulled up to his house.

But instead of hopping out of the truck and saying goodbye, Howard just sat there.

"Are you okay?" Brittany asked.

After a moment, he said, "We'd been separated for a while. Then she took up with my ex-best friend."

"I thought my uncle was your best friend," I said.

He thumped a finger on the steering wheel. "You two and Bob are the only friends I have left."

"We won't leave you," Brittany said.

He sagged, nodding. "*Shonabish.*"

We watched him go into the house and shut the door.

"That was weird," I said.

"It was horrible. Poor Howard." Brittany got into her car. "I'm going to just drop you off. I have to get back home."

"All right." I was disappointed. The day wasn't turning out the way I planned.

We drove with the windows down, music blaring. Traffic was light. Within minutes, we were in my uncle's driveway.

Brittany turned down the radio. "I feel so bad for Howard."

"It could have been worse. He could've gotten into a fight with that big guy."

"I thought he was going to." Brittany sighed. "At least, we got some good information from the Story Keeper."

"Something to think about, anyway."

"Do you have a mark like that? A birthmark like a crescent moon?"

I frowned. "I had something on my back between my shoulder blades, but my parents had it lasered off when I was a kid. I don't think it looked like anything, though. I don't know. I never really saw it."

"Oh." She smiled. "I'll call you tonight."

"Talk to you later." I got out of the car and waved as she drove away. When she was gone, I sat on the porch.

Why had my parents removed my birthmark? Why not just leave it alone? I wondered if they knew all along I'd been touched by this curse. If that were true, I would never forgive them for not telling me about it. I'd never forgive them for rejecting me and sending me away.

Then an image popped into my mind. Uncle Bob had a mark like that on his back. A backwards C. I saw it the morning he'd taken off his bloody shirt.

I laughed, shaking my head. What was I thinking? Like Uncle Bob could be a werewolf.

# TWENTY

Monday after school, we climbed into Brittany's car and drove to her house to study. Brittany chattered nonstop about her day with her mother at the Farmer's Market, and how the flowers were wilted and she made the man go back into his truck to get fresh ones. I made noncommittal sounds, watching her. Her hair was prickly with styling gel. I wanted to run my cheek over it and bury my face in her neck. Of course, she was driving, so I didn't.

When we turned onto the dirt road that ran alongside her house, the topic changed to her brother's report card. He was good in math and miserable in English. There was concern in her voice. She might call him names and bully him, but he mattered to her.

Something pinged off the hood of the car, and I heard the distinctive pop of a pellet gun. I glanced around. Grandpa Earle sat under his favorite tree, pointing his rifle into the woods.

"That man." Brittany parked the car. "He's driving me crazy."

We hurried across the lawn. A naked guy a couple years older than me streaked through the yard.

261

He looked like he worked out. I glanced at Brittany, hoping she hadn't noticed him.

Grandpa took another shot and missed. "Dang jackrabbits."

Brittany raised her voice. "What are you *doing*?"

"Protecting my property," Grandpa Earle said. "That one's been back three or four times."

"I'm surprised the Sunspot hasn't called Sheriff Brad."

"He's already been by. He was in a fine mood." Grandpa Earle chuckled. "It seems the boys got their comeuppance."

Brittany wrinkled her nose. "What boys?"

"That Efrem Higgins and a few of his football buddies got sentenced to community service. Serves them right."

Brittany's eyes met mine. She looked alarmed.

"Brad even showed me a few of the snapshots they were said to be carrying," Grandpa Earle said. "I didn't say anything at the time, but it seems those photos were taken right over there. I'd sure feel bad to know you were keeping important secrets, Missy."

"Don't be silly," Brittany said.

I couldn't let her lie to her grandfather. "You're right, sir. The photos were taken in those trees."

He sat a bit straighter in his chair. "Well, boy, you look hale and hearty to me."

"I am, sir."

"Ah, I get it." He smiled and tapped the side of his nose. "You went to that medicine man. I knew you

262

had smarts in you."

Medicine man? Did he mean Howard?

"The important thing is the boys got what was coming to them," Brittany said.

Grandpa Earle chortled. In a flash, he sighted through his rifle and fired. "Dang jackrabbits."

Brittany shook her head. "Let's get out of here."

We walked toward the house with our fingers entwined. I wished someone were around to see her hold my hand. Behind us, we heard another shot, and someone yelped. Grandpa Earle roared with laughter.

"You don't think there will be retaliation over this community service thing, do you?" Brittany said.

I thought of Eff's face when he called a truce outside Overhill's office. "I expect this is the last we'll hear of it."

"Good." She smiled and climbed the steps. "Although, I don't think they'll be so quick to jump you now that you got muscles."

"What? I don't have muscles."

She laughed. "God, Cody, you really ought to look in the mirror sometime."

We walked across the porch, dodging wicker furniture. The ceiling fans made a lazy thwack-thwack sound. I held the door for her, and we went inside. As usual, the heavy shades kept the living room in darkness, and I blinked to adjust.

"Come on up." Brittany took the stairs two at a time. "I want to show you something."

"Ah, o-okay." Even my thoughts stammered. I'd never been upstairs. Was she inviting me to her room?

I followed, my heartbeat hammering my ears. I smelled furniture polish and bath soap, heard Butt Crack's music behind closed doors. The hallway ended with a sunny window and a vase of flowers.

I stood at the entrance to Brittany's room. It took purple to a new level. The walls were violet. The bed was eggplant. A pyramid of Barney-colored pillows leaned against the padded grape headboard. Several prisms sparkled in the window. A tower of CDs stood in the corner. Dragons and fairies vied for every available spot. I saw the remains of the broken snow globe I bought for her.

A hot blush crept upward. "Are you sure I should be here?"

"Why? You're not going to attack me, are you?"

"Of course not. I—"

"No?" She draped her arms about my neck.

Heat slid down my body. I didn't know where to put my hands. Putting them on her waist seemed too personal, and higher up might earn me a slap.

Then the music became louder, and Brittany's brother jostled past. "Excuse me. Just sharpening my pencil."

"You worm," she said. "There's a pencil sharpener downstairs."

"Yeah, but downstairs is like down stairs."

His pencil whirred. Brittany hit him with a pillow.

I felt sluggish, like I was waking from a dream. I should have put my hands around her waist. I should have kissed her.

"And turn that music down," Brittany told her brother. "We're trying to study."

"Yeah. I saw that." Butt Crack went to his room.

Brittany grinned, her face perfect, looking like one of her mischievous fairies, and I wanted to freeze the moment. I wanted to remember her like that forever.

"Have a seat." She motioned to the bed. Then, shifting books on her desk, she uncovered a laptop. "Let me show you something."

I sat. From my new vantage, I noticed several movie posters on the wall. *Pirates of the Caribbean*. One, Two, and Three. She had a battered, life-sized stand-up of *Captain Jack* taped to her closet door. I figured she got it from work.

"You like Johnny Depp?" I asked.

"He's my man. But don't be jealous. He hardly ever calls me." She spoke with such a straight face, I wasn't sure if I should take her seriously. "I've been trying to find out more about the potion the Story Keeper gave us." She placed the laptop on the bed and sat beside me. "Theriac of viper, aloe, wormwood, and vinegar."

"Do you think there's something to it?"

"I think it's worth a try. Don't you?"

"Sure," I said. *As long as I don't poison myself.* "But where are we going to find the ingredients? I mean, we can get vinegar at a grocery store, but—"

"Read the label. Most of the stuff you buy today is watered down. We need the old-fashioned kind. I've bookmarked a few sites." She turned her attention to the laptop. "We can buy some here."

I gazed at the bookmarks. "That's a lot of research."

"How much do you think we need? A gallon?"

I made a your-guess-is-as-good-as-mine face.

"Wormwood is a bitter herb," she said. "It was used to cure intestinal worms, thus the name. I thought it might be better to buy a live plant. We can grow it on my windowsill. This nursery will ship it overnight. But again, I don't know how much we need."

The plant on the screen was silvery.

"It looks so normal," I said. "Not like something that would be in a magic potion."

"At least it's easy to find. I searched all night trying to figure out what theriac of viper was. Turned out it's several things." She flipped through her *Favorites*. "Here. Theriac of viper is made up of the flesh of a poisonous snake, opium, cinnamon, gum Arabic, and agarics all pulverized and mixed with honey."

"What are agarics?"

She pulled up a dictionary. "It either means a type of gilled mushroom or tree fungus."

"Yummy. Tree fungus."

She looked at me. "I don't know how we're going

to afford all this."

"We'll worry about that when we get to it. First we have to decide how much we will need of each ingredient. We also need some sort of cauldron."

"Do you think we should get a live snake? A poisonous one?"

"Can you get that on the Internet?"

"You can get anything on the Internet," she said. "Do you know how to wrangle a viper?"

I made a face. "Maybe we can buy frozen snake meat from a restaurant supplier."

"Good thinking. I'm sure someone has rattlesnake on the menu. I'll look for that and you research how to make magic circles."

"To trap me? That won't be necessary. I want to stop the wolf."

"But the wolf won't want to be stopped. Maybe it can influence you somehow."

I nodded. "Friday is the new moon. We won't have everything ready."

"Then we'll do it next month. You can stand to shape shift one last time, can't you?"

The thought made me itch all over. Did I really want to stop? Becoming a wolf made me feel powerful. Like a superhero with a secret.

"I still think I should be able to shift on any night," I blurted, "not just the nights of the full moon."

"Now that you mention it," Brittany said, "none of the books on lycanthropy mentioned anything about the moon."

🐕 🐕 🐕

For the rest of the week, the main talk in school was Eff and his friends getting community service. They had to work a hundred and twenty hours at the Palms West Hospital, presumably so they could see pain and suffering firsthand. I didn't know if that would teach them a lesson or inspire them. But Eff kept his word about the truce, and he had enough influence to keep the other guys off me.

I spent my evenings with Uncle Bob. I figured he wouldn't try to kill anyone else with me hanging around. The most exciting thing we did was go to Publix for groceries one night.

As we walked into the store, I noticed a large scale, the kind with a three-foot dial, and I decided to weigh myself. The joke Brittany had made about my having muscles bothered me. I didn't feel any different, although my T-shirts were getting a little tight.

I stared as the dial stopped just short of one-fifty. That couldn't be right. That was football player weight. I still pictured myself as a skinny science nerd. I walked away, glancing over my shoulder at the scale. Maybe this was another perk of being a werewolf.

On Friday, Uncle Bob left a voice mail that he was going to dinner with a friend and would be home late. I had cold pizza for dinner, and was all set to research magic circles when I heard a knock at the door. I opened it.

Brittany collapsed against my chest. "He's gone. I can't find him."

I wrapped my arms about her, too stunned to enjoy it. "What do you mean? Who's gone?"

"My brother." She looked at me, tears like black rivers streaming down her cheeks. "He didn't come home from school. He never stays away this long. He wouldn't miss dinner. I went to all his friends' houses. But nobody's seen him. Where could he be?" She sobbed, her shoulders shaking.

I didn't know what to do. "Don't cry." I patted her back. How lame could I get?

I drew her inside the house and walked her to the kitchen. She sat at the table as if hopeless. I gave her a paper napkin, and then poured a glass of water from the pitcher in the fridge. She sipped, hiccupping.

"What did his friends say?" I asked.

Her voice was weak. "One of the guys, Jeremy, has a couple of motocross bikes, and they took them to these dirt trails out in the Glades. I knew where he meant. I've been there before. Anyway, there were two bikes and three boys, so one had to stay behind and wait."

She blew her nose. I gave her another napkin.

"So they went to give Butt Crack his turn, only he was gone. Jeremy thought he went back to the house. But when they got home, he wasn't there either." She started to cry again, her face red and

269

puffy. "Jeremy said he thought to himself, gee that's weird. But he didn't tell anyone. He didn't call."

I put my hand over hers and squeezed it gently. "Did you let the sheriff know?"

"Grandpa did. They're watching the hospitals."

With a curt nod, I got up to refill her glass. A combination of sympathy and frustration washed over me. "Why didn't Butt Crack have his cell?"

"Mom says he's too young to have a phone." She scrubbed her face with the heel of her hand. "Now it's getting dark, and… Oh, God. There's a killer on the loose."

"Take me to those trails," I said.

"It's no use," she said. "I just came from there."

"Maybe I can track him. I might smell something or hear his voice." I paused, not really wanting to point out how different I was from everybody else.

"All right." She threw her napkins in the trash and walked woodenly to her car.

The sky was bright orange, the sun red. I climbed in beside her. She backed down the drive and onto the road, turning away from town. Several minutes later, we pulled into a new housing development. The homes were large—three car garages, pools in every yard. A few weren't landscaped yet, and they stood out like derelicts.

Brittany followed the winding road. She sat forward against the steering wheel, her lips pressed in a thin line. She didn't speak, so neither did I. Nothing I could say would make her feel better.

She parked at the end of a cul-de-sac. The houses weren't finished, and the ground was rough. "We walk from here," she said.

Without waiting to see if I followed, she took off across the field. Dusk hid the rocks and ruts, and she stumbled. Of course, I could see as well as ever. I took her arm, supporting her until we reached a path leading into the scrub.

It was hilly. Not like the hills you would find up north. It was more like mounds of earth. I realized the construction crews were trucking in fill dirt to keep the Everglades at bay. It smelled old and dusty.

We walked in silence. Night swallowed the sub-division behind us. Bike trails cut through the brush. I imagined motors whining, replaced now by the buzz of mosquitoes.

Brittany stopped on a ridge overlooking the motocross playground. "I went up and down these hills calling his name. He's not here."

I closed my eyes, focusing. I smelled fuel and exhaust, scuffed dirt, and crushed grass. And people. Lots of people.

"Popular place," I muttered.

With my hands in my pockets, I walked away from her along the ridge. I was an idiot. What made me think I could pull out one scent from all the smells around here? I shouldn't have gotten her hopes up. Now things were worse.

As I opened my mouth to apologize, a familiar odor wafted by. Bath soap. I crouched, sifting a handful of dirt through my fingers. "He was sitting here," I said.

Brittany rushed to my side. "Where did he go?"

I took a deep breath, but it was worthless. I could tell where he touched the ground, but I couldn't smell which way he walked. "There are footprints. Look."

"It's too dark," she said. "I can't see anything. Why didn't I bring a flashlight?"

"The prints go this way," I told her, not even certain if they were his. I followed the tracks off the ridge, finally losing them in the brush. "They're gone."

She slapped my arm. "Well, what are you waiting for? Take off your clothes."

"What?"

"You've got to change. You've got to turn into a wolf and find him."

"I can't do that."

"Please."

"Tonight's a new moon. That's like the opposite of a full moon."

She hit me again. "You're the one who always says you should be able to change at will. The moon is always there, you said."

"Yeah, but—"

"Cody, please. I don't know what I'd do if..." Her eyes filled with tears. "He's my brother."

She collapsed inward, shoulders slumping. It was like watching a tower crumble in slow motion— her lips pulling into a grimace, her body quaking. She sobbed against my chest, fingers knotted in my shirt. I wrapped my arms tighter.

How could I say no?

Gently rocking her, I lifted my face to the sky. The moon was always there. I opened my senses, searching for it, reaching for its strength, its power to move oceans. Please take me, I pleaded.

The wolf stirred.

Without warning, the change struck. Heat seared my bones and turned my knees to jelly. I felt my cheek slide down the front of her blouse. My knuckles crackled as they struck the ground, contracting into silver paws.

Pride and awe flooded me. I'd done it. I was a wolf.

A wolf in human clothing.

I looked down at my jeans. Crap. Why did everything happen to me?

Brittany didn't run, but she leaned as far away as she could. Anger flared in the pit of my stomach. This was her idea. How dare she stare at me with...what? Horror? Disgust? Pity?

A growl climbed my throat. I flipped onto my back and wriggled. The shoes came off, but the jeans and T-shirt stayed in place. Double crap.

"Let me help you," Brittany said.

I didn't want her to touch me. Not with that look on her face. With a yip, I scrambled away, tripping on the flapping pant legs.

"Hold still," she commanded. Like she was talking to a dog.

I wanted to bite her.

She snagged the T-shirt, pulling and tugging. By the time it was off my head, my lips were up in a snarl. She fell on her backside with a sound of alarm.

What was I doing? I couldn't hurt Brittany.

I went to her slowly and nuzzled her arm. She reeked of fear and adrenalin. My human side cringed with remorse. I dropped my gaze, trying to look nonthreatening. Like a one-hundred and fifty pound wolf could look anything but. After a moment, she stroked my ear, and I knew she accepted my apology.

The jeans were mostly off, and with them, the socks. That left my underwear. Brittany approached me tentatively, and then peeled them over my rump. I felt a gush of embarrassment. I held as still as I could, letting her work, inwardly vowing never to wear undershorts again.

At last, I was free. I shook myself. Something chafed my neck, reminding me of the necktie I was stuck with the first time I changed. I wanted to sit down and scratch, but that was too doglike.

"Do you see the trail?" Brittany got to her feet. "Can you find him?"

Of course, I saw the trail. It fairly shone in the darkness. Anyone could see where the boy had gone.

I told her to wait there, that she would only slow

me down, but the words sounded like a walrus gargling. Stupid me. So I headed into the brush with Brittany close behind.

There were no trees. This was human land, and they'd scraped it clean. But the Glades fought to reclaim it. Scrub palmetto and sawgrass dragged at my fur. There was no wildlife around. Not even rabbits. But I occasionally caught a whiff of otherness. I searched my memory of zoos and forests.

The boy followed a bear. What was a bear doing so close to civilization?

Eventually, the barren fields gave way to swamp. Shallow ponds sprang around us. I heard crickets and frogs, the splash of fish. I smelled the fetid earth and wanted to roll in it. Of course, there wasn't time.

I tracked the bear's scent down a narrow spit of land. Gnarled trees creaked overhead. Nighthawks screeched, and peacocks sang. After a while, I stopped, nose to the ground. I smelled the boy twice. He'd crossed his own trail. I imagined him circling, totally lost. I quickened my pace.

The dark night hid pockets of water. Brittany splashed, breathing hard, making more noise than necessary. The boy's trail was erratic. I lost his trace several times, but he was near. His scent was on the wind.

We came out from beneath a group of low-hanging trees. The boy was across the clearing, fighting through thigh-high water. I grinned, tongue lolling, mentally patting myself on the back. I watched him for a moment, charting the driest course to his side, when I caught movement behind him. Something swift and as black as the water.

An alligator.

Barking and growling, I charged down the pond's edge. The boy turned to look, lost his balance, and went under. Behind me, Brittany screamed. I hoped she had the good sense to stay out of the water.

Because I didn't.

I jumped in and angled for the boy. He came up waving his arms. The gator latched onto his jacket. With its mighty tail swishing, it towed him toward the deeps. I clambered onto its snout and attacked its eyes. The thing rolled over, knocking me off.

The boy fell backward. He grappled with me, trying to get his head above water. I felt a pop, and whatever had been choking my neck disappeared. The boy coughed and sputtered.

"Give me your hand," Brittany yelled to him.

The gator rolled again, and I pounced on its belly, getting my teeth around its throat. It was like biting a rock. My fangs didn't penetrate at all.

It wouldn't release the boy in its grasp. The twisting jacket tightened, but he managed to shrug out of it and wade for shore. The gator righted itself, throwing me into the water. It snapped at the empty jacket.

Then it came after me.

Brittany screamed, "Cody!"

For a moment, all I saw was teeth. I leaped onto the beast's back, chomping down on its nose. This time, I tasted blood. The gator dove, but the water was shallow. I didn't let go. My hind legs kicked and dug at its eyes. It lifted up, tossing me into the air. I landed hard and heaved myself onto the bank. With a snort, I shook the moisture from my fur.

Brittany stood a short distance away, clutching her brother. She looked terrified. I took a step toward her when something hit like a battering ram square in my ribs. I rolled and spun in time to see the gator come at me again. It sprinted on land like a horse, hind legs gathering beneath it, the armored snout like a lance.

It struck low and flipped me. The sinewy tail sliced across my face. I lay on my side, dazed. It turned to make another pass when Brittany appeared behind it, bashing its head with a club.

It reared back, mouth open. She hit it hard enough to loosen a few teeth. The jaws snapped. She dodged and swung again. The massive animal clamped down on the club. She tried to pull free, but the gator adjusted its hold, drawing the wood deeper into its mouth.

She used the club to push the creature back toward the pond. The thing was heavy, and she had to lean into it. The gator bit the wood again. More than half of the club was in its mouth, drawing her fingers nearer. Perhaps she realized that at the same moment I did, because her expression changed.

I jumped up and barked. *Run away, Brittany. Run so I can run.*

She dropped the club and scrambled backward. The gator roared, snapping at her around the chunk of wood in its mouth. I pounced and dropped my full weight upon its head, ramming the club down its throat. Hot blood bubbled from its nostrils. Its tail lashed. I stepped onto the bank, growling, ready for another round. But the gator withdrew, leaving only splintered wood and a few teeth.

Brittany threw her arms about me and buried her face in my coat. Behind her, the boy clutched her jacket around his shoulders, shivering violently.

"You called him Cody," he said.

She wiped her eyes. "I named him after my boyfriend. Kind of a joke."

"Oh," he said. "That's one huge dog."

I would have laughed, but my ribs were too sore. I strode past him, a slight limp ruining my exit. After a few moments, they followed. We retraced our steps through the swamp. Brittany and her brother argued the whole way.

"It was a bear," he said for the twentieth time. "I couldn't let someone shoot it for getting into their trash. So I chased it. And I got turned around a little."

"Do you know what you put us through?"

"I would have found my way back in the morning."

"That gator wouldn't have let you see the morning."

I was glad when we reached the barren fields. I passed my castoff clothing like I didn't notice them, but Brittany picked them up.

"Here," she told her brother. "Take off your wet things and put these on."

"What? I don't even know who they belong to."

"Neither do I, but they're dry. I don't want you dripping on my seat."

With a snort, I kept walking. He could keep the clothes. Stupid things, anyway. Maybe I should join the Sunspot.

At last, we reached the human housing development. Brittany opened the door of her car and pushed the boy inside. She grabbed her purse from under the seat and took out her cell phone.

"Grandpa? I found him. We'll tell you all about it when we get home. Will you call Sheriff Brad and let him know? See you in a bit." She put the phone away. Then she turned to me, making smooching sounds. "Come on. Get in the car."

I grinned at her. Then I sped off as fast as I could. Why would I ride when I could run? I left the subdivision and headed for the surrounding forest. The thick pine carpeting cushioned my step. I limped, stiff and aching, but I was in a great mood.

The whole fight scene seemed hilarious. Who knew an alligator could run like that? And Brittany was brilliant, whacking it in the head with a stick. But even better was that I had turned into a wolf during the dark of the moon. I could control the change instead of being at nature's mercy. Anything could happen now.

279

Maybe I wouldn't have to be a human at all.

I was chasing rabbits when white-hot pain split my skull. My teeth raged like they were twisting from their sockets. I pawed my face. It felt flat and feature-less.

I was shifting back into a human.

No! It wasn't fair. It wasn't morning yet. I fought the change, searching for the moon's power. I couldn't tap into it. Exhausted, I fell to the ground, whimpering as my limbs elongated and I became a teenage boy once again.

A naked teenage boy.

Man, it was colder than I thought. I stood to brush myself off, and with the dirt and leaves went my sense of freedom. Shivering, I glanced around. I wasn't far from home. The promise of a warm bed spurred me on.

But as I neared my uncle's house, I heard voices. Soft laughter. I approached the yard, peering from the bushes. Uncle Bob's truck was in the drive. He sat on the porch swing, his back to me and his arm around a redheaded woman. Ice clinked in a glass.

I looked longingly at my bedroom window. Candlelight flickered in the darkness. Brittany's candles. The window was locked. I couldn't get in that way.

My attention drew to the kitchen window. Its curtains flapped in the breeze. Could I jump that high? Did I have a choice? Moving in a crouch, I left the bushes and crept forward. My senses were on full. I listened to the rhythmic creak of the swing.

When I was half-way across the yard, the swing stopped. I froze mid-step, expecting my uncle to shout my name. I couldn't stand there waiting for him to find me. I bounded to the house and sprang to the windowsill, pulling myself up and over.

It was easier than it should have been. I climbed down from the sink and snuck to my room. My uncle would never know I was gone.

My bed with the Scooby sheets and the red horse blanket never looked so good. I crawled under the covers without wiping my feet.

It had been a lousy night. But it had been a good night, too. We found Butt Crack. Brittany probably thought I was a hero, fighting an alligator and all. In a way, maybe I was.

But even better, I'd learned to shift at will. The wolf didn't have to control me. I could control it. With practice, I might not have to be a wolf at all.

In the back of my mind, a memory stirred. The wolf had thought the same thing. Was Brittany right? Would the wolf stop me from using the potion? I couldn't let it spoil my chance for a normal life.

A life with Brittany.

I raised my hand to Brittany's necklaces. They were gone. I winced. Must've lost them in the swamp somewhere. She wouldn't be happy. I'd better ride out to that metaphysical shop first thing and replace them. It shouldn't be a problem, although the balance on my debit card must be getting low.

My eyes flew open. Both my cell phone and wallet were in the pockets of the jeans Butt Crack now wore.

# TWENTY-ONE

I awoke to someone rapping at my bedroom window. Still groggy, I dressed in a pair of pants from the laundry pile in the back of my closet. I was stiff and achy, and covered in cuts.

With a scowl, I answered the window.

It was Brittany's brother. "Hi," he said.

I scratched my head and yawned.

"Figured this was your room." He motioned upward. "Brittany's crystals."

I glanced at the dangling prism. "Yeah."

"Can I come in?"

I grimaced. What did he want at this time of the morning? I opened the window wider, favoring my bruised ribs, and stepped back.

He climbed through and stood before me, looking nervous. "That looks sore. Your face."

My hand flew up. A long welt ran across my nose and down one cheek. I remembered the gator's whip-like tail slicing across the wolf's muzzle. Before I could think of an explanation, he showed something in his hand.

"I thought you might like this," he said.

283

My stomach fell. It was an alligator tooth. He'd wrapped the top of it with wire and hooked it to a black cord.

"They say it's lucky to keep a trophy from something you killed," he said. "You didn't exactly kill that gator, but you fought it. It was pretty spectacular, actually."

My head spun. "But I—"

"Besides, I thought it would make up for the one I broke."

He held up a chain. It was the Earth Calm pendant Brittany gave me. I remembered it chafing the wolf's neck. My breath left me in a whoosh, and I stumbled backward to sit on the edge of the bed.

"I never saw a dog wear a necklace before," he said. "But then, you aren't a dog, are you?"

I met his eyes. How was I going to get out of this? The kid wasn't an idiot. He'd catch me in a lie. "Look. Whatever you think happened—"

"I don't know what you are or anything. And that's cool. But you saved my life last night. I just wanted you to know I'm grateful."

What could I say? If I accepted his thanks, I confirmed his suspicions. If I said nothing, I came off like a jerk. "Does your sister know you're here?"

"Nah. She'll probably freak when she finds me gone."

"Are you crazy? We've got to call her." I slapped my pockets for my phone, and then remembered I'd left it in my other pants. My eyes widened.

"Ah, yeah. That's the other thing." He pulled out my cell and wallet.

I nodded, taking them. "Where are my pants?"

"Brit will probably wash them. You know her."

I sighed. "You eat this morning?"

"No. I left before anyone got up."

"Well, let's see if there's something for breakfast. Then we'll call your sister."

I opened my bedroom door just as Uncle Bob came out of the bathroom. He blinked at me, and then at Butt Crack.

"Uh," he said.

I smiled. "Morning."

"Uh," he said again.

I brushed past him on my way to the kitchen.

Butt Crack followed me. "Aren't you going to tell him what I was doing in your bedroom?"

"Not unless he asks. And I don't think he will." I held out a box. "I have blue or red."

"Blue is good."

We sat at the table with blueberry Pop Tarts and chocolate milk. While we ate, I called Brittany.

"You're up early," she said sleepily.

"I had an early visitor," I said. "Your brother is here."

"What?"

I pictured her bolting upright in bed and smiled. "It's no big. He wanted to talk."

"That brat. He doesn't think of anyone but himself. I should have let the gator eat him."

285

"You don't mean that."

"I guess not," she said after a moment. "Did he walk the whole way?"

"Good question." I looked at Butt Crack. "How'd you get here?"

"Bike," he said between bites.

"He rode his bicycle over. Should I send him home?"

"Not on your life." She sounded like she was moving about. "I'll be there in ten. Don't let him go anywhere else."

"No prob." I put the phone in my pocket. "You're right. She freaked. More milk?"

Butt Crack nodded.

He was finishing his third glass when I heard a knock. I caught Brittany's scent as I opened the door.

"Thanks for calling me," she said in greeting. "I have to get him home before anyone else wakes up. Mom went nuts when she found out what happened, and we didn't even tell her about the alligator. He's not supposed to leave the house."

I noticed she'd borrowed her mother's minivan. "Will the bike fit?"

"It better."

"Let's find out."

So while Butt Crack sat on the porch, Brittany and I manhandled his bike inside the van. "You were scary awesome last night," she said in a low voice.

"Really? Because I saw fear and loathing on your face."

"Only for a moment. I don't like that gloppy sound. But the way you tracked him and saved him from that gator. You really came through for me."

"Aww, shucks." I grinned, giving the bike a final shove.

She put her hand on my cheek, looking into my face. "Does it hurt?"

"Nah. But this hurts." I showed her the dark splotch on my ribs.

She winced. "You're a mess."

"I'm fine. Can I see you later?"

She shook her head. "We're staying home and doing the family thing. Right, Butt Crack?"

"I was just gone an hour. Sheesh." He climbed into the front seat.

I rolled the side door shut. As I turned, Brittany kissed me. It wasn't a passionate kiss. I didn't even have time to close my eyes. Her lips were warm and grape soda sweet. Like her.

"Bye." She circled around to her side of the van.

"Hey, man." Butt Crack leaned out the window. "Thanks for, you know, not denying anything."

"Why would I? You're not stupid."

"Depend on it."

I watched them drive away with those words ringing in my ears. Butt Crack wouldn't talk. He'd proven that. Still I wasn't comfortable with him learning my secret identity. Now two people knew about me. At this rate, half the town would know by the end of the year. I'd have to include a wolf boy newsletter with my Christmas cards.

As I walked back inside, Uncle Bob stormed down the hall from his bedroom.

"What's going on, Cody?" he bellowed.

"Nothing," I said. "He's a friend."

He blinked at me, and I realized that he wasn't referring to Butt Crack.

"I heard you come in last night," he said. "Crawling through a window? Why didn't you go through the front? I wanted you to meet my friend."

Now it was my turn to blink. Was the redhead planning to move in or something? "Sorry. I didn't think you wanted to be disturbed."

"Where were you? You're all cut up."

I sighed. The truth was always safer. "Brittany's brother got lost in the Everglades, so Brit and I went out to find him. And we tangled with an alligator. It's no big deal."

"You fought a gator?"

"Yes, sir."

"A *boy* against a gator?"

Did he think I was lying? "There were three of us. Look, can we pick this up another time? I'd like to go back to bed."

Alarm and disbelief crossed his face. It was like he was afraid of me—or for me. "Sure," he said. "We'll talk later."

Not if I could help it. I stomped to my room.

I spent the rest of the weekend under my uncle's watchful eye. I found that increasingly funny, seeing how I was supposed to be watching him. He never mentioned the alligator again, which was fine. He had something to say, though, and I wished he would spit it out.

Once, he almost did. "Made any new friends, lately?" he asked.

"Not really. I don't fit in much at school."

"Maybe someone outside of school?" he asked. "Someone a little older?"

"No." I looked at him, waiting, wondering where this was going.

Evidently nowhere, because he dropped the subject.

The following week, we had the math FCAT at school. The good thing about standardized testing was we had no homework. The bad thing was, because there was no homework, Brittany didn't see the need for study nights. She spent her evenings at home doing the family thing.

I tried not to complain. As a reward, she promised me her full attention on Saturday.

When she got to my place Saturday morning, I was sitting on the front porch looking out at the woods. Spring was coming, causing many of the trees to burst into bloom. Yellow, orange, and even blue flowers filled the branches. It almost looked like autumn up north.

"Hi." Brittany sat beside me.

"Hi yourself." I entwined my fingers with hers. "What would you like to do today?"

"I thought we could follow your uncle around, see if he does anything suspicious."

I shook my head. "He's already gone. Said he had some errands to run."

"Like what?"

"I don't know. He might be picking up supplies for a project he's doing next week."

"We could run by the lumberyard and see if he's there."

"Sure." I stood, pulling her up with me.

"Speaking of next week," she said, "it's spring break, so remember I'll be working."

I nodded. "Do you know your hours?"

"Not yet. But if it's during the day, there's a good chance my boss will be there."

"If it's during the day, I'll probably be working with Uncle Bob. He already asked."

She smiled and got into her car. "Good, then."

We drove past the lumberyard, but we didn't see my uncle's truck. So we continued on to Wal-Mart, Target, and the Home Depot. Then we tried the post office and Publix.

"I wish we knew what kind of errands he's running," Brittany said.

I shrugged. Even if we found him, we wouldn't be able to follow him unnoticed. We weren't exactly inconspicuous in a lime green Volkswagen.

"Why don't we stop at the Coffee Café?" I said. "If we don't see him there, I can at least buy you lunch."

"Deal." She smiled.

By the time we got to the café, the parking lot was almost full. We opened the door to the rumble of conversation and the clatter of silverware.

Anne greeted us as we stepped inside. "Cody. How are you doing, hon? There's a table over in the corner. Better grab it quick."

I spotted the table and guided Brittany to it.

She smiled as she sat. "They know you?"

"It's my uncle's favorite place. I'm surprised he's not here."

Anne placed two tall glasses of chocolate milk before us.

I set my debit card on the table. "This one's not on the tab, okay?"

Her eyes crinkled. "Oh, I see. Who's your friend?"

"I'm Brittany."

"Anne. Pleased as the dickens to meet you." She turned to me. "Will you be having the usual?"

"What's the usual?" Brittany asked.

"Hamburger. Rare," I said.

"Sounds good," she said, "but I'll have mine medium. No bun."

"You got it. I'll be back in a jiff." Anne bustled away.

Brittany picked up the glass of milk. "I thought this was a coffee shop."

"Well, I don't really like coffee, so she started giving me milk." I took a swig. "It does a body good."

"It certainly does yours good. You're like transforming before my eyes."

I gave her a quizzical look. "And I don't even work out."

She laughed and glanced around. "It's really busy in here."

"The food's good."

"I have something to ask, and I don't know how."

I met her eyes. "All right."

"My mother wants me to invite you to Easter dinner," Brittany said. "She wants to meet you."

"Oh." I leaned back in my seat. "She's not scary or anything is she?"

"Hardly. She's frazzled most of the time. Not great at multi-tasking. But she's a really good cook."

"Can she make crunchy cake?"

Brittany laughed. "No one can make crunchy cake like you."

"Here you go, kids." Anne juggled the hamburgers and fries. "One bloody and one pink."

"Yum. Smells great," said Brittany.

"Yes, it does." I looked up at Anne. "Has my uncle been in today?"

"Breakfast. Said he was stopping by Sophie Jackson's to unclog her dryer vent. He never charges that woman a thing, knows she's on a fixed income. I never met a kinder man than your Uncle Bobby. In spite of his birthday."

"What do you mean?" I asked.

"Well, as you know, he was born on Christmas

292

Eve, and I've always found that sort to be rather strange. Standoffish. But not Bobby. He's a real sweetheart. Well, enjoy your lunch."

I watched her walk away without really seeing her. *Christmas Eve*. There was something important about people born on Christmas Eve, but I couldn't remember what.

"Cody? Are you okay?" Brittany asked.

I grabbed the ketchup. "Of course."

🐾 🐾 🐾

Apparently, Spring Break was tree-trimming season in South Florida. Many of my uncle's jobs had us up twenty-foot ladders juggling buzz saws. Uncle Bob said we just had to thin the new growth a bit to let a hurricane blow through. There were a lot of snakes, especially in the palm trees, but my uncle assured me that they weren't poisonous. After they surprised me a couple times, they didn't bother me anymore.

On Monday and Tuesday, I got home so exhausted I just took a shower and fell into bed. But on Wednesday, Uncle Bob decided to knock off early, so I had him drop me and my bike at the Video Stop where Brittany worked.

I walked in with a bag from Burger King. I stank and had leaves in my hair, but when she saw me, her face lit up like I was a rock star. All my minor scrapes and aches disappeared.

293

"Hi," I said. "I thought you might like dinner."

"Got any fries in there?" She opened the bag and took a deep breath. "Heaven."

"Hello." A woman stepped out of the horror section. She had thick black glasses and a mustache.

I'd forgotten the boss would be in today.

Brittany said, "This is my boyfriend, Cody."

Not friend, but *boyfriend*. I smiled. "How do you do, ma'am?"

"Well, Cody," she said. "You look like you work for a living."

"Yes, ma'am. I work with Bob, the Fix-It Guy."

Her heavy brows went up. "Oh? Yes, I know Bob."

"Can I take my break early?" Brittany asked. "There's nothing going on."

"Certainly. Go right ahead."

Brittany grabbed the bag in one hand, my arm in the other, and led me down a short hall into a room lined with boxes. It smelled like cardboard. The light was dim and yellow after the bright fluorescents in the store.

"I'm starved." She set the bag on a table and opened a small, recreational-type refrigerator. "Do you want a Dew?"

"Yeah. Great." I sat at the table.

She set a can before me and opened the bag. "You look tired."

"Not tired enough, I'm afraid. I probably won't sleep much tonight."

She nibbled the burger. "Full moon is Friday?"

"Right."

"Does that mean you'll have to go out tonight?"

"I don't want to," I said. "But the closer it gets, the stronger..."

"Like *the hunger.*"

I nodded and folded half a dozen fries into my mouth.

Brittany frowned and set her half-eaten hamburger on a napkin. "Where's your uncle?"

"He was going home, said he needed to rest up a bit." I looked at her. "Why?"

"The sheriff stopped by this morning to talk to Grandpa. According to him, the coroner thinks most of the murders took place a couple days before full moons. They think the murders were ritualistic. A coven or something."

"Like witches?"

"Sure." She glanced toward the door. "I thought this might be a good opportunity to, you know, keep an eye on your uncle."

"Then you want me to go ahead and shift."

"You don't want to?"

"That's the problem." I looked at the door and lowered my voice. "Every time I change, it's like the wolf gets in deeper."

"It scares you."

"I just want to be rid of it."

She put her hand over mine. "We will."

A gush of warmth ran through me. I smiled, wanting to kiss her, but knowing her boss could walk in at any moment. She seemed to have the same thoughts, because she blushed and pulled away. I covered the awkward moment with a big bite of burger.

"Maybe I won't have to change tonight," I said with my mouth full. "He looked pretty tired. He'll probably be asleep on his old recliner by the time I get back."

"I hope you're right." She crinkled her wrapper and tossed it into the empty bag. "Thanks for dinner. I was just going to get a bag of chips."

"We couldn't have that." I stood, clearing the table. "What time do you get off?"

"Seven o'clock. Call me if you're home." Brittany took my hand and walked with me into the main room.

Her boss sat behind the counter talking on the phone. She looked up and gave me a nod as I continued toward the door. If it hadn't been for her, I would have hung around for a while. I felt better about myself when I was with Brittany. But I didn't want to get her in trouble with her boss.

"Well, have a nice night." I shrugged.

She smiled. "Talk to you later."

I went out into the warm afternoon. The sun hung low, winking at me between buildings. I got on my bike, ready for the ride home, when I spotted my uncle's truck going down Southern.

Disbelief turned to panic. What was he doing? He told me he was going back to the house. I remembered what Brittany said about the murders taking place before the full moon. Was Uncle Bob part of a coven? I had to stop him.

Leaning into the wind, I pedaled after his truck as fast as I could. The wolf inside me howled, strengthening me. I had no trouble dodging through traffic. I stayed two stoplights behind Uncle Bob, turning where he turned. Finally, I found myself on a long, deserted stretch heading west.

Dusk fell over the scrub, giving me enough confidence to pull closer. He didn't have my wolf eyesight. After a while, he pulled onto a rutted dirt road and disappeared beneath the trees.

It was rough going. Rubble and roots filled the road, giving me a workout. Several times, I lost sight of him in the trees. But he was never beyond my hearing. The squeaking chassis and the crackling tires kept me on track. The truck stopped, and the engine cut. I hid my bike in the brush and crept forward.

Uncle Bob stood outside the truck. He loitered like he was waiting for me to catch up. Humming one of his tuneless tunes, he took a fishing pole and tackle from the truck bed and walked into the trees.

Fishing? Frowning with a mix of relief and distrust, I followed.

It was dark when we reached the pond. The water was black, and early stars glistened on the surface. The moon was about to rise. I felt its pressure on the back of my neck. But I would not bow to it. Not until I was certain what my uncle was doing.

Uncle Bob propped his fishing rod against a pile of rocks. He backed to the tree line and stripped naked. I thought he planned to go skinny-dipping. It was a warm night.

But then the moonlight hit him, and fur sprouted from his skin.

I stared with my mouth hanging open. In my mind, the pieces clicked together. Uncle Bob's birthday was Christmas Eve. The book we read at *Ye Olde Bookstore* said all those born on Christmas Eve were in danger of being werewolves. He had a mark like a backwards C on his back. A crescent moon, like the Story Keeper said. There were other things, too, like his nighttime disappearances, trophies on his rearview mirror, and a dead ostrich with no damage to the truck.

He was a werewolf.

How could it be true?

For a moment, I forgot myself. I stumbled into the open, stepping from cover as I stared at him. I'd never seen anyone shift into a wolf.

Uncle Bob's shoulders hunched, and his arms slid forward. There was the popping sound of dislocating joints. The gloppy sound Brittany hated. His hips drew back, dropping him to all fours. His face stretched, and his muzzle grew. Drool dripped in long strands from his fangs.

When he was done, he looked at me, grinning, and bounded into the trees.

Shock held me motionless. My thoughts whirled. Uncle Bob was a werewolf, and he never let on, never told me. How many times I wished I had someone to talk to, someone to tell me I wasn't alone. He could have helped me. But he never said a word.

With my head thrown back, I let out a garbled howl. My own muzzle elongated. I clawed my shirt, shredding it, then fell to my knees. Growling, teeth bared, I ran after my uncle before my own change completed.

# TWENTY-TWO

My paws padded softly as I followed my uncle through the trees. His scent was everywhere, as if he trampled every plant, brushed against every bush, daring me to follow. Eyes glinted in the dark. His eyes. I pounced, but he ran off. I snapped at the grass in frustration.

"Come back here," I barked. Did wolves understand each other? Did he know it was me, or did he think I was just a stray wolf passing through?

The forest deepened, crowding me, blotting out the sky. Branches creaked in the breeze. I walked slowly, ears twitching, taking in the trill of insects, the rustle of field mice. My uncle darted across my path. I tore after him, but lost him in the trees. Nose down, I squeezed between the narrow trunks.

Again, he streaked past and disappeared. Like this was a game. Only I wasn't playing. I needed answers. He was a werewolf. I was a werewolf. It couldn't be a coincidence. But as before, he was holding out on me. I felt his eyes on my back, heard his laughter on the wind, and I never hated him more than at that moment.

I tracked him through the night. Twice more, I saw his golden eyes shining from the brush. Twice more, he bounded out at me. But I never caught him. He was better at being a wolf than I was.

The wind shifted. I lifted my nose and caught a whiff of horses. Stables were nearby. I also smelled wolves. Three wolves had passed not too long ago.

Uncle Bob shot from the brush. He nipped my ear before darting away. I growled, giving chase. Didn't he smell the wolves? Something was wrong. I had a sense of danger. I wanted to warn him but lost him again.

I slowed to a trot. A warm gust of wind ruffled my fur. Blood scent. A lot of blood. With my head low, I crept forward, keeping to the trees. I saw a clearing and a fence with a horse pasture beyond. I froze.

In a patch of moonlight lay a woman. Her stomach was ripped open, and her insides were outside, strewn over the darkening grass. She hadn't been there long. I should have been horrified. Perhaps part of me was. But a larger part felt only relief. My uncle wasn't the killer. He couldn't be. He was with me playing his stupid game of hide-and-seek.

I cocked my head and wondered what to do, if I should do anything at all. There was a rifle beside her. I hadn't heard a shot. She must not have had time to use it. Suddenly, something large dove at me. Uncle Bob knocked me over and held me with a heavy paw, his teeth at my neck.

Was he threatening me? I could have fought him

off. I started to.

But through the trees, I saw three wolves walking along the fence. They had stumpy yellow tails. *Were-wolves*. Blood drenched their coats. These were the true killers. Worse yet, I recognized their scents. They were the intruders who were prowling around Brittany's yard.

They threatened Brittany.

I wanted to leap out of the trees and challenge them. But part of me, my human part, saw the danger. If I fell here, there would be no one to protect her. Fortunately, we were downwind. The trio continued walking, unaware of us. The leader seemed agitated. He spun on his followers, snarling, and bit the she-wolf hard enough to draw a yelp and a whine. All three moved quicker after that.

When they were out of sight, Uncle Bob let me up. He nipped my ear and ran in the opposite direction. I followed. I couldn't help feeling it was wrong. We were leaving a dead woman. But I couldn't help her, couldn't report the crime. All I could do was run.

As the moon set, we reached the pond where Uncle Bob left his fishing pole. He stood on the bank and shifted into a man. Without looking at me, he tugged his clothing from the bushes where they hung. He dressed in silence.

I tried to hold onto the wolf a little longer, afraid that we were followed. Afraid I'd have to fight. But exhaustion overtook me. Unable to stop myself, I turned back into a boy, whining with the pain of my rearranging limbs. At last, I was whole. I stood slowly, feeling dazed.

My uncle tossed my jeans.

I caught them. "You knew it was me?"

"Hurry. We have to get out of here."

"But that woman. Shouldn't we—"

"No. They'll know someone was there. I don't want them to figure out it was us." Fishing gear in hand, he strode away.

I put on my jeans, hopping on one foot, and stepped into my shoes. My shirt was shredded, so I carried it. I had no idea where my socks were. I couldn't get a handle on my thoughts. Had he always known what I was? When we got to the road, I grabbed his arm.

"Wait," I said. "You're a wolf. Like me."

"Yeah. So?"

My face heated with anger. "You knew? All this time?"

"Cody," he said. "Why do you think they sent you to me?"

His words socked me in the stomach.

*Mom knew?* My knees buckled, and I nearly fell. Mom knew about werewolves. She knew there was a chance I might become one. Like her only brother. So she took me by C-section so I wouldn't be born at Christmastime. She had my birthmark erased. And she never told me. Never explained.

"Cody, get in." Uncle Bob started the truck.

I wrapped my arms around my chest to keep my

heart from falling out. She never explained. Just let me think she hated me, as if I'd done something wrong. When all along, it ran in the family. Like a receding hairline.

"Come on." My uncle grabbed my shoulders and frog marched me to the passenger seat. He spun the tires, turning the truck around.

"My bike," I said.

"Where?"

I pointed. He skidded to a stop. I hopped out, pulled the bike from the bushes, and tossed it in the bed. As I climbed inside the truck, he punched it, spraying gravel behind us.

I stared out the windshield, feeling like the world was broken. I wanted to cry, which only made me angrier. "How could you let me keep thinking that I was alone?"

He glanced at me. "You didn't ask for help. How would I know you had questions?"

"Help?" I shouted. "How could I ask for help? I never knew you were a werewolf."

"What?" He squinted like he didn't believe me. "Your mother didn't tell you?"

"She wouldn't speak to me at all. Just sent me here."

He swore under his breath. "All right, then. If you didn't know I was a wolf, why were you following me?"

"Because I thought you were the one killing those women. Because Brittany said the murders took place just before the full moon, and I thought I had to stop you."

"Me? Son of a—" He jammed his fingers in his hair. "Okay, okay. I have a confession to make, too. I've been worried you'd fallen in with that pack."

"What made you think so?"

"The night you crawled in through the window, you reeked of wolf. I was afraid you learned to shift during the dark of the moon. I have reason to believe that at least one member of the pack can do that." He looked at me sideways. "So? Can you—shift on command?"

"Yes."

He slammed the steering wheel with the heel of his hand. "Do you know how dangerous that is?"

"No, I don't. I don't know anything. Haven't you been listening? You and my parents decided to plunk me down in Podunk land and leave me to figure things out on my own."

"I don't believe this."

"Why are you driving so fast?" I yelled.

"We have to get a long way from here."

"Because of the pack? It's morning. They're no threat to us."

"It's not just the pack," he said. "Did you get a look at the woman? Dee Dee Dickerson of Triple D Ranch. She was on committees, a real activist. I'm sure the sheriff's already searching for her."

"Maybe we should tell them where to search."

"I will," he said. "Anonymously. That's what I did

305

for the first one."

"You found the first body?"

He nodded and didn't say more.

By the time we got home, my anger had boiled down to resentment. Still, I took pleasure in slamming the truck door.

"Come inside so we can talk," he said.

I didn't feel much like talking, but I went into the kitchen anyway. I slouched at the table with my feet sticking into the middle of the room. After a few moments, he joined me.

"I made that call," he said. "It's a bad sign when you know the number for the tip hotline by heart."

I didn't look at him. He took my ripped up T-shirt from the tabletop. "This is why I buy from Howard. In bulk." He tossed the shirt in the trash.

I folded my arms.

He poured milk into a Sonic cup and set it before me. "Drink. It's good for your bones. Why do you think I always—" He looked at the ceiling. "I expected your parents to have told you everything."

"They didn't."

"I get that." He sat at the table. "Your mother loves you."

I snorted.

"Believe it," he said. Twisting in the chair, he faced me. His cheeks were pink like he was embarrassed, or maybe he had anger issues of his own. "When our parents died, they left each of us two hundred thousand dollars. I was just getting comfortable with being a werewolf at that time. I'd dropped out of school and was backpacking through the Rockies. Your mother was studying to be a doctor. She planned to go into gene research, hoping to find a cure for her wayward brother."

"She's not in research."

"No. Somehow, she got into brain surgery instead. Anyway, I let her have my share of the inheritance to get through med school with the stipulation that if I needed money she would give it to me. She's kept her side of the bargain."

I thought of the many times I'd heard of Mom sending him cash to get this or that. The last time was to buy the truck.

"She always swore she wouldn't have children," he said. "Lycanthropy follows the mother's bloodline, you see, and she wanted to stamp it out of the family. But then she fell in love and got married. Your dad wanted a family so bad. After a while, she had you."

I closed my eyes. I didn't want to hear this, didn't want to think of her as a regular person with plans and problems.

"I was there when you were born," he said. "She cried, so afraid she'd ruined her only son's life. I guess it was her sense of guilt that kept her from talking to you."

"That's not an excuse."

"No." He sighed. "I have no excuse, either. I should have sat you down and talked to you long before now. I just thought you were the private type, you know? I thought I was giving you your space. It was wrong of me. I should have been there."

I glanced at him, then took a swig of milk. "Did you have someone to teach you?"

"Yeah. Actually, I had an Uncle Bob, too. I was named after him. I would have loved it if we'd gone romping through the woods together. But he was a lot older. He didn't romp." Uncle Bob chuckled as if at a pleasant memory.

I scowled, nurturing my anger. "So what's this about shifting during the dark of the moon being dangerous? Will I get stuck that way? Like Mom used to say, don't cry or your face will freeze."

"No, nothing like that. It's the power of it. You begin to think you can do anything. Like being human is beneath you."

"I don't think that." *Do I?*

"I'm certain the leader of that pack can shift at will. That's what gives him dominance."

"A rogue werewolf," I said.

Uncle Bob raised his hands. "Actually, the two of us are the rogues. We don't belong to a pack, and we don't hunt humans."

"How do we stop them?"

"We don't. Just let them pass through. I've come across violent packs of wolves before, and I've learned to stay out of their way."

"But shouldn't we—"

"No. I like living in Loxahatchee. I'd hate to leave."

I nodded, thinking about the body of poor Mrs. Dickerson. "I don't want to be like them."

"Being a werewolf doesn't make you a killer."

"Real wolves kill."

"Wolves kill to eat. Werewolves are human most of the time and can eat at McDonalds. Werewolves who kill do it for the sheer exhilaration of the hunt and slaughter. They don't make very nice humans, either."

🐺 🐺 🐺

After a short nap, Uncle Bob left to build a chicken coop. I begged off. I had a lot to consider. But thinking about my parents and how they'd duped me all my life was depressing. I grabbed my bike and went to visit Brittany at work.

She grinned as I walked through the door. "What, no fries?"

"Sorry. Is it lunchtime already?"

"Almost." She gave me a peck on the cheek, then peered up at me. "You okay?"

"Your boss around?"

"Not until three. What's going on?"

I sighed. "I've got weird news and weirder news."

"Here. Sit down." She pulled a stool from behind the counter. "Give me the weird news first."

"My uncle isn't the killer. I know because I found a body, and he couldn't have done it."

She paled. "Another murder? Who?"

"Dee Dee Dickerson," I said as if I knew her.

"Oh, my God. Was it awful?"

"Pretty bad, yeah. And I saw who did it. Werewolves. Three of them."

Her eyes widened, and her hands flew to her mouth. I jumped off the stool and helped her sit.

"More werewolves?" she said. "What is it, some sort of secret society?"

"This is where it gets really weird. My uncle knows about me. He's known all along. Because he's one, too."

"What?" She yelped and leaped to her feet.

"I saw him change last night. He was with me when we found the body."

"I can't believe it." She shook her head. "You must feel so...betrayed."

She got it. She understood how I felt, and I didn't even have to explain. My love for her multiplied. I thought of telling her about my parents and their part in the scheme, but the subject was too painful.

"As soon as we got home, my uncle called that anonymous hotline and reported the murder."

She nodded thoughtfully, then frowned. "Why didn't he call Sheriff Brad direct?"

"I think I know why. When Uncle Bob first moved here, there was a string of gas station robberies. The sheriff accused him, although he was innocent. Now, whenever anything bad happens, he automatically suspects my uncle, trying to catch him in something. Trying to save face."

"Yeah."

"Uncle Bob told me we should keep out of it. But Sheriff Brad has already been out to our house twice. I think he wants to pin it on him."

"So you can't keep out of it."

Again, she understood.

I said, "I have to bring them down."

"It should be easy to trace them, three strangers showing up in town. I know most of the cheap motels in the area."

"Do you now?" I grinned.

"Stop it." She laughed and slapped my arm. "I'm in charge of finding the best deal if my father comes to town. I'd be happy to call around and see if I can find them."

I shook my head in amazement. She'd taken the news better than I had. "That would be great. Thanks."

"Three guys?"

"Two guys and a girl, actually."

"A girl?" Her eyebrows went up. "That should make it even easier."

We shared a bag of potato chips for lunch and watched *Aliens* on the overhead television. I kept an eye on the time. I didn't want to be there when her boss showed, didn't want her to think I was keeping Brit from work.

Reluctantly, I said, "I better go."

"All right."

Hand in hand, we walked to the door. We stood

in the open doorway, sunlight spilling around us. An updraft teased her hair. It looked violet in the bright light.

I slid my hands to her waist. "Thanks for listening."

She smiled. "Are you going out tonight?"

"Yeah. Uncle Bob wants to take me into the woods."

"Werewolf lessons, eh?" Her eyes sparkled. "Too bad your uncle didn't fess up earlier. He could've saved you some misery."

"You got that right," I murmured, increasingly aware of her nearness. I didn't want to let go.

She cupped my face in her hands, lifting her lips. My heartbeat quadrupled. We kissed. Not a friendly howdy-do. This was real. I wrapped my arms about her, pulling her close. She seemed to fit against me, her curves filling my empty spots. I squeezed my eyes tighter, falling into the warmth of her touch.

At last, she pulled away. "Bye," she said a little breathlessly.

"Bye."

I left the store smiling. This was a great day. Who would've thought that exile would be the best thing that ever happened to me? I grabbed my bike from against the wall.

There was a red Camaro in the parking lot. A really nice car. I remembered seeing it before. A man sat in the driver's seat, waiting for someone I guessed. I thought about pedaling over to him and telling him what a great ride he had.

Then I saw his eyes.

He stared as if appraising me. It was like he knew all my secrets, all my faults. A shiver ran through me. I turned away and headed home.

My thoughts were so full of Brittany and her kiss that the ride seemed to take no time at all. Before I knew it, I was coasting up the drive. I dumped my bike in its usual spot and climbed the porch steps. Something was tacked to the front door.

My stomach fell. It was my socks. The socks I'd lost in the woods that morning while running from a pack of murderous wolves.

# TWENTY-THREE

"Are you sure they're the same socks?" Uncle Bob stopped the truck.

We were in the forest again, but in a different area than the night before. The sun was setting, and I was itching to get out of my skin.

"Pretty sure," I said. "I can't imagine anyone nailing random socks to our door."

He folded his arms and stared out the windshield.

"What does it mean?" I asked.

He drew a long breath. "It's a warning. They're telling us they know who we are." I nodded, hoping for more. "They must've tracked our scents from the murder site to my fishing pond," he said. "I half expected that. But how did they follow us home? We were in the truck."

I frowned. "Can werewolves recognize each other when they are human?"

"Usually. Why?"

My cheeks heated. I felt stupid. "There's this guy. I've seen him twice. Both times, he gave me the willies. He stared at me like he hated me."

314

"Where at?"

"Brittany's work." And it hit me. He must've seen us kissing. If he wanted to get to me, it would be through her. My mouth went dry. "He drives a red Camaro," I mumbled. "It followed us around one day."

"Do you think he followed you home?"

"What does he want?"

"To recruit you, most likely. Get you to run with the pack. He won't want me. I'm too old. But once he finds out you can shift on command, he'll see you as a threat to his leadership. He'll kill you."

A quiver of panic twisted my stomach. It wasn't what he said so much as the matter-of-fact way he said it. "But if I don't join him, he won't find out. The pack will move on, right?"

"That's what we're hoping."

"There was wolf scent in Brittany's yard," I said.

He frowned. "It's probably nothing. Why would they be nosing around Old Man Meyer's place?"

"To get to me?"

"Nah. I wouldn't worry about it."

But I *was* worried. It was always at the back of my mind ever since the fortuneteller said I would sacrifice something.

It must have showed in my eyes, because after a while, he said, "If it will make you feel better, I'll call Howard, have him check on her."

"That's all right." What good would Howard be against three wolves?

315

"Okay. But remember what I said about him. If you need help and I'm not around, go to Howard. Even in wolf form."

*Howard knew?* I closed my eyes. I should have realized. "He called me *Mai-Coh*."

"It means shape shifter."

"So, Howard knows what I am. Anyone else?" If Anne the waitress knew, I was going to scream.

"No one on my side of things," Uncle Bob said. "How about you? I was there when Brittany found out. Anyone else?"

"Her brother. I was a wolf when I saved him from that gator."

"Well, let's keep it to a minimum. I like living here." He peered out the windshield. "Sundown. Anything you want to ask before we go out?"

"Yeah," I said, struck by a sudden thought. "Is it possible to shift while the sun's still up?"

"In daylight?" He laughed. "Where do you get such crazy ideas?"

"It isn't crazy. Day or night the moon's still there."

"Hold on. I didn't mean to rile you." He put a hand on my shoulder. "It would take a really powerful werewolf, you know? Someone with a strong sense of self. I've never heard of anyone trying it. But, who knows? Stranger things have happened."

🐕 🐕 🐕

It was great to have a companion that night. We chased deer. We ran through a sugarcane field. Fortunately, we didn't come across any more bodies.

At moonset, we dressed and drove home. Uncle Bob took a nap, but I couldn't sleep. I paced my room, thinking about the wolf pack and the threat they posed. It was bad enough the leader might want me dead. I couldn't stand to think they might hurt Brittany. I was so anxious it was all I could do to keep from pedaling to her house right then.

Around nine o'clock, I called her. She groaned. "You don't sleep at all, do you?"

"I thought you'd be getting ready for work."

"I don't have to be there until three today."

"Oh. Sorry I woke you."

She yawned. "That's all right. It's nice to hear your voice. How was your night?"

I leaned back on my pillow. "I ate a rabbit."

"Raw? Eeuw."

"It sounds gross now, but at the time it tasted really good."

"Well, while you were enjoying a rabbit dinner, I was calling in favors," she said. "There are three strangers staying at the Sunshine Motel. Two guys and a girl."

"Wow." My thoughts whirled. I wanted to drop the phone and run out there. "That's great, Brit. Thanks for finding them."

"Are you calling the sheriff?"

"Not without evidence."

"Don't you dare, Cody," she said as if reading my mind. "You stay away from them. They're dangerous."

"I won't let them see me."

"They might smell you or something. Who knows what they'll do. It's better if I go."

My heart flew up my throat. "Oh, no you don't. I don't want you anywhere near them."

"It's no big. My friend works the front desk. I'll visit her and see what I can dig up."

"Thanks but no thanks."

Her voice rose. "Then how are we going to find out about them?"

"Just don't go. Please."

Silence fell. She didn't promise to stay away, and I didn't share my plans with her. Because I intended to confront them, if only to prove I wasn't afraid. Maybe if they saw I wasn't an easy mark, they'd leave us alone.

After a few moments, she said, "I have another surprise for you. I've got all the ingredients for the potion."

I sat up. "You have?"

"Yep. Grandpa took in the last box yesterday. He asked me why I'm getting so many deliveries all of a sudden."

"That's... That's–" I stifled a whoop. Imagine if it really worked. Imagine if I could be a normal kid again.

"Did you tell your uncle what we're doing?"

"He wouldn't understand. He doesn't seem to mind being a wolf."

"Probably just as well." She sighed. "The problem now is how we make a magic circle. I know there are such things. I just can't find any instructions. I talked to some Wiccans, but they got all up in my face about it. Either it's some big secret or they really didn't know."

"Not to worry," I said, feeling important. "I found a book that tells all about them."

"Really? That's a relief." Her voice smiled. "Have you thought about where we should set up?"

"How about in the courtyard where you saw me shift? It's secluded. No one will bother us."

"Is it big enough?" she said. "I think we should have two circles like that book at the bookstore said. A fourteen-footer with a six foot circle inside."

"I'm sure the courtyard is more than fourteen feet across," I said, not sure at all.

"Want to go now and check it out?"

"I'll meet you there."

I closed the phone, excited to see her again. Not that I wanted to touch her or anything. I mean, I did, but just being with her was enough. To know she wanted to be with me. To know she was safe.

I crept to the kitchen, trying not to wake my uncle. There was a tape measure in the junk drawer—a fifty-footer with a metal loop at the end for staking. I even found a long screwdriver to use as a stake.

With the tools in my back pocket, I slipped out the

319

door. Warm breezes met me. No clouds. It hadn't rained in so long, the grass was starting to look and smell like straw.

I picked up my bike and rode to the street. Tonight was a full moon, and all my senses were turned up. It was like waking in a different world—the colors brighter, the smells more distinct.

I pulled out behind a blue SUV. It wasn't going particularly fast, and I kept up with it easily. Probably surprised the heck out of the driver. It would be hilarious if I passed a car on my bike. But my turn-off came before I had a chance.

Full of energy, I stood on the pedals and streaked down the old dirt road. A cloud of dust rose. By the time I reached the courtyard, I was panting, my legs tingling. I let out a loud howl, and it felt so good, I howled again.

Brittany hadn't arrived yet. I left my bike at the side of the road and pushed through the trees into the courtyard. The place felt familiar and comforting, like I'd come home. I stood in the center and closed my eyes. Birds sang, and baby birds peeped. The wind hissed through the treetops. But where I stood, the air barely stirred.

A car door slammed. Nose up, I sniffed. Brittany's scent came to me—her skin, her hair, the toast she ate in the car. I heard her tramp through the underbrush behind me.

"Hi," I said.

"Hi." She sounded surprised. "How did you know

it was me?"

I turned around and smiled. "Lucky guess." I wanted to tell her how good it was to see her, how empty I felt when she wasn't around. But that would sound too weird.

She dropped her eyes, and I realized I was staring at her.

"I was about to mark out our circles," I said. "Want to help?"

"Sure. What can I do?"

"We need two sticks."

She stepped back into the trees. I staked the tape measure with the screwdriver and pulled out seven feet worth of tape. Locking it in place, I stretched it out on the grass.

"Now what?" asked Brittany.

I took one of the sticks she handed me. "Here's what you need to know. There is magic all around us."

"I believe that."

"Good. So a magic circle creates a screen that traps the magical energy within it. If we do it right, nothing will be able to get in or out."

"Okay. How do we make one?"

"Using your stick, you draw a circle on the ground. But you have to focus on your purpose for drawing it. The shape needs to be as exact as you can get it. You make the smaller one, and I'll take the outside."

I got to my knees at the seven-foot mark, half of

the needed fourteen, holding my stick at the end of the tape measure.

She knelt at the three-foot mark. "I can't believe I couldn't find out how to do this. The Internet was useless. What book did you say you read?"

"It was a Harry Dresden book."

"Wait." Brittany looked at me. "Are you saying you're basing this on a novel?"

"He already did the research. I'm just building on his information. Scientists do that sort of thing all the time. Besides, it was a good book."

She shrugged and nodded.

Slowly, I moved the tape measure forward, scratching a furrow on the ground. As I worked, I muttered, "Magic potions. Magic circles. Makes you wonder if there really are wizards."

"Of course, there are," Brittany said. "And fairies. And the Loch Ness Monster. And I know a friend of a friend who actually saw Big Foot."

"Oh." I gaped at her. A lot of strange stuff happened lately, but I didn't think I would ever believe in Big Foot.

I continued drawing. At times, my mark seemed to disappear in the deep grass, but I didn't think it mattered. The intent was there. I concentrated on my need to trap a werewolf within.

When I finished, I sat back. We'd drawn two circles, one inside the other. Outside the larger one, the courtyard continued for another six feet.

I said, "It looks like a miniature crop circle."

"Now what?" asked Brittany.

"We have to invest it with a spark of energy to close the circuit," I said, quoting the book.

"What kind of energy? Fire? Electricity?"

"It didn't say."

"Well, that sucks." She stood, folding her arms and looking thoughtful.

I picked up the tape measure. "Pull that stake for me, will you? Be careful. The end's a little sharp."

Brittany stepped to the center and yanked out the screwdriver. "Ow!" she yelped, her finger in her mouth.

"You okay?" I asked as I reeled in.

She looked at a cut on her finger. "Blood. That's life energy." With her arm outstretched, she dripped a bit of blood onto the line she'd drawn.

There was an almost-audible pop. A prickling sensation washed over me, like I'd hit my funny-bone only all over.

"Cody." Brittany held her hands out like a mime. "I can't get out."

I chuckled, thinking she was joking, but stopped when I saw the panic on her face.

She sidestepped along the perimeter, making patting motions. "Help me!"

"Hold on." I hurried toward her, but as I reached the inner circle, I met a barrier. A silent and invisible tension filled the air. "I can't get through."

Her eyes filled with tears. "What am I going to do?"

I frowned. What would Harry Dresden do? "Break the circle." I scuffed out the line with my toe.

There came another pop, more sensed than heard, and a rush of movement like ghosts fleeing. I grasped Brittany's hand and pulled her toward me. She melted into my arms, trembling.

"You're safe," I said. "I've got you."

"That was scary."

"Yeah. But it worked."

She pulled away, looking at me, and the corners of her mouth twitched. "Too right, it did."

"All we need now is a witch's cauldron."

"It just so happens there's one in my car." She took my hand. "Let me show you."

We walked to her little *VW*. The trunk was larger than I expected. It held a variety of junk, including a black cauldron. Brittany motioned dramatically like she was practicing to be a magician.

"What do you think?" she said. "Is it perfect or what?"

"Nice job." I nodded.

The cauldron was about two feet across and looked to be cast iron.

Brittany drew out a purple backpack. "Let's set it up."

I puffed out my cheeks and set my feet. How would it look if I couldn't carry the thing? I put my arms around it and lifted with all my might.

The cauldron was light. So light that I overbalanced and nearly fell on my butt.

"It looks real, doesn't it?" Brittany giggled. "It's fiberglass. I got it at the garden shop."

"A planter? Won't it melt?"

"Nope. I asked the manager. It's fireproof, melt-proof, and everything-else-proof."

"Perfect." I motioned at her backpack. "Is that the stuff for the potion?"

"No, I left everything at home. I figure, we can't start the potion for another couple of weeks. We can't risk leaving the ingredients lying around. This is just a few things we might need—a big wooden spoon and a box of matches. I brought them to weigh down the cauldron."

"Good thinking," I said. "You know what would be cool? We should redo the circle and leave it running while we're gone. It will keep the raccoons out."

She smiled and crinkled her nose the way I always loved.

As the morning progressed, I began feeling ill with the flu-like symptoms I always got on a full moon. Around noon, Brittany left to get ready for work, and I went home. I didn't pedal as fast going back. As I pulled onto the driveway, I saw Uncle Bob sitting on the porch swing, reading the newspaper.

He looked up and smiled. "Where you been, boy?"

"Just out with Brittany." I clomped up the steps and leaned against the rail. "I thought you'd be finishing your chicken coop."

"It's Good Friday. People don't like a lot of noise."

"Which reminds me," I said, "Brittany invited me to Easter dinner. I hope that won't be a problem."

"Meeting the family. Sounds serious."

"It is, sir."

"Well, I hope you have a nice time." He folded his newspaper. "You free tonight?"

"Ah, yeah."

"Good. I'll take you somewhere special."

"Great," I said without emotion. "I'm looking forward to it."

I went into the house. My palms were sweaty, and I felt sick to my stomach. I splashed some water on my face. Then I pulled my laptop out from under my bed and checked the Yellow Pages on the Internet. The Sunshine Motel was near the new tattoo parlor in town. I must have passed it a hundred times and never noticed.

I thought about the three wolves. What made them kill? Uncle Bob said it was the thrill of the hunt. I thought they were insane. Rabid dogs.

A wave of nausea struck. With a groan, I fell back on my bed, covered in sweat and chilled in spite of the midday heat. I needed to sleep, but something told me to ride past the Sunshine Motel instead. I hadn't promised that I wouldn't go there, although I knew Brittany didn't want me to.

But I had to go. Someone had to stop the pack. I couldn't stand back and let them kill again. I would go to the motel. Not to confront them, just to let them know I was watching. Maybe they'd leave if they knew I was on to them.

I heard Uncle Bob clattering around in the kitchen. At the doorway, I said, "I'm going into town. Do you need me to pick up anything?"

"No, thanks." He looked at me. "You okay?"

"Just antsy. I have to get out for a while." I started to leave, but turned back. "You aren't like me. Sweating. Shaky."

"Over the years, I've become tolerant of the effects. I guess the body adapts. You should stop by Howard's. He has some tea that will calm your stomach."

Herbal tea with snake blood. I remembered. "Maybe I'll do that."

I went outside to my bike. The sun beat down in waves. Its glare was too bright. The racket of the birds was too loud. I flashed them a disgruntled look. Then I hopped on my bike and pedaled away as fast as I could. My thigh muscles burned. My blood surged. And for the first time I was glad Uncle Bob hadn't bought me a car. The bike was better. I needed the exercise.

It was shortly after three when I got to the Sunshine Motel. The building was yellow stucco with rusty sprinkler stains. Brown grass edged the front walkway, and scraggly hibiscus rimmed the parking lot. I leaned my bike against a light pole and crept forward for a better look.

The red Camaro was there.

At the uneven edge of asphalt, I stood and

scratched my head. What could I use as a calling card to let them know I was there? My socks. I could tack them to the door. That would be funny.

Behind me, a voice said, "You looking to steal my car?"

# TWENTY-FOUR

For a moment, I could only stare at the Camaro in the hotel parking lot. My stomach clenched, and I closed my eyes. I smelled the stranger behind me. Why hadn't I noticed the stink before now? He reeked of sweat and unwashed jeans, and something indefinable that I thought was the wolf in him. It made my arms prickle, like my hair was standing on end.

I hated that I'd been caught snooping, hated that I had to face him unprepared. Mostly, I was embarrassed that I'd let him sneak up on me. When would I learn to be more aware?

I turned. The man was about my height but more muscular. He had a thin mustache and long hair that hung in greasy waves. His eyes narrowed, and he smirked.

And just like that, my nervousness vanished. I don't know, maybe it was my inner wolf, but I felt instant anger. I narrowed my eyes and smirked right back. "If I took off in your car, would you chase it?"

"Oh, a dog joke. You are too funny."

"About as funny as a nail through my socks."

329

He chuckled. "Is that what this is about?"

I squared my shoulders. "You've been following me, sniffing around where you aren't wanted."

"Just looking for an introduction is all."

"Why?"

"You stand out in this town." He motioned around him. "You don't fit in. Thought you might like to join with me. See the world. My pack has an opening. You could be my right-hand man."

"I don't want anything to do with you. Murderer."

"Just women."

"No more. It's over. I want you and your friends gone."

"Or what?"

I tightened my fists. "I'll turn you in."

"What?" He sneered. "Over a few bodies? You can't be serious."

"Watch me."

"What's got you so domesticated? Is it that black-haired beauty at the video shop?"

"Leave her alone."

"Maybe I will and maybe I won't. You're the one who threw down the gauntlet." My back stiffened, and he stepped close. "See, here's what I think," he said, his rotten breath in my face. "You don't have a shred of proof to connect me to those kills."

"Maybe I don't. Then, again." I shrugged and lowered my voice. "You get pretty excited, ripping people up. Those little love nips you give your girlfriend can get pretty deep."

"She's not my girlfriend. She's my underling."

"You sure you left those crime scenes clean? No blood or other bodily fluids lying around? Nothing that the authorities could trace to you if someone told them where to look?"

He took a step back, fists clenched. "You don't want to mess with me."

"You're right. I don't want to know you at all. So take it elsewhere."

His dark eyes flared. For a moment, I saw the wildness behind them. Then he strode past me, crossed the parking lot, and went into one of the rooms. When the door slammed behind him, I let out a quavering breath.

Note to self—don't get into verbal confrontations during a full moon. What was I thinking, spouting off to him like that? It was as if the moon took control of my mouth.

I grabbed my bike and headed for home, my arms shaking with adrenalin overload. I was out of my mind, telling off a known murderer. He might have killed me, slashed my throat right there. Groaning, I replayed the conversation. How could I have made that joke about him being a dog chasing a car?

It took him by surprise, though. He didn't know what to make of me. He probably expected me to bow to him like one of his underlings. Pretty funny, actually. He'd think twice before wanting me to join his pack.

I couldn't believe how I stood up to him. Temporary insanity. In any case, it seemed to have worked. I doubted I'd see him again.

By the time I got home, I was laughing. The whole scene seemed funny. I wanted to brag about it, but since both Uncle Bob and Brittany wanted me to stay away from the pack, the only person I could tell was Butt Crack. Or maybe Howard. They weren't around.

Uncle Bob sat before the television, watching the evening news while balancing several cardboard cartons on his knees. He smiled as I came in. "Feeling better? I ordered Chinese."

I sat with him and ate *Moo Goo Gai Pan* and super-fried chicken wings. He showed me how to twist the wing to pull the bones out clean and pop the meat in my mouth. It tasted great. In fact, everything was great. I couldn't have been in a better mood.

"I thought we'd be a little adventurous tonight," Uncle Bob said.

"Yeah? What are we doing?"

"You'll see." He turned off the TV and stood.

I gathered the empty cartons, carried them to the kitchen, and dumped them in the garbage. Then I closed the bag and carried it to the can behind the shed, my unofficial chore. I felt strong and competent. I looked at the darkening sky, reaching with my senses to Mother Moon. Soon I would embrace her once again.

Uncle Bob waited for me at the truck. I got in and

opened the window. It was too nice an evening not to let the wind blow. I settled back, not even minding his lack of music.

He took back roads through fields of tangled scrub and pine. We passed a campground—a nice one with landscaped berths for the RVs. I remembered the old camper in Brittany's front yard and wondered if this was where Grandpa Earle took Butt Crack when Brit's family first moved down.

With my eyes half open, I breathed deeply. The air filled with mingled scents. Deer. Gator. Giraffe? I sat forward.

"Do you recognize where we are?" Uncle Bob asked.

I nodded. "We're near the safari park."

"That's right. Tonight's all about identifying scents. Not killing. We kill to eat. You've already had dinner."

"Gotcha." I bounced with excitement like a kid.

He turned down a road bordered by a rusted chain-link fence. There were coils of barbed wire at the top and *No Admittance* signs every few yards. Beyond the fence stretched a wide field. The grass was long and yellow with drought, dotted with islands of Australian pine.

I heard faraway parrots, peacocks, and monkeys chattering in three-part harmony. Then I heard a deep-throated roar. "The lions are hungry."

"Probably. They're fed in the morning. Nine-thirty sharp."

"How do you know that?"

"It's one of the attractions. Everyone wants to see a lion eat."

"Will we see lions tonight?"

"From a distance." He grinned at me. "We'll see lots of animals, although the handlers move most of them into pens for the night."

"Like cowboys on a cattle drive?"

"Around these parts, zookeepers use Jeeps to round them up. It's not a big deal. Animals are creatures of habit. They practically put themselves to bed. Take the giraffes, for example. Every day when it starts getting dark, they mosey down the trail to the barn and dinner. Pavlov's response."

"Sounds like a cushy life."

"I think they're well treated."

"But they're supposed to be wild. They're so domesticated," I said, wondering where I got that word.

"These are expensive animals," Uncle Bob said. "They need to be kept safe."

"From predators. Like us."

"Thieves, more likely."

I thought about it and nodded.

Ahead, I saw a dingy white van parked on the grass. Uncle Bob pulled behind it. I closed the window and jumped from the truck just as a woman climbed from the driver's seat of the van. The redhead I saw before.

She was of average height and bone thin with a mane of flyaway curls. Not particularly good-looking.

But when she saw my uncle, she smiled, and it transformed her face. She had a wide mouth, showing even her back teeth. It made her look friendly and easy-going.

Uncle Bob hurried me toward her. "This is my nephew, Cody. And this is Rita."

She turned her dazzling smile on me. "I'm happy to meet you, Cody."

I took the hand she offered, and a sense of otherness struck me. "Uh," I said with my usual wit. *She was a werewolf. A she-wolf.* I grinned, proud of myself for figuring it out so fast. I was getting pretty good at this. "Nice to meet you, too. Do you live around here?"

"Just passing through, I'm afraid." She motioned at the van, giving me the impression that she slept in back.

It's strange, but when I saw her with my uncle on the porch that night and thought she was moving in, I felt like she was an intruder. Now that I knew she was a wolf, I was happy to have her live with us. I would have said so, but it wasn't my place.

"Shall we?" Uncle Bob slipped his arm around her waist.

They walked to the fence. My uncle opened a slit in the chain link. It was so well disguised by the fence post, I hadn't noticed it. Rita crawled through on hands and knees, and I followed. My uncle came last, tucking the fence behind him so the hole vanished again.

I faced the stiff breeze and caught a nose full of exotic scents. This was going to be a great night. We walked together across the open field. I figured it was a sort of buffer zone between the zoo and the real world. Gnats and mosquitoes rose from the grass. Stars sprinkled the sky.

"It's almost here." Rita took my uncle's hand. "Can you feel it?"

I could. The moon was cresting the horizon. Its presence was a warm wash of water bathing me.

"Head in that direction." Uncle Bob pointed toward a group of trees.

We stepped up our pace. The copse formed a little island in a sea of grass. Dry palm fronds hung low, creating a shelter. A bird flew as we entered.

"I'll change over there." Rita's fingers slipped from my uncle's grasp. Her smile lit the darkness. "You can't expect me to disrobe in front of your young man."

"I don't mind," I stammered.

They chuckled, and my face went red. All I meant was I would have turned my back.

But she disappeared in the bushes. My uncle stripped off his shirt, so I did the same. I felt hair sprout from my knuckles.

"This isn't our usual spot," Uncle Bob said in a gravelly voice. "We'll have to remember where we left our clothes."

He shifted into a wolf almost before he got the last word out. I was aware of the wet, gloppy sound he made. It really was gross. I closed my eyes and allowed the moon to take me. My face stretched, and my legs twisted. The pain was excruciating—but only for a moment. When it was over, I shook myself from head to tail.

Uncle Bob lifted his leg against a tree, marking it. I thought it was a good idea. The scent would help us find our way back. But before I could follow his example, Rita stepped out of the bushes. Her coat was reddish, and her eyes were gold. She was more beautiful as a wolf than a human. Uncle Bob nipped her ear in greeting, and she nuzzled his chin.

I felt embarrassed. Pushing through the palm fronds, I left. Somewhere, the deer and antelope played. I headed toward their scent at a trot. After a moment, Rita and my uncle caught up. We came to another chain-link fence. It was three times as high as normal. On the other side, I saw a steep trench. Trees grew inside, but the gorge was so deep, all I could see were their tops.

A dirt road ran along the outside of the fence. It led to a padlocked gate. The gate was the only spot that didn't have barbed wire. The road passed through, built up like a bridge across the ravine.

Uncle Bob leaped twelve feet to the top of the gate and clambered over. Rita went next. Giving an inward shrug, I followed, surprised at my ability to jump so high. The dirt bridge had chains stretched over it, evidently to catch the hooves of wayward grass-feeders. We picked our way through it. And just like that we were on the savannah.

We romped over the dung-rich grass, scattering rabbits and armadillos. Bats crisscrossed the sky, feeding on moths. We came across a structure. It was whitewashed cinderblock on three sides; the fourth opened on several stalls. Inside, I saw a water buffalo with horns so wide I wondered how it lifted its head. Its nostrils flared as it turned cloudy white eyes toward us. Old and blind. I padded forward for a better look, but my scent gave me away. It kept its horns pointed at me whichever way I moved.

We continued across the preserve, meeting more roads. One carried the stench of fuel, and I knew that a vehicle had passed recently. Zookeepers or security guards. It reminded me there were humans in the park.

At a water trough, antelope and impala milled about. Another structure stood nearby. Evidently, each pavilion had its own paddock away from the public eye. This one was empty. Perhaps grass grazers were last on the zookeepers' nightly lists.

As we approached, the animals grew skittish. They took off, and we gave chase, barking and nipping their heels. They didn't run so much as bounce, touching down lightly and leaping in a different direction. I laughed as I herded them. Their hearts thundered as loudly as their hooves. Foam flecked their mouths, and their eyes rolled.

They ran far from the structure meant to house them for the night. The zookeepers would have fun trying to round them all up again.

We continued exploring. Here, the trees wore chain-link coats to protect their bark. Many hooves pockmarked the dry ground. I smelled giraffe and knew this was the trail leading to their barns. I wished I could see them, but they were tucked in for the night.

We came to another ravine and a dirt bridge lined with chains. I hated the chains. I tripped and stumbled across. My arrival must have startled an ostrich because she hissed and kicked at me. We took turns goading her and having her chase us about. Finally, we let her run us off.

We were in rhino country. We found several of them in a cinderblock paddock munching lettuce, quite content to ignore us. I wondered if they'd be so complacent in the wild.

Beyond them, we saw the lion pavilion. They were also housed in cells. There was no getting near them. Another gorge surrounded the pavilion, and the road had two gates, too close together to jump individually and too far apart to jump as one. I had to content myself with watching them from across the ravine. They roared at me and paced in challenge, their eyes glinting in the dark.

We left the outlands, approaching the heart of the theme park. Sidewalks led us through an area with concrete dinosaurs. I saw a Ferris wheel, a carousel, and a lake with pontoon boats. We found an island with chimps and another with gibbons. They made a terrible racket as we neared. I was afraid a human would hear. They continued to scream even after we moved away.

The petting zoo used a double gate system to keep the goats and sheep from wandering out. A familiar cinderblock building stood inside. Its doors were open, the animals not yet bedded down for the night. When they saw us, they hurried inside the structure of their own accord. They bleated pitifully, huddling together and staying as far from us as they could.

The wind was in my face, carrying with it their mingled scents. I realized that terror had a distinct smell. I didn't like it. I wanted to go back to the savannah and chase the antelope. Turning around, I saw three werewolves slinking toward us. They showed their teeth and moved in a crouch as if ready to spring. I growled a warning to Rita and Uncle Bob, but the gibbons were making so much noise I doubted anyone heard me.

The wolves had us on three sides, the petting zoo at our back. I planted my feet and lowered my head, picking out the pack leader and locking his gaze. Uncle Bob barked, finally realizing something was up. He stood on one side of me, Rita on the other.

The six of us stared, growling. A standoff. The sheep bleated, and the gibbons screamed. I wanted to run or fight, wanted to do something, anything but just stand there. At a yip from her leader, the female vaulted the double fence into the petting zoo. The animals cried out, trying to hide, but their stall was too small for them to get away. The wolf grabbed a lamb in her jaws, snapping its neck. She shook it, nearly severing the head.

The other two wolves paced as if to keep us from leaving. I couldn't imagine why. A rumble rose in my throat. I would not stand by while this she-wolf slaughtered the helpless. This was not the thrill of the hunt. There was no sport in killing penned sheep.

My hackles rose, and I bared my teeth. I stepped forward, focusing on the leader's throat.

Then a human shouted, "Hey."

In an instant, I realized why they were keeping us there. The pack leader wanted us to be seen. If wolves were known to be in the area, no one would believe me if I said humans killed those women.

I heard another shout and the shot of a gun. We scattered, running in all directions. I was scared I would become separated from Uncle Bob, but after a moment, he pulled alongside with Rita close behind.

We ran the way we'd come, back toward the savannah. A voice inside warned that it was a bad idea. If the humans took a vehicle, they would easily run us down.

There came a distant shot. Rita yelped.

I glanced over my shoulder to see her tumbling. I slowed, barking, afraid to stop, afraid not to. Seconds later, she was up again, running full out, catching up.

I didn't see the other three werewolves. Maybe they'd run the other way into the parking lot. Like we should have done instead of heading deeper into the park grounds.

Another shot, and a bullet whizzed past my head. Its high-pitched whine left my ear ringing. I ducked and dodged, wondering how to get out of this. We reached the first dirt bridge. I leaped, soaring over it, barely touching the chains. Rita had more difficulty. Uncle Bob went back for her, barking encouragement as she stumbled across the ravine. Her coat glistened with blood from her wound.

I watched them, my muscles trembling, wanting to flee. At last, they picked up their pace. I turned, taking point.

I smelled rhino. The ground was pounded flat. Trees were widely spaced. Lions roared in the distance. They wanted out of their cells. I wished they could get out, too. They'd make a great diversion. I urged Rita into a trot and led across the dusty land.

About halfway across, I heard a Jeep. For half a heartbeat, I froze, crushed by hopelessness. I looked back at bobbing headlights. A searchlight speared the darkness, glancing off the trees. It hit me full in the face. The world went white.

"There," yelled a human.

The motor roared.

I scrambled away, following my companions, my

legs coiling beneath me as I pushed for more speed. Ahead, I smelled the savannah.

My uncle angled toward the bridge between the pavilions. He and Rita were across before I got there. I hurdled over the barrier of chains, but misjudged and came down badly. My hindquarters slipped over the edge into the gorge, and for a moment, events of my life flashed before me just like in the movies.

I clung with my front legs, clawing the dirt, trying to lever myself up. Uncle Bob barked and whined, lamenting in wolf talk that he didn't have a hand to grab me. I kicked with my back legs, practically running up the steep slope. Gaining purchase, I clambered to the top, landing with a woof, and then stumbled across.

The Jeep rode over the chains like they weren't there. I ran, and the humans kept right beside me. The tires rumbled. We startled a half-dozen antelope. They galloped through the headlights, forcing the vehicle to veer.

My uncle appeared at my side, pacing me, urging me to run faster. I concentrated on my rhythm, letting my paws eat the distance. A shot rang out and puffed in the dirt before us. I glanced at the car. A passenger aimed a rifle, weaving in his thrashing seat as he pointed the thing at me.

My heart nearly stopped. I smelled terror in my sweat, just like the sheep in the petting zoo, and it made me angry. I was not a penned animal. Taking a lesson from the antelope, I added bounce to my stride. But instead of touching lightly and bounding away, I sprang into the Jeep.

I intended to hit the man with the rifle, but landed on the driver instead. My weight flattened him. As he fell to the side, he pulled the steering wheel with him. The engine gunned, and the car swerved and flipped.

The next thing I knew, I was flying. I hit the grass and rolled for what felt like fifty yards. I tried to remember how to breathe. Rita licked my face, bringing me to my senses. I staggered to my feet, looking at the overturned Jeep. Its wheels spun. The humans stirred. I saw the rifle.

Uncle Bob nipped my ear, and the three of us were off once more, running as fast as we could toward the back gate. I reached the bridge first, soared over the chains, and bounded twelve feet to the top of the fence. In an instant, I was over.

Favoring her front leg, Rita followed. She got over the bridge, but when she tried to leap the fence, she hit halfway up. With a yelp, she slid to the ground. Fresh blood oozed from her shoulder. Uncle Bob barked at her, and she barked back. I didn't know whether to wait or go. I paced, whining. She backed up and jumped again, getting nowhere near the top. Blood streaked the chain-link. She scrabbled, trying to climb, then fell again.

I thought I heard voices.

Her ears perked. She backed up past the bridge. With her head lowered, she streaked forward. She hurdled the barrier chains as I had, and sprang at the gate, hitting the top with one paw over. Struggling, she got her legs beneath her and jumped down to me.

I was so relieved I licked her face. I actually felt my tail wag. Uncle Bob sailed over, and we were together once more, running through the open field.

Rita limped beside me. I knew by her ragged breathing that she was in pain. My uncle ran in a zig-zag manner, searching for our clothes. My initial thought was to leave them. All I wanted was to get home.

But we couldn't drive naked through town. I circled about the dry grass, trying to pick up our scents. I mean, he'd peed on a tree, for cripe's sake. It shouldn't be hard to find.

After several minutes, I caught our trail and led the others to the copse where we'd left our things. But something was wrong. It smelled of wolf. Other wolf. I ducked under the palm fronds. The stench was stronger. The pack had been there.

Our clothes were gone.

Uncle Bob burst into the shelter. His eyes glowed in the dark. We stood for a moment, trying to read each other's thoughts. Then he barked and bounded away. I followed.

He hurried us forward. I saw the fence that bordered the road. Beyond it was Rita's van and my uncle's truck. It was a couple hours before dawn. The moon was setting. It burned like fire.

345

*Just let me get to the truck.*

Rita whimpered. She collapsed, twitching like she was having convulsions. Her muzzle flattened. Fingers grew from her paws. I turned to see my uncle, now a man on his hands and knees.

I could have held my shape a little longer, but there was no point in fighting it. Braced against the pain of my repositioning limbs, I shifted back to my human form. Sweat coated my skin. I got to my feet.

Rita lay motionless. Her body was smooth and slender, like in the magazines.

My uncle leaned over her, feeling her neck. "Get the fence for us," he told me.

I knew I shouldn't stare, but I couldn't help myself.

"Cody," Uncle Bob snapped.

I hobbled away, sticks and stones biting my bare feet. When I reached the slit in the chain link, I looked back. Uncle Bob got Rita up, helping her walk.

"Just a scratch," she mumbled.

I held the fence open and watched her crawl through. My uncle followed. When I got to the other side, I saw Rita leaning against the truck, completely unconcerned that she was naked. She picked at her shoulder.

"See?" she murmured, sounding wobbly. "The bullet just grazed me. The edges are healing."

My uncle jabbed his finger at me. "First aid kit next to the toolbox." He ran along the van and wrenched open the driver's side door.

I vaulted into the truck bed. The toolbox was large and padlocked. Next to it was a variety of stuff—a couple of fishing poles and a tackle box, a Walgreens bag with some candy wrappers and empty Coke cans, and a blue button-down work shirt that looked like it had been used as a rag. I put it on.

Underneath everything was a white case with a red cross on top. I grabbed it and hopped down from the truck just as my uncle burst out of the back of Rita's van. He handed her a pair of cut-off shorts. She bent over, stepping into the jeans, pulling them slowly over her thighs.

I looked away, my cheeks growing hot, and opened the case. I was in love with Brittany. I didn't need to watch anyone else get dressed, especially someone old enough to be my mother. Almost.

"Bring that kit over here," Uncle Bob said. I set it on the hood of the truck. He disinfected the wound and taped a wad of gauze over it. "It isn't bad."

"Told you," she said.

"I'd still like to have Howard look at it."

"I don't want to go there. He always talks me into buying something." She glanced around. "Where's my blouse?"

He helped her slip it on. Instead of buttoning it, she tied it closed.

Uncle Bob looked in the back of his extended cab. He brought out jeans and a T-shirt along with a ratty pair of work boots.

"I don't have anything for you," he told me.

347

"Look in my van," Rita said.

With a determined nod, I climbed inside. Pillows and a mattress took up most of the floor. Boxes sat to either side, filled with everything from bathing suits to parkas. Apparently, Rita was prepared for all climates. But there was nothing large enough to fit me.

As I rummaged around, I heard the crunch of approaching tires. A car stopped outside the van. My eyes widened, and I crouched on Rita's bed.

"Good morning, Deputy," Uncle Bob said.

# TWENTY-FIVE

My stomach sank. Why was the sheriff's department here? All I needed was to be found in the
back of a woman's van wearing a smelly work shirt
that barely covered my behind.

I knelt among the boxes, trying to look inconspicuous. Wind puffed through the open back door,
chilling my sweaty face. I stared outside. Rita still
leaned against Uncle Bob's truck. Neither the deputy
nor my uncle could be seen. Their voices came from
the side of the van.

"Car trouble, Mister Nowak?" the deputy asked.

"Night fishing," my uncle said. "Pond's about half
a mile in the woods there."

"Catch anything?"

"Nothing we kept."

"How long you been here?"

"Got here around, oh...three o'clock." Uncle Bob's
voice shifted like he'd looked around at Rita.
"Wouldn't you say, honey?"

"Sounds about right," she said.

The deputy said, "Ma'am, you're bleeding."

349

I tensed, holding my breath. How would we explain a gunshot wound?

But she just motioned nonchalantly at her shoulder. "Yeah, wouldn't you know it? The stupid hook swung around and caught me in the shoulder. I'm going to need a Band-Aid."

"Humph," said the deputy.

"Anything we can help you with, sir?" my uncle asked.

"Have you seen any dogs?"

"No."

"How about people?"

"Only you. Why?"

"A pack of animals got onto the preserve. Jamie Miller says there were six of them. Biggest dogs he ever saw. They killed a lamb and a couple of antelope."

Rita gasped. "That's awful."

"How could dogs get in there?" Uncle Bob asked.

"That's the question, isn't it?" the deputy said. "I can't see how they *could* get inside. Not without help."

"Are you saying a person—"

"Unusual is all. Animals can't get out but dogs can get in? Anyway, it's not safe. Not with dogs around learning to kill, maybe on command."

"What do you mean?" Rita asked. "You think these dogs are, like, murder weapons?"

"It's an ongoing investigation. Best you don't loiter out here," he said. "Go on home."

His boots scuffed the rocky road. Uncle Bob's face appeared at the back of the van. He gave me a look that clearly said *keep your head down*. The doors slammed. Out the windshield, I watched the deputy's car pull away.

"I'll drive," my uncle said. "We'll leave my truck here."

"Don't be silly," Rita said. "I'm fine."

"You shouldn't be moving that arm."

"Don't baby me. I hate that."

"All right," he said, closing her door. "I'll follow."

She started the van. The engine ran rough. She had trouble fastening her seatbelt, so I reached around and snapped it. Pain radiated from her like an aura. I wished my uncle were driving.

We pulled off the grass and headed home at walking speed. The deputy's cruiser sat on the side of the road. He stood outside it, copying down the license plate of a parked car.

The red Camaro.

I sat back, shutting my eyes. I was an idiot. I hadn't warned the pack leader away. I'd made him angry. It was a good thing I hadn't told anyone that I'd gone to see him.

Rita reached to the passenger seat and produced a cassette tape. I didn't know they made them anymore. She put it in the player, and after a moment, Carole King's Greatest Hits filled the van.

She was my mother's favorite singer. I thought of Mom driving down the street with the top down and

351

that scarf she always wore flapping in the breeze, singing along with her tunes, embarrassing the heck out of me. Sudden tears burned my eyes. I tried to shut out the music, but it was no use. I found I knew all the words.

By the time we got to my uncle's house, I smelled blood. Rita parked on the grass then slumped over the wheel. I squeezed between the seats until I leaned over her. She was out cold.

My uncle wrenched open her door. His face fell. "Undo her belt for me."

I hit the latch, and we untangled her from the straps. She groaned but didn't complain. Uncle Bob lifted her and carried her toward the house. I jumped out of the van, hurried around them, and opened the front door.

Rita was pale and motionless. Her blouse was soaked through. Uncle Bob set her on the recliner. He untied her blouse and removed the bloodied bandage.

I stood in the doorway, staring. This was all my fault. If I hadn't riled the pack, none of this would have happened.

A truck rattled up the driveway. It was Howard. My uncle must have called him on his cell. He got out carrying a cardboard box.

"I see Aunt Fanny is here," he said as he passed me.

"Huh?" At first, I thought he meant Rita, but then I realized that he was referring to the too-short work shirt. Embarrassment rose in a hot wave. But as all my important parts were covered, I ignored him. Motioning at the box, I said, "What's all this?"

"My first aid kit." He grinned. "Why don't you put a big pot of water on to boil?"

I nodded and went into the kitchen. We didn't have a big pot. I remembered the mess I made cooking spaghetti in a skillet for Brittany. After a moment's indecision, I filled a cereal bowl with water and popped it into the microwave.

While it heated, I went back into the living room. Howard dabbed yellow goo onto Rita's wound. Behind him, Uncle Bob paced. His gray hair stood straight up from the many times he ran his hands through it.

"Will she be okay?" I asked.

"We need to keep her still," Howard said. "Whose idea was it to let her drive the van?"

"Whose do you think?" my uncle said.

"Do you have a clean bed sheet? Something we can cut into strips?"

"You can use mine," I said. I hated those Scooby sheets.

"He said clean," my uncle muttered as he brushed past me.

I'd never seen him so upset. The microwave dinged, and I went in to check the water. It wasn't hot enough, so I put it in for another couple of minutes. Then I went to my room and grabbed a pair of sweat pants from the dirty clothes pile.

When I returned to the living room, Uncle Bob was removing Rita's blouse while Howard cut the sheet with what looked like a bowie knife. But he didn't use the strips to bandage Rita's shoulder. He crossed her left arm over her breasts and then tied it there, wrapping the lengths of bed sheet around her chest until she looked part mummy. The wound was in the open. It looked grisly–yellow goop mixed with fresh red blood.

"Do you want the water?" I asked.

"No, I'll make the tea in there." Howard straightened, stretching his back. He looked at me. "How's your ear?"

I frowned, taken aback. "It's ringing a bit."

"Let me take a look." He touched the side of my head. "Ah. The bullet just nicked you."

"What?" I yelped, cupping my hand over my ear.

He grinned at my uncle. "You can't wake a person who is pretending to be asleep."

Maybe he thought I was purposely being dense. But honestly, I didn't realize I'd been shot. I swayed, feeling faint, realizing how close I'd come to having my head blown off.

Howard dragged over the kitchen chair I kept by the television. "Sit down. I'll clean it."

I sank onto the chair, thinking the last time I sat there I was eating Chinese food and laughing, feeling invincible. "How did this happen?"

"You'll live," Howard said. "You will always have a notch, though."

Great. The kid with the notched ear.

He gently cleaned the wound then swabbed it with the yellow ointment. It smelled rancid and stung as bad as vinegar on a paper cut. When he finished, he carried his box into the kitchen to make tea. Moments later, I heard his quiet chant.

Uncle Bob sat on the arm of the recliner. He stroked Rita's hair, murmuring something to her. She looked peaceful, like she was asleep.

"So, is she your girlfriend?" I asked.

"Rita is my mate. Going on fifteen years."

"Why don't you live together?"

"We used to." He gave her a sad smile. "But she is more of a wanderer, and I wanted to settle. She visits me off and on, and I'm always glad to see her."

I pulled the chair nearer, my mouth dry, thinking of Brittany. "Do werewolves only mate with other werewolves?"

"Most do. Some never mate at all. It's a hard life, always looking over your shoulder, always broke."

"Broke?"

"You can't keep a job missing work every month."

"I wanted to be a doctor when I grew up."

"Well, it's possible, but I won't lie to you. It would be tough. I'm fortunate to have learned a trade where I can be my own boss. I could have joined one of the communes in the Appalachians. Of course, they give up their identity to the pack. It's not for me."

Howard came out of the kitchen. "Let's see if we can get her to drink some of this."

355

I gave him my seat. He called Rita's name, holding a mug to her lips. Her eyes fluttered, and she swallowed a couple of mouthfuls.

"That'll do." He set the mug on the floor. "Every thirty minutes. You know the drill."

"Let's go out front so she can rest," Uncle Bob said.

I followed them to the porch. Howard pulled out a pack of cards. "Rummy, anyone?"

"I can't. I've got to figure this out." My uncle jammed his fingers into his hair, pacing again.

"Okay." Sighing, Howard sat on the steps. "You say the pack knew where you were. They followed you."

"They wanted us to be blamed," Uncle Bob said.

"But before they went into the park, they stole your clothes?"

"It was a prank." I leaned against the railing. "We'll find our things buried in a shallow grave."

"Cody, think," Uncle Bob snapped. "This whole thing was a set-up. You heard the deputy. Wild dogs couldn't possibly get on the preserve by themselves. A human had to let them in. Which means they weren't wild at all, but attack dogs on a training run."

I shrugged. "So?"

"So what's to stop the pack from murdering another woman and leaving our clothes at the scene?"

My jaw dropped, and my blood went cold. They wouldn't do that, would they? Just because I threatened to turn them in? All of a sudden, my head swam. I felt my back slide down the rail until I sat on the porch.

"What I can't figure out is why," Uncle Bob said. "I've had no contact with them. Why be so vindictive?"

*My fault. I did it. I pushed until they pushed back.*

"What will you do?" Howard asked my uncle.

"Working on it."

"I think you should give thanks that the three of you survived."

Uncle Bob snorted.

Howard chuckled, shaking his head. "Beware the man who does not talk, and the dog that does not bark."

"The pack needs to realize it's time to move on."

"How will you do that?"

Again, my uncle didn't answer. His jaw worked like he was chewing something distasteful.

"The frog does not drink up the pond in which he lives."

Uncle Bob scowled. "What does that mean?"

"You have a good life here. Don't screw it up."

I groaned. I didn't mean to involve Uncle Bob, didn't mean to mess up his life.

"You look as green as my frog," Howard said.

"I'm feeling..." I buried my face in my hands.

"That's it. Time for bed." My uncle took me by the shoulders and pulled me up.

"No, I can't," I mumbled. "I have to—" *Do something. I have to make it right.*

Roxanne Smolen

"Whatever it is, you can do it after you sleep."

He supported me as I stumbled into the house and down the hallway. I sat on my bed, my head fuzzy.

Howard came in and put a hot mug in my hands. "Half now, half later."

I drank. It hit my stomach like a lead fist. I didn't even know when my head hit the pillow.

🐕 🐕 🐕

I awoke to my cell phone buzzing next to my head. I wanted to toss it out the window and go back to sleep, but I saw it was Brittany.

"Good morning," I said.

"It's lunchtime, Cody."

"Oh." I rubbed my eyes. "What's up?"

"You weren't, by any chance, in the safari park last night, were you?"

"Why? What did you hear?"

"Some animals were slaughtered, and there was a car wreck. It's all over the news."

"I didn't kill anything," I said. "It was *them*. They followed us inside."

"I believe you."

"They took our clothes. I have to get them back."

"Where are you?" she asked. "Wait for me, and I'll bring you something to wear."

"That's not the point. I can't let them have anything that belongs to us. It's really important."

"All right," she drawled. "Where do you think they stashed them?"

"I'm still trying to figure that out."

"I bet they have them in their motel room. I could—"

"No! I don't want you involved. These people are dangerous."

"Stealing clothes makes them dangerous?"

"Diabolical."

"Okay, then," she said with an obvious shrug. "I was calling to remind you about dinner tomorrow. You're still coming, right?"

"Dinner?"

"Easter?"

"Oh, yeah, yeah," I said. "What time?"

"Dinner's at three because Mom doesn't want us to go to bed with a full stomach. So I thought I'd pick you up at two if you have nothing else to do. We can make it earlier if you want, but it can't be later because my mom will freak if I don't help out."

"Two is fine." I smiled at the rush of information. "See you then."

I crawled out of bed and tugged the box of rich-boy clothes out of my closet. I hadn't gone through them since my parents sent them to me weeks ago. I pulled out a yellow-striped shirt and a pair of brown dress slacks. My good shoes were at the bottom of the box. I also found my old pair of Adidas. Since my shoes had been stolen along with my clothes, I grabbed them as well.

I hung up the shirt, hoping the wrinkles would smooth out before dinnertime tomorrow. In the living room, News at Noon blared from the TV. My ears perked at the word dog.

"The dogs were huge," a man told the reporter. "Like prehistoric huge. One of them flipped my Jeep. I'm okay, but my buddy has a busted leg."

"Would you say they were wild dogs, Mister Miller?"

"No, ma'am, I would not. First off, they were organized. When I shot at them, they split up and ran in two different directions as if trained to do that. They didn't scatter like normal animals. Also, their tails were short and stumpy like they'd been bobbed, maybe for identification purposes."

"Are you saying these blood-thirsty animals have an owner?"

"Absolutely. They are smart, bred for size, and nasty as the day is long. And someone must have ordered them into the paddock. No way could they get inside unless someone was able to let them in."

"Did you see anyone, Mister Miller?"

"No, but that don't mean they weren't under someone's control. For instance, a micro-transmitter might be placed under the skin."

Rita laughed, breaking into the newscast. "No one's putting a micro-transmitter under *my* skin."

I was glad to hear her voice. She sounded better. I knew I should go out and say hello, but I wasn't ready to have a conversation. Quietly, I shut my door. Sitting on the bed, I thought about the night before.

I was changing. Instead of dreading the shift, I had looked forward to becoming a wolf, even called the moon my mother. That couldn't be good.

Brittany was right. The wolf *was* affecting my human side. For the first time, I wondered if the magic circle would hold me. Maybe I should have a backup plan—like a leash. I gnawed my lip then told myself to forget it. The whole potion thing happened on the new moon, and that was two weeks away. I had other problems.

Like where did the pack stash our clothes? Brittany thought they took them back to their motel, but I didn't think so. The moon had risen, so they had to be wolves, not humans, when they found our things. It would be difficult for them to carry anything.

Of course, they didn't have to take the clothes far, just move them from where we expected them to be. I'm sure the leader intended to pick them up afterward. But he couldn't. Not with deputies patrolling the streets. He couldn't even get his car.

No, my original idea that the clothes were buried nearby was much more likely. All I had to do was retrieve them before the leader could. Then he wouldn't be able to use them against us.

On hands and knees, I rummaged through my cluttered closet. I pulled out the Scooby Doo backpack that my uncle had bought me for school but I never used because why would I? Staring at it, I

361

chuckled, finally getting the joke. Uncle Bob knew I was a werewolf all along. No wonder he kept buying me things with dogs on them. I slung the bag on my back and climbed out my bedroom window.

I considered taking my bike, but two things stopped me. For one, my bike was in the front yard. I couldn't risk my uncle catching me and telling me not to go. I might circumvent the rules at times, but I was never one to disobey a direct order.

The other thing was it would be easier to keep out of sight if I was on foot. The safari park was a few miles away over rough terrain, not an easy trek for a normal person.

But I wasn't normal.

I took off through the woods, surefooted as a deer. The sun was high and searing as I burst in and out of shade. I crossed empty two-lane blacktops and dirt roads, following the scent of giraffe and gibbon instead of landmarks.

Nearer the park, the stench of exhaust overwhelmed that of animals. Cars lined up three wide waiting to get into the place. Apparently, the loss of an antelope or two hadn't hurt attendance. Perhaps everyone was hoping for a glimpse of the super-intelligent killer dogs.

I kept to the outlying woods as I made my way toward the back. Two deputies stood at the Camaro. Their cars were on the grass, lights flashing. I crouched in the bushes, watching, when a large tow-truck, its own lights flashing amber, pulled alongside.

*That should keep them busy.*

I continued moving until I was across from the slit in the fence. The field beyond looked sparse in the daylight. I gazed toward the deputies, hoping I was too far away for anyone to notice me.

With my jaw tight and my stomach in knots, I darted across the road, slammed through the fence, and sprinted to the nearest clump of trees. I expected to hear shouts of protest, but all I heard was the clank of chains and the whine of the truck's winch.

I leaned against a tree trunk, heart racing, trying to sharpen my senses. I smelled the drought-dry grass, two rabbits, and an armadillo. After a moment, I picked up the smell of wolf. If I could have walked around openly, I would have tracked individual scents. But I had to be discreet.

The deputies laughed with the driver. There came a great clatter as the Camaro was hoisted onto the bed. Under cover of the distraction, I ran for the next island of trees. I needed to find the place where we'd shifted. That would be my starting point.

I peered from my shelter. We'd walked in a straight line. I glanced back at the fence, cutting a path with my eyes. Far ahead, I saw the copse—the same drooping palm fronds, same vine-strangled bushes. I caught the spoor my uncle left behind.

It was the right place. But how would I get to it?

I gazed at the road. The truck driver was on his knees as he worked to secure the Camaro. One of the deputies stood with his back to me, talking to him. The other got in his car.

*No time like the present.*

Bent low, I ran flat out for the little copse. It was farther than I expected. I was in the open for several moments. By the time I reached the trees, I was panting. I burst into the shelter.

At first, I only caught our smells. Then I scented the others. Three wolves. As I figured, they were not human when they entered. That would limit how far they got with the clothing. I peeked through the branches at my surroundings.

With a final clank, the tow-truck assimilated the car. The truck pulled away, and a deputy followed, lights still flashing.

But the other stayed. What was he doing? Paper-work? A phone call? Whatever it was, it took too long. Despite my need to stay hidden, I stepped out of the shelter, keeping my back to the trees. I felt as if eyes were upon me. I hoped I was wrong.

Nose twitching, I located the scents of the three pack members. They'd circled the copse several times, but then they went to the right. I narrowed my eyes, searching. A truck with *Animal Control* printed on its side jangled down the dirt road. The driver pulled next to the deputy, and they held a window-to-window conversation.

Crouched, I stepped into the open, following the trail. But there was nothing.

*Where did they put the clothes?*

Fingers of panic tightened about my throat. I was going to get caught. For nothing. The clothes were gone.

Another patrol car cruised down the road. This one was the sheriff himself. The big man. I flattened, hoping the grass was tall enough to camouflage me, and came nose-to-nose with a jackrabbit under a rotting tree limb.

And just like that, I found them.

Our clothes were tucked beneath the branch and partway into the rabbit hole. I only saw them because I was on my stomach. Couldn't smell them because the rabbit scent was so strong. In fact, the rabbit hadn't run at my approach. Maybe she had young ones inside.

I glanced over my shoulder. The Animal Control truck took off, but the sheriff and his deputy sat side-by-side, their cars pointed the other way. Still on my stomach, I slipped off the backpack and stuffed the clothes into it. Everything was there; even our shoes. I zipped it shut then half-ran, half-scuttled back to the shelter of the trees.

Relief struck me. We were saved. The werewolves couldn't use the clothing against us. And Uncle Bob wouldn't get into a confrontation with them because of something I shouldn't have done.

I gazed through the trees. The deputy pulled his car off the grass and led the sheriff away. Now was my chance. With the bulging bag cradled in my arms like it was made of gold, I sprinted across the open field. I shimmied through the slit in the fence and bent the chain link back in place.

At last, I was on the roadside. I wanted to whoop and laugh. It didn't matter if the sheriff's department caught me now. No one could say anything against a boy walking around with a load of laundry.

The wind gusted at my back, bringing with it the scents of antelope and hay. I breathed deeply, figuring I wouldn't be back this way for a long time.

Suddenly, the sensation of being watched intensified. Across the road, in the shadows of the tree line stood three tall silhouettes.

*The werewolves.*

My heart nearly stopped. I couldn't move. I'd done all the work for them, taken all the risk, and now they would just collect the package. It wasn't fair. It made me angry.

I straightened my shoulders and slung the bag onto my back. It would hamper me in a fight, but I didn't want them to just walk up and take it. With my fists clenched, I faced the watchers.

*Here I am. Come and get me.*

The leader stepped forward, still in the shadow of the trees. His mustache twitched in a sneer. I knew he wouldn't let this challenge to his authority slide. Not in front of the others. He was going to let me have it.

Maybe even kill me.

I couldn't run. Wouldn't get far, in any case. I was

doomed. I only wished I had the chance to tell Brittany how I felt.

The leader flexed his fingers. As if on cue, his two underlings spread out. The woman was blonde. Her face looked hard, like she never smiled. The man was tall and paunchy. I tensed, trying to keep my eye on all three. But before they could rush me, a car rattled down the road.

Brittany in her lime-green Volkswagen.

"Hi," she said as she leaned to open the passenger door. "Fancy meeting you here."

I hopped inside. "Go!"

At the same instant, the pack leader leaped onto the car, hitting spread-eagled on the windshield. Brittany screamed and punched it. I grabbed the wheel. The car veered back and forth, but the leader had a good hold. We couldn't shake him.

Still screaming, Brittany slammed on the brakes. We went from sixty to zero in three seconds. The leader flew for twenty feet then rolled over and over in a cloud of dust. Brittany shifted into reverse and floored it again. We shot backward. Briefly, I saw the other two werewolves staring slack jawed.

The car skidded and turned. Brittany manhandled it until it faced forward, and we sped away from the safari park and the werewolves.

I turned in my seat, relieved to see that they weren't pursuing us.

"Oh God, oh God," Brittany cried, visibly shaking. She kept looking in the rearview mirror. "I didn't think they would get here so soon."

"What do you mean?"

She turned onto the two-lane blacktop doing fifteen over the speed limit.

After a moment, she said, "I did something you aren't going to like. I went to the Sunshine Motel. The plan was I would search their room while the housekeeper tidied up. Only they were there. All three of them. Sleeping. When she opened the door, that guy, the one who jumped on our car, he woke up. He looked right past her. Right at me."

"Why do that? You know I didn't want—"

"Finding the clothes was important to you. So it was important to me," she said. "Unfortunately it didn't work out. I decided to drive around the park instead. I didn't exactly expect to see the clothes lying on the side of the road, and I certainly didn't expect to see you."

"I love you," I blurted.

Her eyes widened, and she gave me a sidelong glance.

I felt myself go crimson. "That didn't come out the way I planned. What I mean is...I love you more than my life. More than the sun or the moon, or—"

"All right, all right. Let's not get carried away." She laughed. Her face was beet red. After a moment, she said, "I love you, too."

# TWENTY-SIX

A grin spread across my face. *Brittany loves me.* My chest swelled and my head grew light. If not for the seatbelt, I would have floated away.

Brittany drove the back roads through scrubby fields as if she knew the area better than she knew her own face. At first, I thought she was taking me to Uncle Bob's—but I recognized landmarks and odors, and soon realized we were headed toward our secret place where we'd set up the magic circles.

She slowed and pulled onto the grass. I was out of the car before it came to a complete stop. I circled around and opened the door for her. She looked surprised but pleased.

As she stood, I cupped her face in my hands. Her skin was pale and flawless. With my heart pounding double time, I lowered my lips to hers. I kissed her gently, lingering. She slipped her fingers behind my neck. We stood for a moment, forehead-to-forehead and nose-to-nose.

"Thank you for risking your life for me," I murmured, "but don't do it again."

"No promises," she whispered.

369

I wrapped my arms around her and held her close. She felt small and fragile. And precious.

"Was my car hurt?" she asked, her voice a little high.

I examined the Bug, expecting dents or a broken wiper, but didn't even find a scuffmark. "No damage."

She gave a shaky smile. "That man was scary."

"Yeah." I hugged her. "I don't know what would have happened if you hadn't shown up."

"Did you get the clothes?"

"Sure did."

"It was worth it, then." She pulled away and took my hand. "Come on. I'll show you what I've done."

We walked together beneath the trees into the hidden courtyard. I saw two circles, one within the other, cut from the rough grass. A pile of supplies sat within.

"You've been busy," I said.

"Do you like? I redid them using a trowel instead of a stick. It works really well."

We approached the boundary of the magic circles. I sensed a vague hum. Brittany motioned as if rapping on a pane of glass. The invisible barrier didn't actually ring, but I got that impression.

"And it's easier to turn off the magic," she said. "You don't have to scuff out the line like before."

With her toe, she flipped over a chunk of the overturned grass, covering part of the perimeter. As soon as the circle was broken, the barrier popped out of existence.

"Excellent," I said as I stepped inside. I looked at the supplies she'd left there—cardboard boxes, a scraggly plant, two cases of bottled water. "I don't know how to thank you. You've done so much."

"Let's hope it works."

*But will it?* I wondered again if the magic would hold me. "Can you bring the barrier up? I want to see how it feels."

"Sure." Brittany knelt. "It's easy. You just concentrate on the purpose of the circle and complete the line."

She folded back the chunk of sod. Then she pricked her finger with a Celtic cross on her keychain and dripped blood on the bare dirt. The barrier sprang into place. It hummed as if it were vibrating.

I stretched out my hand. The surface reminded me of a padded cell—it had a little give, but felt rigid when I pushed. It was transparent, but the curvature caused objects on the periphery of my vision to smear.

Turning sideways, I rammed my shoulder into the wall. I kept hitting and bouncing back until my shoulder ached. Then I kicked, striking heel first.

"Do you want me to let you out?" Brittany asked.

"Not yet." I brushed damp hair off my forehead, overheating in the closed space. "I wonder if I can tunnel underneath."

"Why would you worry about that?"

"What if the wolf in me gets so desperate to survive that it comes out?" I shrugged. "Dogs like to dig."

371

"I'll be with you to apply the potion. If the wolf shows, I'll deal with it." She didn't look happy about the prospect.

I blew out my breath. It really was getting hot. "Mind if I have one of those?" I motioned at the water. It was packaged in squirt bottles, twenty-four to a case. I figured we had plenty.

"Are you all right in there?"

"Don't worry." I flipped the cap and took a drink. The water was warm. Not very refreshing. "Hey, Brit, watch this." I squirted water at the barrier. I thought it would hit like on a window and drip down.

It didn't. The stream of water went straight through. Splat! Right in Brittany's face.

"Cripes," I cried. "I'm sorry. I didn't expect—"

"You did that on purpose," she squeaked. She kicked a clod of dirt onto the circle, dropping the barrier, and dove for her own bottle of water.

I ran, and she ran after, laughing and dousing me. I sent random shots from beneath my arm, but I was low on ammunition and doubted that I met my target. As I dodged around the courtyard, I hit a wet spot and went sprawling. She tumbled over me. We rolled in a tangle of arms and legs.

I landed on top. My heart raced. I became hyper-aware of her body beneath mine.

She squirmed and squealed. "Get off. You're dripping."

I shook my head, sending my wet hair flying, spraying her.

Brittany laughed harder. "Cody, no."

She was so beautiful. Leaning, I kissed her brow, then her nose. She gave a little sigh. Her eyes shone. She stroked the side of my face, her fingers cool and gentle. I took her hand and kissed her palm, the soft side of her wrist. Her pulse throbbed, quickening. A groan escaped me.

I pressed my lips to her temple, sliding them down her jaw, her neck, finally resting them in the hollow of her shoulder. I wanted to stay with her forever. I wanted to just hold her in my arms in the grassy glade away from the world.

But she'd become unnaturally still.

I lifted to my elbows and looked at her. "I would never hurt you."

"I know that. In my heart. But my head keeps screaming that I'm alone in the woods with a handsome boy."

I smiled. "Handsome?"

"The boy of my dreams."

Her words struck low beneath my belly. I kissed her hard, tasting her grape-soda lips, breathing in the mango scent of her skin. Reluctantly, I pulled away, got to my feet and gave her a hand up.

Brittany cleared her throat, looking embarrassed. I didn't know how to respond. I never had a girl say I was in her dreams before. My heart and other parts of me wanted to pull her close and kiss her again. My head knew that wasn't a good idea.

I walked away and looked at the magic circles. "I

wonder why the water went through when I couldn't."

"Maybe it only stops solid matter," she said. "Air gets inside."

"Not very well. It was getting pretty hot in there."

"But you could breathe, right? I mean, we need oxygen to light a fire."

"Yeah, I could," I said, "but just to be on the safe side, I think when we start cooking the potion we should leave the barrier down. We don't want the flames to go out when we aren't here."

"All right. You're the boss." Grinning, she dumped the remainder of her bottle over my head.

"Thanks. Now I don't have to shower for dinner tomorrow."

"Ugh. Dinner." She smacked herself on the forehead. "I'm supposed to be boiling eggs. I have to get home."

"Eggs?"

"Yeah, my mother loves to decorate. Remember to ooh and aah."

I smiled. "I promise to be properly impressed."

"She's going to love you."

We walked arm-in-arm to the car, and she drove me to my uncle's house. She pulled into the driveway, then leaned to give me a kiss.

"Pick you up at two, all right?"

"Should I bring anything?"

"Please, no. We have more food than we know what to do with. Mom always goes overboard."

"All right, then. See you tomorrow." I got out of

the car, slinging my backpack over my shoulder, and waved as she drove away. My damp shirt clung as I moved, and I grinned like it was a secret joke.

Howard, Rita, and Uncle Bob were in the living room as I came through the door.

"Cody," my uncle yelped, hopping up from the arm of the recliner. "I thought you were asleep in your room."

"Nah. I had to go get our clothes." I dropped the backpack onto the floor with a satisfying thud.

Three pairs of eyes stared at me. I wiggled my brows.

"Were you seen?" Rita asked.

I nodded. "They were there."

Uncle Bob groaned. "You're just egging them on, boy."

I bristled. "Would you rather they blackmailed us?"

"I'd rather you let the adults handle this."

I glared at him. Where was my pat on the back, my *well done, boy*? I could have been killed for all he cared.

Howard dumped the backpack onto the floor. There was a puff of dust and a bounce of pebbles. "Looks like everything is here. Problem solved."

"One of them, anyway," Uncle Bob mumbled.

"What other is there?" I blurted.

"You!" He jabbed his finger at me. "I can't have you climbing out your window anytime you feel like it."

"Now, Bob," Rita said.

He waved an arm toward me. "He's a kid. He doesn't even understand the situation."

Howard gathered the filthy clothes. "I'll drop these into the washing machine."

"I'll help," my uncle snapped.

They walked down the hall. It was all I could do to keep from stomping out of the house. "So, now I'm too young? Too stupid?"

"Of course not," Rita said. "He didn't mean it like that."

"Sure sounded like it."

"Sit down." She motioned to the kitchen chair Howard had vacated.

I pulled it closer and sat. She reached to pat my hand. I saw that the movement pained her. "Bob and I have been through this type of thing before," she said. "Some people are animals. You can't go to the police. You're pretty much on your own."

"I know that. Why do you think I went to get the clothes?"

"It was a brave thing to do. But if you had taken Bob and Howard with you, there would have been back up. It would have been three against three."

I opened my mouth then closed it again. My shoulders slumped. If Brittany hadn't happened by, the pack would have torn me to shreds. I was lucky to be alive.

"Bob loves you, Cody. But aside from that, he's your guardian. He feels responsible."

"Well, I feel responsible, too," I told her in a low voice. "It's kind of my fault the pack came after us in the first place. You see, I found out where they were staying, and I confronted the leader."

"You what?" Uncle Bob bellowed behind me.

I jumped. I hadn't realized he was there.

"That does it," he yelled. "From now on, you don't go anywhere without my expressed permission. Do you understand? You are grounded."

"Fine." I stood so quickly, the chair toppled over. "May I still go to Brittany's house for Easter dinner tomorrow? They're expecting me."

"Yes," he hissed, his eyes savage. "But I'll drive you."

I nodded once to show I understood. I was so mad I didn't trust my voice.

"All right," he said, looking away. Dismissing me. "Wait in your room until nightfall."

"I'm not going out with you tonight." I scowled. "I think I'll turn in early."

"Aren't you coming with us?" Rita asked, her eyes wide.

"I don't feel like shifting."

"Don't feel," Uncle Bob sputtered. "Don't you *have* to?"

I glared at him. "No. I don't have to."

Emotions crossed his face—anger, disbelief, but most of all, fear. Rita's eyes widened further, until she looked like a caricature.

I'd said something wrong. I shouldn't have told

them I could control the shift. But it was too late to back down now. I went to my room thinking I didn't fit in anywhere. I was as lousy at being a werewolf as I was at being a boy.

# TWENTY-SEVEN

As it turned out, stopping the shift wasn't as easy as I let on. I spent most of the night feverish and shaky. I remained human, but got little sleep. As a result, it was after one in the afternoon when I finally rolled out of bed.

I showered and shaved, appraising myself in the steamy mirror. I'd need a haircut soon. It was brushing my shoulders. In my room, I pulled the dress shirt off a hanger in my closet. The wrinkles hadn't fallen out as I'd hoped. I slipped it on. It was tight across the shoulders. Then I noticed the sleeves came to only mid-arm. Cripes. Had it shrunk? I tugged the cuffs, but it was no use. The shirt didn't fit.

Frantically, I dragged out the box of clothes from the back of my closet. There had to be a better shirt I could wear. But every one of them was too small. What had happened? I chose a light-blue shirt that was a little roomier, left the collar open, and rolled the cuffs to my elbows. Not the look I was going for, considering it was my first time meeting Brittany's mother, but it would have to do.

I knew my brown pants hadn't shrunk. They still

had tailor chalk on them. Mom bought them just be-fore Christmas for my trip to France, but I decided at the last minute not to pack them. I brushed off the chalk and tried on the pants. The waist fit fine. With a sigh of relief, I looked down.

Three inches of ankle showed. "Oh, no!"

I dove into the box, tossing clothes onto my bed. Every pair of pants I found was too short. What was wrong with them? I couldn't have grown that much in four months.

As I brought out another armload of clothes, my shirt ripped. I felt along the shoulder seam and found bare skin.

I groaned. "Oh, no."

"Something wrong?" Uncle Bob said from my doorway.

"You think? I can't go like this."

He eyed me up and down, looking like he was trying not to laugh.

I jammed my fingers into my hair, not caring if I was making it stand up straight. "Can you drive me to the mall?"

"Don't know that it's open on Easter Sunday. But Howard is. Let's go."

I squeezed my feet into my dress shoes. Tight but wearable. As I tied the laces, my shirt ripped fur-ther.

*This couldn't be happening.*

Uncle Bob waited in the truck. I got in and slammed the door. He was down the drive and on the street before I'd finished belting in. "Did you tell Brittany I was driving you?" he asked.

"Yeah. I called her last night."

"And you didn't shift?"

"No." I raised my voice. "Why is that so awful?"

He took his time answering. I had the impression he was choosing his words. "There are all types of werewolf," he said. "It's just genetics. Usually we feel the urge two days before the full moon, the night of the full, and two days after. Some wolves shift more often. I heard of one or two who could shift even on a new moon." He nodded, brows raised as if repeating something unbelievable. "And then there are those who don't shift at all, just get stomach cramps once a month and never know why. What I'm saying is there are the stronger and the weaker. But that doesn't mean one wolf is better than another. And it doesn't mean being one of us is better than, you know, being regular."

Point taken—I was not better than *him*.

"Did you ever want to stop being a wolf?"

He chuckled. "More times than I can tell you. As I've said, it's a hard life."

I thought of telling him about the potion Brittany and I planned to brew for the new moon, but I was still angry with him for grounding me. Besides, there was a chance it wouldn't work.

We pulled to a stop before Howard's house. He was in the process of dragging his wares back into the garage. Most of the tables were empty. I sighed, never so glad to see him.

As I jumped out of the truck, the seat of my pants ripped. I slammed the door double hard.

"Hullo," Howard called as we approached. "That's a new look for you."

"I'm supposed to be at Brit's in half an hour," I said, "and every decent thing I own is too small."

He nodded. "It's the curse."

"Of being a werewolf?" I whispered.

"Of being a teenage boy," he said.

I blinked in surprise. This was normal?

He walked to a clothes rack at the back of the garage. "I have a few white shirts. Short-sleeved." He took one out and shook it. "Dusty."

"Will you accept my debit card?" I asked.

"I'll pay," Uncle Bob said.

"Nah. I'll just take it in trade." Howard motioned at my ripped shirt. He waited for me to strip it off, then whistled. "Nice label."

I grimaced. "I have a whole box of this junk. You can have it."

"Deal."

I took the shirt he offered. It was a little yellow under the arms, but it fit fine. "Do you have any dress slacks?"

"As it happens, I just got in a pair. They're practically brand new." He rummaged around his inventory. "Here they are."

They *were* new. Still had the tags. They were

also hideous—steel gray with a grid of pink lines forming inch-wide squares. Probably in style twenty
years ago.

"Where did you get these?"

"Woman said her son outgrew them before his
birthday party. I gave her a lamp and a plunger."

*Right.* Her son probably refused to wear them.
"Got anything else?"

"Not in extra tall."

A ball of panic bounced in my stomach. "Are you
sure the mall is closed?"

"Yep," said Uncle Bob.

I shut my eyes. Before I changed my mind, I
changed my pants. Right there in the garage. The
legs flared at the bottom, but they fit. "Yeah. These
will work."

"Much better." Uncle Bob nodded.

I stuck out my hand to shake with Howard. "You
saved my life."

He grinned. "A danger foreseen is half-avoided."

I nodded, pretty sure I knew what he meant.

Feeling calmer, I climbed again into Uncle Bob's
truck. Everything was going to be all right. I was on
time for dinner, and I was dressed like a clown. Brittany's mom would have to take me as I was, right?

My mouth went dry at that thought.

As Uncle Bob wheeled through town, I tried to
think of a conversation starter. I didn't like us being
mad at each other. "Are you spending the day with
Rita?"

"She's gone," he said.

"What? Already?"

"I told her to go. Between the problems with the pack and her saying I was too tough on you..." He blew out his breath.

I looked at him and thought of how it would feel to be separated from Brittany. I didn't think I could stand that. "I'm sorry."

"So am I. In all the years we've been together, I have never asked her to leave."

"Then why did you?"

"You really don't get it, do you?" He threw a glance my way. "These people are murderers. Brutal and unpredictable. You've made this a game for them. And they aren't going to leave until the game is over."

"So," I snapped, "you asked Rita to leave because you're mad at me?"

"I'm not angry," he said. "I'm scared. I'm just trying to keep you both safe."

I folded my arms, scowling out the windshield. What did he think I was trying to do? I'd intended to save the whole town by facing down the killers. It's not my fault it didn't work.

The truck rattled up Brittany's long, pot-holed driveway. Brittany sat on the screened-in porch in one of the wicker chairs. She stood, smiling like she was relieved I'd shown up. I didn't thank my uncle for the ride, just got out and walked toward the house, painfully aware of my too-tight shoes, my garage sale clown pants.

He yelled out his window, "I'll be back at six."

Brittany took my hand. "Is he still mad?"

"Yeah."

"Well, take a deep breath. You're here, now."

"Yeah." I listened to my uncle drive away.

"You look nice," she said.

I cringed like she'd slapped me, expecting her to laugh. But when I looked into her eyes, I saw she wasn't poking fun.

I smiled. "You look nice, too."

"In this thing?"

Stepping back, I took her in. She'd dyed her hair bubblegum pink, and it sat like a puffball on top of her head. She wore dangling earrings with Easter eggs at the ends and a lavender sundress I was sure her mother bought her. It was the first time I'd seen her bare shoulders. I wanted to kiss them.

"Oh, yeah. Super nice."

"Come on." She grinned. "I'll introduce you to my mom."

We went into her house. The curtains in the living room were open for a change, letting in the afternoon sun and making the place cheerful. Rabbit pillows covered the couch, and Easter Bunny plaques hung on the walls. My favorite had the words *Spring Has Sprung* lettered on half a basket and plastic eggs bouncing on springs from inside.

The coffee table held a large vase filled with several dozen tulips. Scattered around the vase were decorated eggs. I picked one up. It was painted to look like a blue rabbit with a doily for a skirt and a cotton ball tail.

"A little much, eh?" Brittany said in a low voice.

"Who made all these?"

"It's a family event. Under pain of death." She pointed to one that looked like a chick with crossed eyes and pipe cleaner legs. "There's one of mine."

"Really? Let me see."

"No." She snatched it up before I could touch it, holding it behind her back. "You'll laugh."

"No, I won't." I slipped my arms around her, trying to grab the egg.

"Stop. I'm shy."

"You? Not a chance."

"You think you know me so well."

"I do," I murmured.

Her lips were a breath away. I caught them with my own. A tingle swept through me; my entire body stood on point.

Someone cleared their throat. I jerked, suddenly remembering where I was, what I was doing. The blue egg toppled from my fingers. It hit the edge of the table with a sickening crack. I winced, turning around.

Brittany's mother stood in the doorway wiping her hands on a dishtowel. She had chin-length brown hair and wrinkles around her eyes. An apron in the shape of a rabbit covered her dress. Its long ears fastened behind her neck.

"You must be Cody." She wiped her hands as if to keep them from wringing my neck.

"Yes, ma'am." My face went hot. I stepped away from Brittany, who was now on hands and knees trying to retrieve the fallen egg. "I like your decorations."

*Wipe. Wipe.*

"Got it." Brittany held up the egg. Its face was bashed in.

"Um, sorry," I said.

"Don't be silly." Brittany stood. "It's good luck to eat the first one. Right, Mom?"

"Welcome to our home," her mother said. "Why don't you two come into the kitchen? We can chat while I work." She bustled away.

Brittany smiled. "That went well."

I groaned. We walked together down the hallway. As we passed the stairs, her brother barreled down.

"Is dinner ready yet?" he asked.

"Bartley, is that you?" his mother called.

I stared at him. No wonder he'd rather go by the name of Butt Crack.

"Bartley, go to the garage and bring in another carton of Coke."

"But, Mom," he said, blocking the kitchen doorway. "I'm trying to finish my homework."

"You had all week to do it. Now, get a move on."

"Yeah. Move it, Butt Crack." Brittany poked him.

"Watch your language, young lady." Her mother looked distracted. "What am I missing?"

387

I followed Brittany into the steamy kitchen. My super senses perked at a barrage of aromas. I smelled maple-and-brown-sugar crusted ham in the oven and cinnamon applesauce simmering on the stove. "It smells really good in here, ma'am."

"Oh dear." She leaned into their cavernous refrigerator. "Brittany, I forgot to have you snap the beans."

"I can do that," I said. "Just let me wash my hands." I headed toward the bathroom.

With my super hearing, I heard her mother hiss, "How does he know where our bathrooms are? How many times has he been here? I thought you only saw him at school."

Brittany said, "Blame Grandpa. He had him in there fixing the sink."

"He did not."

"You always think the worst."

"I would just like to know what you're doing while I'm at work, that's all."

I scrubbed and re-entered the kitchen, holding my hands up like a surgeon. Brittany lugged what looked like a ten-pound bag of green beans to the table. She wore a bunny apron similar to the one her mother had on. It looked cute on her.

My smile faded as her mother held out an apron to me. "You should wear one of these as well. No sense in ruining your nice clothes."

"That's all right, ma'am."

"I insist."

"Don't be a baby." Brittany took the apron, her eyes glinting like a mischievous fairy. "Bend down here."

She slipped the bunny's ears over my head. Then she velcroed its long arms behind my back. Heat rushed up my neck.

At the same time, Butt Crack stepped in from the garage. He burst out laughing, almost dropping the carton he held. "I don't know, man. You must really like her."

"That's enough," his mother said. "Just for that, you can help them with the beans. You'll have to wear one of my craft smocks."

So the three of us settled at the kitchen table—Brittany and I dressed like Easter Bunnies and Butt Crack wearing a smock with humongous red and purple flowers. We broke the ends off the beans, dropping the good part into a pot. I'd never snapped beans before, and I wanted to get it right to impress Brittany's mother. But Brittany kept knocking my elbow and making me drop my bean. Butt Crack flicked stems at us. His fingernails were green. He rubbed his cheek, turning it green, too.

Brittany's mother stood at the sink, her back to us, peeling potatoes. "Cody, I hear you live with Bob Nowak."

"Yes, ma'am. He's my uncle."

"The Fix-It-Guy," Butt Crack said in a deep voice.

"Is that what you want to become?" his mother asked. "A handyman?"

"Actually, I always figured I'd be a doctor. Like my parents."

"Oh." She looked at me. "Have they passed on?"

Might as well have, I thought. "They live in Massachusetts."

"Then why do you live down here?"

"Getting personal, Mom," Brittany said.

"I don't think it's an unreasonable question," she said.

Brittany scowled and opened her mouth as if to answer.

I overrode her. "My parents wanted me to have a different perspective of things, so they sent me to Uncle Bob. I'm glad they did."

I smiled at Brittany, and she took my hand. Butt Crack flicked a stem, binging her in the nose. She snatched the plastic bag and dumped the remaining green beans over his head. Their mother kept peeling as if their behavior was expected. It looked like a mountain of potatoes.

"Anyone else coming for dinner?" I asked.

"Just us." Brittany scooped beans off the floor and tossed them at her brother.

"Where's Grandpa Earle?" I asked.

"Taking a nap."

"I don't nap," Grandpa Earle bellowed as he came around the corner.

I stood. "Happy Easter, sir."

He blinked at me, his eyes traveling slowly from the flared clown pants to the rabbit apron. "You got a bean on your shoulder."

I brushed myself off.

"Never thanked you properly for the job you did on my sink," he said.

Brittany's mother spun around to look at him. "You mean, h-he..."

"Did a bang-up job." He extended his hand, and I shook it. "My thanks is payment."

"Of course, sir."

"Well." Her cheeks colored. "Cody, if you will bring those over, I'll wash them. And Brittany, you need to punch down the dinner rolls so they can rise again. They're right over there in the sunshine."

Brittany lifted a cloth, exposing globs of dough. My eyebrows rose as I watched her punch each one with her knuckles. Shrugging, I carried the pot to the sink, then helped her brother pick up the mess on the floor.

Before long, dinner was on the table. There was enough food for twenty-five people instead of just five—mounds of mashed potatoes, string beans with slivered mushrooms, buttered corn, warm applesauce, and of course, the ham.

Grandpa Earle and Brittany's mother sat on either end of the table. Brittany and I sat across from Butt Crack. I held Brittany's chair for her as she settled in, more for her mom's benefit than because I thought she needed help. I knew it was something old people liked.

As I took my seat, I noticed the blue egg with the

smashed-in face beside my plate. All hope of scoring points left me. I felt like it was a statement, like I had to pay for the stolen kiss.

Brittany's mother said, "Cody, will you do us the honor of saying grace?"

My jaw dropped, and my mind went blank. Grace? Like a prayer? I didn't know any. My parents were agnostic.

Silence fell over the room. The others bowed their heads. Waiting. My hands grew clammy.

"Four score and seven years ago," I said, "our forefathers brought forth a new nation, um, in order to form a more perfect union—" No, wait! What was I doing? That was for Thanksgiving, wasn't it? "Um, conceived under God and to the republic, with liberty and justice for all. Amen."

"Amen," said Brittany.

She and her brother dove for the bowls of food.

Her mother said, "Thank you, Cody. That was quite... patriotic."

"Bah," grumbled Grandpa Earle. He reached for the basket of rolls "There are no patriots anymore. The government's full of lies and conspiracies."

"Grandpa wears a skunk skin hat on the Fourth of July," Brittany said.

"Tell him about the flying saucer you saw last year, Grandpa," Butt Crack said.

"Bartley, no," his mother said. "Not in front of guests."

"You can laugh." Grandpa Earle waved his fork.

"But I know what I saw. It was big and silver, and it tried to take over my mind."

"Grandpa was most insistent on that point," Brittany said. "He bypassed the sheriff's department and went straight to the press."

"Durned right," he said. "And do you know what they had the gall to tell me it was? A runaway hot air balloon from the State Fair. In Tampa, for Pete's sake."

"They probably believed what they were saying," Butt Crack mumbled around a mouth full of potatoes. "Mind control, you know."

"Maybe so," Grandpa Earle said. "Never thought of it like that."

Brittany smiled and rolled her eyes at me.

Her mother said, "Cody, tell us what it's like to live in Massachusetts."

"It's nice," I told her. "Big trees. Bigger hills. Traffic's worse there. Everything seems to move at a faster pace."

"Do you miss living there? Your friends?"

"The first week or two was hard. I had a lot of friends in school. I was president of the Science Club. Teacher's pet. But I was in a rut. Taking the safe route. It's exciting living here. There's always something new to see."

"Good boy," Grandpa Earle said between bites. "You're never too old to see something new. I saw my first yeti this morning."

Brittany laughed. "Aren't they supposed to be in

the mountains?"

"I know what I'm talking about. It was right outside the kitchen window. I came in for some water to take my rheumatism medicine, and I saw it."

"What did it look like?" Butt Crack asked. "Big and hairy?"

"It was huge. Like a dog, only not exactly."

Brittany dropped her fork. She looked at me.

"A dog?" her mother said.

"Like no dog I never seen. It was down on all fours, poking around the yard. Then at first light, it just rose up and stood there on its hind legs, manlike but shaggy. Then it shambled away. I looked for footprints, but there weren't none. It's so dry out there."

My stomach lurched, and all the good food I'd eaten turned sour. He'd seen a werewolf, not a yeti. Someone had been in the yard. I wanted to believe that it was my uncle keeping watch while I was tossing in bed.

But I knew it was one of the pack. Maybe they'd split up, looking for me. Only I hadn't shifted. Why did I have to be so stubborn? If I'd become a wolf, I would have realized Brittany was in danger. I would have been there to protect her.

"Maybe we should think about fencing in," Brittany's mother said. "I don't like the thought of animals doing their business in our yard."

"If it was as big as Gramps said it was," said Butt Crack, "it would probably break through a fence."

"Then we'll electrify it," she said.

"Excellent idea," I said. "You should get an extra tall one. My uncle and I can put it up." I glanced at Brittany for confirmation and noticed she wasn't eating.

"Drumming up business for the Fix-It-Guy, eh?" Grandpa Earle laughed. "Good boy."

We got through dinner without further discussions of yeti and flying saucers.

I leaned back from the table. "Everything was delicious, ma'am."

"Thank you, Cody. I'll put a plate together so you can take some home to your uncle. And don't forget. We have rabbit holes."

Butt Crack and Grandpa Earle stood at the same time and began clearing the table. It seemed to be a ritual. I wondered if I should join them.

But Brittany tugged my hand, practically dragging me from the room. "We'll be on the front porch," she told her mother.

"Rabbit holes?" I asked as we passed through the living room.

"Our traditional Easter dessert. Mother loves crafts." She stopped to look at me. "Was that you Grandpa saw in the yard this morning?"

I shook my head. "I didn't shift last night. But I'm sure it's nothing to worry about. Maybe Uncle Bob stopped by to keep an eye on you."

"Maybe." She didn't sound convinced.

We stepped out onto the porch. I tried to think of a way to change the subject when my blood went cold. At the end of the long driveway, I saw a shiny black Mustang. Leaning against the hood was the pack leader.

Brittany gasped. "Oh, no."

I wanted to run back into the house and lock the door—but I couldn't show weakness in front of her.

"Stay here," I said.

I walked as if my legs were numb, as if I were in a dream. The driveway stretched longer with each step. The pack leader crossed his arms, smirking.

*Don't let him sense how scared you are.*

"There's the little pup," he said.

I stopped about ten feet away and put my hands on my hips. "I see you got another car."

"There's always another car."

I paused. *Thief.* "What do you want?"

"You didn't come out to play last night. I wanted to see if you were okay."

"You watching the house?"

He shrugged.

"Now, you see?" I said. "I don't appreciate that."

His eyes flashed. "Do you think I give spit for what you appreciate?"

"Is that supposed to convince me to join your little gang?"

"We're way beyond that." He dropped his arms and took a stance.

I didn't move. Frankly, I was too scared to, so I just waited to see what happened next. After a moment, he screwed up his face. "You really aren't afraid of me, are you? Maybe you should be."

He got into the car and gunned the motor. I stood there, knowing I could never jump away in time if he tried to mow me down. He didn't. With a spray of gravel and dirt, he backed out of the drive and took off.

Shaking inside, I walked to the house. Brittany looked stricken. I put on my brave face. "He's gone." I shrugged. "No big."

"What did he want?"

"He's just a jerk."

Her mother came out carrying a tray. "Dessert time. Cody, would you like a cup of coffee?"

"He drinks milk, Mom. I told you."

"Oh, that's right." She set the tray on a wicker table and rushed back inside.

Brittany and I sat down. I couldn't meet her eyes. I knew I'd put her in danger.

Instead, I inspected the tray. It turned out that rabbit holes were cupcakes with green coconut along the rim and a circle of fudge on top. Two white feet were drawn with icing on the fudge—the rabbit jumping into its hole. They looked delicious, and I knew she'd gone through a lot of trouble to make them.

But I couldn't eat one. My stomach turned at the thought. All I wanted was for Uncle Bob to show up and take me home.

# TWENTY-EIGHT

Uncle Bob wasn't bluffing when he said I was grounded. For the next week, I had little time to myself. He drove me to school, picked me up afterward, and hung over my shoulder in the evenings. Brittany and I couldn't have a phone conversation with him always within earshot.

But the week that followed, he hired on to re-roof Mrs. Portland's barn. He asked Howard to drive me home after school, and Howard was happy to delegate that honor to Brittany.

That was when I noticed the pack leader and his stolen black Mustang everywhere. He cruised past the school when I was in class. He honked and waved going the other way on Southern Boulevard. On Tuesday, he followed us home, but when I hopped out of the car to confront him he squealed away.

Tuesday night, I slept with my bedroom window closed, although it was stifling in my room. I was unnerved, but couldn't let on to anyone.

"Why can't he leave us alone?" Brittany said Wednesday at lunch.

I shrugged. "Why don't you just drop me off at the Sunshine Motel and I'll ask him?"

"No way," she snapped. "Don't even think it. Besides, I have to stop by Walgreens to pick up some salve for Grandpa."

So after school, we headed to Walgreens. Brittany drove in silence, not her usual talkative, bubbly self. We parked in the lot. It was crowded, but we found a good spot.

As we unbuckled our seatbelts, a black car screeched to a halt behind us, blocking us in.

"Oh, God." Brittany stared in the rearview mirror, her face paler than usual.

"Go into the store. I'll talk to him."

"But—"

"Go on."

She got out and, trembling visibly, walked forward between the cars. Her cell phone was in her hand, and I wondered if she planned to call the sheriff. That thought gave me courage enough to walk to the passenger side of the Mustang.

The pack leader grinned. "Hello, pup."

I leaned to look in the open window. "What do you want?"

"I want you to be afraid of me."

"And you'll accomplish this how? By harassing me?"

"Is that what you think I'm doing?" He chuckled. "I'm just trying to get to know you, learn your routine, your weaknesses."

His words landed hard in the pit of my stomach. My hands shook, and I rested them on my knees. "Seems like a lot of work. Why bother?"

His smile faded. "Because I don't like feeling you'll be talking about me after I'm gone. Now, I could kill you, but I hate to deprive the world of another wolf, even one as housebroken as you. I could rip out your tongue, but I'd much rather teach you to hold it."

Try as I might, I could not think of a witty comeback. I could only stare. My uncle was right. The guy was dangerous and unpredictable. And I'd dissed him off.

At that moment, a green-and-white sheriff's cruiser pulled into the parking lot.

The pack leader scowled. "Don't be talking about me behind my back, you hear?" He put the car in gear, merged with traffic on Southern, and disappeared.

I gulped my heart back out of my throat and walked with shaky knees to the drugstore.

Brittany threw her arms about me. "What did he say?"

Should I tell her he wanted to kill me, or that he was going to rip my tongue out? I hooked my thumb. "He said to stay away from the sheriff's car that just pulled in. Did you call them?"

"I said there was an altercation in the parking lot, but I didn't give names."

"Thanks. It got me out of a boring conversation."

I didn't let on that I finally realized there **was** no reasoning with the pack leader.

🐺 🐺 🐺

Thursday after school, Brittany had another errand to run for Grandpa Earle. This time she stopped by the Sheriff's Office in Royal Palm Beach to leave a package for Sheriff Brad.

"He probably won't be there," she said as she parked before the County Building. She was much more animated, probably feeling safe with all the sheriff cars around. "I think he's at the main headquarters in West Palm today. I'll just leave the box with the lieutenant. He knows me."

"It seems everyone knows you." I closed my door and met her at the front of the *VW*.

She opened the trunk and showed me a box containing three mason jars. I picked one up. It held some honey, a chunk of honeycomb, and a few dead bees.

"Sheriff Brad likes honey, does he?" I asked.

"Gramps and the sheriff had an argument. Do you remember the old shed in the backyard where we took you when… um—"

"The one with Butt Crack's comic book collection?"

"Yes. Well, some bees started a hive inside. You couldn't get near it. Butt Crack was beyond bummed. I guess it was like his clubhouse or something.

Grandpa called the sheriff's department. Sheriff Brad said, 'Now Earle, you can't be calling me for bees. I've got murders to solve.' And Grandpa told him that his job was to serve and protect, and he needed protecting."

I laughed. "Did the sheriff rush over?"

"He didn't show. So Grandpa rigged a contraption that held burning newspaper and shot smoke out a spout, and he went back there himself. Only the hive was bigger than he expected, and he got all stung up. He dropped the smoke contraption, and it caught the shed on fire."

I gasped. "With all those vintage comics?"

"Mom had a fit. She said he could've burned down the forest with the drought going on. Anyway, the shed is gone, and all that's left of the hive is half a dozen jars like these. He's sending some to the sheriff as a statement. He should've been there."

I picked up the box. "That's quite a story."

"There's always something happening when Gramps is around."

We walked into the welcomed coolness of the building and went up to Suite 300. Brittany stopped at the front desk. "I'd like to see Lieutenant Koombs, please. He's expecting me."

The officer at the desk picked up the phone. "Lieutenant, there's a young lady here to see you. All right." She smiled at Brittany. "Go on back."

"Wait here," Brittany told me. She took the box. "I'll just be a minute."

I watched her walk away, appreciating the sway of her hips, until she disappeared down a hallway. With a sigh and a smile, I glanced around the room. It looked like any other office space, full of desks and activity. Two deputies passed, escorting a man in handcuffs. An older woman who had to be a hooker judging by her abbreviated outfit entertained onlookers with her colorful language.

There was a waiting area of sorts, but I didn't feel like sitting. I headed for a water cooler along the far wall, dodging people and desks. No one stopped me, so I figured I wasn't breaking any rules.

I pulled a paper cone from a dispenser, nearly crushing it in the process. The cooler gurgled as I siphoned the water. It was cold and refreshing. I refilled my cup and started back across the room. As I wound through the obstacles, I noticed a fax on a desk. It had a photo of a black Mustang—a stock shot you might see in a magazine. Underneath was a police report—model, year, plate number.

"Hey, I've seen that car," I said a little loudly. "Yep, that's the one."

That garnered the attention of several deputies. "Where?" said one man. "Here in Royal Palm?"

"No, in Loxahatchee. At the Sunshine Motel. I was cutting through on my bike. Couldn't help but notice a car like that. It's a real beauty, isn't it? Stolen, eh? You never know."

They looked at each other. I slurped my water.

Just then, Brittany came down the aisle accompanied by a man with short, curly hair. They both laughed, probably at Brittany's story of Grandpa and the bees. I nodded at the deputies clustered around me and walked toward her. By the time I reached her, the man was gone.

She turned her smile on me. "See? That didn't take long."

"I was just getting some water. Want some?"

"No, thanks. We better hurry and get you home before your uncle misses you."

I crumpled the empty cup, pocketed it, and followed her out. We passed the front desk and entered the elevator. Brittany hugged my arm, and it tingled down to my knees.

"Tomorrow night's the big night," she said.

"Yeah. The new moon is coming. We have to start the potion." Like I could forget. "I don't know how I'm going to get out of the house."

"Just tell your uncle the truth. It's Friday night. We want to spend some time together."

"I'm grounded," I said. "He won't care about that."

"It's worth a try."

I shrugged. And if it didn't work, I'd climb out my bedroom window and face the consequences later.

We stepped from the building into bright sunlight and crossed the parking lot. Brittany still held my arm. It felt natural and amazing at the same time. But then her fingers slipped and she missed a step. I looked at her in alarm. Then I followed her gaze.

Parked in front of the library next door was a black Mustang. The pack leader leaned against the hood.

"He'll have the wrong idea," Brittany whispered. "He'll think we told the authorities about him, and we didn't."

But I did. When the deputies stop by the Sunshine Motel, he'll know I sent them. I hoped they were good at their jobs, because I didn't want to find out what he'd do if they failed to arrest him.

🐺 🐺 🐺

The next morning, I sucked up my courage and walked into the kitchen. Uncle Bob sat at the table with his coffee and newspaper. A breeze drifted through the window and circled the room.

I stood in the doorway with absolutely no idea what to say—which was funny because I'd played and replayed the scenario all night long.

When he looked up, I stammered, "I-I would like to take Brittany out tonight. With your permission. It's Friday night. I don't want her to get tired of waiting and find someone else to go out with." I thought that last bit was a stroke of genius. Make him feel guilty.

"Where did you plan to take her?"

"Somewhere nice for dinner. Like the Olive Garden. Then maybe hang out."

"Well. I appreciate that you didn't climb out your window." He made a show of turning the page and folding it just right. "I want you back by eleven."

"Yes, sir." I grinned. "I can do that."

I went to school in a better mood than I'd been in some time. Even the mass of kids clogging the hallways didn't dampen my spirits. As I rounded a corner, I ran into none other than Efrem Higgins.

We stood for a moment, staring at each other. His eyes narrowed with hatred. I understood. If I hadn't come to town, he'd still be on the football team, winning girls and terrorizing anyone who crossed him. But with everything going on—the potion, my uncle, the pack leader—I found that what good ol' Eff thought of me didn't matter very much.

I shrugged. "Hey."

He nodded and passed without the traditional slam into my shoulder.

It was a fun topic at lunch with Brittany.

"He didn't have his thugs with him?" she asked, wide-eyed.

"No. He was alone."

"For the first time in his life." She laughed. "He's really changed."

"Because of me."

"He did it to himself. You were a victim. I'll never forget seeing you tied up in that tree."

I closed my hand over her warm fingers. "It's over. He doesn't matter."

"All that matters now is you. We have to get that potion brewing, get you back to normal."

My stomach did a little flip, partially at the prospect of becoming a normal kid again, but mostly because she said I mattered. "I talked to my uncle about letting me out tonight. He said I have to be back by eleven."

"That's great. We'll be done by then."

"I told him I was taking you to the Olive Garden." I looked down at our hands. "So, do you want to? Go to dinner with me?"

A mischievous smile crossed her face. "And do our magic stuff afterward?"

"As magical as you want." My cheeks heated. "It will be kind of like our first date."

"Unless you count the Valentine's dinner you cooked for me."

"Yeah." I chuckled. "I'd rather forget about that one."

"I wouldn't." Her eyes sparkled.

I wanted to cup her face in my hands and kiss her right there in the cafeteria. But the bell rang, breaking the moment. I settled for her peck on my cheek as she hurried to class.

After school, I dressed in the clown outfit I wore on Easter, vowing to buy myself new clothes. Brittany picked me up at five so we would beat the crowd at the restaurant. The building looked like every other Olive Garden in the country. Which was a good thing—I knew what to expect.

"I'm going to have bowtie pasta," Brittany told me as we waited to be seated.

"You don't have to settle for that. Get whatever you want. A steak, or the fish special—"

"That *is* what I want. Their pasta is delicious. And you can order two kinds of sauces, one on each side."

So we dined on alfredo and marinara. It was great. Brittany chattered on about her Computer Graphics teacher telling her she had a real knack. She talked about her mother's addiction to crafts, and how she once tried to redecorate Brittany's room. She retold the story of Grandpa and the bees, this time with embellishments.

I was content to listen to her laugh and watch her perfect face. But after a while, I kept glancing out the window at the fading light.

When I apparently failed to laugh at an appropriate spot, she said, "Do you want to leave?"

"I'm sorry. I'm just worried. What if the potion doesn't work? What if we do something wrong?"

"We followed the instructions. I went there this morning before school. Everything's set."

Gratitude and love mushroomed inside me. "I don't know what I'd do without you." I meant it. I couldn't imagine my life with her gone.

"It's dark enough to keep away prying eyes." She pushed back from the table. "Let's get started."

Brittany drove in near silence to our hidden courtyard in the woods. At first, I thought she was mad at me for cutting dinner short, but maybe she was just as nervous as I was.

"So, you came out this morning?" I said in an attempt to break the ice. "Must've been at the crack of dawn."

"Yeah, and you'll never guess who followed me. Our friend in the black Mustang."

"What? You're just telling me this now?"

"It was no big deal. I drove about a mile down the road before I stopped. There's an old rock quarry down there. I pulled to the side, and he went by real slow. When he didn't come back, I got out of the car and ran through the woods to check our stuff. Then I had to run back again. I barely made it to school in time."

"This is bad," I said. "We have to call it off."

"No way."

"He might have tracked you from the quarry to the cauldron."

"He wasn't there. He kept on driving." She shook her head. "See, this is why I didn't want to tell you."

"But you did. You knew something was wrong."

She parked on the grass before the courtyard. "All I know is it's important to you and I don't want to call it off. If anyone's been nosing around, you'll smell them, right?"

"Sure," I said, not sure at all.

We got out of her car. The area was dark so far from city lights. The air was damp and cool. I smelled the hot engine, heard field mice and ground owls and crickets.

"Is he here?" she whispered.

"No. We're alone."

"Good."

We walked hand-in-hand through the trees into the hidden clearing. I saw the shadowed outline of boxes and bags.

"Watch where you walk," she said. "I left the barrier up."

I nodded. "I hear it."

The hum was annoying. I stretched out my hand and rested my fingers on a wall of thick air. The surface gave slightly beneath my touch. With my toe, I kicked a flap of sod onto the magic circle carved in the ground. The circle was broken, and the barrier popped out.

Brittany took a hesitant step. "Was anyone here?"

"Rabbits," I said. "An armadillo. You came in there."

"Yeah. I did."

"But no one else."

"That's a relief," she said. "Take a look at what I've done."

My mouth dropped. Besides the boxes of supplies, there was now a fire pit with stones around the rim and a large rock in the center, presumably to hold the cauldron. Neat piles of kindling surrounded the pit.

"You did all this for me?"

"For us," she said. "After all, we're partners."

I felt overwhelmed. It was really happening. In

two days, I would rid myself of the curse of the were-wolf. Because of Brittany. Because of her belief, her perseverance, her caring.

"I love you," I said.

She glanced up. "I know. Can you build a fire?"

"I've seen it done." I knelt at the edge of the pit and layered it with wood. "Did you bring newspaper?"

In the dark, I saw her nose crinkle. "You'd be amazed at the amount of chemicals in a single page of newsprint. We can't risk polluting the fire. This is an old potion. It has to be done the old way."

"What, by rubbing two sticks together?"

She laughed. "No. I brought a bag of dry leaves from my yard. And I got wooden matches. I've heard regular matches and lighters leave a residue."

While I tucked leaves around the kindling, she struck a match. The fire caught and flickered. She set the cauldron in place.

"I can barely see what I'm doing," she said.

"I can see. Tell me what you need, and I'll pass it to you."

We started with a gallon of pure vinegar. It looked and smelled like molasses, nothing like the vinegar sold in grocery stores. To that, she added a pound of freeze-dried rattlesnake meat, a handful of cinnamon sticks, and a package of gum Arabic, which looked like rabbit pellets.

Then came the live plants. She put in whole poppy blooms. She pulled the silvery leaves off the

411

wormwood herb and crushed each one as she dropped them in. Then she skinned the fleshy limbs of an aloe plant and squeezed the gooey parts into the mix. Lastly, she opened a block of powdery tree fungus and crumbled it inside.

She stirred the mixture with a large wooden spoon then tapped the handle on the edge of the cauldron as if cooking a pot of soup. "That should do it."

I peered inside at the muddy-looking lumps. "It looks pretty thick. Are you going to add water?"

"We don't dare. It's not in the recipe. I bought the water for fire control. It hasn't rained in so long."

"Yeah." I smelled the drought in the surrounding forest. The green scent was gone, replaced by a stench like the inside of an old straw hat. "What happens next?"

"We have to make sure the fire doesn't go out. I'll stop by mornings and evenings."

"I can take the night shift. I'll drive out on my bike after Uncle Bob goes to sleep."

She shook her head. "Too risky. If you get caught, he'll never cut you loose on Sunday."

"About that," I said, "I'll need a good excuse to get him to let me out again. How about we say you forgot to do a book report and need to copy mine?"

"I don't think he'd approve of cheating. Maybe we can tell him I'm studying the human form in Graphics and need a male model."

I laughed. "Yeah. That'll work."

"Or, I can make you dinner to thank you for the nice time I had at Olive Garden."

Warmth spread through my body. "Glad you enjoyed it."

"Then, it's settled. I'll call you around three on Sunday to invite you to dinner. After we eat, we'll head out here." She fed a few more sticks into the fire.

The potion made a *blurp* sound.

"That stuff will be hot enough to take my skin off," I said.

"Okay, how's this? I'll come here before I call you and take it off the fire. The cauldron can cool while we eat our dinner."

"Deal."

She glanced around. "Help me pick up. I don't want to leave any trash."

We spent the next few moments gathering empty boxes and wrappers. I could see perfectly in the firelight, so I did most of the work. By the time we left, the potion was bubbling, and my stomach was dancing right along with it. I couldn't believe it was finally happening.

🐕 🐕 🐕

We decided I should hang out with my uncle all the next day to keep him from getting suspicious. I wasn't happy about that. It was difficult enough being away from Brit on a normal day, let alone one when so much was happening. I woke on Saturday morning knowing I would have to find something to do or go insane.

Fortunately, Howard showed up with a bucket of fish. While he and I cleaned the little beauties, my uncle dug a trench in back and filled it with charcoal briquettes. We wrapped the fish in banana leaves from our yard and tossed them onto the glowing coals. Uncle Bob covered them up again. Wisps of smoke outlined the layer of dirt.

While the fish cooked, we played gin rummy. I had trouble paying attention and lost every hand. They teased me about it, so I told them the aroma of baking fish put me off my game.

At last, Uncle Bob dug up the cooked fish, flipping the blackened pouches onto the grass. We carried them to the kitchen. Howard cut the banana leaves with scissors to reveal perfectly cooked fish, steamed in their own juices.

I went to bed with a full stomach and a mind that wouldn't rest. Although it was difficult to keep my word, I did not climb out my window to check on the potion. I tossed and turned with nightmares. In one dream the cauldron melted, spilling the potion and putting out the fire. In another, a bunch of squirrels got together and carried the cauldron away. Even worse, I dreamt the pack leader put something into the potion and when I used it, I turned into a chicken.

By Sunday morning, I was a basket case. I wanted to pace the house. Uncle Bob kept watching me over the top of his newspaper like he knew something was up.

I had to keep busy, so I offered to wash and wax his truck. He seemed grateful, so I went to work. I unpacked the truck bed then put everything back again after I scrubbed it out. It took hours, which was a good thing.

At three o'clock, I was showered and staring at my cell phone. Brittany would call at any moment. I wondered how she planned to put the potion on my skin. Maybe a big paintbrush? Would she expect me to take off my pants, too? I grinned. I'd better wear undershorts just in case.

Three-fifteen. Still no call. She couldn't have forgotten. Maybe we got our signals crossed. Maybe I was supposed to call *her*. I flipped open the phone.

Uncle Bob appeared in my doorway. "Anything wrong?"

"Just checking the time." I put the phone away.

"Thought I'd take you to Sonic tonight. My treat."

My stomach plunged. How would I get out of this one? "You don't have to do that."

"Well, you did a nice job on the truck. This is my way of saying thanks."

I nodded, wishing he would go away. "Sounds good."

"All right." He tapped a quick drum roll on the doorjamb and walked back to the living room.

I blew out my breath and leaned against my pillow. Why was everything so complicated? He probably thought I washed his truck in an attempt at reconciliation. While I'd like to be un-grounded, I didn't think we were going to be buds anytime soon.

What would he do if he knew what I was attempting? Would he take it as a slap in the face, or would he want to use the potion himself? He always said life as a werewolf was hard, but when he shifted, he was the happiest wolf I ever saw. Not that I knew many.

I waited until three-thirty sharp before I punched in Brittany's number. I felt in my gut that something was wrong—maybe her mother was ill or something happened to Butt Crack.

The phone rang twice, then a man's voice said, "Hello, pup. I wondered when you'd call."

# TWENTY-NINE

I blinked, the phone held loosely at my ear. That was the pack leader's voice. How did he get Brittany's cell? I was about to ask when it registered. He had Brittany. Oh God.

"What did you do to her?" I asked, my voice stronger than I felt.

"Your little pink-haired beauty? She's fine. For now."

My hands shook so hard, I had trouble holding the phone. "Where is she?"

"And I should tell you, why? So you can run to your sheriff pals? I don't think so. They'll find her soon enough."

I struck my forehead with the heel of my hand. Brittany. Oh God. All my fault. "Let her go, and I'll join the pack. I'll do anything you say."

"We're kind of beyond that, don't you think? Besides, I need her to help me make a point. I want you to understand what happens when you set the cops on my trail."

"But I didn't. I haven't—"

"Then why did they confiscate my wheels?"

417

Roxanne Smolen

I fell silent. Tears filled my eyes. Uncle Bob was right—I never understood what I was up against.

"You don't appreciate me or my power," the pack leader growled. "A demonstration is in order. So tonight, I'm going to shift into my wolf form. Impossible, you say? Not during a new moon? Nothing's impossible for me, pup. I *will* shift, and I will tear your girlfriend to pieces. The only way you'll be able to identify her is by—"

I threw the phone across the room. It smashed against the wall. Lifting my head, I let out a throat-rending scream. I ran into the living room as Uncle Bob leaped to his feet.

"They've got her!" I yelled. "He's going to shift tonight!"

"What? Who?" His face fell. "Brittany?"

"Oh God. What am I going to do?"

"Where?" He pulled out his cell. "Cody, where are they?"

"I don't know!" I jammed my fingers into my hair, feeling like my head would explode.

"Why would they take her?" Uncle Bob shouted. "What have you done?"

"They've been following her," I shouted back. "A black Mustang. She told me that she was followed on Friday, said she kept driving to throw them off. I knew, and I did nothing to keep her safe."

My hands clenched. Hair sprouted on the back of my knuckles. My body seemed to ignite.

"We can't track her," he said. "Not as humans.

418

Even if we knew where to start, we'd never get to her in time."

I felt like I was on fire. With clawed fingers, I grabbed my neckline and ripped my shirt in half. Bare-chested and heaving, I howled. Drool ran down my chest as my muzzle elongated.

Uncle Bob backed away, eyes wide. "No. Oh God, Cody. No."

My fur rippled as I shed my clothes.

"No one can shift during the day! No one!"

I growled in answer, then ran into the kitchen and barreled out the window.

"What *are* you?" he shouted after me.

I ran flat out through the trees, head down, ears back. My senses were on overdrive, especially the one I depended on the most—my sense of smell. Uncle Bob said we couldn't track them as humans. But I was more than human, more than wolf. I wouldn't rest until I had the cur's throat in my jaws.

The swampland was dry and reeked of death. I flew over it in great strides, barely touching the ground. I felt certain I knew where they were. Brittany said she would take the potion off the fire to cool. They must've jumped her there.

I reached the dirt road and paused outside the hidden courtyard. My nose twitched. Brittany's scent was hours old. She hadn't been there since morning. Now it was almost nightfall.

Alarm raced through me. I was running out of time. Focus. Where could she be? I lifted my nose

419

and caught the lingering stench of car exhaust. The vehicles hadn't stopped. If she were being followed, Brittany would have driven past as she had before. She'd go to the quarry.

With a determined bark, I ran down the road. The trees thinned, giving way to boulders and sand. I came to a field of gravel penned by a broken-down metal guardrail. A blue Lexus sat at the lip of a drop-off.

At the bottom of the gorge, I saw Brittany's lime green Volkswagen.

I yelped and skidded down the steep slope, finally reaching her car. It listed against a large rock. I was tall enough to look directly inside. Brittany wasn't there, but a window was broken and I smelled her blood.

I also smelled three other humans. The pack. Rage infused me. Nose down, I followed their scent. It led across the flat floor of the basin to a rocky trail along the far side. The trail would've been treacherous for a human, although I had no problem on my four feet. As I climbed, I noticed the sky turning pink. It would be dark soon.

I got to the top and looked down upon a moonscape of craters and boulders. The only green was a fringe of trees along the edge. Brittany and her three abductors stood a short distance away. The leader had her by the arm. Brittany's forehead was bloody. Her clothes were torn.

My lip curled. I followed the ridge until I was right

above them, hoping for a surprise attack. But I dislodged a stone.

Brittany looked up. "Cody!"

"Look out!" cried the blonde woman.

The leader's face fell to disbelief as I leaped. I hit his chest, knocking him away from my mate. He sprawled upon the ground. I was on him again, snapping at his throat. I caught his face in my jaws and squeezed.

He threw me off with surprising strength and was on his feet in a flash. Blood streaked his shirt. He pulled it over his head and wrapped it around his arm as if it would protect him.

I was more interested in Brittany's safety. The other man held her like a shield, her arms wrenched behind her back.

"I knew this was a bad idea," the woman wailed. "I knew it, I told you. We had no idea who we were dealing with."

"Shut up, Nadine," the man said.

"Look at him! It ain't even dark yet."

I growled, advancing on the man.

Nadine scrambled up the ridge. "Let go of her, Hank. He's going to kill us all."

"Hold!" bellowed the leader. "Or I'll kill you myself."

"Hank! Come on!" Nadine yelled, and then disappeared over the ridge.

Hank grimaced, backing away, drawing Brittany with him. Brittany's gaze met mine. She nodded once. Then she collapsed. The sudden movement ripped her arms from Hank's grasp.

I sailed over her, slamming into him. His head snapped back. I rode him down, my weight on his chest, and heard a crack as his head hit the rocks. He didn't move.

"Cody!" Brittany screamed.

The leader stood over her, blood pouring from his mauled face. He looked at me and smiled. Then his jaw narrowed, and his ears slid up the sides of his head.

He was shifting.

With a high-pitched growl, I sprang at him, hoping to catch him while he was still human. He threw out his padded arm. I latched on, shaking it. Suddenly, all I had was the foul-tasting T-shirt.

A large black wolf rammed into my side and bowled me over. He dove onto me, fangs flashing. I got my hind legs beneath him and flung him back. He was on me again before I could get up. I squirmed, biting wherever I could, tasting fur and blood.

His fangs sank into my shoulder. I yelped and struggled. Brittany looked horror-stricken. Then she ran away.

What? I fought with renewed strength and threw him off. Brittany ran across the rock yard. Not for the road, as I would expect, but for the encroaching line of trees. What was she doing?

I turned to follow, but the wolf jumped me from

behind. He snapped at my wounded shoulder. I caught his ear in my teeth and shredded it. He howled and backed off.

I charged. We fought on our hind legs like two grizzlies, holding each other for support as we jockeyed for an opening we could sink our teeth into. He had experience, but I outweighed him. I bore him backward until he lost his balance and scrambled away.

Brittany was out of sight. I tore after her, kicking up gravel. The pack leader ran behind. I wanted to spin about and finish the fight—but Brittany's safety was more important. The other two pack members were out there somewhere. I had to find her first.

I burst through the tree line. Her scent was strong. I smelled fear and adrenalin. Where had she gone? I lowered my head, zigzagging through the underbrush, trying to keep the leader off my tail. He caught me, his heavy paws swiping my haunches. I yelped and veered, taking a new route, expecting him to follow. Instead, he ignored me and continued on Brittany's trail.

Now I was the one bringing up the rear. I flattened my ears, running for all I was worth, trying to cut him off. I came at him at an angle and sank my teeth into his hip. He cried out, snapping at me, but I held fast, lifting his hindquarters into the air, his back legs working as he tried to get away. I shook him. His flesh tore. He took off running, although slower. I spat out a hunk of his hide and followed.

Familiar odors seeped into my awareness. I knew this area. Then it hit me—Brittany wasn't running in blind panic. She was leading him to the potion that turned a werewolf into a man.

I burst into the hidden courtyard a second behind him. Brittany looked up. She was crouched beside the cauldron. Her face was dark with blood, her eyes white. I halted, but the leader kept running.

He leaped at her just as she brought up the barrier. He slammed into it and bounced, shaking his head. Then he jumped at her again, standing on his hind legs, frothing at the mouth as he snarled and clawed to get inside.

Wide-eyed and teeth bared, Brittany picked up the cauldron and threw the contents at him. The dark liquid passed through the barrier and struck the wolf in the chest.

He howled, steam rising as he writhed on the ground. Within seconds, he reverted to his man shape.

Silence fell over the clearing. I stepped forward. He wasn't dead. His chest rose and fell in slow even breaths. He was covered in bite marks, from his mauled face to his shredded ear to a nice chunk I'd taken out of his butt. As I watched, however, the wounds faded and disappeared.

Brittany dropped the cauldron with a clunk. She gaped at me. With her gaze on the unconscious man, she released the barrier and tiptoed out.

I stepped toward her. When she passed the

larger of the two circles, she dropped to her knees, swiped her still oozing forehead, and touched the blood to the magic circle. The second barrier sprang in place, trapping the man inside.

Brittany wept. I nuzzled her. She wrapped her arms about my neck and sobbed into my fur. I wanted to say something comforting, wanted to hold her close. But all I could do was sit there.

After a time, she pulled away. "I'm okay," she said to my unspoken question. "I need my cell phone. I think he had it in his pocket."

I got to my feet to show I understood, and we walked back to the quarry. Brittany moved as if she were exhausted. She stumbled several times. I could have gone on ahead, but I stayed at her side. I wasn't letting her out of my sight.

We left the darkness of the trees and crossed the stony yard. As we neared the spot where the scuffle began, I saw that the human I had knocked down was no longer there.

"He's gone," Brittany whispered. "Hank, or whatever his name is."

I ran my gaze over starlit crevices.

"Do you think Nadine came back for him? Are they waiting for us in the rocks?"

I walked to where I'd left Hank for dead. Nadine had indeed come back. Her scent was fresh. They went down the trail that led into the basin. I sat and looked at Brittany to signify all was clear.

"Here's my phone." She tossed down the

leader's pants. She punched numbers with her thumb. "Hello? Yes. My name is Brittany Meyer. I was run off the road and— What's that? I was reported as kidnapped?" She looked at me. "Yes, that's right. Two men and a woman. I'm in a clearing about a mile before the old quarry. Yes, ma'am. I'll wait for the sheriff." She pocketed the phone. "Apparently, your uncle got a hold of Gramps, seeing he has an in with Sheriff Brad. They're already looking for me. We have to get back."

I picked up a shoe and dropped it onto the pants. She frowned, then gathered the leader's shoes and clothes and carried them with us.

When we got back to the courtyard, the leader was still out cold. Brittany lowered the barrier and approached him. She scattered his clothes around. Then she brought the cauldron down hard upon his head.

Lights flashed from the direction of the road. An amplified voice called from a police bullhorn, "Brittany. Brittany Meyer."

"I'm here," she shouted. Then she hugged my neck. "Thank you for saving me. Now go."

I stepped into the shadows and crouched within the brush. My senses were on high. I smelled the stench of the potion, exhaust fumes from the road. And men. Many men.

Boots tramped through the dry grass. Several deputies, spaced strategically apart, stepped from beneath the trees. Sheriff Brad came out. After a moment, he ordered the others to put away their guns.

Grandpa Earle hurried into the clearing. With a cry, Brittany ran to him. When I saw her safe in his arms, I backed away.

I was bruised and bitten and weary to the bone. I didn't know if I would make it back home, didn't know if I had a home any longer.

That hurt more than I expected. I really liked Uncle Bob. I liked living in Loxahatchee. Where would I go if my uncle disowned me? The way my parents had.

I circled the edge of the clearing and came out onto the road. I saw three sheriff's cars and an ambulance, lights flashing. By morning, the area would be crawling with deputies gathering evidence.

"Cody!" came a harsh whisper.

Uncle Bob rushed toward me along the side of his truck. I was so relieved, so happy to see him I shifted back into a boy on the spot.

He pulled me into a bear hug and said with a catch in his voice, "You scared the life out of me, son."

I closed my eyes, smiling, feeling the pent-up tension dissipate and turn my muscles to jelly.

He took off his shirt and put it on me. It felt warm and comforting.

"Come on. Let's get you home."

# THIRTY

I stepped into the sunny hospital room. Its silence warred with the bustle of the hallway. There were two beds. One was unoccupied. Brittany slept in the other. She was pale, even paler than usual. She wore a bandage across her brow and an IV line in her arm.

I winced, knowing how close I'd come to losing her. I might lose her still after she heard what I had to say.

Grandpa Earle slept in a chair, his head against the wall. I grabbed the remaining chair from across the room and carried it to Brittany's bedside. As I settled in, she opened her eyes.

"Hi," I said.

She yawned and stretched. "I thought you'd be in school."

"Took the day off. Uncle Bob and I were up all night. Talking."

"You two okay, then?"

"I think so. He's downstairs waiting in the truck. He said to tell you he's glad you're all right."

"He should come up."

I shook my head. "I understand why he doesn't want to. This place reeks."

"I forgot about your sensitive nose. You won't have to worry about that much longer."

"Brittany, I–" I took her hand.

"Ooh, ow. Scorched fingers."

"From the cauldron? I thought it was fiberglass."

"It was hot toward the bottom."

My shoulders slumped. "I'm sorry. You've been through so much."

"Don't be silly. I'm fine. The doctor wouldn't have admitted me if Mom hadn't insisted."

"Yeah. I thought she'd be here."

"She went home to check on Butt Crack. I think she's sending him to school."

"So, she'll be back? I don't think she likes me very much."

"Well–"

The sound of jingling pockets interrupted her reply. Sheriff Brad entered the room.

"Hello, Sheriff," Brittany said.

Grandpa Earle snorted and woke. "Brad. 'Bout time."

"I understand you'll be released from the hospital later today," the sheriff said to Brittany. "Happy to hear it."

"Thanks."

"I came to tell you that your car has been retrieved and is in Eric's Body Shop."

"It'll be fine." Grandpa Earle patted her arm.

"I also wanted to reassure you that the perpetrator," the sheriff checked a notebook, "Lonzo Pascal, is behind bars, awaiting arraignment."

"Any sign of the other two people?" I asked.

"Not yet. A blue Lexus was reported stolen. It may be the vehicle you saw, Miss Meyer. We have a plate number. A search is ongoing."

"They're long gone," Grandpa Earle said.

"Don't stop looking," said Brittany. She appeared anxious, like she thought the two wolves might come back for her.

"We'll find them," the sheriff said. "I know you've been through an ordeal. You did a fine job recounting everything for me last night. Unfortunately, I have to ask an additional question."

"All right."

"In our search of the area, we've come across several animal prints. Did these people have dogs with them?"

"Yes," Brittany said as if she'd just remembered. "There were two dogs. Huge things. They snapped at each other like they wanted to fight. The leader, Pascal, turned to settle them down, and that gave me the chance to hit him over the head with the cauldron."

"Are you willing to testify to that in a court of law?"

"Absolutely."

Sheriff Brad smiled. It was the first time I'd seen him do it.

"What are you saying?" Grandpa Earle sputtered. "Is this Pascal guy the one who murdered those women?"

"We suspect he ordered the dogs to kill them, and then he put their blood in that cauldron of his for whatever nefarious purpose."

"And my granddaughter was next?"

"If not for her quick thinking." Sheriff Brad nodded at Brittany. "And it was at that point the other two people fled?"

"Yes. I don't know what happened to the dogs."

"That does it," said Grandpa Earle. "I'm never letting you out of my sight again. What were you doing by the old quarry anyway?"

"I told you, Grandpa. I planned to make a rock garden for Mom's birthday."

"At night?"

"It was the middle of the day when the whole thing started."

"Come on, Earle. I'll buy you a cup of coffee," Sheriff Brad said. "You look like you could use one." He clapped him on the shoulder as they left the room.

I gnawed my lip. "You're really going to court over this?"

"Of course. I don't want him to get away. He's an evil man." She sighed then grinned. "But he did make a good guinea pig. He'll never change into a wolf again. And now that we know the potion works, we can–"

431

"Here's the thing," I said. "I don't want to use the potion. I want to stay like I am."

She blinked. "A werewolf?"

"I just feel it's who I'm supposed to be, you know? I understand if you don't want to be with me anymore."

"Please. Do you really think I'm that shallow? I'm not going to stop seeing you just because you're a little different."

"But I don't want to cause any—"

"If this is what you've decided, then we'll deal with it. Together."

Relief washed over me. I leaned forward. "I love you."

"You better," she whispered.

Our lips barely met when someone cleared their throat. I looked toward the doorway. Brittany's mother stood with her arms folded and her eyes narrowed.

"Oh, h-hello, ma'am," I stammered. "We were just, um—"

Brittany laughed, and then pulled me close for another kiss.

432

Excerpt from Book Two of
The Amazing Wolf Boy

# WEREWOLF ASYLUM

## ONE

April 8, 2008 Loxahatchee, Florida

When I shifted into my wolf form that balmy April night, all I wanted was to escape the hassle of the day. You know, romp through the sawgrass, maybe chase a rabbit or two. I never expected to run into a bear. But there it was, up on its hind legs like it wanted to give me a big hug.

I froze, staring, my teeth bared in greeting. I knew there were black bears in Florida. I lived in the northernmost region of the Everglades. We had panthers, gators, pythons, and bears. But I'd never seen one before. All my fur stood on end, trying to make myself appear bigger, but the bear had me on weight alone.

It swatted me with one frying-pan-sized paw, catching my shoulder. I yelped and tumbled. At that point, any sane person would have run. Unfortunately, the wolf in me took offense. With a low-

i

pitched growl, I leaped at it.

Here's the difference between bears and wolves. Bears fight with their claws, and for good reason. They're like a fist-full of daggers. Wolves fight with their teeth. I caught its forearm in my jaws and clamped down. The bear roared. It swung around, trying to shake me off. My backend swished through the air. Blood filled my mouth, hot and slick. I lost my grip and flew against a tree trunk.

Floridian forests aren't like the forests up north. Back home in Massachusetts, I remember feathery grass, carpets of pine needles, and smooth-barked trees. Down here, we have porcupine palms and saw palmetto. The ground is spiked with spiny cones. I struck an Australian pine, which isn't a true pine tree at all, and slid down the trunk. The bark felt like concrete wrapped with razor wire. Tufts of fur scraped off as I fell—which only served to make me madder.

I launched myself at the bear, my jaws snapping at its throat. It batted me away with the strength of a major leaguer. I sprang again, this time spinning in mid-air and striking its chest with my hind legs—a move sure to impress any ninja warrior. My attack staggered it, and it came down on all fours. I climbed aboard, biting the back of its neck. My fangs penetrated the heavy fur. The bear rolled to knock me off, exposing its soft underbelly. I dodged its weight and went for its gut. My teeth caught something strange. I pulled back with some sort of belt in my mouth.

As if it were melting, the bear morphed into a kid.

My jaw dropped, and the belt hit the ground. The boy scrambled to his feet. His expression went from shock to alarm and then to determination as he took a fighting stance before me.

My wolf chuckled at that, but my human side filled with questions. Who was he? How did he shift into a bear? I couldn't wait to tell Brittany, the girl I secretly loved. I started the change back to human before I even made a decision to do it. My muzzle flattened painfully, sinking into my face. My fangs receded. With a liquid sensation, my ears slid down the sides of my head. My transformation was not as smooth as his, but moments later I got to my feet as a sixteen-year-old boy.

His eyes widened, and he took a step back. He looked like he feared me more as an unarmed kid. Then he squared his shoulders and lifted his chin. He was about my height with a weight lifter's build. Probably had twenty pounds on me. He looked a bit older than I was. We faced each other, and it was weird because we were both naked, yet we weren't in the shower room at PE or anything.

"Hi," I said, trying to sound nonchalant. "I'm Cody Forester."

"William." The boy eyed me warily. "I never met a werewolf before. I thought your kind only changed on the full moon."

I felt a twinge of panic. True, most werewolves only changed with the moon. My ability to change at will made me an oddity. A super wolf, my Uncle Bob called it. And a super danger if it got out. Like gunslingers of the Old West, everyone would want a piece of me.

I shrugged, then motioned at the blood dripping down his arm. "Sorry I hurt you."

Anger flared on the kid's face. "You didn't hurt me."

"Well, you hurt me." I rotated my shoulder, wincing at the score marks. With a grunt, I picked up the bear hide belt and sat on a nearby log. "So, what are you, like a were-bear?"

William gave an indignant snort and raised his chin even higher. "I am a medicine man, like my father before me. We can change into many animals."

"With this?" I held out the belt.

His eyes flashed, but then he seemed to deflate. He took the belt and sat at the other end of the log.

After a few moments, I said, "Medicine man, eh? What tribe? Miccosukee?"

"I am half Navajo," he said as if challenging me to deny it.

A creepy feeling crawled into my stomach. My uncle's best friend was a Navajo medicine man. Without looking at him, I said, "Really? Who's your father?"

"Howard Shebala."

"Garage Sale Howard?" I blurted.

He jumped up. His face darkened, and his hands clenched. "My father is a great man."

"Chill," I said. "I just know him, that's all. He's my

iv

uncle's best friend."

"Then speak of him with respect."

"Does he realize you're out here turning into a bear?"

William shook his head and slumped back down on the log. "He was voted out of the tribe. An outcast. The tribal council says I cannot see him or make contact."

"That stinks." I knew all about being an outcast. My parents banished me to Loxahatchee the first time I showed fang and fur.

William said, "Now my mother has taken up with another."

"Top knot guy." I remembered meeting Howard's rival during a trip to the *Miccosukee Indian Village* in the Everglades.

"Joseph Achak." William scowled. "I hate him."

"No doubt," I said. "But why are you here?"

"I left. Wanted to be nearer my father. Sometimes I see him."

"So you live here? In the woods?" I remembered news reports about bear sightings in the city. "Hate to see the media blitz if Child Services finds out."

"Do I look like a child?"

"Okay," I said, "so you get hungry and you turn into a bear to eat. I get it. But where do you sleep? You can't be a bear all the time."

"I found an old fishing cabin in the Glades," he said, then looked sorry he told me. "That's a secret. I don't want anyone to come looking."

v

I nodded. Now we both knew secrets about each other. "You could stay at my house. I live with my Uncle Bob. Howard stops by pretty often."

"No." He stood. "No contact."

"So you'll defy the tribal council enough to run away from home, but you won't risk seeing your dad?" I rose to face him, royally ticked off. How could he act like that? I would do most anything to see my dad again.

"Don't comment on what you don't understand." With a final glare, William stomped off into the trees.

All I could do was watch him go.

# TWO

The next morning dawned blue and breezy. Since I was out late the night before, I overslept my alarm. I made a Cap'n Crunch sandwich to eat in the truck as Uncle Bob drove me to school. Uncle Bob had steel gray, over-the-collar hair and a thin build. He was known as the *Fix-It Guy*, a handyman who did odd jobs around town. In his spare time, he was a werewolf, although not many people knew that. I'd lived with him for only four months, but I felt pretty comfortable. He didn't try to replace my parents. He was more like a friend looking out for me.

Seminole Bluffs High School seemed blindingly white under the bright sun. Its expansive concrete courtyard had small holes cut out for trees to grow through. The only grassy area was the football field. Home of the Hawks. As we pulled into the drop-off area, I noticed Maxwell and Lonnie hanging around. They looked decidedly nerdy in their button-down shirts. It made me smile. At my prep-school back in Cambridge, all the kids looked nerdy. I wondered what they'd think if they saw me now in my garage-sale T-shirts and jeans.

I hopped out of the truck and circled around to pull my bicycle from the back. I'd have to bike it home. My uncle drove me to class most mornings, but he was rarely able to pick me up again. Usually I made plans with Brittany after school. We were study partners, but in my head, we were more. Since she had just gotten out of the hospital, though, she'd probably take off for a few more days.

My wolf sense seemed to be on high. I heard laughter and conversation as far away as the buses. The stench of car exhaust assaulted me, mingled with a miasma of hair gel, perfume, and cigarette smoke. I bounced my bike onto the curb and raised a hand in farewell. Uncle Bob drove away as Maxwell and Lonnie approached.

"Hey, where you been, man?" Maxwell asked.

I was ready for that. I'd missed the past two days of school, and I'd concocted a story about having the stomach flu, complete with illustrations. But Maxwell didn't give me time to get into it.

He said, "Is it true your girlfriend was kidnapped by a serial killer down by the old rock quarry?"

"B-Brittany?" I spluttered, not knowing how to answer. I couldn't tell him the whole story, that the serial killer in question was actually a murderous werewolf, and Brittany was kidnapped to punish me for not joining the pack.

Lonnie said, "Don't try to deny it, man. It was all over the news."

"No," I said, "I mean, she's not my girlfriend." Not

officially, my thoughts added.

Maxwell blinked and gave his glasses a shove. "Really? I thought you were together."

"I'd like to be, but—"

"Hi, Maxwell," a female voice purred. Alitia Carpenter smiled over her shoulder as she walked by, her blonde curls ruffling in the breeze.

"Later, man," Maxwell told me.

"Seeya," said Lonnie.

I grinned, shaking my head. As I walked my bike to the rack, I thought about Brittany being my girlfriend. It would be too good to be true. She once told me she loved me, but I couldn't count that. We were running for our lives from the pack of werewolves at the time. However, when I visited her in the hospital on Monday, she kissed me. In front of her mother, no less. Did that mean we were together?

I glanced at the student parking lot. Brittany's lime-green Volkswagen Beetle wasn't there. Her car was wrecked in the kidnapping. I felt as responsible for that as I did for her safety.

No. I wouldn't tell anyone that she was my girl. I didn't want to jinx it by blabbing it around school.

I left my ratty old bike unlocked, certain that no one would bother to steal it, and headed to Trig. As I had been absent for two days, I was a little behind and had to pay attention in class. It was torture. Mr. Varney had to be the most boring teacher in the world.

But I was rewarded for my efforts when I got to

World History an hour later and found Brittany there.

She was stunning. Her hair was black and streaked with purple today, and her lips were deep violet. Her dark tank top showed off her pale shoulders and long slim arms. Her miniskirt accented her perfect legs. My heart skipped in circles as I stood there watching her. She was surrounded by a group of chattering, giggling girls. Perhaps they thought she was cool for having her life threatened. She looked up, saw me, and rolled her eyes. I smiled and let her have her moment of fame.

I didn't see her again until lunch. She sat at our table with her customary tray of yogurt and an apple. I felt so relieved to see her there. It was like everything was back to normal. I picked up a bag of chips and a couple of *Dews*.

"Hi," I said as I reached her.

She motioned at the chips. "Is that all you're having?"

"Hey, it's potatoes. It counts as a vegetable." I sat across from her, basking in her smile. Her long bangs trailed into her eyes, not completely hiding the *Band-Aid* over the stitches on her forehead.

"What?" She laughed, and I realized I'd been staring.

"I like your hair," I said, "much better than the pink."

"Oh, I only did that for my mother."

"Your mother likes bubblegum hair?"

"No." Brittany grinned. "She hates it."

x

I opened my *Dew*. "I'm really glad to see you, but don't you think you should have taken off a little more time?"

"I couldn't stay at home with Grandpa Earle hovering over me. He means well, but…" She cut a slice of apple with a plastic knife and handed it to me.

Earle Meyer was old but a decent guy. He took in Brittany, her little brother Butt Crack, and their mother after a messy divorce.

"Anyway," Brittany said, "I feel much better. Except my stitches are beginning to itch."

"Hear anything about the car?" I remembered the panic I felt when I first saw Brittany's Beetle at the bottom of the cliff at the old rock quarry. Double that when I realized she wasn't inside.

"It's not totaled or anything. The bumper is dented, and the trunk is dinged. One headlight is smashed." She took a bite of apple, leaving purple kisses on the skin. "Because it's a bug, they've had to special order everything. They've already got the windshield in. They tried to talk me into the tinted kind, but that didn't suit Baby."

"Baby?"

"Yeah, as in come on Baby, you can do it."

I chuckled. I never knew she named her car.

"The problem is that the tie rod is broken. It will take time to get the part in," she said. "Mom got a loaner from the insurance company, but she won't let me drive yet. She's making Grandpa chauffeur me around like a little kid. Parents can be such pains."

"Speaking of parents," I said, "did you know Howard had a son?"

"He does?"

"I met him last night. I was—"

"Hi, Brittany," a girl said.

Brittany looked up. "Oh, hi, Katie."

"I couldn't believe it when I heard about you on the news," Katie said. "Are you okay?"

"I'm fine," Brittany said. "Glad it's over."

I smiled and nodded as Katie walked away. "Anyhow, I was in the woods and I came across this bear. Only it wasn't a bear, it was—"

"Brittany, I'm so glad you're all right."

Two more girls stopped at our table.

One of them asked, "Were you scared?"

Stupid question. I closed my eyes and rubbed my forehead.

"Maybe we can go to the mall after school today," the other girl said.

"I'd better not," Brittany told them. "I still get really tired."

"Oh," they both crooned and patted her back.

After they left, Brittany said, "So, you met a bear in the woods."

"William the Bear," I said.

"He talks?"

"No. He turned into a boy. He uses some sort of magic belt."

She nodded. "A hide belt. Remember? We read

about those when we were researching were-wolves."

"Ohmygod, Brittany, you were kidnapped?" a girl squealed as she led three more to our table. "Was he cute?"

"No, Amber. What are you thinking?"

"What kind of thing is that to ask," I said, my voice rising. "Get out of here. Leave her alone."

"Well, check out Mister Jealous," Amber said, although she seemed more amused than miffed.

They walked away.

"Don't look now, but you have an admirer," Brittany said.

I glanced around and saw Efrem Higgins sitting at a nearby table. I hated Eff. He hated me, too. Enough to call his football-playing cronies together to play piñata with me. When Eff posted pictures of the beating on MySpace, his coach found out and turned him in. He was saddled with community service. And he was kicked off the school football team.

"Yeah," I said, "he was hanging around in PE, too. All his friends seem to have abandoned him."

Brittany muttered, "Serves him right, the psycho-path."

"It's no fun being alone."

"You're too forgiving," Brittany said. "Anyway, I didn't know Howard had a son, and I think he would have told us. After all, he introduced us to his ex-wife. Maybe we should talk to him about it."

"Yeah," I said, and finished my Dew.

Lunch ended, and I reluctantly said goodbye. I kept Brittany in my thoughts the rest of the day–the crinkle of her nose when she smiled, the tilt of her head to keep her bangs out of her eyes. It was almost as good as having her with me.

My last hour was Shop. I dreaded taking the class at first, but I found that I liked working with wood. Besides, all you had to do was show up and you got a passing grade. I joined Maxwell and Lonnie at their worktable. We'd finished making birdhouses and had progressed to decorative mail caddies, the kind you might set on the kitchen counter to hold the day's bills.

"No, stupid," Maxwell told Lonnie as I sat down. "The top is supposed to look like waves, not pumpkin teeth."

"So," Lonnie said, "my waves are a little choppier than yours."

Maxwell jostled him. "Let me fix it."

"No." Lonnie pushed back.

"What do you think, Cody?"

"Well," I said, studying the misshapen box. "If you paint it yellow, it would look like the sun. You know, the way little kids draw it. Your mom would love that."

"Yeah." Lonnie smiled as if with fresh inspiration.

Just then, an annoying tone crackled from the intercom, and Vice Principal Overhill said, "May I have your attention, please."

Maxwell gave Lonnie another shove, and Lonnie hip-checked him, sending him staggering. They laughed in hissing whispers.

"Boys," said Mr. Conklin, the Shop teacher.

"Because of recent tragic events," said the intercom, "grief counselors will be available to all students for individual sessions from eleven until two. We encourage everyone to make an appointment."

In an undertone, Lonnie said, "I'll be grief stricken if it gets me out of class."

"Right," Maxwell said. "Our poor, dear friend Brittany. She might have been killed."

I smirked. "You guys don't even know Brittany."

"We know she's hot," Maxwell said.

"Double hot," said Lonnie.

"Besides, what do you care if we get to know her better? Seeing how you two aren't together."

"Yeah, man. Study partners. Lunch buddies. You better make your move."

I nudged him with my shoulder. "I'm working on that."

Eventually, class ended. I hung around in front of school, hoping to wave goodbye to Brittany, but in the crowd, I must've missed her. Disappointed, I hopped on my bike and pedaled down the street. I didn't feel like going home to an empty house, although you'd think I'd be used to it. I grew up that way. Both my parents are doctors, and they were never home when I lived with them. Now that I was older, I had choices, so I headed to Howard's house.

Howard Shebala lived on a street lined with pink and aqua houses. Between drought and water restrictions, the usually immaculate lawns looked brown, the flowerbeds sparse and wilted. In Howard's front yard, the shaggy grass lay in worn out lanes between rows of tables. The *Garage Sale* sign was a permanent fixture.

As I pulled my bike up the driveway, I noticed only one shopper, a woman with a small boy. The kid kept reaching on tiptoe to drag items off the tables. I leaned my bike against the garage door and walked to where Howard sat with his customary lemonade. He stood as I approached, his ponytail swinging onto his shoulder. He was short and stocky—and a Navajo medicine man.

"Howdy. Good to see you." He shook my hand. "I'm sorry to hear of your recent trouble. Is Brit all right?"

"She's amazing," I told him. "So brave."

"The rest of the pack got away?" He said it as if he thought they were a danger, but I knew they weren't. They were followers. Sycophants. They wouldn't be back.

"The sheriff has the leader," I said. "He'll never get out. Brittany plans to testify against him, but even if she doesn't, they still have him on the other murders."

Howard shook his head. "The wolf in him cannot be incarcerated. Come the full moon, who knows what will happen?"

My face grew warm. This was the first time Howard spoke to me about werewolves. It was a touchy subject, not only because he knew my secret but because I should have realized he knew. His pet name for me was Mai Coh, which meant shape shifter.

I said, "Between you and me, I don't think that wolf will be coming out any time soon. You see, your wife, er, ex-wife, Chelsea, told Brittany and me about a potion to change a wolf back into a man. We used it on him."

Howard stared at me. Then he threw back his head and laughed. Great resounding guffaws. I'd never seen anyone laugh so hard.

When he quieted, I said, "I didn't tell my uncle that part." I hoped Howard would take the hint and not mention it. I didn't want to have to explain to Uncle Bob that I'd been trying to cure my own lycanthropy; he seemed quite content with his werewolfism.

Howard wiped his streaming eyes and slapped me on the shoulder. "A wise decision. So, young Mai Coh, what brings you to these parts?"

"Socks. I'm running low."

He nodded and led me through tables of neatly folded Levis and stacks of T-shirts. He stopped at an open box. "I know I saw socks around here somewhere." He pulled out belts by the handful and draped them over the table, trying to peer to the bottom of the box. "Nope. Not this one."

As I watched him replace the belts, I said, "What

would you do with all this stuff if it started to rain?"

"Not likely. Worse drought I've seen in many years."

"Has it ever happened?"

"Certainly. But not often. Florida weather is predictable. It hardly rains in winter, and in summer it rains everyday like clockwork. I just set my alarm clock and clean up when it goes off."

I shook my head, gazing over the many tables. "You need an assistant."

Howard grunted and moved to another box. The lone shopper waved to him and, kid in hand, walked off without buying anything. They left a trail of fallen Tupperware and paperbacks on the grass.

Howard muttered, "Never picks up after him."

"Do you have kids?" I said as if just thinking about it.

He buried his nose in the box. "Why do you ask?"

"The first time I saw all this stuff, I thought you must have a whole slew of kids to have so many castoffs."

Howard grunted again. "EBay."

"Excuse me?"

He looked up. "I'm running a business here. Most of my inventory comes from EBay. I stock the items I figure I can sell, up the price a bit for profit, and make a living."

"No kids, then."

Howard sighed. "I have a son."

"Really? What's he like?"

"Dead."

I blinked, not sure if I should apologize or call him on it. Before I could respond, he held up two white socks bundled with a thick rubber band.

"How many do you need?" he asked.

"Five or six pairs."

He pulled more socks from the bottom of the box. Some had red or blue stripes on the tops and some were plain white. "Two dollars a pair."

I grimaced. "But they're used."

"No, they aren't," he said. "My friend's an amputee, gives me all his left-handed socks."

I pulled a five-dollar bill out of my pocket. "This is all I have."

"The magpie flies even in rain." Howard muttered one of his indecipherable sayings and took the five. "Don't tell anyone I gave you such a good deal. They'll all want something."

He walked back to his lemonade, pulled a *Publix* grocery sack from under the lawn chair, and placed the socks inside.

"Thanks," I said, accepting the bag. "See you later."

"Tell Bob my Rummy cards are lonely."

I slung the bag of socks over my handlebars and took off, feeling bemused. I didn't really need socks, but I knew there was no getting information from Howard without buying something. Only I hadn't gotten much information. All I knew was that either Howard or William were lying to me. Maybe both.

It was late when I got home. My uncle and I live in a small, two-bedroom house with almost no furniture. It's set back from the road, surrounded by woods. The neighbors can't see or be seen. A perfect den for a couple of werewolves.

I dumped my bike in its usual spot on the grass. As I clomped up the wooden steps to the porch, Uncle Bob arrived. He parked his truck on the gravel drive and climbed out with several *Publix* bags of his own. His held groceries—chocolate milk, instant coffee, bread, and what smelled like a family-style fried chicken dinner. I opened the door to the house and held it for him, and my stomach growled as he passed. It smelled great.

We didn't often cook in my new home. Of course, my mother the brain surgeon, rarely cooked either. Our housekeeper, on the other hand, could've been a Japanese chef. Lots of greens. Fresh seafood. I missed the comforts of my home. But I was pretty much a vegetarian then. I couldn't go without meat now.

I followed my uncle into the kitchen, and we sat down to fried chicken, potato salad, and baked beans. A breeze blew through the open window, flapping the curtains. Uncle Bob insisted on keeping the window open regardless of the heat, a habit I was coming to appreciate.

"Heard you go out last night," he said as if reading my thoughts.

"I just needed to unwind."

"Have you heard from Brittany?"

"She was at school today. Looks great."

"Good. Now you can stop worrying about her." He poured me a tall glass of chocolate milk.

Glasses were a recent addition to the household. I guess Uncle Bob felt more domestic now that we both decided I would stay. The adjustment period was as difficult for him as it was for me. I hated Florida at first, but now I couldn't imagine living anywhere else. I would never run away.

Which made me think of William.

"I stopped by Howard's today," I said, tossing chicken bones into the empty bag. "I asked him if he had any kids, you know, with all the junk he has around, and he said he had a son but he was dead."

"Willie." My uncle nodded. "I suppose he *is* dead, figuratively speaking. I don't know if Howard told you this, but he's a full-blooded Navajo. He lived among the Miccosukee for many years. When his wife divorced him, the tribal council banned him from their land."

"They can do that?"

"Guess so. Willie was thirteen at the time. A tough age. A tough situation for both him and his father. He must be seventeen, now. Lives with his mother. Howard never talks about him."

I took a long pull of milk. How could Howard neglect to mention he had a son? Was he happy to disown William, or was it too painful to think about him? I wondered if my dad ever spoke about me. Did he tell people I was dead? "What would happen if Howard defied the council and visited his son anyway?"

"Who knows? Maybe they'd excommunicate the entire family." Uncle Bob got up to make a cup of instant coffee with hot tap water.

I watched him for a moment, then shook my head. "That's brutal. What did Howard ever do to them?"

"There was an incident," my uncle said, slurping his mug.

When he didn't elaborate, I knew the subject was closed. I gathered the trash from dinner and carried it to the garbage can behind the shed. My unofficial chore. The sun was down, and the surrounding trees looked black against the pink sky. I listened to birds settling in for the night. Field mice scampered through fallen leaves. Farther off, I heard peacocks calling, making the place sound like the set of a movie.

For a moment, I wanted to slip out of my clothes and into the wolf, romp through the trees and swampland. But that was a dangerous habit to get into. Just because I could change into a wolf anytime I wanted didn't mean I should. After all, I had a human side, too. I couldn't be a wolf all the time.

I wondered about William living in the woods as

a bear. Why would he refuse to see Howard when clearly he loved his dad? It wasn't like he had parents like mine. My parents banished me to Florida without a clue. They never told me that lycanthropy ran in my family or what to do if I suddenly turned into a wolf, like I had in that restaurant in France. They were all about secrecy. From their neighbors, from society. From their only son. I would never forgive the way they abandoned me. Still, I wished I could see them, if only to tell them that.

When I went back to the house, I found Uncle Bob in his beat-up old recliner in front of our twelve-inch black-and-white television. Watching *Jeopardy* was one of his nightly rituals. We exchanged nods, and I hurried to my room to call Brittany. *My* nightly ritual.

She picked up on the second ring. "I wondered when you would call."

I smiled as I always did when I heard her voice. "Did you miss me?"

"Always," she said, "but that's not it. I have to tell you that I won't be at lunch for the next few days because I have appointments with the school grief counselors at that time."

I winced as if she'd slapped me. "You're still that upset?"

"Not me. It's my mother. She thinks I'm repressing the horror of the ordeal and need to let it out. Her words."

I groaned. "I feel so responsible."

"That's silly. You couldn't know what they'd do. Maybe you should talk to a counselor, too."

"Yeah, I can see it now."

"Don't make fun. I wonder if they have werewolf therapists or werewolf doctors."

"Why would they? There's no such thing as werewolves, remember?"

"Or were-bears."

"Now who's poking fun?" I said. "I'm telling you, he's out there. He said he's living in an old fishing cabin."

"I know where that is. At least, I might. There's a fishing cabin in the Everglades out on State Road 80, kind of community property. Grandpa took Butt Crack and me there when we first moved down. The original owner must be long gone. Of course, you can't really own anything in the Everglades."

"Howard told me his son was dead. That really bothered me."

"Because he lied to you?"

"Sounds kind of harsh, that's all."

"I can't imagine how anyone can live by themselves in the woods," Brittany said. "We should take some groceries to him."

"Whoa," I said. "I'm not sure that's a good idea. I was supposed to keep the whole thing a secret."

"It's no big. I'll just raid the pantry."

"But–" My mind whirled, searching for a way to derail her. "You aren't driving yet. How are we going to get there?"

"Maybe my friend, Eileen, can take us."

I frowned. "Does she go to our school?"

"No, she's homeschooled. Eileen Beamer. I've known her since I moved down. She lives at the Sunspot."

"A fulltime nudie?" I blurted. The Sunspot Naturist Resort bordered Brittany's house. I had a quick image of Brittany's grandfather sitting with his pellet gun, shooting nudists who strayed from the nature trails into his yard. "I thought only tourists stayed at the Sunspot."

"Not all the residents are tourists," Brittany said. "Remember the fortuneteller we went to? She lives on the resort."

"The grandmaster. How could I forget?" The grandmaster scared the life out of me by predicting that I would sacrifice Brittany for the greater good.

"Then it's settled," Brittany said. "Let's plan a trip to the old fishing cabin on Saturday morning."

I ran my hand over my face. William the Bear wouldn't be happy.

# About Author
# Roxanne Smolen

Roxanne Smolen became enamored by werewolves after watching the movie Abbott and Costello Meet Frankenstein when she was a girl. The pathos of the wolfman character touched her even then. As she grew into her author shoes, the idea of a conflicted werewolf character grew as well until she knew his story had to be told. Her wolf boy series takes place in Loxahatchee, Florida, not far from her home. You can connect with her on Twitter, Facebook, and Google+.

# Books by Roxanne Smolen

## The Amazing Wolf Boy

The Amazing Wolf Boy

Werewolf Asylum

Wolfsbane Brew

Werewolf Apocalypse

The Bear, the Werewolf, and the Blogger

The Amazing Wolf Boy Box Set


## Dark Angel

Satan's Mirror


## Colonial Scouts

Alien Worlds

Alien Jungle

Alien Seas

Alien Beginnings

## The Resort Debauch Trilogy

Resort Debauch

The Resort Debauch Trilogy

## The Violet Series

Violet and the Missing Laptop

Violet and the Missing Puppy

## The Adventures of the Power Girls

Keepers of Magic

Island of Magic

# Dear Reader,

Thank you for reading The Amazing Wolf Boy. I hope you enjoyed the adventures of Cody and Brittany and will look for the next book in the series, Werewolf Asylum.

Readers today have the power to make or break a book via reviews. Without reviews, a book will go unnoticed. I hope you will take a moment to leave a short review wherever you bought this book. If you have questions or comments, feel free to contact me directly at smolen.roxanne@gmail.com.

Again, thank you for reading.

Roxanne

www.roxannesmolen.com

www.ingramcontent.com/pod-product-compliance
Lightning Source LLC
Chambersburg PA
CBHW071633260626
47170CB00001B/82